I0778856

THE KINGLESS CROWN

KINGDOM OF THE WHITE SEA BOOK ONE

SARAH M. CRADIT

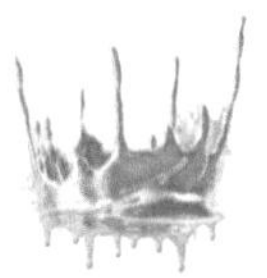

Cover Design by Regina Wamba of ReginaWamba.com
"Midnight Flight" Art by Art by Steffani
Portrait Art by Lauren Richelieu
Map by The Illustrated Author Design Services
Editing by Emily A. Lawrence of Lawrence Editing

Publisher Contact:
sarah@sarahmcradit.com
www.sarahmcradit.com

INTRODUCTION: THE KINGDOM

There exists a kingdom set upon an isle, surrounded by a sea that no one has ever traveled beyond. The Kingdom of the White Sea it is called, or simply the kingdom, for they have no other name for it. The kingdom consists of Five Reaches: Northerlands, Southerlands, Easterlands, Westerlands, and Hinterlands, with an honorary, if one can call it that, Reach referred to as the Wastelands, for reasons that will become quite clear.

The kingdom is nearly two thousand miles long, half as wide at its widest point, and far less so at its narrowest, an inlet dividing north from south called the Wulf's Neck. Travel within the kingdom happens along the Compass Roads, and to some extent, by sea, though this is not the type of sea where travel happens easily, or safely.

Following the death of his father, King Eoghan of the Rhiagains has recently taken his place as the wearer of the crown, though he was not the intended, and many suspect his involvement in the death of its rightful bearer, his twin brother, Darrick. The Lords and Ladies of main Four Reaches (the Fifth, the Hinterlands, living by laws that predate all other current inhabitants) have long enjoyed varying degrees of amity with the Rhiagain crown, but Eoghan and his father, Khain, have pushed the kingdom to a point never seen before in all its history.

Two decades earlier, King Khain designed a ceremony upon the back of deception. When the Lords and Ladies of the Four Reaches arrived to what they believed was a celebration of the birth of his heir, they were instead commanded to give over their children, sons and daughters, and a series of marriages proceeded without hesitation. These marriages united families that were sometimes at war— families that had previously only wed within their own Reach. Khain claimed this clannishness was the cause of their enmity, though it wouldn't become clear what his true motivation was for the Epoch of the Accordant until he was dead, and his second son ascended.

The parents and grandparents of the brides and grooms would not live to learn this for themselves, for within two years of the Epoch, all were dead of mysterious illnesses. One by one they fell, and with each death, the enmity between the Rhiagains and the Reaches flourished to levels never seen before in the history of Rhiagain reign. The fervent denials issued from the crown of their involvement only gave the new ladies and lords of the Reaches confirmation of the truth they already held in their hearts.

We enter this story only a fortnight away from the culmination of Khain's ultimate vision: The Right of Choosing, wherein the young, but cruel, King Eoghan will exercise his right to take the eldest daughter from four of the unions born at the Epoch of the Accordant, and where the Lords and Ladies of these great houses are expected to comply without recourse.

But the Rhiagains were not always the kings of this kingdom, and there are many who still pass down tales of a time before them... a time where the Reaches ruled unto themselves, and where tyrants had no place. And somewhere in Duncarrow, the seat of the

Rhiagains, there are those who know the true fate of Darrick Rhiagain.

As the Derehams, Blackwoods, Warwicks, and Quinlandens prepare their daughters—some willing, some not—to be queens, not all is well.

Not all is well at all.

Complete character guides by location can be found at the end of the book. These are spoiler-free and include only information that is true at the start of the book.

You can find a complete list of content warnings on my website: sarahmcradit.com

OWLING
SEA
N
W
E
S
MIDNIGHT CREST
ICEBOLT MOUNTAIN
MIDWINTER REST
WITCHWOOD CROSS
WHITECAP
FOREST OF LYCANA
NORTHERLAND RANGE
WULFSHEAD HAVEN
9
TORRIN'S PASS
6
WESTPORT
EASTPORT
DUNWOODE
1
DARKWOOD RUN
SALTHILL
WULF'S NECK
7
MAYKE
SALEEN
ASGILL
2
DRUMAIN
BY THE SEA
TERMONGLEN
RUSHWOOD
WHISPERING WOODS
12
VALLEYBROOKE
EVERLEIGH PIKE
STREAMSTOWNE
EVERHART THICKET
WILDWOOD FALLS
THE SEPULCHRE IN THE SKIES
10
PARTH
RESPLENDENT RELIQUARY
5
BRIARHAVEN
THE SEVEN SISTERS
GAP O' EVER
GREENFEN
RIVER RUSH
WINDWATCH GROVE
PINE BLUFF
FIONN'S PASS
WHITE SEA
WHITEWOOD
OLDCASTLE
OAK HILL
3
EAST DERRY
IRON HILL
BLACKPOOL
STONE MAWR
NEWCARROW
4
SANDYMOUNT
GREENCASTLE
GOLDTHORPE
SANDYCOVE
LEECASTER BAY
11
HORNSEA
PORT WORTHING
CAMP ATONEMENT
GREYSTONE ABBEY
WHITECLIFFE
8
CAMP RESTITUTION
1.) NORTHERLANDS
2.) HINTERLANDS
3.) WESTERLANDS
4.) SOUTHERLANDS
5.) EASTERLANDS
6.) ISLE OF BELCARROW
7.) DUNCARROW
8.) WASTELANDS
9.) WULFSGATE
0.) LONGWOOD RUSH
1.) WARWICKTOWN
2.) WHITECHURCH
KINGDOM
OF THE
WHITE SEA

For Melannie, Holly, and Madeleine
My lights in dark places, when all others have gone out.

For Pam
Since the very beginning.

For Becket
For the right words when they were most needed.

For Gladys
You embraced my strange vision and helped me blaze new trails.

For Queen Melian (Mellie Smells), King Aragorn (Guvvy Bear),
and Millicent Boleyn (Missy Sis)
My sweet pugs who are at least partly responsible for the end result.

And for James
My constant.

PROLOGUE

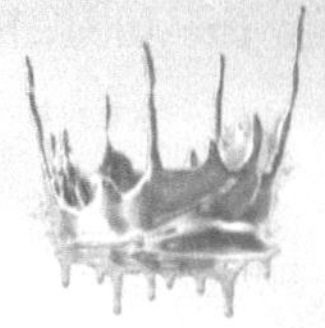

Shadows bounced along the dampened walls as Gretchen Dereham hurried down the stairs to the crypts of Wulfsgate Keep. The air was cooler down here and her breath unfurled in small clouds as she descended in haste, torch clutched in hand, one eye cast over her shoulder with every panicked step. Every sound was an enemy yet to be discovered. The dark fingers dancing into shapes on the stone never let her forget what was at stake.

Sweat dripping into her eyes obscured her vision. The whoosh of flame moving across the air nearly caused her to drop the torch as she spiraled downward, into the darkness.

Spies weren't her problem anymore. She'd seen to that, casting subtle, but final, punishment in the direction of anyone who even dared suggest they might know her deepest, darkest secret. And Holden was no threat. He never ventured down into the Dereham family tombs. He didn't possess a sentimental view of the past. He was also not fond of the dark, or anything resembling the unknown.

Gretchen thrived in the dark. It was the opposite to all she'd known growing up in the trees of Whitechurch, and the antithesis to what she was most afraid of; that strange world of her past that suffocated her in all its promise. But this darkness came with the shroud of a truth she'd shared with no one, and never could. A hell she'd brought upon herself, but couldn't seem to stop seeking with every step.

Her harried breaths were the only sounds greeting her at the bottom. Mossy patches bursting through cracks in the stone dripped murky condensation on her plaited hair. She'd always wondered where the water in the mausoleum of the Derehams came from, but feared more the idea that there was no satisfying answer. That coming here was akin to going elsewhere, or even Beyond.

Another rush of urgent sound as her flame passed left to right, painting light across the dusty, cobwebbed tombs of her husband's ancestors. They were all here, even Holden's brother, who'd been the true heir of Wulfsgate. It was a most macabre tradition to Gretchen, who had watched all deaths in the Easterlands pass forth to the Guardians in the form of flame and ash.

Ash. She turned as she exhaled, and he was there.

His eyes were always first to greet her. They were his name-sake, a color she knew only from the embers of a fire long spent. Pale, searching. She remembered being ensnared by these eyes even as a girl, when as children the two of them swung from the branches of the great trees of Whitechurch. They bound her entirely by the time he kissed her for the first time, by the weeping well.

"Sparrow," he whispered, taking her at once in his arms. It was the worst of names, but it was the best, because he'd given it to her before they'd ever whispered of love. He called her as such because, he claimed, she flitted through their years together, beckoning him to follow. That wasn't quite her recollection of things. They both remembered the past through different eyes.

Gretchen allowed his comfort with careful distance. She sought him out, night after night, while understanding that each night could be their last night should his presence be discovered. Twenty years she'd been meeting him like this. Seventeen of those years meeting him on these terms.

Always, she held her torch to the side, where only half his face was revealed to her, and half of hers to him. The half of her that was his belonged to the half of him he could still give.

"Holden has agreed," Gretchen said, voice low despite her relative confidence that they were alone. "He's going to send Lisbet to the king."

Even in dim light, Ash's deep lines were clear to her as he furrowed his brow. "That doesn't sound like Holden."

"It sounds exactly like Holden," Gretchen shot back. "What else could I have expected from a man who claims family first, but relents at the first sign of danger?" The venom for her husband, laced with a love even Ash wouldn't understand, interspersed her words in a way that scared her. In a flash, she imagined herself taking Holden's life, hands clutched around his neck, while he slept. She shook it off, forcing a replacement in her mind of how safe she felt riding the rise and fall of his chest. Nothing in her life had ever been simple.

"I don't think that's fair," Ash said, ever her diplomat. Thoughtful, like her second son, Drystan. He always looked for the center of a situation and attempted to bring her there. "Holden must feel as if he has no other choice. The lords of the other Reaches are complying. To not fall in line would invite war. You know this king would fight all of you before allowing a slight to his delicate pride. He wouldn't trouble himself with whether he could win."

"War brings resolution to matters of great need. And is now, when the king demands the daughters of the Four Reaches in his bed, not a matter of need? How is complying a more preferable outcome than the sacrifice of children we nursed at our breasts and raised in love?"

Ash brushed the back of his soft hand across her brow, pushing stray hairs away again. "Sparrow, my dearest, you and I have never seen war. We can't make such a comparison."

Gretchen scoffed, recoiling from his touch in punishment. But he'd done what she knew he would, attempt to instill reason in a kiln of chaos. Is that not why she sought him out? To reassure her? To give her heart permission to do what it refused?

"Eoghan is a cruel man," Gretchen argued. She settled her torch in a nearby sconce. "He isn't the king his grandfather was."

"I've not forgotten," Ash said softly. "Nor am I ever in absence of the reminder that the king's father ripped you from my arms."

Gretchen slipped her hands around his waist and tilted her chin. "Am I not now in your arms?"

Ash's kiss cured everything, for the moment. No, it wasn't the truth she'd come here for, but this, a softness she'd not only given up when the dead king forced her to marry the Dereham heir, but one she'd surrendered from her own constitution. Gretchen was one woman below and another above. Only one was of use to her, but this… this comfort…

She allowed Ash to love her atop the crypt of Holden's father, Hadden, and when it was over, she whispered in his ear the demand of a promise.

"If things shouldn't end as we expect, and I cannot hand over my daughter like an animal to a man who will crush her beneath his cruelty, then it is you I will look to, Ash. You who will look after all my children while I pick up a sword and do what my husband cannot."

Ash regarded her in the flickering darkness of the musty crypts for some time before he answered.

"I've always looked after your children, Sparrow. And will do so as long as the magic holds."

If there was an unspoken rule between them, it was to never mention the magic. To give voice to it was to remind her of a truth so terrible she couldn't resist the pull back to the moment her entire world crumbled beneath her. Even when she slept, she was tortured with the image of her lifeless love, her Ash, dead against the stones of her chamber after taking one of her own poisons. After she'd persuaded him to do that very thing, in a moment of terrible rage.

She lost many months beyond this, until she met the Enchanter who could restore her Ash to her.

Not to life. Never that. Dead was dead. But it was a return, none-theless.

"You have to go," Ash said, as he always did. "You have to return to the living."

"Sometimes I don't know how," she whispered. Her eyes blurred with tears. "And what use am I to the living, if I cannot even save my own daughter? If my eldest son left me?"

Ash pressed his lips to the top of her head. "When the time comes, you will know what to do. Not Holden. You, Gretchen. Just as you did when you whispered life back into what remained of me."

SEVERAL PACES FROM THIS TENDER MOMENT CROUCHED ANOTHER figure. It wasn't the first time Drystan had followed his mother to the crypts, but he'd never come so close to her subterfuge. He strained to see in the darkness; somehow the tickle of torchlight was harder than the pitch blackness of night. Her voice carried, her inflections indicating an ongoing conversation with another, but he heard only her.

As Drystan edged closer, he saw her arms reach out to embrace the air. Her head caved to the side as she sought comfort from something that didn't exist.

His heart surged so hard he thought for sure she could hear the thrumming echoing off the walls.

"My love," Drystan heard her say, to no one, to nothing, and that was enough to make him wish he'd left his curiosity at the top of the stairs.

FEALTY AND SECRECY

I

THE LOT IS CAST

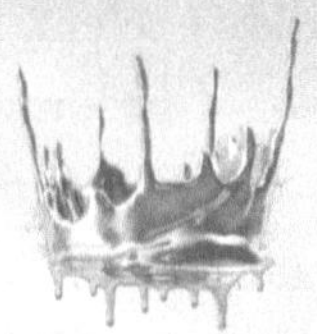

Ravenna Ravenwood stormed through the moonlit halls of The Rookery, her rage echoing in every strike of her jeweled heels against the sodden stone.

Brilliant white light flashed beyond the open arches of the upper gallery. Thunder dutifully followed moments later, splitting the sky. It had been storming all day, and now night, but this was midwinter, the tempest season, and if it wasn't crackling skies and ice storms, it was snowbolts. High in the Northerland Range, at Midnight Crest, they almost always received the worst of whatever the gods sent down.

She loved and hated these storms. They brought her peace, soothing her own natural tempestuousness, but they also meant no escape from the castle. Being so high in the mountains, there was only one way to swoop down into safer territory, and there was nothing safe about flying through the wrath raining down upon their world that night.

"Ravenna!"

The voice calling her name, only a pace away, was the very one she now fled. If he thought she'd change her mind, or soften her heart, he was destined for disappointment. If he thought there was ever any going back to the way things were, he was—

"Come on, Ravenna! You know the way of things!"

The shock of lightning pulsing the sky as Ravenna rounded a corner caused her heel to miss a step. That brief change of stride was enough for her brother to reach a hand out and snag her arm in his palm.

"Let me *go*, Alasyr," she hissed. She wrenched her arm so hard his fingers bruised her, but he didn't relent. She didn't turn. Looking at him again, now or ever, would be unwise. If she did, her hatred would burn through them both. Turn him, or her, to stone.

"You knew this day would come." He didn't let go, but he lessened his death grip. Alasyr, her truest of friends, until today. Her confidante, playmate; pillow for tears, or rage, or sometimes both. Ryandyr, Ashara, and the twins were too young as she'd come screaming from childhood and forward, dwindling over the precipice that would change her designation from enfant to woman. But Alasyr had understood. He protected her on bad days and laughed with her on good ones.

Now, all of that was past. It was snow on the wind of yesterday. It was beyond meaning or consequence.

"This day," she said, staring defiantly into the murky sky beyond the balustrades. "Not your part in it."

"How could you not know I would put in my lot?" Alasyr reached forward with his other hand, and this touch was more tender. "That I wouldn't at least try to protect what we have, forever?"

"What we have?" Ravenna laughed. The sound found sharp edges as it bounced off damp stone. The howl of the accompanying wind was animalistic. Rain pummeled hard enough to sweep in sideways, stippling the ground near their feet, while the thunder clapped almost in tandem with the light now. The storm roared heavy upon them, yawning in from the darkness. "You believe what we have would be the same, then, do you? That it would not be spoilt by such an act? Even if you did emerge victorious from the night?"

Alasyr stepped closer. His breath was a humid rush against the cool, charged air. "What would you have had me do?"

"Not that!"

"Then *what*, Ravenna? Let it fall to one of the cousins? Uncles? Men, boys, none of whom know a whit about you, who you are? The things you love? What makes you smile?"

Love was a peculiar word to a Ravenwood, and an even more twisted sentiment. Love wasn't meant for the priests and priestesses of Midnight Crest, because love could only amount to disappointment. What was the opposite of love? That was what a Ravenwood should expect from life. There were other rewards designed for their ilk.

Except, Ravenna Ravenwood *did* know love, and the source of that love, and what it meant, or could not mean, was the true font of her rage as the moon entered its fullest form.

The skies tore open. Rain formed a wall in the night, hitting the castle so hard it drove both of them farther in. Alasyr pivoted in the retreat and covered her with his body protectively. "Ravenna. This is who we are. This was always your fate, but it doesn't have to be so beyond your control. It doesn't have to be Aryc, or Sandyr." He reached inside his violet cloak and withdrew a vial. "I had this made. It's for virility. It could improve my chances."

Ravenna turned her face away. She winced as her cheek connected with the icy stone wall. "You're lifetimes away from the point, brother. Even if you win, Aryc and Sandyr and the others, they already cast their lot, and they'll get their chance. What's the difference between once and forever? Once is enough to change everything. As for you... for us... if you lose, everything dies, because of a single act. If you win, everything dies, because of many acts. At least if you stayed away, you'd still be my Alasyr. Now, no matter the outcome of Langenacht, you'll be no better than the rest."

Alasyr stepped back. He slipped in the growing puddle, but

steadied himself. He looked wounded. "I treasure you, Ravenna. You above any. Above all."

"You can't be my protector, my brother, and my husband. Not all three."

"Why not three, when I've always been two?"

Ravenna sighed. She pulled the velvet hood tighter around her dark hair. Violet eyes glowed from within. If she transformed now, she'd be knocked about by the storm, and there was no magic she'd yet learned to protect her from a perilous fall into the jagged, snowy mountains. But if she stayed…

"You say you treasure me, but you haven't listened to me. You haven't heard anything I've told you about this day, about what the Langenacht means to me."

Alasyr twisted his mouth into a frown. "That's not true. You've never wanted it. Not like Mother did, or Grandmother. I know that, Ravenna, that's—"

Ravenna pressed a finger to his lips. "You talk, talk, talk, Alasyr, but you don't listen. I never wanted it, no, but I know who I am, and I know the inevitability of taking my own blood as a bridegroom. But that does *not* mean I have to like it, or to treat it as some great honor as the High Priestesses who've come before me have done. Until today, I looked at you and saw my escape. I saw my brother, my confidante, the one who knew me. Now, I see only another Ravenwood casting his lot to lay with the future High Priestess, in hopes of securing his own power and legacy."

"That isn't why I did it!"

"I know that," Ravenna said. The chill biting the air came with sharp sprays of icy rain now, and if they didn't seek greater shelter, farther inside The Rookery, they'd be inundated. "But your motivations mean nothing to me. Only the inevitability of laying with my own brother, my only friend, and tarnishing the very last pure thing I still had."

It wasn't the last. That was a lie. But this was a truth she kept even from Alasyr, because she couldn't bear the idea of him one day choosing between his loyalty to the Ravenwoods and his loyalty to her. Either choice would destroy her, and them.

Ah, but it no longer mattered, because Alasyr, her beloved brother and only true friend, had cast his lot in with the other eligible male sorcerers of the Ravenwood clan, and he, along with the others, would get their chance to lay with her by the greenlight fires on the Langenacht. If Alasyr's seed proved strongest, she would take her brother as her husband, and they would rule Midnight Crest together, as High Priest and High Priestess. If he failed to ignite a child within her, her hand would go to the male who didn't fail to fill her womb. The magic blessing the cold cliffs would go to the man most worthy, and only the gods knew the outcome.

The Langenacht was the one and only means of deciding the divine rulers of the Ravenwoods, and as the eldest daughter of the reigning High Priestess, she had but two choices on the anniversary of her coming of age: surrender to the blessed tradition of her ancient forebears, or be thrown from the mountain to a disgraceful death. So it had been for thousands of years, and so it would be for thousands still. No one questioned. No one changed.

Whichever way the wind of fate blew, the innocence of her bond with Alasyr would be no more.

"I didn't know." Alasyr's face collapsed, and she couldn't discern the rain from tears. "I only saw a chance for things to be as they always had. To keep protecting you, as I always have." He ran a finger over the edge of her velvet hood. "I'll withdraw. I'll tell Mother I've changed my mind."

"The lot is cast. It cannot be changed."

"But I'm her son! If I tell her I didn't mean it, that I was sleep-deprived, or drunk on brandywine, or—"

Ravenna pressed two hands to her brother's chest and gently pushed him back. "You cannot. What's done is done. You offered your own blood, and it's written in the stars. Only death can undo a cast lot, as you well know."

Alasyr stepped once, twice, thrice. He held open his arms. "Then

I'll fling myself from the ramparts, Ravenna, if that'll end your pain and quench your hatred of me."

"Don't be a fool."

"Would it make you look at me as you used to? If instead of calling down all your curses on me, you were crying over my broken body?"

Ravenna shook her head. She needed to be free of this moment. Peril or no, she couldn't remain here. There was no use in prolonging the torment, or debating a solution that didn't exist. "You *can't* die, Alasyr. Not that way. I bound you in safety years ago. No fall would harm you, no sword could sever you. You'll die old, in your bed."

Alasyr regarded her with bleary, sad eyes. "Alone?"

"Only the gods know," Ravenna said, but the last of her words were lost to the current of wings as she soared over him and into the peril of the storm. She didn't turn her raven's head to see if he watched, but instead navigated south, bracing against the driving rain, toward Wulfsgate.

2

WCNM999

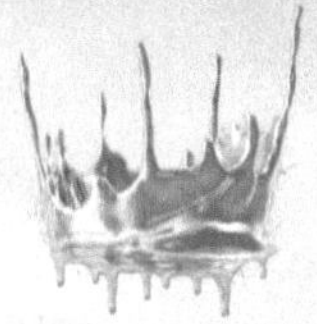

"Food allotment for Prisoner W-C-N-M-9-9-9," a deep voice called out. Cap made his way through the throngs of dusty prisoners, pushing against filth and despair. He hadn't eaten in three days and hadn't passed a wet cloth over his flesh in as many weeks. He could no longer pretend the sores on his feet and thighs were from the grueling labor schedule. This was a disease he'd never seen before in his past life, but he knew of it. It was common in the Southerlands, where they ate more fish than they did things grown from the ground. Cap had been to the Southerlands, in his youth, but he wasn't from there.

"Thanks," Cap said as he accepted the crumbling clay bowl, overflowing with gray matter. He wasn't convinced what they served was even food, but it was warm and it staved off death. Five years he'd survived on it, if one could call this Wastelands existence surviving. Many didn't make it that long.

He tried to find a place under the shade, but there were no trees in Camp Atonement, or anywhere in the Wastelands, only tattered tents and ramshackle lean-tos. Cap settled in at the edge of the makeshift screen that encircled the area where the men went to lay their waste. The smell didn't bother him anymore, not really, not like it did. Like it should. He didn't think about what life was like before. He'd stopped comparing the food of this world to the heady scents of boar and spice; stopped recalling what his flesh felt like against *hers*, clean and soft and inviting.

"Lucky day for you, Cap," another prisoner, Hill, said, pointing with jealous hunger at the nondescript meal. Truth was, it smelled as good as it looked and tasted worse.

"How long's it been?"

"Aye, a week?" Hill rubbed at the dirt on his face. Dark purple crescents dipped along the underside of his eyes, and he had the belly bloat that signaled the path had begun. Thin and frail in the limbs, but a gut that grew until the only thing to look forward to was the dead-given rites.

Wouldn't be long, then.

"Ahh, Hill," Cap said with a shake of his head. "Have some of mine."

Hill smiled as he kicked at the red dust at their feet. "Nay, it wouldn't do to take a meal from a man living, not for a man dying."

Cap lowered his voice. For some reason, the gaolers didn't like them talking about the camp for what it was. "It doesn't have to be that way. Maybe I can finish some of your work instead. Bring up a few more barrows from the mines and say they're yours. I can do more than I'm doing." This last was a lie, and they both knew it. No one could do more than they were doing, or they would. Their food was measured in tandem with their efforts.

Hill clapped him on the back, but it lacked enthusiasm. His bony hand fell back to his side. "But then you'd starve, and we'd both die for the effort."

There was no use complaining to the gaolers about any of this. They'd find more prisoners, probably from the Southerlands, where the king saw fit to steal men from the Warwicks in the crown's ongoing efforts to punish them. Men, they could replace. Food was a finite resource. Food was a reward for labor, and once a prisoner grew too old, weak, or weary for labor, he wasn't worth feeding. Hill was one of the first to come to the labor camp opened by King Khain before he died. His prisoner number was SHNT1—the very first thief to come here from Salthill, in the Northerlands. He'd outlasted nearly everyone, including many who'd come after. But you could only starve a man for so long.

"New batch came in a week or so ago." Hill squinted against the unforgiving noonday sun. It brought the flies with the heat, which were already gathering everywhere; against their flesh, along the gummy surface of the gruel Cap had no choice but to eat if he wanted to survive.

"Oh, yeah?"

"Most from the Southerlands."

"Seems the way of things." Cap swallowed down another spoonful.

"Warwick's a fool, but he's not the one who starves when he squares up against the crown. At least here, his people can eat." Hill scratched at his brow. "Well, sometimes."

Cap didn't like talking about the crown. "Any bets on the unluckies?" The unluckies were what they called their fellow prisoners in those first days when they realized every terrible thing they'd learned about Camp Atonement was wrong—it was all far worse than they could've ever imagined.

"A few squirrely ones, but they'll knock that out of 'em quick."

"I'd say so."

"One from Sandycove has a real swing in his step. Young'un."

"What did he do?"

"Thievery, according to the crown guard. But, like most here, prolly nothin' other than the misfortune of being born under a Warwick reign in the Southern Reach." Hill spat at the ground, but almost nothing materialized. If the lack of food didn't kill him, the dehydration would rise to the task. "Goes by Andy."

"Andy." That wasn't his name, of course, any more than Cap was really Cap and Hill was really Hill. They had names before this;

some even came from the Greater Families. In here, those names meant nothing, and so they were quickly forgotten. They weren't enough to shield them from the horrors of the Wastelands. Hill was called as such because of his Salthill roots. Cap, from Whitecap. Andy, a nod to Sandycove. The call back to where they hailed from was the only whisper of home allowed.

"There's also the matter of The Right of Choosing."

Cap winced. The king was a fool for going forward with the ceremony. Khain's death should have freed Eoghan from imprudent choices, but instead he was pushing forward along the same course. "He really intends to go through with it, then."

"Aye. I think he'd take all the lasses if he thought the houses would stand for it. Greedy bastard." Hill spat again, and this time nothing left his mouth. "Hell, might be war anyway. Warwick's only daughter is with the Guardians now, and no chance he'll send his wife in her stead."

"Mother's blood."

"Aye. The Dereham girl is still a lass, too. None of it feels right."

Cap would miss Hill for a lot of reasons, but his ability to glean any and all news, from within and without the camp, was among the top.

Even the painful news. He'd stopped fighting so hard, but Cap couldn't forget who he was.

Cap licked at the remnants of the bowl. When he considered how far he'd fallen in five years, it was never in the big moments, but in these, where his desperation for anything warm in his belly overrode any semblance of humanity left in him.

"That'll be the bell," Hill said, followed by a curse under his breath.

Cap was overcome with a powerful sense, and he'd come to trust these feelings. He'd never see Hill again. He knew it, just as he knew his own name. His real name. "Hill," he said, as the old man turned away. "I'm not a murderer. I didn't kill anyone, least of all my family."

Hill blinked away the sweat from his eyelids. "Aye? Wha' brought this on today?"

"We both know," Cap said. "And, if no one else believes me, let me leave the words with a dying man, who can take them to the Guardians and write them on the sky."

Hill snickered. He ran his hands over his head and came back with a tuft of white hair. "I know who ye are, Cap. I've always known. But it was never me ye had to convince. You're a good man, but that means feck-all in a place like this. And unless you can see your way out of it, you'll die a good man, and that'll mean feck-all, too."

"There is no way out of it."

Hill shrugged his bony shoulders and slumped off to complete his final day of labor.

THE EARLY DAYS HAD BEEN HARD.

Cap fought through his mornings and noondays, and nursed his wounds through his sleepless nights. The gaolers made a sport of his beatings, looking forward to them with increasing zeal. No other prisoner goaded them quite like Cap, as most learned their lesson after the first two or three sound thrashings. Most eventually figured out that the gaolers had no such rules against killing them. Men were replaceable, and the Wastelands was a lawless land.

For a year, he went to bed bruised, broken, and bloody. But he worked hard, and so he ate, and the energy emboldened him, and the emboldening led to more fighting, more whipping.

Eventually, the bloodlust in the eyes of the gaolers turned to pity. A man needing the spirit knocked out of him had come to the prison camp, but what remained was an empty shell of what once was, and there was no fun to be had in that.

They left him alone after that. Not only from the beatings, but in all things. When he walked past, they made a wide berth, as if afraid of the one man in the Wastelands who had nothing to lose and was no longer afraid of losing it. The soulless one.

But this wasn't true. Cap still had a soul, and it was the only thing that still kept him lifting the pickaxe, day after day.

CAP PAUSED FOR THE FIRST TIME IN HOURS TO CATCH HIS BREATH. He'd been pushing the carts up the mine all afternoon, owing to the brief rush of energy from the colorless gruel. Sweat covered every inch of his skin, running the dirt from his flesh into the floor of the cavern.

"Careful. I hear the gaolers are real cockmongers," someone said.

Cap winced and turned toward the sound. A young man, standing fully erect with soft arrogance coursing through his virile limbs. Not yet broken by the yoke of labor under the crown's worst. New, then. "You heard right enough." He uncapped the waterskin and took a deep sip. "Some are worse than others. You'll learn."

"I don't intend to learn feck-all here, but I may teach 'em a thing or two," the young man with the sandy blond hair and ruddy cheeks said, before extending a hand. "Andy. Not really my name, but you know that. Feckers made me check it at the door, along with anything else of value."

Cap frowned at the clean hand in front of him. They didn't observe pleasantries here, but of course most of the unluckies didn't know that coming in. They didn't know anything at all, but they learned.

"Right." Andy pulled his hand back and dug it into his pocket. "Well, I know who you are."

"Yeah?"

Andy's bright blue eyes twinkled. "The infamous murderer of Whitecap."

"So they say."

"What say you?"

Cap, in his delirium of hunger and desperation, often wondered if the crown sent in spies disguised as prisoners, and he couldn't decide if Andy fit that delusion, or was simply too new to realize the futility in wasting words. If they didn't get them food, rest, or water, they had no use. Merely energy misused.

"I say nothing matters but their truth. And you'll do well to remember that if you want food in your belly."

Andy grinned from one corner of his mouth. "You're looking out for me. That's sweet."

Cap shrugged. "I don't even know you. And now, we both better get back to work, because, as you say, the gaolers are real cock-mongers."

"We should be mates."

Cap didn't know what to make of this strange young man. Even in the real world, the outside world, no one talked the way he did, not that Cap could remember, anyway. In fairness, he'd forgotten more than he'd like. "Why?"

"You need one," Andy said, and then said no more. He walked off, picked up an axe, and went about his first day of labor.

3

THE DEAD-GIVEN RITES

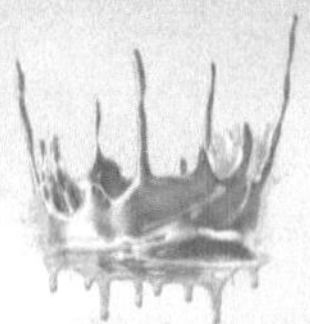

"The sea lives within us. We live within the sea. On land, as on sea, we persist in dualities. Salt. Flesh. Blood. Foam. Stone. Bones." Minister Allen drowned in the heavy crimson robes of the Reliquary. He was neither boy nor man, from what Khallum could see. If he had hair on his balls, it had come mercifully early. He wasn't ready for the magnitude of a day like this, or for any great task of adulthood, but yet here the man-child was, delivering the dead-given rites, for what was undoubtedly the first time in his fledgling career in the clergy.

That the Grand Minister hadn't attended this requiem was yet another slight against the Warwicks and the Southerlands, and he'd no doubt of the source. Sending this little pube in his place was a direct hit with a morning star, meant not only to wound, but to cripple. Under orders from The Pretender or no, he would pay a price for this choice. Khallum would see to the task himself.

"That poor kitten never seen blood, t'wasn't his own," Hamish Strong muttered to Lem Garrick. The men stood at Khallum's side, as all the men of the great houses of the Southerlands were compelled to do by the ineffability of tradition. Gwyn was elsewhere in the crowd, with the other children, the ones who'd lived. He found himself searching for her in the sea of robes and gowns, but they were all where they were meant to be, and even his authority held little sway against tradition.

More so, his eyes were drawn to the milky cliffs of the Golden Coast. The tidal surge brought the seafoam of the White Sea up and over the jagged edges, though by most accounts it was a good day. The sun shined overhead, and there was naught but a light midwinter chill, the kind people would say reminded them more of springtide.

Esmerelda, Khallum thought, and as if on cue, Minister Allen said the same name aloud to the assembled mourners.

"Although we cannot consecrate Lady Esmerelda's terrestrial remains to hallowed ground, or to the blessing of the flame, we beseech you, Guardian of the Unpromised Future, ye who have weighed the life of Esmerelda Warwick and deemed its promise ended, to protect her from your kin, the Guardian of Trial and Tribulation. Surely, the soul of the young and spirited Esmerelda has earned her peace eternal."

Khallum spotted Gwyn across the rocky span. Her red hair caught the wind like a flag, blowing sideways over the heads of their three sons. Even Ransom, though grown, could not match the height of his Northerland mother. She didn't see Khallum. She wasn't looking in the direction of the requiem, but elsewhere, toward the sea. Esmerelda's broken vessel belonged to the waves now. Was she thinking of how it was her child the sea chose not to return? Hers, when so many others found their way back, rolling lifeless to the shore?

Minister Allen fumbled with the Great Codex of the Reliquary. If he hadn't had the words written upon a page, there would've been no end to the disgrace of this bairn barely removed from his swaddling, struggling through the dead-given rites for Khallum's only daughter.

If he fails at her name even once, Khallum forewarned, in the Hall of Warring, just before Strong rolled the mourning cloak over his shoulders. The thing was hefty, a mess of black ermine, woad-dyed wulf's pelt, and raven's feathers sent down from Gwyn's people in Wulfsgate. Too much for the milder winters of the Southerlands, but it looked fit for a king, and if The Pretender had his spies about today, all the better. Eoghan's men had stolen as he pleased, plundered and raped as he pleased, but today, Khallum Warwick looked as kingly as a Rhiagain, and ten times more formidable.

Garrick responded by reaching one hand over his back, to caress the battle-axe, his most especial promise of fidelity. He'd do it, too. Slice the little pube's head clean off, or perhaps not so clean. Khallum loved him for it and would use his childhood friend's unquenchable bloodlust for as long as it suited him.

Save it for the Grand Minister, Strong growled. *Tha' craven bastard.*

Aye. I have another thing planned for that lowborn grasper. Leave him for me. Khallum would deal with the matter of Grand Minister Maegar another day.

Today, he was releasing his only daughter to the uncertain afterlife of the Unpromised Future.

KHALLUM SHED THE MOURNING CLOAK WITHOUT SLOWING PACE. IT hit the stone floor with a heavy, gratifying thud. He'd worn it, as he promised Gwyn he would when her fair-haired moralist brother had it sent with haste on one of his antiquated whaling ships. His duty to the matter of the oddly trussed cloak was ended.

Someone, probably Erran Rutland, stopped and swooped the monstrous thing from a future of dust and obscurity as they all followed Khallum back to the Hall of Warring.

His men, to the last. And the last might not be so far ahead now.

"Khallum." Samuel Law. The only one of them with the courage and strong head to know business was the order of the noonday. Even today. Especially today.

"You never quit, do ya? Not even t'day?" Hamish Strong, his soft but effective freebooter of Sandycove. Hamish's loyalty pulsed in his heart, not his head, and there was no one, not even Khallum himself, so devoted to the Southerlands and her prosperity.

"Tomorrow doesnae slow down when today gives pause," Law rejoined.

"Be still, Hamish," Khallum said as he sank into the deep chair at the head of the darkish table he and his father built with their own hands from the teakwood growing along the black sand shore at Port Worthing. Salt had corroded the exterior, and it now bore a milder, milkier patina than the original design, but it reminded Khallum that everything he possessed came from the land that belonged to him and his forebears. A land that had, only recently, fleetingly, belonged to someone less worthy.

Hamish squared his hard features at Law, but was still, as his lord asked.

Khallum ran his hands over the rough surface of the table. They'd shaped it into the resemblance of their finest sea vessel. The corners were roughly hewn, a stark reminder never to lean in too far when you paid counsel to the Lord of the Southerlands.

His ten men took their own seats once he was settled. Five steorbord, five larboard, with him, the eleventh, at the helm.

"Speak, then," Khallum said, and it came out nearly a groan, but more truly a sigh. "Taxes, I presume."

"We're two seasons behind," Law replied. He rested both hands atop the table, but carefully. Barne Holton had, just that past autumnwhile, sliced so deep into his palm during a passionate discourse that the blood loss rendered him light on his feet. Later, the black fingers spread up into his wrist, and the doctor promised he could save him, but not his hand.

"Tha' all? Wait till they see the rotting fish sent their way!" Strong cried, and several of the other men grunted in pleasured agreement. Proud of their freebooting they were, though until someone could figure out what was really out there to be had, in the

World Beyond the Sea, there'd always be a limit to great achievement.

"Two seasons, and King Eoghan sent our messenger's ear back when we asked for a reprieve."

"An ear," Khallum fumed, far too exhausted to disguise his wrath. His eye convulsed in tandem with the veins throbbing in his neck. "I'll take more than an ear, should the craven ratsbane find the mettle to show himself in the Southerlands."

Garrick twitched, but resisted the urge to give his battle-axe another loving stroke.

"He'd never," Rutland answered. "The king isnae the man his grandfather was."

"Aye, and is that not the point? His grandfather restored to us these lands. Eoghan would see them taken away."

"He wants a more agreeable lord is all," Law said. "One who would do as he was told."

Waves crashed against the cliffs beyond the stone castle. Khallum could taste the salt; it burned through his nostrils. He wasn't like these other men. He wasn't even really a Southerlander, not in the way they were. He'd built his fortress in Warwicktown to harden himself against the elements, but his skin never leathered and his lungs struggled against the gritty sea air. If his men knew it, they never let on, but they missed very little.

Khallum ran his tongue across his perpetually cracked lips. "You're on his side now, Sam? The man whose father was behind the deaths of my parents, my grandparents? Who drove my own daughter to the sea like a troubled fishwife?"

Law recoiled. "Never, my lord. But you've always asked me to think like the enemy. I'm thinking like him now. His patience is thin, and even a craven ratsbane will act upon slighted pride. He'll send in others to avoid dirtying his hands, but he won't tolerate another season of rebuke." Law glanced cautiously at his peers, as if they'd all convened ahead of the council session, and he'd pulled the unlucky short draw of wheat. "And then there's the matter of Esmerelda's absence."

Khallum pressed both palms into the rough tabletop. Yes, Esmerelda. Eoghan would've taken her, too, if she hadn't taken her own life. But her unavailability to serve at the king's pleasure didn't mean the Warwicks wouldn't be held to account.

"There is no matter of Esmerelda. Not anymore. There is only the matter of Gwyn, as I have no other daughters, and these are the rules in the season of pretenders."

Most of the men gaped at him in confused horror, even Nye, who never reacted to anything except when a cold snap took them unawares. But it was Strong who had the courage to ask, "Ye donnae really mean to hand over your wife to tha' fiend?"

"Of fecking course not," Khallum replied with a look that turned the room to stone. "But that'll be the ratsbane's expectation. My daughter is with the Guardians now. I have no others. Gwyn nearly died bringing little Garrick along, and she willnae be bringing another."

"In any case, the ceremony of the Right of Choosing is in less than a fortnight," Law reminded them. "Hardly time to usher in a replacement."

Khallum blinked the heaviness from his eyes, aiming a stony gaze at his sophistic friend. "Do ye not hear me? There willnae *be* a replacement. There willnae be an offering to the king at the Right of Choosing from the Southerlands."

"What about the other three houses? Will they deliver?"

Khallum grunted. "That bootlicker Aiden will ensure the Easterlands complies, and he'll do it with shit in his smile. My brother says Asherley would smite the crown, but she isnae prepared to let Eoghan turn an eye to the Westerlands, for fear he'll seek the richness of her resources."

"And Gwyn's brother?"

"Holden," Khallum echoed. "Aye, the Northerlands will deliver.

He shouldn't, but he will." He curled his upper lip. "To protect those enchantresses in the north."

"What then? Do we go? Do we stay?" Rutland asked.

"We'll be the only Reach without an offering," Law said, and you would've thought someone suggested he run through his neighbor's handfast ceremony in the nude. "For the very first Right of Choosing! Like it or not—"

Garrick rolled forward, looking down the table at the man he'd never gotten along with unless his lord commanded. "Do ye not hear Lord Warwick? Anything he says? Ever? He doesnae *agree* with the Right of Choosing. None of us do. He *loathes* it. It's an affront to each of the kingdoms, and an affront to what the crown once was. And ye remember the last time a king summoned them to Termonglen, do ye not? All four Reaches still mourn their mas and pas." Garrick launched something yellow from the back of his throat across the room. It slid down the wall, next to the streaky white trails of sea salt. "And on the day he submits his sweet wee lass to the Guardians, you lay this guilt at his feet."

"Steady," Khallum warned, but he loved Garrick, in a way he could never love a man like Law. But he needed Law, in a way he'd never need Garrick. "We go. We spit in the face of the ratsbane, and tell him no Southerlander will be sucking his cock, today or ever." He spat on the stones at his feet. A prophetic demonstration.

Cheers from his men. The table rocked as their pounding enthusiasm mingled with the crash of the flow tide building outside.

"Then there will be war," Law said.

"War." Khallum snorted. "The little pissant doesnae know the word beyond the pages of books written within a kingdom he knows nothing of."

"The most promising soldiers in the kingdom join the Rhiagain Guard," Law countered. "There is no greater honor in our realm than to be elevated to a Knight of Duncarrow."

"The Rhiagain Guard grows fat upon inaction. The Knights of

Duncarrow are naught more tha' pretty costumes. All bluster, no blow."

"I would not underestimate their numbers. They're thrice ours, and that estimate is conservative."

"Aye, and the Easterlands will fight for him," Strong said. "They're sworn to him."

"Since when?" Khallum demanded.

Strong glanced at a handful of others. So, this wasn't news. Not to them. "In the springtide, my lord. Aiden laid Rowanwen, their ancestral sword, at Eoghan's feet, swearing especial fealty. 'Twas no empty promise."

"Nay. No empty promise," Khallum mused, and with a wave of his hand, dismissed them.

Strong and Rutland hung back when the others departed. His dearest boyhood mates, now his most trusted advisors. Khallum moved to the balustrades lining the Hall of Warring. The weather was agreeable enough that he rarely regretted building a room so open to the elements, but there were other foul things traveling across the air that day.

"My lord," Rutland ventured. "Khallum."

"Aye, I meant it." Khallum dug his palms into the stone counter, stained white from the perpetual stream of seabirds swarming overhead. "Eoghan and his father have forgotten their forebears."

"So it has been, from time to time, throughout history," Rutland replied. "Are we prepared for war? Much as it aggrieves me to say, Law was right. Not that you were wrong. Eoghan isnae the man his grandfather was. He's worse than his father, Khain, in some ways. And his reign is only just begun. Only the Guardians know what other horrors lay ahead when he finally finds his sea legs."

Khallum rolled his head forward. Below, miners covered in black filth bustled like ants, dredging gold, ore, silver, and now something else, something new that glittered in the noonday sun. The glory of the Southerlands. "Fynne would look you in the eye as he drove the sword into your belly. Khain and Eoghan are cowards, who sent their men slinking into the Reaches to pluck the life from our ancestors until it was only us left. Cowards are dangerous. Unpredictable."

"We could extract my son from the Wastelands. My Ryan," Strong said, voice low and cautious. A light tremor passed through his words.

"Nay. Ryan's been in there nary a fortnight, Hamish. He willnae have finished his task. Not yet." Khallum turned halfway and cast a look at his old friend over his shoulder. The work Hamish's son did now was important work, but there was a reason it was a Strong, and not some lowborn, chosen for it. It wasn't Hamish's fault his son Ryan reached beyond his means, letting his heart lead him to Esmerelda. And now, the matter of his crime was stricken from the great record of life. Yet, it was true that the work he'd do in the prison was the work of a hero. Perhaps Ryan Strong could redeem himself with Khallum in the end. "We willnae abandon him. On my word."

"We were *promised* shipments of grain from the Easterlands a calendar cycle ago. Our men have eaten nothing with roots or stems in ages," Rutland interjected. "Our people are starving. A foul illness sweeps through them. One we've seen only in our darkest times."

"If the lowborns want to take up broken promises with someone, I suggest they sail for Duncarrow and ask the king himself."

"If we only paid the taxes—"

Khallum's voice thundered across the rocky walls. "I will *not* send even *more* money to a crown that delivers nothing in return! Every season, Khain and his demonling have asked for more of us. Every season, we've delivered, trusting that they would deliver on their own promises of supplies. The King's Decree is meant to work both ways, not one. They never intended to live up to their end, Rutland, so we should bend over now and deliver even more? Give them free rein of our lands, our riches? When they've already taken a quarter of our men, swaddling them with false charges and throwing them in labor camps? Eoghan Rhiagain would destroy everything his forebears built, and I willnae help him along on this craven fool's errand. I willnae allow him to take without giving, even another day!"

"There willnae be riches if our men are too ill to take to the mines."

"Khallum is right," Strong said. He sounded shaky and unsure, probably still thinking of his youngest son in the crown labor camp. "We're Southerlanders. We donnae bend. We donnae break. We donnae do anything if 'tis not a benefit to us or our people."

Rutland ignored him and turned to Khallum. "I know Quinlanden is licking Eoghan's boots, but do you truly believe the others won't stand with us? Asherley Blackwood? Holden Dereham?"

Khallum returned his gaze to the sea. "Asherley is a riddle, even to my brother. I've already sent word to Holden."

"When?"

"When I found Esmerelda's letter." Khallum swallowed. The emotion ebbed back down, where it belonged. "He is Gwyn's brother. He cannae sit back and let the boy king take her. His own daughter, Lisbet, only turned fourteen. He cannae really mean to send her to Duncarrow."

"And if he willnae stand with us? If the Southerlanders are the only ones at Termonglen without a bride for the king?"

Khallum filled his lungs with the coarse air of the sea. "Garrick has been keeping the blacksmiths sharp and practiced."

4

THE SPARE

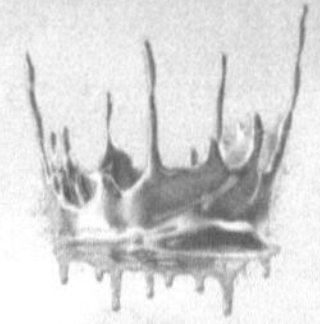

Drystan Dereham crossed out yet another line in the book he referred to as his diary when his mother wasn't around. Her soft, but commanding voice echoed in the back of his mind with every word he penned to life. *This is not a poem, Drystan. This is an accounting of your day. Your life recorded for posterity. Your future reader does not desire dressing, only facts.* He then tried to imagine his words one day written in *The Book of All Things*, within the chapter *Histories of the Great Families*, sub-chapter, *Northerlands*, section, *Dereham*. Of course, he'd never witness this. The words would be inked upon his death, and not a moment sooner, as was the way. On that day, they'd throw the old copies of the *Dereham* section tomes in pyres, replaced with the new.

He didn't envy the copyist responsible for transcribing the mundane thoughts of all the highborns of the kingdom. His mother reminded him, when he forgot to stifle his groans, that if not for these writings of prior generations, they would not know their own histories. That they didn't want to be like the Rhiagains, who claimed to know nothing of who they were. That every detail, no matter how small, was important. *It's these details that make the story, Drystan. Not the words announcing a new chapter.*

He enjoyed details too, just not the same ones.

Gretchen Dereham rarely wasted so much of her energies on her other five children. Christian left for the Sepulchre when he was young and never returned, Lisbet was a dutiful student—or, smart enough to pretend—Pieter enjoyed the rigor of regimen, and the twins were as yet too young to be held to the responsibility of chronicling. And Drystan knew for a fact there were sometimes weeks where her mother wrote nothing in her own chronicle.

Your words will matter one day, Gretchen liked to say, even before they knew Christian wouldn't return to prepare himself to become the eventual head of the Northern Reach. It was as if she knew Drystan, who was born the spare, would be forced to find within himself that which he had not been born with. She knew that as well, of course. Who he was. What he was not.

Drystan sighed and returned to his least favorite duty. *Last night I dreamed of Ravenna. She came to me in the sliver of moonlight easing across my windowsill, her hair of midnight streaming behind her, vying to keep pace with the luminous energy she unintentionally, but purposefully, brought forth into every step. I dared not wake, not even for the hunger tickling through my dreamscape.* He crossed this out, too. Tried again. *Slept fair, awoke just after dawn and broke fast with the family. Boar, quail egg, and bread fresh from the oven. Father was indisposed, so I sat for two ticks of the sun in the Hall of Hearing, considering the petitions from the working class and guilds of Wulfsgate. Resolved two border disputes and granted aid to a farmer whose crops were lost to a rare run of blight. Approved a tanner's solicitation for new business, along the market quarter bordering the southern gates. Collected monthly rents.*

Drystan set the quill aside. He looked up, almost desperate for his dream image of Ravenna to appear, which was no replacement for her presence, but was still most welcome. It was akin to the light scent she left upon his pillow; her, but not enough.

He hadn't seen Ravenna since the day they agreed the only

option available to them was to leave before the Langenacht. But that discussion was nearly a fortnight ago, and less than a fortnight separated them from that fated night where she would bed the virile men of her clan, marry the one who sired her child, and, together, rule Midnight Crest until their own daughter came of age and went through the same sordid tradition.

It wouldn't come to pass. It couldn't. It was impossible for Drystan to imagine the woman he loved laying with *any* man not himself, though he'd never lain with her, either. Not out of a lack of desire, but fear. Her brood had a way of knowing certain things, and the discovery of the loss of her maidenhead would cause her to be cast from The Rookery to her death. There was no crime amongst her ilk like that of betrayal to tradition.

Until they were safely delivered from the Northerlands, they could not be safe in their love, either.

For Ravenna, the prospect of the Langenacht was even more painful than anything Drystan could imagine. She'd accepted her fate, as all future High Priestesses of Midnight Crest eventually did, until the strange friendship budding between her and Drystan became more than shared giggles and the comfort of childhood acquaintances. Her apprenticeship in Wulfsgate, which like many Ravenwood children involved healing and other useful tasks to help prepare for maturity, lasted far longer than it should have, and she was running out of excuses for why she continued to visit the town of men, when she belonged upon the jagged peaks of Midnight Crest with her own. She couldn't possibly tell them about the long talks, lasting through the night and well into the morning. She didn't dare mention the stolen kisses and the tears of longing. She blamed the volatile Northern weather and the sharp crags of Icebolt Mountain for the evenings she didn't make it home.

Drystan said nothing to anyone either, except Lisbet. His punishment might or might not be equal to hers—he very much doubted the Ravenwoods were foolish enough to go up against the might of the Northerlands—but the fallout would change everything. It would destroy the careful alliance between Wulfsgate and Midnight Crest; between man and sorcerer. The two had little in common but much to gain from keeping civility intact, and Drystan felt the weight of this piercing him in places he couldn't reach to ease.

The only option was to leave.

Yet there was a problem Drystan, in all his hours and hours of daydreaming, had yet to solve, and that was how he might accomplish this without tearing apart centuries of alliances and bringing the world down upon both the Derehams and Ravenwoods.

Drew my bow for one tick of the sun, out past the edge of the Forest of Lycana where the foothills begin to rise up and become mountains. Did not fell any beast, but our kitchens are stocked so we are not in need of surplus. Following this, I took Nyssa and Torrin to the armory to be fitted for their twelfth year armor, though by the time it is needed for practical use they will have outgrown it. Drystan, frowning, scratched out the last part because he heard his mother tell him he was being contrarian again. Sometimes he struggled to separate her voice from his own. *Does it matter if there's no looming war, son? Those from later days will know this by the time they come to read it. Your opinion is of no concern to the historical record.*

Drystan disagreed entirely. Opinions *started* wars. They shaped worlds. But there was no use arguing with his mother on any subject. He wasn't Lisbet, who could wrap Gretchen Dereham around her fingers like silk, or Pieter, who knew when to speak and when to keep his counsel.

Drystan had a heart that wanted to lead his head, and the greatest challenge of his entire life had been learning when to listen to this instinct, and when to suffocate it.

"MOTHER'S BLOOD, SIT!" HOLDEN BOOMED AS THE TWINS, NYSSA AND Torrin, ran circles around the wooden slab where the family gathered to sup. The boom of his piqued voice, reserved for those who had pushed him to his greatest displeasure, and almost never for his children, stirred Gretchen from her reverie.

Torrin looked stricken and quickly stumbled into the bench across from his mother. Nyssa just gaped at her father's outburst, backing away in an instinctual retreat. Drystan caught her before she fell back into the roaring fire of the Great Hall.

Gretchen should soothe her little ones. They certainly looked to her for exactly that, their wide eyes as confused as she was. But instead she locked her curiosity on her husband. She had half a mind to provoke him to see how far he might take this unusually foul mood, but she wouldn't do it at the expense of the children.

"Where's Lis?" Holden asked, calmer now, as if the past few moments were erased from the record of life. He reached for an ewe leg off the platter in the center of the table, eschewing the root vegetables altogether. She'd asked the kitchens to prepare meals that would sit with his constitution better, but she couldn't make him eat them. Her mother had told her once that having a husband and having a child were quite similar, except children occasionally behaved. "And Eavan?"

"Playing," Torrin said with a glint of mischief, happy to take the focus off his own misbehavior.

Holden's tension returned. "Playing?"

"They aren't playing," Gretchen quickly clarified, with a quick, sharp look to her youngest son. Holden was in no mood for coy exchange. "They're in the stable, with her mares. Lisbet asked for a bread and cheese basket from the kitchen so they could spend the evening brushing and tending them."

"And why are they not sitting here at the table with the family?"

"She's going to miss them," Drystan blurted. "She can't take them to Duncarrow. There's nowhere to ride there. It's all rocks and darkness. You know how she feels about her horses." To himself, he muttered, pushing snow peas on to his fork, "That's not all she's giving up."

Pieter's lips twisted in surprise at his brother's words. He buried his face in his plate.

Gretchen swallowed a measure of pride at her son's courage to bring this up now. Guardians knew she could not. She'd argued this point with her husband until she was lost for breath, and he'd made up his mind. Even now… even after Khallum and Gwyn's sweet Esmerelda went to the Guardians, which could have changed everything, Holden stuck steadfastly to his stubborn resolve.

"Hmph," Holden replied. He refilled his ale from the jug. "I don't like it. This table used to be full of Derehams."

"You're the one sending her away," Drystan said. "Better get used to it."

"Son," Gretchen whispered in a hush. The only thing worse than Holden's resolve was pointing it out.

Holden dropped his hands to the sides of his plate. "Drystan. You'll be the one making these decisions someday. And when you do, your judgment will not be so easily maintained. Pray you never have a son who makes that harder."

Drystan flushed. Nyssa and Torrin stopped eating, wide eyes passing between their father and brother. Pieter continued his intimate acquaintance with his meal.

"Drystan will miss her. As we all will," Gretchen said. Peacemaker. Another role she'd never excelled at but was expected to serve. "But this day was inevitable. Lisbet would leave us to marry someone else if it wasn't the king."

"Not at fourteen," Drystan said, but the fight had left him. The one thing he'd always sought and rarely received was his father's approval, and he'd brought the ire upon himself this time.

"There's nothing to be done," Holden said, voice heavy with the weight of authority. "Lisbet will be your queen. *One* of your queens. Fourteen or forty, her age changes nothing."

Gretchen herself hadn't even reached the age of forty, and it brought chills to her spine to consider what her oldest daughter might experience in the years before she did.

Again she wondered, had she not fought hard enough? Not used what little real authority she had as the Lady of the Northerlands?

She reached for the tray of vegetables and rebelliously placed some on her husband's plate, before doing the same for the children, who had also avoided them. "At least she will have Eavan," she said. These were the same words she repeated to herself for false comfort. Sometimes they even worked.

"Eavan *wants* to be queen," Drystan said. "She's been playing pretend as one her whole life. But even she doesn't know what she's getting herself into."

"Your mother and I were both happily betrothed to others before the Epoch," Holden replied. "And now we're happy to be wed to one another."

Torrin snickered. Nyssa looked scandalized.

"What if he hurts her?" Drystan asked, and a hush fell over the table. The question said aloud was a reiteration of the fear underpinning the entire affair. The crux of the decision Holden had agonized about for weeks, before sending his raven to King Eoghan with their affirmation of The Right of Choosing.

"He won't," Holden said, but his eyes were now solely focused on the feast in front of him.

"Real men don't lay hands on their women," Torrin recited. "A king is a real man, so he can't hurt Lissy."

"They aren't even from the kingdom. We know nothing of the men the Rhiagains truly are," Drystan said to his little brother. He pushed back from the table and stood. "I'm not hungry anymore."

Gretchen watched him leave the Great Hall, but still jumped at the sound of the heavy door swinging shut.

"He's too emotional, Gretchen," Holden said, casting a careful glance at the twins and Pieter. "He's seventeen. The responsibility of this Reach could fall upon him at any time. We can't abide these whims of his."

Gretchen looked away. As always, the act of saving, small and large, fell to her.

If only Holden understood that Drystan's sensitive side was only enhanced by his father's unwillingness to be the one to talk to him about it.

DRYSTAN FOUND LISBET ALONE IN THE STABLES. THE DOORS WERE flung wide on both sides, snow falling in sideways, collecting at the edges of the hay piles.

She stood upon a chair, head lying against the mahogany neck of Starcaller. Lisbet had four horses, but Starcaller was her favorite. She'd been riding the mare since she was old enough to walk. Starcaller was older now, and not as nimble as the younger ponies Holden showered her with, but nothing could replace the bond of friendship.

Lisbet wiped at her tears when she saw her brother. She forced a smile.

"Where's Eavan?" he asked. He knew better than to ask her what was wrong.

Lisbet sniffled, rolling both eyes. "She didn't stay long. Said she wanted to pack her trunk more neatly, but I suspect she's with Argus."

Argus, the armorer's son. Just the other day, Drystan had heard Eavan remark that he was far too handsome to be a laborer. She'd cast similar opinions and aspersions on most of the workers at Wulfsgate Keep throughout her month-long stay.

"She should be careful," Drystan said. "Who knows what the king might do if he finds one of his brides has been unchaste."

"She's not that foolish. She only wants him to fall in love with her," Lisbet said, returning to Starcaller. She pressed her lips to the soft mane and backed away. Starcaller neighed and backed into her stall. "Father send you?"

Drystan dropped his eyes. "I walked out."

Lisbet's mouth parted in surprise. "You walked out? In the middle of mealtime?"

"He's not the same man I remember growing up. He's changed."

She tilted her head. "*You've* changed, Drys. You never used to fight back."

Drystan kicked at the hay. "He likes to remind me I'll be in his chair someday, but that doesn't mean I'll make his choices."

She reached forward and grabbed her brother's hand. "I know what you speak of, brother, but you, too, would've sent me to the king."

"Lisbet, there's no wa—"

Lisbet kissed his hand. "Yes, you would have. Because to do otherwise would be to invite the king's eye and army to the Northerlands, which you're sworn to protect. Because sometimes there's no other choice."

Drystan hated himself for the tears trailing down his cheeks. Of all of them, Lisbet would understand, but he didn't *want* her to understand. He didn't ask for this tenderness of heart that made him utterly ill-equipped for anything of substance. Father had failed Lisbet, and Mother had too, and now, here he was, following their lead despite the resistance burning in his chest. A betrayal wasn't always a direct action. Sometimes it was inaction.

"How am I supposed to protect you?" Drystan whispered as he crushed his sister to his chest. "If I can't even find the words to convince our own father?"

"There were never words capable of doing that," Lisbet told him. "But you're wrong, Drystan. You've protected me all my life, by teaching me to be true to myself. And I can't think of a better weapon to take with me to Duncarrow."

5

THE LONG-TRODDEN MULE

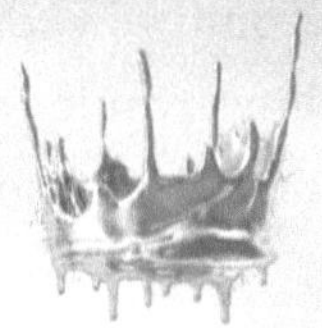

"Nightfall was an hour ago," Esmerelda whined. She sagged atop the nag in demonstration of her exhaustion. Jesse expected no less from her and was surprised she'd even made it across the border into the Westerlands without surrendering and going home. "Come on, Jesse. Please."

He waved his hands around the forest without turning. "Do you see a place to stop for the night, Princess?"

"I wish you wouldn't call me that."

"I wish you hadnae gotten my brother thrown in the traitor king's prison camp. So, we both suffer."

This shut her up for the time being. Truth was, he was tired, too. They'd hidden in an abandoned fortress just outside Goldthorpe for nigh a week, waiting for her father to announce the dead-given rites. Until then, there could be no confidence that Khallum had fallen for the ruse. That was to say nothing of the Rhiagain Guard who would use Esmerelda's absence at the upcoming Right of Choosing as an excuse to send even more men into the Souther-lands. They had to be absolutely certain no one was after them.

But unless they planned to sleep amongst the flora of the forest floor, they had another hour, perhaps two, before their next destination, the inn at Greystone Abbey. Westerlands, it might be, but the Abbey and Goldthorpe had alliances that ran deep, and Esmerelda, despite her attempts at disguise, was a vision in any land.

Crying, she'd sliced off her brilliant obsidian hair just below the shoulders with Jesse's sword the night before. There was nothing to be done about the color. Any lighter and he could've crushed berries, like his father's second wife did, or even woad, like his mother had done, but nothing would work against the black. He gave her his own cloak to drape down over her face, the only cure for her emerald eyes. They were playing a dangerous game until they arrived in the Hinterlands.

Beautiful or no, Esmerelda Warwick was now Jesse's burden, and if he hadn't sworn the sacred oath to his brother, he would've left her to meet the consequences of her feigned death by the sea. Ryan would be better for it, even if he'd hate him for the rest of their days.

But an oath was an oath. It was sacred, especially when given between men of the same blood. A man was nothing without the bond of his word.

"How far are we from Greystone Abbey?"

"Do I look like a mapmaker, Princess?"

"You know, and you just won't tell me."

"That's a real possibility," Jesse admitted and continued on, weaving through the roots and undergrowth. Their slow pace was a liability, but staying on a road, or even a well-worn path, was a risk too great. Whispers of the gloaming twilight pierced through gaps in the upper veil of the forest to light their way, but it wasn't enough. Shelter or no, they'd be forced to stop if the forest grew more dense.

"I know you don't like me."

Jesse snickered. "I donnae know you." And, though it was cruel, he couldn't help adding, "all I do know is my brother is in Camp

Atonement for loving you, and it was your father who put him there."

"That wasn't supposed to happen!" Esmerelda grunted, shifting in pain from the long day's ride.

"No? Tell that to your daddy."

"If you think me so abhorrent, why didn't you tell Ryan to find someone else?"

"Donnae say his name aloud," Jesse snapped. "Or mine. Or yours. Not until we're safe. You hear me?"

"You didn't answer my question."

Jesse adjusted in his worn saddle, travel sore. He'd thought about taking the newer one, but his father paid a pretty penny for it, and his disappearance was supposed to raise no suspicions. Same reason he borrowed two horses no one would miss. He was away on the usual business. That's all. "And who else was there, Princess? Who else would've risked their neck for you?"

"You might be surprised."

"Or you might," Jesse countered. "The Warwicks aren't as well-loved in the Southerlands as you want to believe."

Her shoulders shot straight back in a flash of pride that Jesse found astonishing in their current situation. There was a saying about this, but it escaped him.

"Your father has thrived at my father's side," she countered. He didn't dare look at her, but could feel her pout from feet away. "Without my father, most of the Great Families would be in the mines."

"So says you."

"So knows everyone!"

"Will you keep it down? You trying to wake the trees?"

"The trees a threat now, too, are they?"

"Donnae be so overly confident our plan was foolproof, Princess. As you said, *this* wasnae supposed to happen."

"We wouldn't have made it out of Warwicktown if anyone suspected a thing."

"If you cannae keep your mouth closed, you can at least stop yourself from telling the whole world who you are."

"You're the one who pointed out my family's reputation."

Jesse navigated his nag around a copse of fallen trees. Esmerelda nearly ran into it, and he resisted the urge to chuckle as she cried out. She was a mess. Pretty, maybe, but not the type of woman a Strong man married. Ryan wasn't thinking straight at all where this one was concerned, but he'd always been guided by the head not on his shoulders.

"We aren't safe until we're safe," Jesse said. "Why don't you leave the planning to me? My brother, at least, seemed to understand that wasnae your strength."

Esmerelda blew some stray black hairs out of her face. She tugged at the hood, which she hated, but knew better than to remove it after the reaming Jesse had given her last time she'd tried. "Ry—your brother is overprotective. He treats me with delicacy, and I don't require it."

Jesse laughed. "No?"

Esmerelda looked away. At what, Jesse could neither guess nor care to. The only light to guide their way now was the spill of moonlight that washed across the makeshift path. When he reached for his waterskin, he realized he hadn't seen her drink a drop since they'd left Goldthorpe. A groan that started from deep within him breached his lips before he could speak to say the painful but necessary words.

"Princess. You should have some water."

"You care now, do you?"

"I care for my brother," Jesse corrected gruffly. "And my brother cares for you. And if he returns to a shriveled corpse that might set us on the wrong path when your father finally sees fit to letting him come home." Not that it mattered much whether Ryan was there or here. Esmerelda was promised to a king, and if ever anyone discovered her death was feigned, she'd return to her fate as a queen. If there was a world where Esmerelda Warwick and Ryan Strong could be happy and wedded, they weren't living in it now.

"I'm fine," Esmerelda lied.

Jesse slowed his nag. He reached for the reins on her own and she made a soft, shocked sound when her horse did the same. He held the skin out, looking half-away. "Come on. Drink."

"I said I was fine."

Jesse shoved the skin under her nose. A slosh of water spilled over the lip. "We aren't moving until you do."

Still refusing to look directly at her, Jesse nonetheless felt the pride burning from her, as she reluctantly did as he demanded. When she shoved it back his way, he reached around until his hand settled over the skin, and he pulled it back, capping it. He was already moving again when he slipped it into his saddlebag.

"Greystone is nigh an hour, barring any problems," he mumbled and pushed on. "Push through your stubbornness and then we can sleep."

Greystone Abbey was once a vital trading port, some five miles off the coast, though this changed in the past fifteen years. Someone came along and built something bigger and better, closer to the water, as Greystone should have been from the start, and Greystone's population eventually migrated there, leaving the shells of another time in their wake. In today's world, the only remaining were the ones who couldn't afford the rents in the more bustling Newcarrow, which had almost overnight become the most important port along the southwestern shore of the Westerlands.

A dark pall hung over the derelict village. Even the name, Greystone, seemed appropriate in a way its forebears couldn't have foreseen. The mud along the untended main road was hardly touched, though an abandoned cart stuck along the side of it was a reminder some still passed through. Smoke billowed from the chimneys of the occasional house, but the foliage beyond most doors grew up and around, sometimes poking through windows, or bowing doors.

"What *is* this place?" Esmerelda whispered, suddenly alert once more.

Jesse hadn't the heart to sting her with another barb. He hadn't been to Greystone himself since he was but a lad, and this wasn't how he remembered it. Back then, Stanhope was just building his trade kingdom near the sea, and Greystone still held out hope that it wasn't the end. A true end would've been kinder, Jesse thought, as he watched the crows pecking at what remained of the carcass of a mare long-dead. That was a sign of the times as much as anything, that no one had bothered to move it off the main road.

"It wasnae always like this," he answered. "But keep your head down, Princess. A place forgotten by civilization isnae forgotten by robbers and beggars. Stay close to me."

Esmerelda had no retort, either, and did as asked, pulling in so close he could smell her fear and sweat. He hoped she couldn't smell his. Friends here or no, it was a world time had forsaken, clearly manifested in the abandoned shops along what was once a village of prosperity. Signs dangling or stuck in the ground, overgrown, made him wonder if he could even find the place anymore. Would Kaslan even still be here? The rest of the world had moved on. Why not him?

Ahead, Jesse spotted a denser billow of smoke above a structure of wood and moss, tucked into the corner just off the path. He heard the voices next, and as they drew closer, the sign, perhaps the only in town still neatly intact, read *The Long-Trodden Mule.*

"I don't like this," Esmerelda said.

He didn't either, but replied, "My brother trusted me. You should try it as well."

"Are you sure the person you're wanting to meet is even still here? No one else is."

No, I'm not sure at all. "I've known him and his family all my life. If he's here, he will aid us."

"If he isn't?"

Jesse grunted in response. No use telling her that if they couldn't find what they were after in Greystone Abbey, their journey north would be fraught with dangers beyond prediction.

He tied up his own horse first, then helped Esmerelda with hers. She handed the bridle over with tense hesitation, and he could almost read her thoughts: *What if someone steals them?*

After securing the bells, their alarm against theft, Jesse planted a hand against his sword. "Food. Drink. Sleep. It's all here, Princess. And if it isnae, I'll know that straightaway and we'll be gone before trouble finds us."

Esmerelda answered him with a deeply skeptical look, but she was right at his heels as he entered the only sign of life in all of Greystone Abbey.

THE MOONLIGHT PAINTED THE FIELD BEYOND THE LONG-TRODDEN Mule. The way it lay at the edge of the rotting fence line told Jesse that they were well past midnight. All respectable laborers had given up their spots at the bar for sleep, as the world would wake in less than a few hours.

Jesse scanned the tavern for signs of life. One man at the bar, another behind it. Some sounds from a back room, indicating at least one other. Three, perhaps more.

The one behind the bar came to life when Jesse and Esmerelda passed through the door, bringing with them a strong wind and a spray of fresh rain. He was old, wearing the signs of that age in pocks and brownish marks dotted along a weathered face that resembled the warbled rings on a tree trunk. Whatever remained of his hair clung desperately to an environment no longer hospitable. His unreadable expression wasn't the immediate ease Jesse searched for, but the look wasn't hostile, either.

Without turning, the man seated asked, "You lost, travelers?"

Him, Jesse couldn't so easily assess. He wore a wide-brimmed hat and a heavy cloak that he hadn't bothered to remove. His deep voice could be that of a man, young or old, and his hands, the one thing Jesse might use to confirm the truth, were sitting on the bar, blocked from view.

"Not lost. Only looking for food and a night of reprieve, if both still exist. We'll be on our way tomorrow."

"If they exist," the old barkeep said with a snort. "As if you've been here before. As if you'd know what once was."

"I have been here, though it's been some years," Jesse said carefully. He hoped his effort to mask his accent and speech pattern, unique to the coastal Southerlands, wasn't in vain, either. "We want nothing more than a hot meal and a bed for a few hours."

Esmerelda was stiff at his side.

"She your wife? Your mistress?"

"Sister," Jesse replied, sticking to the story they'd agreed to. "But one room is fine."

The barkeep erupted into subdued laughter. "Aye, that kinda sister, aye."

Jesse ground his jaw but didn't rise to the bait. He hoped Esmerelda had the good sense to keep her trap shut, too. "So, do you? Have a room?"

"Aye, I've a room," the barkeep replied. He uncorked an amber liquid and took a swig, wincing. "But it'll cost you." He leaned forward. "Mayhap your sister there don't need a room at'all. Mayhap she can come with me, and I'll keep her warm into sunrise."

Esmerelda gasped. Jesse laid a hand at her back, steadying.

"Easy, Hogger," the stranger sitting at the bar said, and the barkeep did an odd thing then. He seemed to shrink back, moving away and almost inward toward the wall of liquor. "If the girl is anyone's, she's mine."

A shrill metallic shriek rang across the empty tavern as both Jesse and the wide-brimmed stranger drew their swords in sudden tandem. Esmerelda screamed and backed into a nearby table, toppling a chair.

"You lay a hand on my sister and you're a dead man," Jesse said, using the entirety of his focus to quell the trembling. His father, Hamish, once said, *ye donnae draw a sword if ye donnae intend to spear a man to the wall wit' it.*

The stranger's face remained obscured by a hat that was unlike any Jesse had seen. The brim was even broader than it had appeared from behind, almost like the ones some of the clergy wore. His cloak was nicer, too, than it had seemed in the shadows, and Jesse could see now that it was bespoke, as would befit a man of means.

Esmerelda's soft cries behind him broke Jesse's concentration. The steel wavered in his hands. "Who are you?"

Glass broke behind the bar as Hogger crab-walked away from the scene, pressing his weight into the lower half of the door and disappearing into the room behind the bar.

"You come into a land foreign to you, a bar foreign to you, and you ask me who I am?"

"Yes," Jesse replied. Sweat beaded on his nose and he twitched, dying to wipe it away. "Yes, I do. I came only for succor. It is your intentions that need clarifying."

"You're scaring your sister," the stranger said in oddly soothing tones.

"I'm not s-scared!" Esmerelda insisted, and Jesse didn't blame the stranger for laughing at her unconvincing protestation.

Jesse put a hand behind him to caution her to stay, and then put it back on the hilt of his sword. He'd forgotten how heavy it was; the burden of holding it for longer than a few moments was one requiring more training than he'd had. The stranger never wavered. His arms strayed true. His mouth—the only part of his face visible to Jesse—showed a calm that scared Jesse all the more.

"Sister, go outside and ready the horses," Jesse ordered. He didn't take his eyes off the stranger. He didn't dare.

"But J… Brother…"

"Just go."

"She tries it and she'll be dead before she reaches the door," the stranger promised.

"What do I do?" she whispered at Jesse's back.

"What do you want from us? Money?"

The stranger lowered his sword so the sharp end was inches from Jesse's neck. "I want your names."

"Elizabeth and John Dunn."

"Your real names."

"I told you our real—"

Jesse gasped as he felt the tip of the stranger's sword pierce the hollow of his neck. "You're not from Greystone. You're not a Westerlander. I hear the lie in your voice. I know where you come from. When I have your names, I'll know why."

"We only wanted food and a bed!" Esmerelda cried out, and Jesse wanted to tell her to stop, that she wasn't helping, but this *was* her way of helping, and she was determined to prove she could do just that. "We're passing through, and this is how you treat kind strangers?"

Jesse only hoped the Guardian of the Warrior's Aim was on his side of the bar this night.

"Father, that's enough!" cried out a new voice. No, not new, but new to the escalating situation. "They're here to see me."

Kaslan James.

Father?

The elder James lowered his sword, but slowly. Easlan James, this was, the head of the Great Family who reigned as stewards over Greystone Abbey—or what remained of it. Easlan had been steward long enough to remember Greystone for what it was, and had the displeasure of seeing it fall into ruin. There were whispers that the Blackwoods were considering removing Greystone from its list of key cities, and the James family from the book of Great Families, but Lady Asherley Blackwood had a soft spot for Easlan James and valued loyalty above all else.

Jesse cleared his throat, pressing his hand to the bloody, burning spot left by Easlan's steel and skilled hand. Another man might have taken away his voice. A less adept one.

"No one comes to Greystone Abbey anymore, Kaslan. No one stumbles upon us by accident. Most avoid us intentionally."

"His raven came a week ago. I was expecting him sooner, but better late than never." Kaslan leapt out from behind the bar and laid a hand against the shaft of his father's sword. His hand slid down the steel as he approached Jesse, first with a serious look that gave Jesse pause, and then, face spreading into a beaming smile, arms wide.

"Old friend," Kaslan said. He waited for Jesse to sheath his sword before swallowing him in an embrace. "You haven't changed a bit."

"I should hope thasnae true, seeing as I still had the voice of a soprano last we played together," Jesse said, laughing through the bear hug.

"And Ryan?"

Jesse sighed. He cast a look behind him, at Esmerelda. Her green eyes peered back from the darkness of the hood still covering her face. "We have much to catch up on. First, let's eat and prepare a bed for my traveling companion."

"You're safe here," Jesse promised Esmerelda, standing at the door. She sat upon the hard mattress, looking straight out the window ahead of her. Now that their lives were no longer in mortal peril, she was back to being furious with him.

"You still have blood at your neck," she hissed.

The wound would need a salve, but would be healed by the time they reached the Hinterlands. No use in telling the princess that, though. If there was reason in her, it was down for the long sleep. "Yes, thank you."

"Curse you for not letting me stay and palaver. For thinking I'm not suited to sit at the table with the men," she shot back, swallowing back a yawn. He almost smiled, but he quickly remembered that this, all of this, was for her, and her foolish decision. She was no better than a child.

"I need to determine the safest passage for us through the Westerlands. And you, as you pointed out hours ago through your whinging in the forest, need rest."

"And you think these unfortunates have anything that will help us?"

"I think you'd do well, Princess, to remember that the 'unfortunates' make up most of our world. They keep it running, and they can stop it from running, should they choose."

Jesse closed the door before she could find even more complaints to sling at him and made his way down the rickety stairs, to the main room of the tavern.

Hogger had lowered the closing bar over the door, and when he was done bringing the pitchers of ale to the large table in the corner of the room, Easlan dismissed him for the evening.

Easlan James removed his hat, and Jesse at once understood why he chose to wear it. Without it, he'd be forced to explain the mountains of scars dotting his face. Many looked as if they'd been earned in combat, but there'd been no war to speak of, though Jesse deduced that the James family had seen their own kind of war as they fought to protect their land and status from the progress and ambitions of another.

"It's been a fair few years, Jesse Strong," Easlan said, pouring a mug for each of them. "And Hamish, he faring?"

"Faring as well as you'd expect," Jesse replied. He broke off a hunk of bread from the stale loaf, washing it down with a swig of ale. "Under the circumstances."

"You said Ryan is in the Wastelands? In the crown camp?" Kaslan said, whistling through his teeth. "Where will the king's punishment of the Warwick loyalists end?"

"This one wasnae the king, I'm afraid," Jesse said. "Lord Warwick himself ordered this one."

Easlan frowned. "Khallum is a tempestuous man, but a fair one. And no one has been more loyal to him than your father."

Jesse's attempt at a grin pained him. "Loyalty only goes so far when that same man's son is presuming himself upon your only daughter."

Kaslan's face paled. "Ryan and Esmerelda?"

Jesse nodded. This, at least, wasn't so much a secret. Perhaps a shock outside the Southerlands, but within, it was the main source of gossip leading up to the events that brought Jesse to their doorstep. "Donnae ask me to explain it. I cannot. She's a petulant, spoiled... ah, it doesnae matter now. She's not right for Ryan, but try pushing that truth through his stubbornness. He wouldnae let the matter go, and when Khallum found out... well, let's say there was no crime to speak, so he framed it as a way for Ryan to serve the Southerlands. Lord Warwick believes there's something more going on in the Wastelands. The real reason the crown willnae give the land back to the Warwicks. He wants Ryan to find out."

"But... no one ever *leaves* the camps, Jesse," Kaslan said, wearing a look of growing horror.

"Aye, so they say."

"And Esmerelda, bless her, has gone to The Guardians," Kaslan went on.

Jesse said nothing.

"You're a long way from the Wastelands, if you're intending to spring your brother from the clutches of the king's men," Easlan observed. He ran his fingers down the valley of scars on his cheek, tracing a familiar path. "And though my memory has suffered alongside my body, I don't recall you having a sister. Not one who survived, anyway."

Jesse emptied his mug and poured another. To say what he needed to say was to create great risk for his quest to deliver Esmerelda to safety. But he knew now, as he'd known when he made the promise, that what he needed to do couldn't be done without allies.

"The woman I'm traveling with is Esmerelda Warwick."

The revelation delivered the shock Jesse expected. Easlan's hands ceased their voyage through his battles, and Kaslan fell back in his chair, gaping, eyes focused elsewhere as if needing to return to several moments before to ensure his ears hadn't failed him.

"Donnae look at me as if I'm the mastermind behind this," Jesse said quickly. "This wasnae my plan. Ryan and Esmerelda are both fools, but Ryan is my brother, and I made him a vow."

"But how?" Kaslan asked.

"How?"

"How did she… that is, to say…"

"She left her father a letter announcing her intentions to take matters into her own hands, spending her promise before the Guardians were ready for it. She had reason enough, with being sold off in marriage to the pretender king. They believed she'd thrown herself to the mercy of the sea. An absence of a body makes for simpler explanations, and a greater level of acceptance among those who loved her best. As a Southerlander, we lose many of our own to the sea, both by accident and by a man's own hand. Women in particular fill their pockets with the biggest rocks they can find and walk until the sea takes them. She isnae the first or the last."

Easlan shook his head. "I don't know who the bigger fool is. Your brother, for loving Warwick's greatest treasure, or you, for trying to secret her away, across the kingdom."

"Fool or no, Ryan is my brother. And I made a vow."

"What *is* your plan?" Kaslan asked. His wild eyes were no longer worried, but excited. Jesse feared he might ask to join them. Jesse needed Kaslan, but not at his side. The veil of secrecy was harder to cast over three than it was two, and even bringing a man he trusted into his design made it that much less destined to succeed.

Now, Jesse had to reveal something of his own self. There was no way around it, or through it. This was the corner he had settled himself into by accepting this promise. He had no place in the

Hinterlands, and these men would know it. The explanation required would leave him as vulnerable as Esmerelda.

"I'm taking her to my mother's people," Jesse started. His tankard was again empty, but days of eating so little had left his wits blurry from the drink. He needed them now. "In the Hinterlands."

Easlan balked. "Only Medvedev reside in the Hinterlands. And The Hinterlands is the only place Medvedev have ever resided."

Jesse said nothing, letting the implication of his silence wash over both men.

"Yanna was a Rosewood. From Greenfen, in the Easterlands," Easlan said.

"I believed that, too, for most of my life," Jesse answered. "As far as everyone else in the Southerlands is concerned, she was Yanna Rosewood, from Greenfen. But that isnae who she really was. She was Yanna de Medvedev, and my father met her when he became waylaid on a sea voyage to Witchwood Cross. He was on his way back when the weather turned, and the sea followed."

"Witchwood Cross? Up near where the sorcerers live? Only fools travel that far by sea," Kaslan said.

Jesse grinned. "Or Strongs."

"Go on," Easlan said. "About your mother."

"She told us her truths as she lay dying. We all knew she was dying, though my father refused to believe it until long after they put her on the pyre. Why she never told us before, or even why she did tell us then, I cannae say. All I know is, she had to color her pale green hair every fortnight, and when she brought her fox with her from her homeland, it took some convincing for others to believe it was a pet and not a nuisance. But her familiar died when she did. Down to the very second. We burned him alongside her."

While Kaslan was busy affecting the shocked look of scandalized youth, Easlan was processing. Nodding. "Did Khallum know?"

Jesse shook his head. "No. His pride wouldnae have allowed him to give her leave to stay. Warwicks are as old as the Southerlands, but there are men who still call them outsiders, and he has no tolerance for anything resembling the word. My father knew that. The stress of keeping that secret weighted him all her life. Isnae a shock, I suppose, that he married a simpler woman when it came time to take a new one."

"Do you and Ryan have familiars?" Kaslan asked.

"No, and neither did our baby sister before she died."

"So how do you know this story is true?"

Jesse met his eyes. "Because I know."

"And you think they'll welcome you and this foreign princess with open arms?"

"I believe they'll welcome me," Jesse said. "And I hope to convince them that welcoming Esmerelda is a service to Ryan, son of Yanna. She and Ryan are husband and wife in all but the name of law. Laws the Medvedev donnae even follow or recognize."

"It's a risk," Easlan said thoughtfully. "The Medvedev leave us alone, and we leave them alone. That's the agreement. One of the few absolute truths of the kingdom. One that not even a Rhiagain would violate."

"Until now. No telling what this *boy* king would do," Kaslan countered in disgust. "His balls haven't even come down yet, what makes you think his sense has?"

"He wouldn't. If he tried, he would discover in haste the reason the idea was a bad one."

"Aye, and that's what I'm counting on," Jesse said. "It's why it might be the only safe place in all the kingdom for her."

"And where do the others think you are now? Lord Warwick? Your father?"

"Rushwood. And they willnae be expecting me back anytime soon, as they know I cannae take to the seas in midwinter and must travel by land. I'll return through Rushwood and conclude the business I said I was there for. That part was true enough. But first, I have to get Esmerelda safely to the Hinterlands."

Easlan folded his hands and leaned back. "How can we help you, Jesse Strong?"

Jesse released a long-held sigh of relief. "I need safe passage through the Westerlands. The paths that'll lead us true but are not etched upon common maps. I need to know who's loyal to the king, and who's loyal to their Lady of the Reach."

Kaslan looked giddy with excitement, but Easlan only nodded. "Get some rest, Jesse. Guardians know you'll need it."

6

QUEENS-IN-WAITING

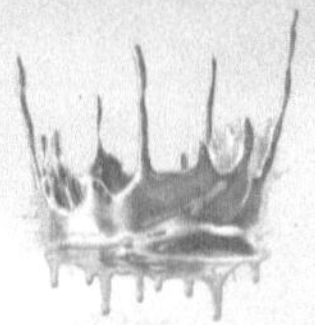

"**C**ome *on*! It's my last night here, Lisbet!"

Lisbet Dereham set about neatly folding her gowns and cloaks. She tried to place them in the two trunks her mother designated for her journey to Termonglen, but the unwieldy fabric only sprang back. Or maybe it was her own stubbornness about the days ahead seeping into the task.

"You had three fortnights, and *now* you want to soak in the springs?" Lisbet squished her emerald gown down into the softness of the yew lining the trunk. Her mother, when she wasn't in tears about the whole affair, reminded her that a queen wouldn't need the quaint trussing of the Northerlands anymore; that her new husband, King Eoghan, would buy her any dress she pleased.

Eavan looped both arms around one of Lisbet's. "Come on, Lis. Aunt Gretchen is right. You won't need any of this when we're married to the *king*."

Lisbet dropped the fabric. She didn't like discussing this with her cousin. Eavan failed to see what Lisbet did not: that a king demanding four brides, from four Reaches, wasn't an attempt at unification but domination. Subjugation. One that should be no surprise to anyone. It was an effort that began with the Epoch of Accordant, grew legs with the suspicious deaths of the matriarchs and patriarchs of the kingdom, and was now coming into full form with the demand of the realm's daughters. It wouldn't end there, either, but begin anew, again, in some new sinister form.

But Eavan's parents were unfailingly loyal to the crown, in a way that reminded Lisbet to always tread around her own disenchantment with caution.

Eavan danced across the bearskin pelt that covered most of Lisbet's room. Wind whipped through the curtains. The candles flickered. "Truly sisters, just like we've always dreamed."

"Won't be only the two of us," Lisbet muttered. She pressed her fists into the pile of fabric, heart racing. Even the edges of the subject caused her distress. It was so unfair. So wrong. So unlike the world her grandparents told stories about over the midwinter fires. "There's also Hollyn Blackwood, and…" Lisbet pulled herself erect. "Who will Uncle Khallum send, with poor cousin Esmerelda gone to the Guardians?"

"Why, his wife," Eavan replied. She tilted her head to and fro, leant over the bowl of water set out for Lisbet's nightly wash. Her smile spread across the surface of the water.

"Aunt Gwyn? Truly, you're not serious?" Did her father know? Surely he'd find a way to stop the king from ripping his own sister from her marriage bed. Holden Dereham was a man of honor, a man of his bond, and his bond was the protection of his family in all things. He was a man who might say all his people in the Northerlands were his family, but for his blood, he'd move the mountains themselves.

"Those aren't my rules, cousin." Eavan rolled her wavy blond hair forward, admiring it in the reflection as she wove loose braids with her fingers. Like all Quinlandens, Eavan was a vision of purity and unfiltered beauty. Like all Quinlandens, she was excruciatingly aware of this fact.

Lisbet was a Quinlanden as well, through her mother, but no one cared who your mother was.

"They weren't rules at all, until King Khain took it upon himself to make a new world," Lisbet muttered. "If Prince Darrick had lived—"

"He would've made a finer husband than Eoghan, for certain," Eavan replied, in a dreamy tone. She rippled her fingers across the surface of the water, giggling at the distortion in her reflection. "Father says Eoghan believes as his father did, that a kingdom united is a kingdom strong. That we'll reach new heights under his rule. And that we, as his queens, will play a glorious part in this new world."

"You really believe that?"

Eavan stopped smiling. Her expression was as dark as the night beyond. "No. Of course not. But what *choice* do we have, Lisbet? Ah, yes. That's right. We have but one, unless we want to see the heads of our parents lining the walls of our castles as midwinter ornaments."

Lisbet weighed the costs of sharing her secret, the one involving her brother Drystan and the enchantress from Midnight Crest. Drystan prepared to take his destiny into his own hands, and with it, risk everything. Not only for himself, but for her, the raven princess. The price of this freedom, if discovered, was both their lives. The current radiating from such a choice might sunder the alliances of the Northerlands forever.

But love, as they said, overcame all.

"It might not be."

"What?"

"Our only choice."

Eavan stopped swaying to the soundless rhythm. "Well, Mother's blood, why didn't you say so?"

A smile so wide it burned spread across Lisbet's cheeks. "Too many ears here. You get the springs after all, it seems."

. . .

"You cannot intend to let the king take your sister from her marriage bed without answer."

Holden ran his hand across the short beard tickling his chin. "When I know what I intend, Gretchen, you'll be the first to hear the report."

Gretchen resisted the urge to scream, beyond the stone balustrades and into the snowy night. She and Holden were not well matched. That was the truth for all the Derehams, Warwicks, Black-woods, and Quinlandens paired together almost two decades ago at the Epoch of the Accordant, the concept King Khain employed to quell the bickering between the Reaches. But from strange pairings love could grow anyway, as it had between Gretchen Quinlanden of the Easterlands and her husband, Holden Dereham of the Norther-lands. Where she was a barrage of ripples at the edges of the lake, he was the calm center. There was no war in his blood. But there was war in hers.

"He is no king of mine," Holden added quietly, not to her, or perhaps even to himself. He was a man beholden to his deeper conscious, a place where even she couldn't go.

"Precisely my point. Yet you'd allow him to take from us. You have allowed it." She put up a hand to his scandalized expression. "I understand the politics, Holden. We cannot fight every battle with this broken, kingless crown. We've never been able to prove they were behind the deaths that followed the Epoch. But Gwyn is your *sister.* Her husband doesn't possess your reason. He will bankrupt his entire Reach fighting the Rhiagain king, because the king has left him deplete of resources for the fight. You think that was an accident?"

"Of course it wasn't. But you cannot blame the king for Esmerel-da's death."

"Can't we? Was there another reason she took her life, before she'd even had a chance to live it?"

"We don't know what was in her heart."

"And why should we allow him to take child *or* mother?"

"An old refrain with no winner." Holden turned. "Gretchen. Our daughter... our nieces... will be in Eoghan's mercy in a fortnight. We have to think of them. Gwyn will do what she has to do, because she has no choice. Neither do we."

Gretchen set her jaw. She recalled the day Holden was chosen for her. On that day there were marriages across all the ruling families, marriages dictated by the crown, leaving other betrothals destroyed in the process, including her own. Her father had a grudging, if intermittent, respect for the Derehams, but didn't want his daughter marrying one. *They are steadfast, Gretchen. True. They honor their bonds. But they will die on the battlefield of their own morality.*

The morality of a Dereham centered around their loyalty to family and crown, and Gretchen could see within her husband the swirling tempest pulling him back and forth. He tried to sound assured with her, even now, but she knew him. He was soft and hard at once, impenetrable and yet transparent to the core. Her wulf, decked in the heavy furs of beasts known only to their realm, slaughtered and treated by his own hand. Meat he often prepared without aid, and ate with relish.

Quinlandens, by contrast, were known for their symmetry to the crown. They seldom agreed with the decisions of the Rhiagains, but understood the benefit in aligning themselves with the central power of the kingdom. There was nothing to be gained in isolating oneself. Nothing to be gained in creating enemies. Quinlandens valued education, and they valued neutrality. Yet they valued neither more than their own prosperity.

Gretchen witnessed this as if belonging elsewhere. Her marriage to Holden had opened her eyes, but he could not be credited with this. She was neither Quinlanden nor Dereham. She was something else entirely. With a heart that beat faster than it should, and a sense that their world was coming swiftly to an end.

That it should be her, and not her husband, advocating on behalf of Holden's sister, wasn't a new occurrence in their marriage. But it was especially troubling to see Holden so firm in his belief they do nothing to aid the Warwicks. This was bigger than all the young girls going to Eoghan's bed at the Right of Choosing. Bigger than the wheels that started these motions back at the Epoch of the Accordant. Bigger than the tremendous losses that followed. There was no sense at all in reliving what was, but there was every sense in predicting and aiding what should be.

A foul wind swept in from the east of Wulfsgate. Gretchen shivered and reached for her tankard of ale. "What if... stay with me, husband... what if none of the daughters of the realm were forced into marriage with the Rhiagain boy king?"

Holden, leaning against an open window with his weight rested upon his hands, heaved himself backward. "There are ears everywhere!"

Gretchen grinned halfway. There used to be. She'd caught some of them herself and dealt with them as the master poisoner she was raised to be in Whitechurch. Word spread. Now there were fewer ears. "You've become too cautious in your middle age. It doesn't become you."

He returned his gaze to the snowscape outside. "You know your brother laid Rowanwen at Eoghan's feet? Swore especial fealty."

Gretchen swallowed a hard knot. She knew. Her brother took after their grandfather. Spineless. Sycophant. But his was the richest of all the realms, and that was the price. A price he paid, and his realm enjoyed. "I'm not surprised, only at the timing."

"Meaning?"

"Why now? Unless war was expected. Unless Eoghan expressed an anticipation of such. A need for such a public show."

"And why..." Holden sighed. The sound reverberated across the stone walls, stopping when it hit the far wall tapestries. "We have six children to fear for. The Northern Reach has thousands more. Khallum has never been able to keep his tongue, and he put himself in the eye of Khain and Eoghan. That was his own doing."

"Only after he caught the crown falsely accusing his men of

crimes so they could be thrown into Camp Atonement, for the crown to enjoy free labor off the backs of innocent men."

"Rumor only. There is no proof of this."

A silver swirl appeared in the air as Gretchen laughed, humorless. "What proof is needed? Do you suspect the crown of better intentions? On the land *stolen* from the Warwicks and the South?"

"No, but it isn't our business."

"Aye, Holden, and *that* should be on your banners. *'Tis none of our business.* For it will surely be etched upon your grave."

Without turning, Holden asked, "Do you think Khallum wore the cloak?"

Gretchen almost laughed, but held her tongue. Holden was done talking about this, but she wasn't. "Of course he did, though I expect it's now lying in a heap, never to be touched again. He never wanted your cloak, anyway. And it's not what he needs now."

Holden closed his eyes and leaned his head back against the glass. "I can feel your judgment from here, Gretchen. I've always felt it most acutely in the moments I've found myself in the tightest corners. But words are no balm for me. They never have been." He swept across the room, pausing to brush his lips at the corner of her mouth. "You have my love, wife."

"And you have mine."

"I'm saddling up Sorcha and headed into Witchwood Cross for the night."

"With this storm!" Witchwood Cross was due north of Wulfsgate, at the base of the mountain where the sorcerers did whatever it was they did. But Witchwood Cross, for her husband, was a place of reflection. Where he could draw his bow and answers in the same held breath.

"I was born in a storm," Holden replied, with a wry, distant smile. "And, Guardians willing, I will die in one."

. . .

Eavan lowered herself into the hot spring with all the enjoyment of a man served warm food after a stint in a prison camp. Lisbet told her as much. Eavan swatted at the snowy air in protest, rolling her head back against the cool stone.

"How is this different than you always wanting to climb to the tops of trees in Whitechurch? Eh?"

"You can see the skies!" Lisbet cried as she watched the fluffs of white snow dance across her prickled flesh. It fell in soft sheets from the sky, disappearing under the steam.

Eavan waved at the sparkling night. "Look at the twinkles here, Lis. You can't see the twinkles this bright in Whitechurch."

"We call them stars here. But they're more truly the Guardians, standing sentry."

Mist rose between them, twisting into white curls that disappeared into the dark air. The low moon lit the ground, but it needn't have bothered at the height of midwinter. All around them, the only thing the eye could see was snowy landscape and the beckoning darkness of the Forest of Lycana. Midwinter was too chilled for venturing out in, so they'd taken one of the caravans instead of a wulf sled. Her father wouldn't miss it, or the ponies they'd relegated for the task of pulling them along. She'd seen him ride off on Sorcha, likely for Witchwood Cross. If so, he'd be gone until morning.

For the ponies, with their long manes crowning their heads and limbs, this weather was a treat. They frolicked under a nearby tree.

Nobody had followed them. When Lisbet told her cousin there were ears, that was a guess rather than something she knew with certainty. Someone trailing them to the spring would have been easy to confirm, but so far they were alone.

So much alone that a wulf, or even a snowbeast, could take them before anyone was the wiser.

"We can't climb the mountains here without taking the risk of never returning," Lisbet countered. She sank further into the heat of the bath, wondering why she didn't make more time for this luxury.

It was one of the very few they had in the Northerlands. She liked to think she was immune to needing such things, and she realized this might be the reason she'd kept away. She had many tests ahead. What did it say if this one wasn't so easily passed?

"You wouldn't put so much excitement in climbing trees if you lived in them."

Lisbet scoffed. "It isn't as if you live on the branches, princess. The Quinlandens built kingdoms in the sky."

"Listen to us. I long for the land, while you long for the skies. Neither of us will ever be satisfied, it would seem."

The night was unusually quiet, save the wind rolling down off the snowy mountain pass. This meant the eagles had descended from their eyries, pushing all other birds into cowing retreat. No raven's caws or even the buzz of the little fairies, as she called them, that lit up the night as they zipped to and fro. The snow rabbits retreated to their warrens, so there'd be no bringing in an easy meal for the kitchen staff with her bow.

But no, not all the birds had hidden away. A lone raven raced across the sky toward Wulfsgate.

Better watch yourself, little one, Lisbet thought, but then an immediate darkness descended over her heart, as she realized that was no ordinary raven.

"Eavan," Lisbet ventured. She changed her tone, so Eavan would know their playful banter was over. Maybe for a while. "There's something I want to tell you, but if I do, it comes at great risk to me. And someone I love more than all the world."

"I don't want to marry the boy king either, Lisbet." Eavan liked to assume she knew exactly where Lisbet was headed with a topic, and, as usual, came close to the mark but missed. "But what choice do we have?"

It didn't matter. She was close enough, and sometimes to get where you needed to go, you had to start somewhere else.

Lisbet drew in a hard breath of steam and ice. "My father always said... he said that he wished his parents had stood against King

Khain when he demanded the Epoch of the Accordant. That if they had, there wouldn't be a Right of Choosing now."

"Our grandparents acquiesced and the crown still killed them. They had no power." Eavan laughed. "And do you see Uncle Holden doing a damn thing now to stop it? My parents? Any of the Reaches?"

"They're afraid for us."

"Do you really think so? Or are they afraid for themselves? For the riches and titles they'd lose if they went against the crown? Or that they'd end up poisoned and discarded, like their own mothers and fathers?"

"Don't be so cynical," Lisbet chided. The pendant her mother gave her, a rare purple gem mined from the Snowcap mountains, floated atop the steamy water. It had been passed down from Gretchen's mother and grandmother, women Lisbet would never meet, thanks to the crown. Lisbet wasn't supposed to bring it outside, but she always did, because she couldn't bear to be parted from it. It was a connection to a past she would know only from her mother's stories. She pushed it under, but it returned to the surface, over and over. How many times would it take before the gem sank forever, never to return? "He also said, not to me, but to my mother, which I overheard—"

"You really are such a naughty child."

"You don't listen to your parents when they're talking serious?"

Eavan sank her head half into the water and grinned through the break in the surface.

"He said to her that if he had it all to do over again, he would've resisted."

"And not wed Aunt Gretchen? Not have you, or Drystan, or the others?"

Lisbet frowned. "You're missing the point. What's done is done. But the Epoch emboldened Khain and Eoghan. It paved the path to the Right of Choosing. You understand?"

"I understand, but as you said, what's done is done. We can't go back in time and watch our parents find the courage for a rebellion."

"They're afraid for us," Lisbet said again. "Khain was a monster, but Eoghan is young and tempestuous. He has some sort of defect... something that stokes his anger and cruelty. I heard my father telling my mother that if they fight this, Eoghan will throw us all in his dungeons. Or the Wastelands. Before, Khain had the parents destroyed, but Eoghan will use the children toward that destruction instead."

"We aren't children anymore," Eavan pointed out. "Children aren't selected to marry kings."

"*You're* not a child, but I'm hardly fourteen." This was always a startling reminder to Lisbet, who'd often felt like the older of the two, though Eavan was eighteen now.

Eavan slid higher against the stone. Her golden, wet hair clung to her cheeks. "You said there was a risk to someone you love. Not just you."

"First, tell me this. If there was a way out of this, would you take it?"

"I don't know."

"It's an easy question, Eavan."

"But it's not a simple one. What if it meant someone got hurt because of it? Someone we love?"

"That's no answer. Everyone gets hurt."

"I don't want to see my parents sent to one of the labor camps, Lisbet. They're awful places."

"Eoghan wouldn't send them there. To do so would be to undo everything his father believes he accomplished in the Epoch. He has to show the rest of the kingdom that the Reaches are all aligned in unity. But he'd send us, because our parents do have more children, after all. What are we, but replaceable lasses?"

Eavan considered this. She submerged entirely in the scalding water and then surfaced once more. "So, our choices are wed and bed the boy king, or toil in the Wastelands under his prison guards. I don't want to die in a prison camp, do you?"

"There's a third option. But you have to swear a vow."

Eavan groaned. "You don't trust me?"

"I trust you," Lisbet replied. "But it isn't my secret to share. A vow helps me keep my word with the person who entrusted me."

"Fealty and secrecy, the breaking of which means my untimely death," Eavan recited swiftly. "Tell me already. I'm getting hot."

"You're the one who wanted to come here."

"And now I'm done. My delicate skin is burning."

"It's Drystan. He's fallen in love with someone," Lisbet said in a rush, thinking of the lone raven racing the sky. "Someone he can't have."

Eavan leaned forward. "Ooh! Who is it?"

Lisbet looked at the jagged crest of Icebolt Mountain. She couldn't see Midnight Crest from down there, but she knew precisely where it was, on the map of the sky. She'd never been, but the young Ravenwoods were a staple in Wulfsgate. They were sent down, amongst the men and women, to practice their healing magic in the Northerland capital before they came of age. This arrangement was at the core of the centuries-old alliance between the Ravenwoods and Derehams.

We protect them; they protect us.

Protect them from what, Father?

Everything. Everything outside the Northerlands is a threat to them and their way of life.

But never, that Lisbet was aware of, had either dared toward dalliance with one another. The Ravenwoods had their traditions, and the Derehams theirs. Some ventured toward friendships, but anything beyond that was asking for trouble neither side wanted.

"No. No way," Eavan replied, following her meaning as her eyes traveled with her cousin's. "He can't be so foolish. Not Drystan."

"The Ravenwoods don't yet know," Lisbet said. "Or Ravenna's

corpse would be frozen against the mountainside by now, alongside my brother's."

"He's going to stop this foolishness, right? End it?"

"He's not," Lisbet said. "He loves her, Eavan. And, though he hasn't told me this, I believe he's planning to leave with her." She remembered the lone raven in the sky. "Perhaps tonight."

"Leave? And go where?"

"I don't think he knows, but he's racing time. The Langenacht is soon."

Eavan rolled her eyes. "For believing themselves so superior to us, they sure have archaic traditions."

"If they don't leave soon, Ravenna will be forced to endure it. And I'd rather they leave than see Drystan take his sword to the men who cast their lot for her and start a war no one can win."

"You think he would?"

"He loves her," Lisbet answered. "He loves her that much."

"Mother's blood," Eavan whispered. A slow realization came over her dark eyes. "You want to go with them."

"I'm considering that it may be an option preferable to the one ahead of us."

"And… if we did go…."

Lisbet's relief caused her to sag in the water. "You'd come?"

"If we did go," Eavan repeated. "It would have to be a place the Rhiagains can't, or won't go. You know my father swore especial fealty to that fool? He laid Rowanwen at his feet?"

Horror settled over Lisbet's flushed face. "No!"

Eavan nodded. "My father's people are now the king's army. The Easterlands aren't safe anymore."

"Mother's blood." Lisbet looked at the sky, toward the Guardians. "The Southerlands are already under his watchful eye, with Uncle Khallum refusing to pay taxes. We can't stay anywhere near here, for Ravenna's sake. Her people won't venture out of the North. Drystan will want to get her across our borders. There's the Westerlands, I suppose. Knowing my brother, he won't have gotten half this far in his considerations, though. That's another reason I want to go with him. He needs me." She sighed.

Eavan was only half-listening. She'd gone somewhere else, as she sometimes did in moments of extreme contemplation.

"You have an idea," Lisbet ventured.

Eavan nodded slowly. "I have an idea, but I'm not sure you'll like it, and I'm even less sure of its success."

7

THE CONSORTIUM OF THE SEPULCHRE IN THE SKIES

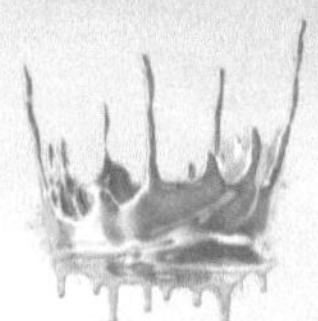

Brandyn Blackwood lifted his palm to the wind, the way his father had taught him. At first, he didn't know what he was looking for. Byrne Warwick always seemed so confident when he did this, so sure of the answers gleaned.

An icy wind rolled off the Seven Sisters of the West. He didn't need a palm-in-the-wind trick to deduce that bit of truth. But what he didn't know, and his father would, was what it would bring.

Because if Brandyn did *not* know better—and, at twelve, he was resigned to the reality he didn't know much—he'd say behind that wind would be snow.

He adjusted his cloak tighter, pulling his hood well over his face to block the onslaught of ice in the air, and pushed forward.

Barring anything too unfortunate, he'd be home in the morning.

ONE WEEK EARLIER

THE GLOVE WAS ITCHY. BRANDYN HAD NEVER LIKED HAVING TO WEAR it when thumbing through the *Chapter of The Consortium of The*

Sepulchre in the Skies and Magic Practitioners, one of only a hundred reproductions of this particular chapter of *The Book of All Things*, but it was compulsory. He'd been at The Sepulchre less than a year, but he learned this lesson vicariously when he witnessed the punishment of a fellow Adherent who'd dared touch the vellum with his unwashed hands. That was the last time Brandyn ever saw him in the library again.

The Adherents were only allowed an hour a week with The Chapter, as it was known in casual speech. Like all chapters in *The Book of All Things*, it was the most comprehensive—only, really—accounting of the intended topic, including names, dates, histories, and everything in between. Reproductions were not allowed, beyond what already existed, without express permission from the Head Magus of The Sepulchre, and they took The Chapter more seriously than just about anything.

Brandyn had never enjoyed reading. The youngest child of Lady Asherley Blackwood, he had access to an impressive library back at the Halls of Longwood, but had always preferred to play with what he could touch and feel. He and his three sisters had access to entire worlds where they were from, or so it seemed. That was enough.

He didn't choose to be sent to The Sepulchre, but then, most didn't. Magic was forbidden in the kingdom, and any born wielding it were sent here for proper training. Even that didn't mean you could go around burning down trees or reading minds at your leisure, because magic practice was heavily governed. Even a benevolent act, like healing, was branded treasonous and punishable by death unless done under proper assignment.

Longwood Rush had several Enchanters and Enchantresses in employ, tasked with various things. There was, of course, a healer, but that wasn't all. His mother's army also had among its ranks a man named Joran, a seer, and she spent the most time with him, though she never said why. Ember told him in her last letter that their mother had been with Joran all the time lately.

He understood a lot of things, but he did not understand adults.

At his side, Esther Rutland nudged him. "You went somewhere again."

"I did not."

"Thinking about asking Magi Christian for leave to go home again?"

Brandyn scoffed, though that was exactly what he'd been thinking about all morning. Unlike some of the great universities in the Easterlands, where children were sent from the best families, the Adherents at The Sepulchre, or the Consortium as it was sometimes called, weren't given leave to return home until their tenure was complete, usually around five to seven years, depending on how long it took them to pass their trials. Families could visit in nearby Briarhaven, at the base of their school of magic, but the Adherents couldn't spend the night outside the Sepulchre or risk expulsion. Expulsion wasn't the trouble, though, it was what came after. If you escaped with your life, it would be spent in exile. Branded a traitor, a magic dealer, and any number of sellswords, bounty hunters, or lawmen looking for a reason to take your head off.

These rules weren't in place to make their lives miserable, Magi Christian explained, but to protect them, and to protect The Sepulchre. It was far too dangerous for an Adherent to leave the womb of the great consortium only partially trained.

Although Brandyn received one letter a week from his mother, he hadn't seen her in a year and didn't expect her to come visit him. The distance was harder on her. And although there were rules, there were exceptions. Death, sickness, and other urgent familial matters were among the reasons they might grant an exception.

No one had died, but something was definitely amiss back in Longwood Rush, and Brandyn had the desperate pull to return. He knew, in the way he'd always known things, that his presence would be needed. Beyond that, he knew nothing at all.

"You're doing it again!" Esther accused.

Brandyn carefully closed The Chapter, which was the size of a large tome, as all chapters in *The Book of All Things* were.

"Sure, I was done studying," she said with an eye roll. Though the boys' and girls' dormitories were on opposite ends of The Sepulchre, they could mingle and study when not in class, or engaged in instruction. Esther was from the Southerlands. She was a Rutland, one of the Great Families, and her father was a favorite of Lord Khallum Warwick. She insisted she'd probably be expected to marry one of the lord's sons. Brandyn met her on his second day, when he found her trying to skip rocks across the sky. She hadn't succeeded.

"I do need to go home," he answered with a hearty sigh. "But I don't know how to ask."

"Ask what?" Magi Christian said, approaching with a smile. Christian Dereham was their youngest teacher, hardly a man himself, but that wasn't what made his assignment as a Magi of The Sepulchre so unusual. He had also been Lord Dereham's heir in the Northerlands, a role that would ordinarily exempt an Adherent from a life of service, but Christian had fought all objections and chosen his path. He was a favorite of the younger ones, because he hadn't yet had the playfulness wiped out of him. The older ones carried their yoke of tenure with measured disdain, alternating between great seriousness and incurable weariness.

"Brandyn wants to go home," Esther said, the brat.

"I do not!"

"I sense that you do," Magi Christian replied. "But you must have your reasons, Brandyn Blackwood. You decide nothing lightly."

"It isn't my decision, anyway," Brandyn said, his heart sinking. He liked Magi Christian. He didn't want him to think he was a big baby.

"No," Magi Christian said with a thoughtful look. "But it's one I can help along, should your reason be compelling enough."

Brandyn shrugged. "That's the thing. It's just a feeling."

"A feeling?"

"You know. Like the ones I get."

Magi Christian nodded. "Ahh, yes. Your intuition. And what is it telling you?"

"Nothing clear," Brandyn said, shooting a look at Esther, in case she was thinking of doing something dumb like getting in his head. She was a healer, but the way she looked at him made him wonder if she could also read minds. She was his closest friend here, but she was also a brat. "Just that feeling, Magi. Like… like I'm needed there. Soon." He shook his head. "My sisters, I think. They need me. I don't know."

"I see. And what do we teach you here at the Consortium, Brandyn? About your powers?"

"Um…" Brandyn searched his brain. "A lot of things."

Magi Christian smiled patiently. "Specifically about our connection to them."

Esther smirked. "I know this one."

Brandyn glared at her from his peripheral, but brightened. "To trust them."

"Yes, to trust them. Reading them is another matter, and that takes years. It's why you're here with us. But your inability to read them as of yet does not make them inaccurate, or misguided."

Brandyn mused, not for the first time, at what must have pushed the young, handsome heir to surrender his life to a stuffy, magical college in the skies of the Easterlands. Maybe it was that pretty Magi Aylen Wynter, but he didn't think that was all of it. There was something special in Magi Christian. Something he hadn't experienced very much in his life and suspected was rare enough he wouldn't experience it much in the years that lay ahead, either.

Magi Christian rested a hand on Brandyn's shoulder. "I'll take it up with the Head Magus this afternoon. If he grants your leave, we can talk about how to use what I've taught you to protect yourself out in the world for a few days."

"He's so handsome. Too handsome for a place like this," Esther mused in a dreamy voice when Magi Christian was halfway down the corridor, but Brandyn was thinking something else entirely about their teacher.

Except it wasn't so much a thought as a premonition. Unclear, like all the others, but the underlying emotion rang so strong it stole his breath.

Magi Christian's family needed him, too.

He just didn't know it yet.

CHRISTIAN RETURNED TO HIS CHAMBERS AND CHANGED INTO HIS formal robe. Like the informal one, it was silver, but the hood was lined in purple fleece, with a sash to match. It was silly, but all tradition was silly if you didn't take it seriously. He'd been at odds with himself on this topic most of his life. Tradition was what he'd run from in Wulfsgate, dreading the day he'd one day have to take over duties from his father. But he'd traded one set of rules and guidelines for another, and the requisite wardrobe change for visiting the Head Magus was a sharp reminder of this irony.

Unlike the Adherents, the Magi were allowed leave to return home, or even to take pilgrimages, should they choose. But Christian hadn't been home to Wulfsgate even once. He last saw his mother and father at his convocation three years ago, when he graduated from Adherent to Magi, but the visit wasn't a happy one for any of them. He'd known even before that what he planned to do, and neither his father nor his mother had taken the news well. Neither understood. They didn't want to.

Holden and Gretchen Dereham had five other children, and Christian had made his choice.

They'd accused him—like the rumors around here that never quite died—of following his heart. He did love Aylen Wynter. Had since he was a boy, playing with her when his family would visit Witchwood Cross, or hers to Wulfsgate. He wouldn't deny he'd been happy to follow her to The Sepulchre, where they were free from the bonds of everyday family life and could explore things as adults would, despite that they'd entered as children. They were married now.

No heir would ever be denied their right to return, no matter how strong their magic. This had always been the way of things at The Sepulchre, for how could you disrupt a system that was thousands of years old? They'd never considered Christian for assignment because of who he was, and had he chosen to return and take his rightful role, no one would have denied him bringing Aylen as his wife and ruling as Lord and Lady of the Northerlands when the time came.

He had his reasons for refusing that life. They were his own.

More important on his mind was ensuring Brandyn Blackwood could return home before his entire world was toppled.

"For I, too, have seen the future," Christian whispered to the mirror, and, sighing, turned to employ whatever magic needed to allow the boy to return to his people while he still could.

8

THE RAVEN

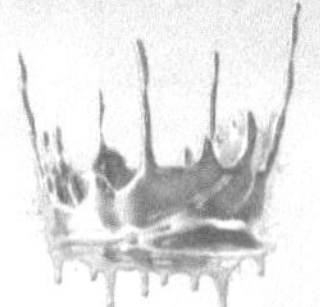

Ravenna slowed her flight as she approached Wulfsgate Keep. A discerning eye could glean the difference between an ordinary raven and a shapeshifted priestess, and while those eyes were less prevalent outside Wulfsgate, the capital of the Northerlands was used to the Ravenwoods and their oddities. She wasn't supposed to be here outside of the sacred agreement between Ravenwoods and Derehams, which for her had already ended as she ceased her training in Wulfsgate and returned permanently to The Rookery to prepare herself for maturity and the Langenacht. Every visit now was a risk. A careful calculation.

Unless she and Drystan could agree on a way forward, there would be no more visits. The time they'd viewed with such dread was upon them, and they must either face it, or flee.

She'd stayed the night atop Icebolt Mountain. That wasn't the plan, but she hadn't intended to leave so abruptly, and the snowbolts were merciless.

Ravenna made a few laps around the battlements, past the flags waving the symbol of the jagged mountaintop in the furious wind, dipping low over the Wintergarden, surveying the snow-coated world for any risk. It was late, and the storm was at its peak. As hoped, most were inside, sleeping or seeking shelter.

All except Holden Dereham, that was. She'd seen him on his horse headed for Witchwood Cross. He was an odd man. A second son, like Drystan, who was never meant for what he was given. But he'd always been kind to her, and kindness was a unique commodity in her world.

Ravenna eased herself upon the sill of Drystan's window. His velvet curtains were drawn to keep out the cold, so she slipped herself between the light crack and pressed gently against the glass to further open it. When she was safely inside, she unfolded into her usual form.

Drystan sat at his desk, quill hovering over that record-keeping that was about as useless a task as Ravenna could imagine. Memories were passed through kin; through late nights around fires. What were the words of a stranger to another?

His quill hovered above the page. It dropped, and he pulled himself erect.

"Ravenna," he whispered, relief pouring through each syllable.

She'd hardly straightened her cloak before he had her in his arms, spinning her wildly with a haphazard joy that was only possible now, when everything they wanted was on the verge of being ripped away by duty.

"Drystan," she purred against his ear, that familiar stirring within her both welcome and a torture. The pull toward him was indescribable. Her desire blasphemous. She could neither explain it nor define it. She snaked her hands up through his soft hair. "I had to come. I can't stay there anymore."

Drystan ran his lips across her face, inhaling as he peppered her with the purity of his affection. "I worried... no, it does no good now to say it. You're here."

"That I wouldn't come? That I'd changed my mind?"

Drystan's gaze dropped slightly. "I tried very hard not to think that. I know you have so much more on your mind than I can understand."

Ravenna led him to the edge of his bed, and they sat side by side. "Alasyr cast his lot."

Drystan edged back. "Oh, no… but why? Why would he do that?"

"It doesn't matter. He had his reasons, and his intentions are irrelevant to the outcome. I cannot sit and listen to his childish rationalizations. That's what I understood tonight. I cannot stay there, with him, with the others."

Drystan rested the back of his hand against her cold cheek. "You can stay here. You're welcome here, always."

Was this why she loved him? His idealism? His momentary lapses into a world where anything was possible?

It was one reason.

"No," she whispered, wrapping her hand around his, dropping them both to the bed. "I cannot. And this is a truth we've always known. This is a day that has been coming since you first kissed me in the armory." She grinned. "Kissed me, apologized, and then kissed me again before I could forgive you."

He looked briefly away, and she saw in his eyes that he, too, had been considering that they were imminently upon a time they'd both ached for, but also feared with everything sensible within them. They'd be free in their love, but they'd never be free.

She knew, though, that he needed a push. He might always, her Drystan, but tonight he needed one only she could offer, and it was one she desperately, desperately wanted to give.

Ravenna rolled her face against his soft, milky neck. "Love me tonight, Drystan. Like we've wanted for so long. Let it be tonight."

Her dearest stiffened, but also came alive, in another way. "You know what happens if—"

Ravenna silenced him with a kiss. "Not if. It's done. I cannot go back. We cannot stay here. If you love me, then love me tonight, Drystan."

Drystan turned, angling his whole body toward hers. His hands trembled as he took her hair in his hands, as he sometimes did when fighting against his own desires. "I live in constant fear of losing you, Ravenna."

Ravenna slid her limbs atop his, rolling atop and over him with such skill, he had no time to perceive or halt her intent. She squeezed her thighs against his, looking down at his cradled head. "Save your fear. Tonight, we are free."

DRYSTAN FOUGHT DESPERATELY AGAINST SLEEP, BUT THE BLOOD coursing through him brought with it the reminder of the sin they'd created over the ticks of the moon. The soft demand of her silken heat as he buried himself within her was something even his dreams hadn't prepared him for. The mastery of her own lovemaking, a skill she hadn't learned anywhere, and he wondered if she'd been born with it. He was exhausted, utterly, but his fears had never reached higher than they had with his great love sleeping softly at his side, her supple flesh peeking from under the ermine blanket as both a reminder and an invitation.

We cannot go back. Only forward, she'd said, before surrendering to her own need for sleep. He usually loved her wisdom, which wasn't terribly original, but said with such conviction every time. But wisdom without direction was just words. Yes, forward. But where? How?

He went to reach for his clothing when the door to his chambers slammed open.

The intrusion stirred Ravenna, and she was the first to identify the interlopers, as Drystan bounced around in his trousers.

"Lisbet… Eavan."

"Lis, would you say our timing is terrible, or right on the mark?" Eavan said to their cousin in a petulant, teasing tone.

"The Guardians would certainly appreciate the coincidence," Lisbet muttered. She closed and bolted the door behind her. "What it does mean is that we haven't even a moment to waste."

Ravenna looked at Drystan with a dozen questions in her eyes, but he needed answers, too. She wrapped the ermine tighter.

"What are you doing here?" he asked, flushed, struggling with his buckle. "Shouldn't you be sleeping?"

"You forget you have a lock on that door, Drys?" Eavan, still amused, perhaps the only one. "Or do you enjoy putting on a show?"

Lisbet shot her a scathing look from the side. When Lisbet set her mind to a task, humor ceased to be welcome. Her expression was grave. "In a fortnight, all of our lives change, and not for the better. If we stay, we surrender to a fate others agreed to on our behalf. If we leave, we choose our own fate."

"Leave..." Drystan's mind was still trapped between bliss and confusion. But leaving had been on his mind, too. He hadn't realized it had also been on Lisbet's. "And go where?"

Lisbet stretched her palm out toward Eavan. "Eavan has a plan."

When Eavan started talking, Lisbet quietly moved to Ravenna's side with her gown and cloak in hand. Ravenna offered in return a confused, but grateful, smile.

"It's not so much a plan as an idea," Eavan started.

"It's a plan," Lisbet replied firmly. "Now, *hurry*."

"Right. Well. We know any land ruled by Quinlanden, Dereham, Blackwood, or Warwick is out of the question. We can't be sure any of them would protect us, since all four agreed to send us to the king in the first place, and it seems unlikely many of *their* men would defy them. We'd be in a lion's den, wondering which had eaten already. It isn't safe," Eavan said, no longer smiling. "But there is one place where their rule has no voice. Where the king's rule has no weight."

"The Hinterlands," Ravenna said, a break in her shocked silence. "Or do you mean Beyond? You cannot."

"Yes, the Hinterlands," Eavan said. "I grew up with... that is, to say, I know some of the Medvedev. Yseult... the Chieftainess... she was always very welcoming, and her son, Kian, was a childhood companion of mine."

Ravenna, now dressed, rose to join the conversation. "But you said it yourself. They have no loyalty to the crown, to any of the lordships of the Reaches. Why would they aid you?"

"Us," Lisbet said. "We're all going."

Drystan gaped at her. But he was starting to understand and accept that this conversation was real, and what it would lead to.

"Kian, as I said..." Eavan faltered. "The truth is, we didn't part last on the best of terms. But I believe he would help us. You're not wrong, about their loyalties. But I'm in the unique position to have spent a fair amount of time getting to know the Medvedev and their ways. They have no loyalty to the crown, because they have no use for it. Who they are, what they are, it goes far beyond our idea of rule and law." Eavan paced the room, her confidence blossoming once more. "They are magic. They are... unlike anything you've ever known. Even you, Ravenna. They aren't troubled by the things that trouble us. I believe Kian, and Yseult, will see that we only wish to live in harmony and will shelter us, to that end. That's the way of their people. It's the one language we have in common."

Drystan pulled Ravenna to his side. He believed wholly in the leading hand of fate. Fate was often about timing, and about the Guardians conspiring in a way that came together, in spite of, or even working against, your doubt. That his sister and cousin had come to them on the very night his heart was most troubled affirmed the direction he'd been searching for, but failed to find.

Ravenna looked at Eavan. "And if you're wrong?"

Eavan bristled, but Lisbet stepped forward. "What are our choices, priestess?" Drystan's sister said, assuming command. He had the sense she'd be in charge now, from here forward. He didn't know if he should take that from her, or let it be. Once more, his confusion over his own role in this world, this family, confounded him. A riddle with no answer. "We stay, and Eavan and I are at the mercy of a king who killed his own brother and is renowned for his terrible cruelty. They'll force Ravenna to bed half the males in her family and marry one of them, and you'll never see her again. Not if you value her life." Lisbet stopped before the couple. "Or, we go. We risk our lives on the whisper of a promise, one that gives us a future where we can make our own happiness. Staying is its own form of death, so if the Guardians deemed our quest to be wrong and we found ourselves caught and facing punishment, what, really, is the difference? To leave... to leave is the chance that, maybe, we could find ourselves on a better path."

It was decided. It had been decided before they entered the room. He had his questions, and Ravenna had hers, but to hesitate would be to give more power to risk, and to dull the unquestionable authority of fate.

Drystan suddenly felt a potent sadness filter through him. He had the sense he'd never see his mother again, and their last words had been a persnickety exchange about his chronicling. His father; when had they last spent time together? And Pieter... the twins. Even Christian, though he'd come to terms with that separation years ago.

Lisbet reached her hand forward, as if reading these thoughts. "Drys. None of us know what this will bring upon the kingdom. When only one bride shows at the Right of Choosing, that'll be a slight that changes our whole world. But this world *needs* changing. If we play into the hands of this boy king, one who isn't even from our world, but Beyond, then we accept that our complacency has powered his evil. Maybe... maybe we do this not only for ourselves, but for all of the kingdom. Maybe we're the only ones with this control."

"Or maybe if we had parents less willing to sell us into slavery," Eavan muttered, and Drystan felt terrible for her in that moment. The Quinlandens had been the first to agree to send a bride, and all too eager for another opportunity to cement their role as crown favorites. The Derehams had agonized for a fortnight, and even then, felt sick as they released their raven toward Duncarrow, hours from the deadline. They agonized still.

"Or... maybe war is the equalizer needed to restore our world to one where we all again prosper," Lisbet whispered. "Maybe fate is relying on our action."

"We're children, Lis, none of us have that power," Drystan countered, but without bite. He didn't care about her ideals of war. War or no, she was right when she said they only had this one option if they didn't want a life akin to death.

"I saw your father headed toward Witchwood," Ravenna said, turning toward Drystan. "The best of his guard followed. This is an opportunity we might not get again, before it's too late."

Lisbet pointed toward the door. "Bags are packed. Ravenna, you're tall and slender, like my mother. I prepared a satchel with some of her things for you. More… erm… practical. Her riding gear, for one. Drystan, I packed the clothing Christian left behind so as not to interrupt your… activities."

"You knew we would go," Ravenna said.

Lisbet grinned.

"We saddled the horses. Lisbet *insisted* upon taking Starcaller, but other than her mare, we've chosen a few stallions no one will miss," Eavan said. "If we go under the cover of darkness, it will be easier to get some distance from Wulfsgate, so we're not followed. The Compass Road would be the quickest route, but we'll never make it in the open, so we will have to aim ourselves in the right direction and hope that aim is true."

On another day, another circumstance, any one of them would've decried the inanity in the suggestion. But on this night, the eve of the rest of a life they would choose for themselves, for better or worse, it was all they had.

"I can help keep our trail clear. Create diversions that prevent our trail from being discoverable," Ravenna said. "They'll work long enough to create distance from Wulfsgate. It may work the whole way, if the magic holds."

"Food and other provisions are loaded," Lisbet went on. "We're as ready as we can be, Guardian willing."

Ravenna turned to Drystan. "What did I say to you earlier?"

Drystan flushed, and she laughed.

Eavan groaned and rolled her eyes.

"No, not that. About tonight."

He recovered himself and gave her a lazy grin. "We are free."

"We are free," Ravenna repeated, sealing the words with a kiss. "And now we know the path that leads us there."

9

VELLUM

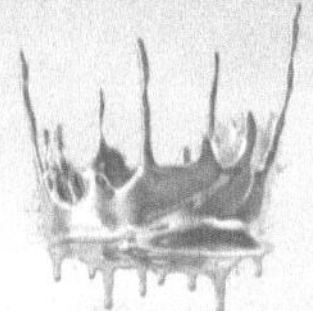

I begin this in the fifth year of my captivity, though I long ago ceased to count the days, or the hours. I know the time only by my son's growth, which is both a joy and the sun ticking down toward the beckoning end.

I do not know why I didn't consider doing this sooner. He won't miss the vellum. Wastefully, The Pretender stacks the precious resource ceiling to floor in my chambers, which he almost lovingly calls my suite, but has always been an equitably decorated prison. The great Sky Dungeons at Duncarrow. I gave birth to my son here. I expect we will both die here.

The vellum is for the letters he demands I write him, professing a love that is the opposite of any emotion I could ever feel for the man responsible for my greatest sorrow. He is not even a man, but something less than, who uses my son as a weapon to ensure my fealty, and so I write these letters, day after day, with a silver in my pen so convincing that I hardly recognize my own words. It must be someone else constructing them. Perhaps I go somewhere else. I sign them, Isa- my beautiful. The name he gave me, not The Pretender, but the other one, whose name I cannot bring myself to say or even write. But I will. One day, I will again.

The Pretender makes me sign them this way. He makes me do many *things that have changed me. The last time I refused to unlace my bodice so he could enjoy himself in the corner, he lifted my son and made as if to squeeze him out the tiny window to let him dangle. My boy cried and cried, unable to tear his eyes from the jagged rocks and sea below, and though I could not see them myself, I instinctually envisioned his broken body splayed against them, and I never refused The Pretender again.*

No eyes will ever see these writings, but it would not take a great scholar to deduce that The Pretender and Eoghan are the same. The second son who murdered his own brother as the only cure for his childish jealousy. I call him The Pretender not to feign pretense on his identity, but because I cannot stomach calling him by either his birth name or his stolen one. I will find that strength, though, for this story is about him, too. I must face his atrociousness to keep truth in my words.

But, ah, it was not always so. The Rhiagains were once decent kings, and some, decent men. Their origins remain obscured by time, or so they would like us to believe. They are not from our kingdom. They are from Beyond, though where, no one knows. Nary three centuries past arrived a ship of them, an entire clan, and the wreckage washed upon the rocks below what is now Duncarrow. The king's seat. My prison.

They claimed to have been buried by storms, and their direction obfuscated. They called the place from which they came Duncarrow, but could not say precisely where it was. Many believed this, because they wanted to believe in the promise of Beyond, but were frightened of the potential. It was simpler, safer, to accept that it had all been left to chance. With no means by which to return—and if it is to be believed, no idea where their old home was—they built their new home upon these unforgiving rocks and named it after the old.

By the time a hundred years had passed, no one lived who could confirm or refute their version of events. It became lore, no longer a memory. Even the Rhiagains claimed ignorance of their past. It was this that prompted the Council of Universities to begin work on The Book of All Things. *To never again lose the histories that shaped us.*

Kings they became. In the days of early, they were treated as the Ravenwoods, those elusive sorcerers in the mountains. Left alone, and even feared for their otherness, though their reputation as gods was already building, even then. Their strange magic was at the heart of this belief. It was like ours, but also very different, and many believed the Guardians had sent them to restore order. In those days, there was not one but four kingdoms. The compass points ruled unto themselves, with their own customs and culture. There were wars along borders and fierce competition for resources, which the Rhiagains witnessed. My father once said to me, when I was but a girl, that we were all our own undoing. That our behaviors demanded a king, and an opportunist only seized an opportunity. I suppose there is sense in that. My father also said that no fair intention ever ends as such, and there is sense in that, too.

There were so few of them, too few to be of any threat—if only our ancestors had foreseen our present times. Perhaps they did, but could do nothing.

I am not old enough to remember the reign of Fynne, though I was raised with the image of him as fair as a Guardian itself. Fynne the Good. Fynne the Fair. He had many nicknames, all bathed in golden light, and perhaps the Guardians were involved in the irony required to deliver him an heir who was all the things he was not.

I sometimes ask myself, had Fynne lived longer, would Khain have been allowed his foibles? The Epoch? The Great Massacre of The Houses? Is there any sense in the energy wasted on such a thought?

Why do I write this... why do I relive history... my father would say it is my natural curiosity bubbling to the surface. That I always had to know how things worked, and to do so, I had to know how things were.

There is no power to be found in this dungeon of the skies, but there are words.

My son watches me as I write. I swore when he was born that I would get us out of here. I lied to him. The first lies were my own misconception of my reality. Now I lie because, after five long years here, he is still not ready for the truth. And once The Pretender takes his four brides, he will lose interest in his plaything in the sky dungeon, and we will die of hunger, if we do not first perish of thirst. He is not so kind as to fling us to the stones. He is unacquainted with mercy.

The knife stitched into my bedding is another secret I keep. I have not the strength to use it against him. *I would pay, though not with my life— no, with something far worse. It is for me, for my boy, for a death more merciful than the hopeless one our gaoler would abandon us to.*

And so here we are.

Here I am.

Here my boy is.

All I have are my words, and there will be a day—soon, I sense, yes, soon—where I will not have those, either.

The world outside might as well not exist for me anymore, and so I will recreate what I do still remember, after this cruel captivity, for as long as I can.

I beseech The Guardian of Rebirth and Renewal. No matter my own fate, the kingdom cannot fall to the malicious whims of this man.

THE PRISONER FROZE AT THE FAMILIAR DREAD STEMMING FROM THE Pretender's footsteps. She quickly rolled the vellum and slid it into the drain at the edge of her room, which emptied into the sea… and obscurity. She hurried back to her desk, set to the darting eyes of her son who had never once in his short life seen the sun from the outside. Through his careful observations, her reality had always been the clearest.

The tension from shoulders to toes cut like a sharp knife as she hurriedly signed the other vellum, the love letter that kept the worst of his cruelties at bay. He would like this one. The more she sang his praises, the less he asked of her. And one day, he would ask for everything. This she never doubted.

She was almost ready for that day. The waiting was harder, she thought.

She would as soon face the Guardian of Anguish and Tribulation than fear his arrival. With him would come swiftly the Guardian of the Unpromised Future.

The Betrayer was worst of all. She'd been raised, as all in the kingdom were, believing this. No death, no torture, could be worse than The Betrayer's eye falling upon you.

But the prisoner had already met The Betrayer. She knew him well.

He was their king.

IO

THE HIDDEN CAVE

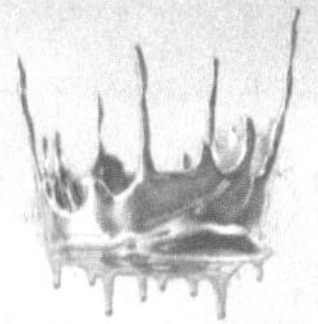

Emberley Blackwood, known by most simply as Ember, in large part due to the sparks she brought to nearly every situation in which she was invited, and also those she was not, awaited her brother's arrival at The Hidden Cave without a shred of patience.

Once she was certain Brandyn was on his way from the Sepulchre, she'd intended to share the plan with her sisters. Honestly, she had. Gabrianna would defer to her wisdom, as she typically did. Hollyn, on the other hand, wearied by her now long-term illness, never had time for whatever her younger sister had up her sleeves. Gabrianna would comfort her in her skepticism, Hollyn would rail in her protest, Gabrianna would cave and take her side for a spell, and then on it would go, until they finally acquiesced, but not before giving her the headache of her life. Always a fight. Always a win. Always at a cost.

Emberley resisted the terrible urge to tell Hollyn that she, too, was weary—of the delicate dance she had to do around the eldest Blackwood child whenever her impending wedding to the king was mentioned, which was no less than twelve times in a day. But it couldn't be helped that Hollyn had a blindness for the world she was so eager to jump into. They had bigger problems at present, and of a more immediate nature.

Such as the fact that Hollyn had become violently ill anytime sunlight even tickled her porcelain skin.

She'd always burned in the sun. They all did. It was the curse of the pale Blackwood skin, one of the few traits they'd never quite shaken when they split their ancestry from the Ravenwoods generations back. But this was not that. Great black spots spread across her flesh within seconds; whatever meals were left in her belly regurgitated onto the floor, across the room, or anywhere, really, without discrimination.

It was almost funny, the first time. A curiosity in a world where all the Blackwood children were each afflicted with their own brand of it. But then Hollyn was bedridden for days. The next time weeks. The fourth episode left her near death. Their mother, Asherley, paraded in healer after healer—both magical and not—looking for causes and cures, and all left without providing either. Their father, Byrne, insisted she'd grow out of it, sounding entirely unconvinced, and it turned out he was both right and wrong, depending on whether you listened to what he'd said outwardly, or believed inwardly.

Hollyn's affliction only worsened. Curtains had to be drawn at all times until sunset. There was no more playing in the gardens and forests of Longwood Rush. Hollyn came of age locked in a dark room, growing paler and more miserable each day, while everyone else in the family looked on helplessly.

While Gabrianna waxed on about how the love of a king could perhaps cure their sister after all, Emberley focused her mind on practical solutions. It was time to be realistic, not flit from daydream to daydream, thirsting on the sweet creams of blind idealism. There was little chance a king who had murdered his own brother would welcome a defective bride, and his rejection was assuming he reacted in the best way. At worst, and what Emberley had resolved herself to as the most likely outcome, he'd have Hollyn locked away, and their parents punished for daring to present such a "gift."

Emberley, being the second daughter, would then be plucked as the replacement and *that* was most certainly not happening.

She'd kept her own counsel on the matter until now, when she intended to present her plan to all of them. Once Brandyn arrived.

The Hidden Cave. It wasn't so hidden, but no one else bothered with it, on account of having to wade through waist-deep salt water at high tide to even reach it. Once inside, one could climb to higher ground, but there was the risk of being trapped. If the adults knew their children played there, they would've had the place sealed off years ago.

Gabrianna huddled, arms around Hollyn, at the back, shrouded in the darkness. The midwinter chill unsettled Emberley, too, but she kept it to herself, eyes peeled for any sign of Brandyn. The Sepulchre hadn't yet sent a raven, but Mother would be looking for him just the same. Joran would have seen it by now, and come straight to her to inform her that her youngest child was on his way home. If Brandyn were wise, he'd know that, but Mother was wise, too. Wiser than all the kingdom. Her wisdom buoyed Ember in ways she knew she'd miss when it was time to put her plan to action.

"He'll probably wait till morning. Sun will be here in two ticks," Gabrianna whispered. She'd always whispered in the cave, as if she expected the whole thing to come crashing down around their heads. "We can't keep her here much longer, Ember. We shouldn't risk it."

"I have the dark blanket for her if the sun comes before he does. But it won't. I did the calculations. He'll be here tonight," Emberley insisted.

"Voyages that long are not so precise."

"Have you studied long voyages, Gabi?"

"Have you?"

"Yes," Ember said, drawing a firm emphasis across the word.

Gabi's lips twisted in a pout. She, of course, had no response to this, so she asked something else. "But what if he goes home first?"

"He won't."

"You only said he *was* coming, not when," Hollyn said, followed by a cough. She coughed a lot now, and it seemed less a symptom of her malady and more to ensure others didn't forget for a second. "We can't be certain he'll come to the cave first. Or that he will come at all, to be quite frank, as we're relying wholly on your whims."

Ember sighed against her cold fists, letting her breath warm her before answering. "He will. He sensed it."

"You always say that. He doesn't even know how to use his powers yet," Hollyn said. "He's only been at the Sepulchre for a year."

"Brandyn's instincts are stronger than any ability he might have now," Ember said, her tone indicating there'd be no more on the matter. The frigid air stabbed at her bones. She didn't have the energy to waste when so much was needed for what lay ahead. In a way, she looked forward to what would come next, because the burden of upholding their faith would be someone else's for a while.

As such, she'd known better than to tell them that when they left this cave, they wouldn't be returning home.

BRANDYN CAUGHT HIMSELF BEFORE THE HOWL ESCAPED HIM. THE ICY sea sent a shock to his head that pulled his balance off course. Had he only come at low tide... but it couldn't be helped. He'd come as fast as he could, and alone, which, when his mother found out, might cause her to murder him.

"Brandyn!" Ember cried, before his eyes could adjust to the dim cave. She enfolded him into a hug that caused a well of emotion to surge forward. Home. He was home, after all this time.

Hollyn struggled to stand, so he rushed over to her instead. He rolled himself between the girls, accepting their hugs with powerful relief.

Relief that wouldn't last. He'd seen it in Ember's eyes as he peeled himself from her embrace.

"I've packed a bag for each of us," Ember began, forgoing even the pretense of pleasantries. "You'll find everything you need for the journey ahead."

"Journey?" Gabrianna rocked forward. "What are you talking about?"

Brandyn watched in silence. Listened.

"You brought us all the way out here, in the freezing cold, to play silly games with us. Even from you, I expected better," Hollyn said in exasperation. She grasped at the cavern wall, searching for purchase. "We waited here, and now we're going back. Brandyn, come, Mother will want to see you straightaway."

Ember stepped into the center of the path leading out to the sea. "We are leaving, but we're not going back to our home. We aren't going back to Mother." She turned to her brother. "Brandyn, tell me what you saw."

He tried not to look at the two sisters huddled in the darkness. It would be too easy to be pulled into their doubt. He'd come, and he knew, as he'd known before deciding the trip was needed, that Ember would have the answers.

"I didn't see anything. I felt… I felt drawn home." He shook his head. "Not to the Halls of Longwood. To you. The three of you."

Ember nodded, looking off somewhere else. "Yes. As I suspected."

"Oh, stop it!" Hollyn cried. "You are not all-knowing!"

"I don't have to know all, Hollyn. I only need to know enough," Ember replied, as evenly as if they were discussing supper plans. "I know what happens if we stay. There is no world where you become queen. Not anymore. And if you're not gone when Mother and Father attend the Right of Choosing, you might also find yourself devoid of freedom. Or life. And if you refuse to believe me,

Gabrianna will tell you she heard Mother and Father whispering about the very same thing."

Gabrianna glanced away, dodging Hollyn's incredulous glare.

"We have to find you a cure, and we have naught the time anymore. The Right of Choosing isn't even a fortnight away." Ember reached her hands over her head, looping them over the crisscross of plaits. "The kingdom has failed to provide a solution for us sisters, and so we must take matters into our own counsel. There is the Sepulchre, of course, even if the healers they've sent haven't been helpful. The Medvedev also have healers among them, and there are also the Ravenwoods, of—"

"You cannot be suggesting what I think you are," Hollyn said, whipping her neck toward their other sister for an ally. But Gabrianna always listened to Ember in the end. Her fight never lasted very long.

Brandyn spoke up. "You want us to go to all these places? That would take months."

"Not months if we split up."

"What? No!" Hollyn cried. "Alone? We've never been anywhere alone. Without Mother, or Father…"

Gabrianna remained silent, but her eyes filled with tears. Tears of fear, but also acceptance, Brandyn realized. She'd do whatever Ember suggested, no matter how scary, because she trusted her. Just as Brandyn did.

"Yes," Ember said. "But not alone. I've arranged for travel partners for all of us. They're fully aware of the plan, have all sworn the sacred vow, and await you at the rendezvous spot."

"Travel partners?" Brandyn scratched his head. "Who?"

"Why, The Hidden Crew, of course." Ember looked first at Gabrianna. "Gabi, Meadow and Brook Ashenhurst will be accompanying you to the Hinterlands, where you'll seek the aid of the Medvedev. I'll be taking Marsh Tyndall with me to Midnight Crest, where I can only hope they won't toss me against the cold mountain." With a humorless laugh, she added, "Be fortunate I chose the most dangerous task for myself. Don't ever say I don't think of your well-being. Hollyn, you'll go with Brandyn back to the Sepulchre, to Christian Dereham, who I believe will break rules, if needed, to do what he can. I don't believe for a moment the healers did all they could, only what they were allowed to do. Storm Wakesell will join you, because you'll have to be clever in how you travel with Hollyn, given her condition, and she wearies easily, so it will be easier if you can split that burden."

Brandyn was astounded.

"And they all agreed to come? Leave their homes? Their mothers? Their beds?" Gabi asked.

"You all remember the blood bond between The Hidden Crew. I called upon it. They know that failure to answer is a pox upon their very honor."

"Honor," Gabi repeated. "But they're children. Can children have honor?"

"Honor isn't t shackled to age," Ember said. "Honor is in our bones. Our souls. We either have it, or we don't."

Brandyn watched his siblings volley their questions, already knowing the outcome. He hadn't seen it before, but he was beginning to sense it now.

Hollyn laughed through her fear. "You can't make us do this."

"You're right. I can't," Ember said.

"Mother will track us down before we can even leave the boundary. She'll... she'll send wulves and hounds, and I've heard tell of that going badly, at times, you know, where the wulves instead of rescuing someone tear them apart. They are wulves, after all."

"Mother is already asleep. She'll be expecting Brandyn just after the morning meal. Only then will she realize we've all slipped away, and by that time, we'll be hours from even the best trackers."

"Christian has been kind to me. I don't want to get him kicked out of the Sepulchre," Brandyn said.

"It's his kindness I'm counting on, but we don't need to rely on it. You'll go on ahead when you reach Briarhaven, and Storm will be the one who brings Hollyn to the doors of the Sepulchre. She'll be the one to drag her in, claiming the rights granted all of us in the rules of the Sanctuary of Need. None there should recognize Hollyn as your sister, and you can privately enlist the aid of our cousin to see she gets whatever help they can provide."

Brandyn shook his head. "You've thought of everything."

"Yes," Ember said, without modesty. "And now if we want to maintain an advantage, we need to act on it."

Gabrianna leapt from the floor and rushed to her older sister. Sobs shook through her tiny body. Instead of the hug she seemed desperate for, Ember reached an arm out and steadied her. "Gabi, your strength will guide you."

"*You're* my strength."

"I'm your sister, and that's sometimes the same, but not always." Ember smiled and pressed her other hand to her face.

"Why can't we ask Mother and Father to help?" Hollyn asked.

"If Mother and Father knew what to do, they would've done it."

It was Gabrianna who asked the final question, the one reflecting in everyone's eyes, unasked. Brandyn already knew the answer, but he wanted to hear Ember say it.

"Why can't we send Brook and Storm and the others to these other places? Why can't we all be together, as we've always been?"

Ember dropped her hands. The glance she flashed Brandyn was conspiratorial, and a warm flush passed through him. She somehow knew he'd understand, and he wouldn't prove her wrong.

"Because the king will be very unhappy when the Blackwoods arrive without a daughter to give him. I guess you're waiting for me to promise you what we're doing will be okay, but I don't know, Gabi. Hollyn. Brandyn. I don't know." Ember's confidence wavered for only the briefest of whispers. "And should the worst happen, and one of us is caught, and punished, then we'll take that punishment knowing there are still Blackwood heirs in the world who can return home and take their place in the Westerlands when the time comes for our return."

Hollyn wobbled as she rose. "You're serious about this."

Ember nodded. Brandyn slipped his hand through hers in the darkness, returning the confidence.

Hollyn exhaled. Gone were the tears and the indignation. "Oh, curses of Rowan." She moved across the cave like a wraith and, joining her sisters and brother, they wove their arms into an unbreakable knot, bowing their heads, wordless in their goodbyes.

As they slipped from the cave and toward their journeys ahead, Hollyn pulled Ember aside once the others were safely around the bend.

"I know you're doing this for me," she said. "So I can marry the king in peace and full health."

No. Not that. "I'm doing this for us all."

"Which wouldn't be necessary if not for my affliction." Hollyn pressed her forehead to her sister's. The roar of the sea behind them turned her voice into a whisper. "Guardians bless you for always having the strength to do what I never can."

Ember twisted her mouth to trap the emotion within. It was useless to her. Anything with the power to cast doubt had no place in her world. At fifteen, she'd learned this in ways that had already changed her. "Maybe I just don't want to have to go serve The Pretender in your place."

Hollyn laughed. "Guardians help the man you one day serve, sister."

II

THE MISSING

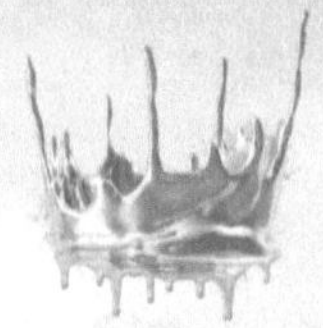

Asherley Blackwood received two ravens that morning, and both sent her straight to Joran Rosewood.

She found the old seer tending his indoor garden, in a small corner of the castle grounds she'd bequeathed him after several rounds of begging that was beneath him. It was a silly little hobby, and rightly unnecessary, living amongst the splendorous fauna of Longwood Rush. It seemed almost an affront to what the Guardians had given the Westerlands in plenty, and a poor imitation at that. But Joran was a man of his whimsy as much as his visions, and keeping him happy was of utmost importance to her. Although to deceive her would cost the seer his life, she could never be certain of his fealty—and thereby accuracy in what he conveyed —without first earning it.

She supposed it wasn't his fault that he was such a dreamer, being from a land ruled by Quinlandens, with their castles in the trees and their inflated sense of self-importance.

Asherley slammed both rolls of vellum on the wooden bench where he mixed his soils. "Your services are required."

Joran, kneeling by a patch of purple blossoms too foul to be native to the Westerlands, jumped back. He landed in a pile of plucked stems. "Lady Blackwood. My apologies, I did not hear you come in."

Asherley rolled her eyes behind his back. Here it began, the games they would play. He'd hem about the rules, she'd remind him of the alternative, and on it would go, until they were both weary, and the conclusion set before they'd even began. Would that she could trade him in, but he'd need to commit an egregious violation first, and while he was a fool, she didn't wish him into a death sentence, either. "We had ravens this morning. Two."

The man, now closing in on sixty, winced as he solicited a nearby tree trunk to pull himself to his feet. He stretched his arm out, and a shaking hand appeared from behind the swath of silver robe. "May I?"

Asherley passed the notes, and the old seer read one, and then the other. His patchy silver brows made several dramatic curls.

"Ahh. Yes, I see why you might have questions."

Asherley set her jaw, resisting the urge to grind her teeth. Her healer told her if she kept it up, he'd have to pull some in the back. "I need your guidance," she said in a rush, brushing her hand toward the curling scrolls. "Tell me. Tell me what they mean."

Joran gave her a rather stupid look, brows knit into a single line of haphazard hair, and said, "Lady Blackwood, I believe the messages are quite clear. The Dereham and Quinlanden brides are missing, along with Holden's heir apparent, and the Sepulchre wishes to confirm your son Brandyn has made it home safely."

She could feel now the burning red rage lighting from her toes, traveling as if on a restless sea toward her belly. Suffering fools seemed to be the Guardians' way of pinning her back from greatness. "I can read, Joran. You know what I'm asking of you."

Joran's feigned ignorance melted from his face. "Yes, mistress, I do. And you know well that I cannot."

Asherley loaded a hand, ready to slap him, but slid it inside the pocket of her hunting trousers. She hadn't even changed into something more suitable yet. She caught him staring at the smears of blood on her thighs. "It wouldn't be the first time you did what you could not."

"My life could be forfeit—"

She nearly howled the next words, and with every one, Joran shrank further into himself. "It *will* be forfeit if you don't tell me why my son would leave an institution that never allows such things, and why he is not, as the vellum suggested, home. If you don't tell me what happened to the other children, and what this means when we convene at Termonglen with no daughters to present!"

"There is Lady Hollyn."

Asherley gaped at him, open-mouthed. "We both know Lady Hollyn will not be a queen."

"How many years have I been in your service, Lady Blackwood?"

Asherley scoffed. "Too many."

"Twenty," Joran answered. "Since the Epoch, if I recall."

Of course it was the bloody Epoch. The Epoch was the end of everything. The beginning of everything. The beginning of the end. "Your point, Joran."

"I've always served you well. More than well. I have given you all I can give, and sometimes more." Joran affected a slight bow. The top of his head gave her shivers. His silver hair, once lush and flowing about his shoulders, was a sparse garden of decaying weeds. He was too old for a man of sixty, and she thought, not for the first time, he might be close to dying. "The rules forbid me from revealing news of your own blood. You know that now, as you always have. And yet you ask me this, knowing I would give you anything but that."

"Tell me, Joran." She inched closer, pulling the vellum from his gnarled hands. She pressed them to his face. "You and I both know the implications of two brides missing. If there's to be war, I will *not* be caught waiting for it to land upon my doorstep."

"War," Joran repeated. His eyes became glassy. "I've seen war, but it is hazy. Not war as, you or I would recognize it. I cannot say more, because I do not know."

Asherley's arm shot out, her fist wrapped soundly around his throat before he could gasp at the intrusion. "My son, Joran."

The old seer dangled from her strong grasp. Asherley was a warrior in ways her husband, Byrne Warwick, could only dream to be. It was an exhausting business, but she'd always done what was needed, and she didn't need to be a mind reader to know Joran knew this, too.

He flailed around, gesturing for a truce, and she dropped him. He flew back, sputtering.

"My son. Lisbet. Eavan. Drystan."

"I do not know why..." Joran coughed, face still red as a beet. "Brandyn returned to you. I know only that it was his request."

"Returned? So he is already here?"

"He was..." Joran shook his head. "Now I'm quite confused, Lady Blackwood, for it seems he has come and gone."

She wasn't confused at all, but it wasn't the time to let him know that. "His request, you said. The Sepulchre doesn't allow requests to return home, unless..." Asherley knelt before her seer. If he had seen the truth, then others had, too. She had to know. "Has someone died? Is someone dying?"

Joran shook his head, not meeting her gaze. He'd always been fearful of her, but had never been afraid until now. This she read in his bloodshot eyes. "I cannot see. But Brandyn believes his presence is necessary, and the Sepulchre encourages us... seers... to trust our instincts, even when unclear. This is why they granted his leave."

Asherley saw her hands at his neck again, but it would be no use. As she was painfully aware, seers did not see all. They saw what they saw, and naught else. Brandyn might not even know the source of his fears, but they were strong enough to bring him home. She knew why he *should* have come, but that wasn't the same as knowing. Nothing short of confirmation would be acceptable.

She paced the small garden, thinking. Rolling this all around in her mind, the tactician within her forming her assessments. She intentionally kept her own daughters from her thoughts. How they'd missed breaking their fast; how she'd not checked their beds. "And Lisbet and Eavan? Drystan?"

"I have seen nothing, other than the powerful sorrow of Gretchen Quinlanden, and the fiery rage of her brother, Aiden."

There were few men in the kingdom Asherley loathed, as she did Aiden Quinlanden, but his sister was a puzzle. She was neither Quinlanden nor Dereham. She was more like a Warwick, really, though she shared no blood with them. And like Asherley, but perhaps in a way that was more subtle, Gretchen, too, was a warrior.

She turned back to Joran. "What we talked about before. Our shared visions?"

"Yes?"

"It makes sense now. With this new information. I can see Termonglen more clearly now."

"As can I, mistress."

"And the king? What does he know?"

"Nothing. But he will."

"And?"

Joran dropped his eyes to the side. "And it will all be well, mistress, as it always is."

Asherley's heart dropped into the dust.

For the first time in two decades, her seer had lied to her.

KHALLUM STOOD AT THE EDGE OF THE QUARRY WITH ERRAN RUTLAND when Gwyn came running down the patch of dead grass, something clutched in her right fist.

"Grant me a moment, Erran," he muttered. All around him, the eyes of starving men regarded his every move. He wanted to scream to them, *blame the king! You give all, and he returns nothing!* And had

Khallum, too, not given all? While they still breathed and blinked, ripe with their judgments, Esmerelda did not.

"What shall I tell them, Lord Warwick?" Rutland struggled with the title. He only used it when among the mine rats and fishmongers.

"Nothing. I said a moment, not a lifetime," Khallum answered over his shoulder as he trudged up the steep hill his wife was easing down sideways, with frightening haste.

"News from Dereham," she sobbed. "Khallum, my brother—"

"Let me read."

Gwyn whimpered, shifting from one foot to another as the warmish midwinter wind from Leecaster Bay whipped across the hills. It wasn't from the cold. Gwyn often bemoaned missing the true iciness of the Northerlands. He'd never seen her so anxious.

Khallum brushed the filth and sweat from his brow and unfurled the tightly coiled vellum.

Lisbet, Drystan, and Eavan have gone missing.

The wulves are in pursuit, and my best men cleave to the task. Yet we are at least a day disadvantaged.

You understand that in tandem with our fears for our children is another fear.

Requesting a convocation three days ahead of the Right of Choosing with the lords and ladies of the Reaches. Termonglen.

"Guardian's cock," Khallum breathed. He read it again. Again. "Missing isnae dead."

"Khallum! The children have run off! We both know why. It is the same reason the Guardians have taken..." Gwyn buried her face in her gloved hands.

Khallum grunted. Esmerelda had said as much in her final letter. No one wanted to bed the king. The farce of his ascension to the crown could not be borne, but Khallum had given little thought to how the young women would bear this until Esmerelda had ended her sorrows over the matter. He supposed he didnae give any of them enough credit.

"This raven may carry old news. Perhaps another is on the way announcing their return."

"I'll find no sleep in the realm of 'perhaps.'"

"And Drystan? Why go with them?" Khallum had no skill in soothing his wife. Questions were all he had.

"Protecting them, of course!"

Khallum snickered. "That boy never stopped suckling his mother's teat."

"He's more Holden than Gretchen," Gwyn said, straightening. "But he is all heart, no sense. They'll be all alone in the world. Afraid. We have to do something."

"What? Do what?"

"Attend the convocation, for one."

Khallum looked away. Gwyn wasn't the ear for what he needed to say. That when he called for Holden, Holden answered with a cloak. Now Holden called to him, and the spite burning in his limbs had an even better answer.

"This isnae about that," Gwyn said, with the curious instinct she'd always had for the contents of his dark heart. She even said it in his language, her way of reaching him. "I willnae ask you to love my brother, Khallum, or even like him. But these children are my blood. And what happens, pray, when the usurper arrives to claim his brides and finds none?"

"There's the Blackwood girl," Khallum grumbled, because it should be he, not his foreign-born wife, providing the logic. Khallum knew fear. He could hardly look Gwyn in the eyes these days for fear he may not be man enough to keep her from Eoghan's slithering grasp. And now the Dereham and Quinlanden girl would also be missing from the king's gift. One bride wouldn't be a consolation, it would be an insult.

"My ears tell me she has a defect. That Eoghan will find her wanting," Gwyn answered. "Half a wife."

"Byrne has said nothing."

"Why would he? This is his child, his eldest. He'll see it as a failure of his own."

He understood he'd sent the Strong boy too late. Even if Ryan did discover what Khallum had sent him to the Wastelands for, less than a fortnight stood between their present shock and The Right of Choosing. There was no time.

"We'll leave for Termonglen in a week."

"With or without the Warwick Guard?"

Khallum squinted against the salty breeze.

Aiden Quinlanden stretched his arms over his head. With gently closed eyes, he listened to the world come to life in the trees. The trill of birds, humming of insects. Even the pitter-patter as the evening rain broke through the branches, easing a mist over the kingdom of Whitechurch. Inhaling. Home. Peace. Ahh, yes. This.

His attendants served him his morning meal on the Perch. As always, he ignored the burning loathing in their eyes, these displaced Medvedev he'd had the good fortune to rescue and put to use. Maeryn was always on him about her perceived crime against a peaceful people, but Aiden knew what a woman could never. Peace wasn't possible without subjugation and alliance. You subdued those whose alliance didn't bring you the appropriate prosperity. Survival wasn't as simple as breathing. Understanding this had kept Aiden from ever mourning his parents, or grandparents. Their promise had ended so his could begin.

The two Medvedev slaves hobbled off, dragging behind them the weight of their chains. The sound was *such* a disruption to his otherwise euphoric morning. If only they'd accept that he'd given them a chance at another life, he would not have to listen to the grating clinks and clunks as he partook in his meals made for a king.

He was not a king, but with the offer of Rowanwen, he could be the Lord Chancellor. The right hand of the king. Eoghan had no care for rule, only power. Aiden could offer him a reprieve from these niggling duties, assuming the functional role so the king could affect the symbolic one that meant so much to him.

The Quinlandens were once greater than any Rhiagain dared to rise. They were admired by all the other Reaches, elevated upon their perches of alder and oak. It would be so again, starting with the Right of Choosing.

His daughter, Eavan, had been due back the evening prior, but the midwinter storms were at their peak, and a delay of a day or so wasn't unexpected. He didn't miss her presence and was eager to see her become the burden of another great man. She had too much of her mother in her. She had the beauty of a Quinlanden, but lacked the iron spine needed to protect it.

Aiden ripped the edges of the starfruit with his incisor. Juices dripped down over his green cloak, which he would throw to the other attendants to wash. His eyes shuttered closed once more, drowning in the lilting melody of a world that lived to serve him.

A sharp scream from his wife broke his peaceful reverie. Rage. That fool Maeryn. Marrying a Blackwood had been the bane of his life, those upstart offshoots of the Ravenwood clan. Only for Eoghan would he tolerate her, but his tolerance was not in abundance. Even the sound of her voice could send him into a violent rage, though he was ever careful never to leave evidence. That would not do. Whispers were more powerful than anything you could confirm with your own eyes.

"How many years, Maeryn? How many years have I *explicitly* told you to never, ever, ever disturb me as I break my fast? How many?"

The question was rhetorical, but as he affected his slow, furious turn in her direction, he would demand an answer even if it came with his hand wrapped at her ebbing, whinging neck.

But her appearance startled him. Her face was white as a ghost. Her dark hair uncombed.

"It's Eavan," she pushed forward, into a mix of a whisper and a cry.

Aiden flung his fruit into the forest and marched toward her, cloak flying behind him like wings upon the sky. He gave her a hard look before ripping the vellum from her bony fingers.

Lisbet, Drystan, and Eavan have gone missing.

The wulves are in pursuit, and my best men cleave to the task. Yet we are at least a day disadvantaged.

Rest assured, we do all we can, but it is advised you consider how you might calm the king in the event we arrive without them.

Aiden's hands pressed so hard into the vellum it ripped and shredded, floating around in the breeze as Maeryn watched him, soundlessly crying, awaiting his counsel, like the weakling she'd always been.

"He's lying," Aiden decided, turning back to the beautiful song of his most loved subjects in the branches, birds dancing atop the trees.

"But why—"

Aiden reached back and sent his fist into the belly of his wife. He'd done this only once before, with grievous results, but she was past having children now, having long ago left the marriage bed, and her suffering pleased him.

He heard her connect with the soft wooden platform as she fell behind him.

"Holden, Khallum. They're the same. This is an excuse for war."

Maeryn gasped for breath.

"They never intended to send their daughters to Termonglen. Khallum probably killed his with his own hands, because he's an uncivilized grasper who knows nothing of duty or honor. And Holden would take my own child from me, too, thinking I'd have no choice but to align my own army to his, to save her." Aiden laughed, but the sound had no humor, and if Maeryn were present enough in the moment, it was a sound she'd recognize as one preceding some of her greatest terrors. "He has no inkling the hell he's called down upon a world he'll come to find unrecognizable by the time this is over."

Aiden kicked at his pathetic wife. "Bring Assana to me at once."

"But why? What do you want with her?"

"Why do you think? Eavan is lost to us. Assana will be wife to our great king."

HOLDEN DEREHAM WAS WEIGHED TO THE IRON CHAIR IN THE HALL OF Hearing. He used this only when in service to his people. It wasn't an especially comfortable chair. Most remarked that it was even too small and homely for a great lord. Gretchen liked to say it was crafted by someone who must have at one time been kicked in the head by a mule, with its lumpy edges and poor smithwork. He didn't really know the origins, or care, but his brother, father, grandfather, and probably great-grandfather had sat upon it to show the reciprocal fealty of lord to landowner, and if it was fair enough for them, it was fair enough for Holden.

It was also the only place in Wulfsgate Keep where he couldn't hear the keening, feral sound of his wife's wailing.

As a man, there were few things more terrifying to him than that which he couldn't solve. His wife's intermittent melancholy was high on the list. When she was present, she was a force. She had the makings of an heir. But when "the ache"—as she called it—took hold of her, she went to places he couldn't go. The last time, when she'd found that poor blacksmith's apprentice dead on the floor of her bedchamber, she didn't return to Holden until he sent her away for a healing he couldn't provide. *You can't go this time, not this time, Gretchen!* he'd pleaded when she refused to release the note left for them, in Drystan's scrawl. *This time, I need you.*

How she'd begged for him to resist the king! Ah, if only. There was no greater honor than a son joining the Rhiagain Guard, topped only by his elevation to the Knights of Duncarrow. It was one of the few calls to greatness available to anyone not highborn. But even a few dozen trained cavalry were better than what they had in the Northerlands. Farmers with rusting swords propped against the corners of their barns. None had swung metal in actual combat, because there'd not been a war since before any of them were born. It would take a decade to train a proper legion, and King Eoghan had given them mere weeks to return their answer.

Gretchen. Khallum. Both led with their hearts, and if Holden had followed, what remained of their ways of life would be blood seeping into the soil of the land they loved. Wars weren't won on desire alone. He couldn't will a resistance into being, any more than he could convince them of the same.

The convocation would provide answers. Perhaps the Southerlands or Westerlands had resources Holden was unaware of. The crown had been stealing Khallum's men since before the Epoch even. It wasn't impossible to consider he might have taken the intervening years to train his guard and ready them for battle.

If Khallum Warwick had an army, he would've used it by now, you fool! He would've used them when Khain picked off our mothers and fathers, one by one, without answer!

Even elsewhere, his wife's words lingered.

Holden ran his hands over the uneven metal of a throne chair fit for no one. A chair meant to represent a kingdom that was nothing of the sort, not since the Rhiagains washed upon the shores of their realm from the World Beyond the Sea.

But Holden Dereham was descended from kings. And kings, they could be again.

"But not me," Holden said, trying out his voice in the empty chamber. "And not Drystan."

How swiftly all had changed.

Holden turned his head to the side to regard the position of the moon. It was late, and tomorrow he and Gretchen would leave before dawn to reach Termonglen a day ahead of Aiden and the king.

It wasn't where he wanted to be. He belonged out there, searching for his children with the party he'd sent hours before. It should be him observing the hounds for even the slightest change in pace. He should be at the front with the brightest torch, commanding the charge. It should be him to bring his family home.

But if Holden, and Asherley, and Khallum couldn't come to a consensus on a way forward, there wouldn't be a home to bring them to.

THE SILENCE OF COWARDS

12

SCST8769

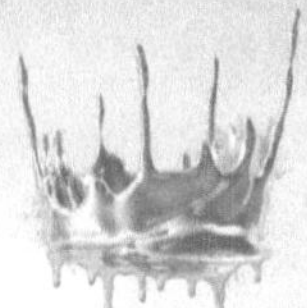

"Prisoner S-C-S-T-8-7-6-9, if you don't retake your pickaxe, your meal allotment for today will be forfeit!"

"You can fecking have your gruel," Andy muttered, shoulders so heavy he could do nothing but rest his hands upon his knees. His back was a field of fire, like what he imagined the ground at the base of the nearby mountain to feel like when it occasionally belched up its meal. Red and black, dancing, fighting, co-existing.

And how did these good-for-naughts remember so many combinations of letters and numbers, anyway? The brutish louts didn't take their education at a university. Most boasted the sea-worn leathered flesh of the Southerlands, which was a real feck-you upon an entire season of feck-yous. So the king didn't only take them for prisoners, then. *Eoghan should be paying the Southerlands' taxes on their behalf, he owns so many of them outright.*

"Pick it up," Cap warned, hissing through clenched teeth. The wild look in his eyes faded the smile on Andy's face.

But Andy didn't reach for the pickaxe.

"What are you doing?" Cap, still swinging his own. Like most men in the Wastelands, he'd learned to exist in dualities. "Pick it up!"

Andy pulled both his arms behind his back into a gratifying stretch. The popping sounds were welcome signs of life. Hard work had never scared him away, but where he came from, hard work was a means to an end worth working for. The end here was humiliation or death, in either order, often together.

"Prisoner S-C-S-T-8-7-6-9, this is your last warning!"

"Dinnae bother. Starvation will knock the fight right outta tha' one," the other guard said, and they laughed together. Iron Hill, Andy supposed from the accent. How long had it taken him to forget where he came from and suck on the balls of the king who put him here?

Andy winked at an incredulous Cap and said to the guard, "Aye, I wasnae hungry for your mother's milk anyhow. 'Tis spoilt."

Something hard and metal connected with his back. His next inhalation of breath made him feel like he was on rough seas, and he stumbled right into Cap, who seemed completely torn between wanting to help and his animalistic, instinctual need to eat at the end of the day.

"Sorry, mate," Andy said, grinning at the two guards as the shovel made fine work of his face. Now his grin was bloody. "Ah, no, not you. See, I was apologizing to this fine worker beside me, who never misses a step." Cap closed his eyes with a sigh as Andy clapped a hand on his shoulder. "Didnae mean to disturb your most inspiring dedication."

He saw it in Cap's eyes before he felt the blow that sent him to the ground, and somewhere else.

WHY THEY'D LET HIM TAKE ANDY back to their barracks was a wonder in a place possessed of none. None had ever tended his own broken bones, except for time. Cap had a theory he'd been working against. Most of the deaths here were of those who'd given all the best of themselves and had naught left to give. Like Hill. They could beat a man like Andy, but they couldn't kill him, because he had five, maybe seven years' worth of half-starved labor in him alive. This same thing had kept Cap alive until he'd had the piss knocked out of him for good.

Andy might need the same lesson. He reminded Cap of himself in the early days, using his resistance to protect his humanity. Cap had watched the young man mouth off daily, and subsequently pay for this, in varying ways. Today had been the worst. He'd been building to this one.

The barracks weren't a marked improvement from the mines. They stacked the rotting cots almost on top of each other, with the privy buckets just outside the tent flaps, day and night. It was too much to expect the privilege of privacy in such a godless place, but it was the *smell*. Cap was used to it, but he never forgot it, like a persistent illness that nagged at your every step. The flies left traces of shit on their blankets, clothes, flesh. Their only form of décor.

Clean water was a scarcity. Even the river that ran adjacent was suspect, from the constant use by the prisoners and guards to cleanse the worst of the filth from the camp. He swiped a flagon of mead from the small stash he'd socked away and used it to clean Andy's wounds. The fool. He wasn't much younger than Cap, but he had a lot to learn before they were matched in wisdom.

Andy slept through the first few minutes of Cap's ministrations, but when he finally did wake, he launched himself forward in such a powerful surge that Cap almost mimicked him in response.

"I nearly lost my bowels," Cap muttered, pushing him back against the burlap satchel filled with hay that counted as a pillow. "You don't do anything halfway, do you?"

"Not if I can help it." Andy winced, arching his spine for relief. "I hafta remember not to turn my back on the ratsbane. There's a lotta me can take it, but my back may as well belong to a woman."

"A woman? What's that?"

Andy's bloody lips curled into a smile. "Are you cracking wise over here, Cap? Nah, cannae be. You don't have it in ye."

Cap shrugged. He twisted the lid back on what was left of his precious mead and buried it under his cot with his second and only other item of clothing. It was a jumper identical to the one he now wore, expected to serve his needs in midwinter or springtide alike. There were no coats allocated, and only when his boots had worn across all toes and both heels were they issued a replacement pair, often from the feet of the recently departed and in hardly better shape than the ones discarded.

"Is there a woman waiting for ya, where ya come from? White-cap, no?"

Cap scowled and looked away. "There's nothing waiting for me in Whitecap."

"Five years, it's been?"

"More or less."

"How do you keep track of the time passed?"

"You count off the days in your head, until everything in there is a blur and you forget your place. And then you guess. When you're tired of guessing, you realize time ceased to be important, just like everything else in the world before this one."

Andy squinted in the direction of the tent flap. "By the sun I'd say it's suppertime. Where's your hog shit?"

Cap had given that up, too. That was the choice the guards had given. *Him, or supper.* How desperate he'd been for sustenance as he gazed down at the broken, arrogant lad at his feet. His humanity danced back and forth across the half-second it took to say, *Him.* A word he regretted in the next moment.

Andy propped himself up on one elbow. "Aw, Cap. Come on. I wasnae trying to pull ye down with me."

Cap threw the filthy, bloodied rag into the corner pile, where one of them would be on duty in a week or so to take them for washing at the river. "I know."

"Go on and get it. I'll be fine."

"I know you'll be fine. But there's no food for me now."

Andy's face fell. "I didnae intend it that way. I'm sorry."

"Your contrition isn't necessary. But your adherence is." Cap leaned in. "I won't make that choice again. And if you do what's asked of you, I won't have to."

Andy dropped his head back against the crude pillow. His eyes took on a glassy sheen. "You may have no one awaiting ya in White-cap, but I have a girl in Sandycove. With the darkest hair and eyes like the seas upon a violent storm. Verdant. That's the word. When the foam turns green. Ye know it?"

Cap said nothing.

"And I'll nae break her heart again when she has to sign for my body."

Cap rolled himself to a stand. This was the natural end of this conversation, where the small talk that promoted survival had slipped into the sentimental; a place that didn't exist anymore, not for them. "Aye, well, rest, and remember this feeling, for the next time. Pray it gives you better sense."

Andy's eyes blinked once, twice. Cap had the odd feeling he intended something with it, but mystery was another thing the Wastelands had no time for. "There won't be a next time. Thank you for helping me see it, friend."

When Cap had left, Andy started to laugh. He knew better than to launch himself into the real gut-busters he and his brother used to lose themselves to, despite that the urge was present, but he laughed nonetheless.

He laughed for Cap, who he guessed had done nothing like it in years.

He laughed for his long-suffering, loyal brother, somewhere out there, along road or trail, with his love and her wicked temper and silver tongue.

He laughed for the dead, and for the living.

For the Southerlands.

For himself.

Especially for himself. For what had he even come here? It

should be him accompanying his Esmerelda to his mother's family in the Hinterlands, not Jesse. And that's if the plan even worked. The Wastelands was a place devoid of news of the world. He had no confirmation Esmerelda made it out of Warwicktown at all. If she was discovered, Ryan would have no place in the Southerlands awaiting him. His life forfeit.

He didn't think Esmerelda had failed. He'd know. If nothing else, Khallum would've sentenced some of his own men to the prison just to have them come and deal with the issue of the meddling Ryan Strong once and for all. When he'd discovered their love, Ryan really thought Khallum would kill him.

But he hadn't. He'd somehow restrained his anger while reciting reminder upon reminder that Ryan wasn't suited for the daughter of a lord. And then he'd given him an opportunity for redemption. It wasn't a choice, but a chance. *A chance to save the Southerlands, Ryan, and perhaps the kingdom with it.*

Khallum was a man of few words, but he'd spent a handful on Ryan before the guards came to take him in chains to a new reality.

'Tis more than the minerals we're after, Ryan. And then he told him what the *'tis more* was.

How can you be sure? Ryan had asked, because he would sacrifice for the Southerlands, would do it happily for a cause that could save it. *How can you trust what you were told?*

There is a force... a force for good. A small force, but 'tis powerful. That force would see us all restored. To tha' end, you go to the king's lawless prison and you return with our salvation.

What if I cannae do as ye ask? What if I fail?

If you fail, I send your brother in your stead. These, the last words Khallum spoke to him, were both a reminder of why they all served him and why they equally feared him.

But Khallum Warwick was not his enemy. The Southerlands and all within her boundary had prospered until the Rhiagains began their reign of terror on their men and resources, on a land that Fynne the Good had only recently restored to the rightful owners, only to have his descendants threaten it once more. Khallum exerted the only power he still had, and in doing so, made it harder for all.

But Ryan Strong knew that doing nothing would have been worst of all.

Khallum might not believe a marauder's son from Sandycove was a suitable groom for his daughter, but what about the savior of the realm?

Sewn into the hem of the narrow strip of ripped cloth holding the sweat from his head was the only thing he'd come in with that he'd been allowed to keep. Sleight of hand was how he'd held on to it when they'd robbed him of everything up to the socks on his feet.

It wasn't yet time to extract it, but today was the first day he'd had in this hellscape where he could imagine that day coming to pass.

I3

SNOW

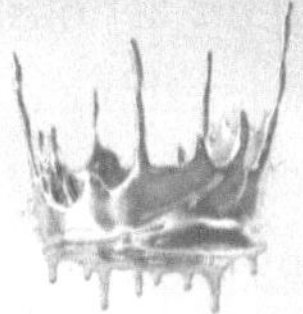

J esse tugged at the reins, slowing his nag. To his right, Esmerelda, daydreaming as usual, took a few extra seconds before following his lead. He shook his head. If he'd been avoiding a trap, she would've fallen right into it.

"Why are we stopping?"

"For once you want to keep on, Princess?"

"Only wondering."

"I ken I'll tell ya when I feel like there's something you need to know."

"Something's wrong," she said.

For a moment, Jesse wondered if she, too, could sense what he felt. But it wasn't so. She was only reading his hesitation and searching for another way to retrieve an answer to her question. Just one more question, topping a mountain of them in the weeks he'd spent as her guardian. And, like with all the others, he would keep his counsel this time, too.

Jesse dismounted. He pressed a hand in her direction, indicating he didn't want her to follow. The path they'd taken was the one Kaslan and Easlan indicated would give the most cover, but would also be the hardest to traverse. Their path ran a jagged parallel alongside the Seven Sisters of the West, and already they'd come across a foothill so steep they had to lead the horses over it, hoods over their heads to fight their uneasiness. Even the flat land was covered in fallen trees and untended forest floor growth. They'd covered half the ground Jesse hoped for, and if his senses hadn't failed him, they had a different challenge ahead.

"What is it?" Esmerelda pressed. She leaned forward in the saddle, listening. Mimicking his actions, as if she understood at all what it was to surrender to something bigger than herself.

Jesse's hand went up again, this time with more force. He stepped into a small clearing in the trees, where he could see the sky, but not far enough for him to lose sight of her.

His eyes closed as he let the chill in the breeze pass over his skin. Palms up, Jesse forced himself into stillness. His feet lightened and the forest floor fell away, separating him from the world in order to bring him further into it.

A memory of a choppy sea voyage in the Northerlands entered his mind, and he let it take over, as his father taught him.

A Northerly wind. A heaviness to the world, like a great pressure descending from the sky. The ice in the clouds grates upon something unseen and the results fall upon us.

Who had said these words? Not a Southerlander. No one Jesse had been raised with spoke this way. It must have been their Northerland guide, the one from Westport who could say nothing without waxing poetic. At another time, Jesse might laugh at the memory, but he needed it for something more important now.

But what is it? What are ye cracking on about? Hamish had asked, speaking for all the Southerlanders.

"Snow," Jesse whispered, as the first flake landed upon his eyelash. Esmerelda appeared beside him, holding her own hands out to receive the grated ice from the skies.

"I've never seen it with my own eyes," she mused. Her head fell back, and with it, the hood hiding her remarkable hair. Short black waves tumbled out. "I don't know if I believed it was real. Like a dream. Snow." She said the word slowly, musing over it.

"It cannae be," he said, though he knew it was. He knew because his instincts had guided him to this answer, but now he'd seen it with his own two eyes. "This far south."

"It's beautiful." Esmerelda extended her tongue to catch the few rogue white flakes; the start of a storm. "How I wish Ry—"

Jesse yanked her away from the clearing, marching them toward their horses. "Don't you dare say his name out loud. What's beautiful to you is dangerous to those with sense. And we're heading straight into it."

"How can it be dangerous? It's so soft!" She cried out as she stumbled over the underbrush.

He urged her up into the saddle before climbing into his own. "It can be, and it is. And as I've seen a snowstorm and you have not, ye can cease it with the questions and you'll see for yourself soon enough."

STARCALLER WAS THE FIRST TO RESIST. SHE CAME TO A HALT, planting her hooves with a fierce neigh. Lisbet ran her hand over her soft mane, cooing in her ear, but her old friend was stubborn in her twilight years. She was also wise.

Lisbet pulled at her rabbit-hair hood, tightening it. She squinted against the wall of white. Maybe Starcaller was right. The old mare's sensibilities weren't plagued by the pride of a Northerlander, who always insisted there was no storm strong enough to stop them. This wasn't true, but the sentiment pushed them into this belief, and now it might have pushed them into danger.

"Where's Ravenna?" Lisbet shouted over the whistling wind. "She going to be okay up there?"

Drystan's worried face turned toward the sky. "She knows what she's doing."

"Great, well, are you both ready to swallow your pride so we can get out of this mess?" Eavan yelled as she struggled with the reins of her restless nag.

"The wulves aren't even a day on our trail. We're losing our lead," Drystan said.

"What trail?" Eavan, disappearing into the bulk of her coat, waved an arm around. "Every step we take is covered by a fresh layer. And there's Ravenna's magic, for whatever good that's done keeping them off our scent."

"She's right," Lisbet said with a sigh. She didn't turn her head to see Eavan gloat. And if they weren't treading on dangerous ground, Lisbet never would've given her the pleasure. "We have to find cover. You know how it is. Once the worst is past, we pick up our pace. Any trackers will have slowed, too." She reached for her brother across the space between their horses. "This could work to our advantage, too. Rest by day. Ride by night. Even wulves can't track as well in the darkness."

Drystan nodded, moving his head across the snowy scape before them. She sensed in him several confusing emotions. Regret. Fear. But most of all, Lisbet sensed her brother's disdain for himself, and his own ineffectualness. She would have to be more careful with her suggestions going forward. Make them seem as if they were his own.

"What's that?" Eavan pointed to a cluster of stones. They resembled a chimney separated from its base, though larger. "Almost looks like a home of sorts."

"An abbey, my father calls them. They're all over the Northerlands," Lisbet answered. "Remnants from the time before the Resplendent Reliquary took over leadership for the clergy. The monks lived away from the people to strengthen their connection to the Guardians. They aren't unique to our part of the kingdom."

"You know how sheltered I am, Lis."

"The abbeys were torn down when the Reliquary came in, and the clergy sent to serve within the towns instead, where they could be available and present with the people," Lisbet said, and, as it was often the case when talking about something she'd never experienced, she let her mind explore the potential for the briefest of moments. Of a world where faith was bigger than the organization binding it to the world.

"That's all very nice, but will it keep us warm?"

"As well as anything else, I suppose," Lisbet said, reverie lost, and angled Starcaller toward the ruins of the abbey from another time.

Drystan paused before following, eyes searching through the blinding snow for his love.

GABRIANNA TUGGED AT THE MULE. CURSED THING WAS STUCK IN THE mud *again*. Ember hadn't mentioned they'd be contending with rains. She hadn't mentioned which direction they should go, or how to get to the Hinterlands. And the Hinterlands weren't small, she presumed, any more than the Westerlands were. So what happened when she got there? Ember had offered nothing of use, issuing her commands with a confidence that made Gabrianna strong when she could bask in it, and weak when abandoned of it.

"It's cold out here," Brook whined. He was supposed to be tracking. Tracking *what* Gabi didn't know, but all he'd done so far was stand around while she tried to figure things out.

"I'm... aware," Gabrianna grunted, throwing all her weight into the resistance of the stubborn animal. It wasn't even all that stuck. The mud was annoying, but not cloying. If she didn't know better, she'd say the stupid thing was being dramatic.

"It's not too late to go home," Meadow added, so bright and chipper it was clear she was putting it on to counter her brother's melancholy, though her sentiment matched his.

"Go home then," Gabrianna replied, panting through her efforts. She'd die if they actually left her, of course. But they wouldn't. They just wanted her to tell them everything was going to be fine.

Well, she needed that, too. She needed Ember's stalwart reassurances that no matter the challenges, all would be well. But Ember couldn't even give that in her parting words. *I guess you're waiting for me to promise you what we're doing will be okay, but I don't know, Gabi. Hollyn. Brandyn. I don't know.* She should've lied. Gabrianna wouldn't have known the difference, but she could have moved forward into the unknown with *something.*

"We can't," Brook said with a heavy frown. "We swore the blood oath."

"Fealty and secrecy, the breaking of which means our untimely deaths," Meadow joined in.

"Might get to experience that anyway," Gabrianna muttered, giving one more heaving yank that yielded no ground.

The first day, the trio had argued for hours about where to go. Meadow was supposed to be good with direction, but had planted herself on a tree stump to cry instead of pointing them true. Gabrianna knew Ember had chosen the Ashenhurst siblings because Gabrianna would need the aid. The Ashenhursts were known for their instincts. Not magic, because that was illegal, but a prowess with the flora and fauna honed over generations.

Maybe they were defective. It was simple to brag to your friends about all you could do, and another thing entirely to prove your worth.

In the end, Gabrianna had decided, through her own tears, which path to take. The Hinterlands was north and east, according to Ember. The sun started the morning to the left of her and ended it to the right, so she angled herself to the last place she remembered the sun setting and made a silent prayer to the Guardian of the Unpromised Future that she wasn't leading them instead to the salt and sand of the Southerlands.

Following one unfortunate tug, the mule bucked, and Gabrianna went flying face-first into the mud. She heard the gasps of the Ashenhursts behind her, and then their unsure steps as they debated how to help her.

Gabrianna drowned them out. She couldn't hear them anymore, and their petulant indecisiveness. She buried herself deeper in the mud, pretending it was the softness of her pile of pillows at home in Longwood Rush. She could almost smell the rich saltiness of a hog on the spit, waiting for her to break her fast. The citrusy sharpness of the juice at her bedside luring her away from her restful sleep.

"Gabi!" One of the twins. She didn't care. Gabrianna was slipping her soft heels into the plush slippers her father got her for her last birthday, her twelfth. They were fluffy, like the tail of a bunny, and she hopped around in them, delighted by her father's chuckles. She loved to make him laugh. And her mother said Warwick men never did.

"Gabrianna, get up and *look!*"

And then her father wrapped her in his arms and told her she was his most favorite bunny. The best of all the bunnies, and would this bunny like some roast pig with freshly baked bread? Oh, and there was honey, fresh from the hive. Extracted just that morning.

Gabrianna felt the soft spun sweetness across her tongue. This was its own kind of magic, this nectar mined from the world for their own enjoyment.

Honey turned to dirt. Gabrianna inhaled just as a spray of mud flew into her mouth and she stumbled back, sputtering and wiping at her mouth. No, no, no, she was a bunny, and her morning meal was so wonderful, and her father was there, and—

Brook took his jacket and wiped the rest of her mud from her face, then held her face in his arms. "Will you look?"

Her protests turned to wonder at the soft white tufts falling from the sky. Like curls from a bunny's tail, but smaller and more perfect. She was again in the warmth of her home, dancing around the room with her father, his most favorite bunny.

"Is that snow?" Meadow asked. "In the Westerlands?"

"Are we even in the Westerlands?" Brook asked.

"We haven't gone that far, Brook!"

"How would you know, you didn't even know where the Hinterlands was?"

"Have you even been covering our tracks? Is that wulves I hear?"

"Hush, both of you," Gabrianna hissed, tearing herself from Brook's wary grip. "Help me get this mule free, and then we'll go until we find a place to hide."

"Hide?" Brook asked. "Why do we need to hide?"

Meadow chimed in. "Is the snow dangerous?"

"Everything we don't understand is dangerous, you fools," Gabrianna said, and with the help of her friends, she freed the stubborn animal easily.

STORM HELD HOLLYN AS SHE SLEPT, PRESSED AS FAR INTO THE shallow cave as they could. Brandyn felt Storm's eyes boring holes in his back. He ignored it. The snow poured from the sky like the stuffing from one of his old baby blankets, and he wished he could enjoy it. When they were much smaller, they played pretend and when they found themselves in the most contrived peril, snow arrived to save the day. How they'd jump and land in the pretend tufts, which Brandyn now realized, must have looked different to all their imaginations. They'd never seen it for real, until now.

He wondered how Ember and Gabrianna were faring. He didn't think they were far enough away yet to have escaped the rare storm, and Ember, on her way north to Midnight Crest, headed straight into the worst of it.

What would happen if he ran from the cave and right into the snow? He had half a mind to find out. His senses had been absent since they'd scattered from The Hidden Cave, and without them, he was lost. His stomach clenched in an endless knot, and the swimming feeling in his head hit him when he least expected it. He could bear peril when it was known.

Brandyn jumped when Storm appeared at his side. He hadn't heard her stir.

She slipped an arm around his waist. He looked at it, confused.

"Beautiful," she said, and Brandyn felt a new fluttering in his belly. Storm tucked her flaming red hair into her hood. "But we have a problem."

Brandyn spun to face her. "What?"

"Hollyn is burning up. Did you bring anything for her?"

"Um…" Brandyn broke away and knelt by the satchel Ember had provided. He'd never looked inside it until now. He had no idea what was inside. When he found the pouch full of what he knew to be his mother's herbs, he handed it to Storm with a blank stare.

Storm laughed. Her pale cheeks blazed. "You think I know what to do?"

"I…" He, what? Had another excuse for not knowing what he should? True, he'd been away for a year, but before that he'd been his mother's shadow, always underfoot, whether she liked it or not. He sometimes wondered if her eagerness to brand him for study at the Sepulchre was for her own peace, because he knew, even if others pretended not to, that his mother had magic of her own and had never stepped foot into the Consortium. She wasn't the only one, either.

"Surely you watched Lady Blackwood?" Storm asked, clearly sidestepping the question she wanted to ask, which wasn't as nice.

Despite the howling, icy wind, Brandyn's brow was doused in sweat. He looked over at his helpless, sleeping sister. A deep redness spread across her cheeks and down into her chest. Anything could have caused it. That was the worst part of this illness Hollyn carried. No one knew what it was. No one knew what it would do. There was nothing preventative they could do for her, other than avoiding the one thing that *always* made her ill: the sun. But it wasn't the only thing.

Moonseed.

Brandyn brightened. Whether through memory or sense, the word came to him suddenly, and he knew it was right.

"Moonseed," he said, rifling through the bag. "That's what Mother used for fever."

"Oh, I know it!" Storm said. She dropped to her knees at his side.

"It's shaped like this." Storm cupped both her hands into a heart, pressed against her chest.

Brandyn blinked through the swift skip in his heartbeat and went back to searching. "Ah, here." He held up two leaves. They were already wilted, but now he remembered them and could find them again by sight, once the storm passed. "We need to start a fire."

"The wind will blow it out."

"Then we stand in front of the wind."

Storm nodded. "I'll venture out and see if I can find any dry wood." She looked around. "We can't afford to spare water from the skins. We don't have enough to last us until we can get to the next stream." She disappeared half out of the cave and returned with a handful of snow. "We can use this."

"Snow?"

"Snow turns to water when it warms."

"How do you know this?"

Storm grinned. "I know everything, Brandyn. Why do you think your sister chose me?"

Brandyn flushed. He knew good and well why Ember had chosen Storm Wakesell for his particular voyage, and it had nothing to do with her usefulness. He'd spent the last year at the Consortium trying to forget how silly he felt in the presence of their strong, beautiful friend.

"Right. So, get some snow into the stone pot, I'll find out if there's any dry wood left in the world, and we'll pretend to be adults until it no longer suits us."

"Tell me again about the Ravenwoods." Marsh Tyndall, knees to his chest against the tree Ember had built her lean-to against, watched as she stoked the fire.

"I've never met one."

"You seemed pretty confident they'll help you."

Ember dropped the stick into the dying flame and eased back on the canvas blanket she was now so grateful she'd had the foresight to pack. The branches lying across the makeshift fort weren't enough to keep the snow out, and even if they had been, it blew in sideways with each gust of wind. She'd accounted for a lot of potential challenges, but she didn't expect to see snow before they hit the Northerlands.

"I have no idea if they'll help us, Marsh."

His eyes widened as he watched her over the fire. "You have no idea. And yet, we're going to see them."

"And yet," she answered lightly, taking a bite from her ration of the dried ox.

Marsh laughed. He shook his head. "I should've known you'd send us into danger. Your whims are always ten steps ahead of the rest of you."

Ember grinned from the side of her mouth. "They're not going to kill us. They might turn us away."

"It's a long way to travel for rejection."

"Longer still, if this is what we have to contend with."

He leaned forward over his knees. A warm light fell over his face, and his eyes, one purple, one green, regarded her with bemusement. "Truly, though. There must be a reason you chose them."

Ember shrugged. She tossed another twig from their dwindling stack into the fire. The night would be a cold one. Maybe Marsh would let them pool their warmth. "You know the Blackwood history, don't you?"

"Not very much."

"We were Ravenwoods once. That ended when one of them fell in love with a Westerlander and left Midnight Crest. To ease her transition to the Westerlands, he combined their names into one. Blackrook and Ravenwood became Blackwood. We share blood and history."

Marsh's lips twisted, as if deciding whether to believe her. "How far back? Hundreds of years, or dozens?"

"My great-great-grandmother was Rhosyn Ravenwood," she said.

"Did she live long enough for you to meet her?"

Ember swallowed. "None of them did. Not my grandmother, great-grandmother. Before I was born, the king killed them all. He and his men wiped out every last bit of our heritage, prior to my mother. It's as if none of them ever existed."

Marsh dropped his eyes. "I'm sorry. I forgot."

"Why do you want to know about Rhosyn?"

"I suppose I'm wondering if the Ravenwoods are still holding a grudge toward the Westerlands, is all. Of the kind that might have our heads on pikes."

"That's far too rudimentary for the priests and priestesses of Midnight Crest. They would use magic to dissolve our bones and scatter us to the winds."

Marsh laughed again. "You're not scared at all, are you?"

I'm frightened. "No."

"Are you afraid of anything, Emberley Blackwood?"

"Not that I've been made aware of."

He released a long sigh between pursed lips. "Guardians help us."

"The Guardians allowed the Rhiagains to run their hands over our kingdom and turn it into their own. You believe they're with us now?"

"Of course I believe."

Ember scoffed.

"Come on. You can't tell me anything?"

"You assume I know everything. It's flattering."

"You said they were your relatives."

"My mother doesn't talk about it," Ember said, pinning down the shiver that started at the base of her spine. "I think she's ashamed. The rest of the kingdom holds the sorcerers in low esteem. She likes to pretend we've never had anything to do with it. That we've just always been the Blackwoods. I don't know for certain, but I think that was her way of dealing with her mother's and grandmother's deaths. By reinventing who we were."

"And you?"

"I'm not ashamed of who I am, or where I come from."

What she didn't tell Marsh was that she'd chosen Midnight Crest not only because it was the most dangerous and she felt she should take that burden herself, but because, if the Ravenwoods did *not* turn them out, they might bring her into a part of herself that called to her, but had so far given no answers.

"All I know is that they're powerful, but not enough to exist without the protection Lord Dereham and the other Great Families of the Northerlands offer them," she said, hoping to put his curiosity to rest alongside the rest of him. She was exhausted. "And the women are the rulers of the family."

"Some things didn't change when your great-great-grandmother came to the Westerlands."

"My mother broke that chain when she made Brandyn the heir. She's never said why, but I think she wanted our lives to be easier than hers was."

"Wise woman, turning things back over to a man."

Ember tossed some weeds at him, but the attempt failed utterly. He pretended to dodge them anyway, despite that they'd landed right near the hand that threw them, arcing his mouth into a mock, terrified O.

"A warning," she teased. "Next time you won't be so lucky."

Marsh pulled his bedroll out of his knapsack. Instead of rolling it out, he covered himself with it, leaning against the hard bark of the tree.

Ember threw the last of the sticks on the fire and crawled in beside him, pulling her own bedroll behind her. Ignoring his shocked look, she said, "We'll be warmer together. Don't be a silly boy."

She thought she felt him smile as his arm slipped around her, easing her closer.

. . .

RAVENNA WAITED UNTIL THE GIRLS WERE ASLEEP BEFORE ROLLING atop Drystan in their shared bedroll. He pretended to be surprised, but she knew he was wide-awake, lost to his thoughts. He never turned them off. Perhaps she could succeed at that tonight.

"Shh," she whispered, reaching lower, slowly, with the dexterity of a cat slinking through the night. She covered his mouth when her hand pulled him inside and she rode the rhythm against the song of the soft wind.

Ravenna was eleven when she was first sent to Wulfsgate. She'd come to her assignment with excitement and wonder, having never walked among the men and women of the kingdom before. Her only voyages from Midnight Crest were upon her own wings, and she never unfurled, to her true form, anywhere but home.

They sent all Ravenwoods to Wulfsgate, or sometimes Witchwood Cross, or even the village at Torrin's Pass, when they reached an age where they were expected to practice their magic enough to master it. This wasn't possible to do in their sky kingdom, where everyone had magic. An agreement, now centuries old, with the Lord of the Northerlands, traded their services for security. In the early days, Ravenwoods had much to fear from the curious and the fearful of the kingdom, but they'd lived in peace for so long there were no memories of turmoil. At least, not from the outside world.

Ravenna came into her healing gift before any others. Her very first day in Wulfsgate, as she marveled at hulking, furry beasts she'd never beheld with her eyes, at grass and hay and other delights she couldn't wait to run her hands over, she was called to the bedchamber of Lady Dereham. It was Drystan who dragged her by the hand, forgetting even to introduce himself in his panic. *Come, come, you must come. Father is gone, and Mother is dying.*

Gretchen didn't die, but her unborn child wasn't meant for this world. Ravenna rushed behind her new nameless friend, striking each stone with rising thrill and panic intertwined. But when they arrived, the child born too soon had already gone to the Guardians.

It wasn't too late for Gretchen, and Ravenna had acted purely upon instinct as she laid hands on the Lady of the Reach, desperate for an outcome that would bring honor upon her and not shame.

"I've never seen anything like it," Drystan said after Gretchen had surrendered to healing rest. He dabbed a cloth in a basin of water and gently cleansed the blood and grime from Ravenna's fingers, ever careful in every brush. She thought later, how decisive he was. How unapologetic in his actions. Not like her mother or father, but in a softer, more commanding way. As if Drystan didn't understand he *should* ask permission to touch her, to cleanse her, because to do so was the right thing.

"Can I tell you something?"

"You can tell me anything," he said, and Ravenna believed him.

"I've never healed before."

He paused his gentle ministrations.

"I didn't know if it would work. I only knew it had to."

Drystan nodded. He wrung out the cloth, staining the water red. "Is that how magic is? Working when you most need it to?"

Ravenna smiled. "That's what I'm here to find out. I'm here to learn. I hope, to help all of you in your moments of need."

Drystan brought her hand to his mouth. "You saved my mother. If you do nothing else here, you'll have succeeded."

Ravenna flushed, dropping her hand with some reluctance. Drystan seemed nothing like how her mother and father had described the men of the kingdom. *They are brutal. Unrelenting. They understand only pain, and they deal well in it. Be cautious and fall not for their deceptions.*

She met Drystan's father the following week and immediately liked him as well. She learned to love all the Derehams, from peculiar Gretchen, to spirited Lisbet. Serious, strong Pieter. The playfulness of the twins as they moved effortlessly through something she'd never experienced herself, childhood.

She never forgot the words, but their hold on her lessened as she began to understand that blood and family were not the same. That you could be bound by heritage and duty, yes, but also love; by joy and laughter. She wondered if these discoveries had enchanted any of her forebears. None had ever surrendered to them.

Drystan climaxed and was asleep in seconds. Her sweet boy, who had never acted without his heart leading—who would one day be lord, if their fool's journey didn't prove to be their end.

But there was no world where Ravenna would ever be Lady Dereham. This cruel reality never left her thoughts for a moment, even if Drystan spent his every waking moment denying it to the point of delusion.

She pressed her lips to his, inhaling a whisper of his warm breath, and lay back to prepare for another sleepless night.

14

TERMONGLEN

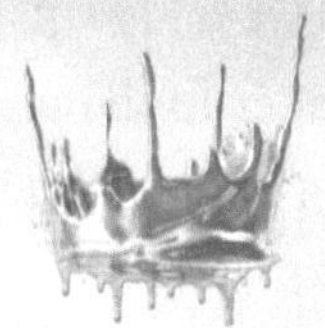

When men and women of the kingdom referred to the Reaches, they were really talking about only four of them—Northerlands, Southerlands, Westerlands, and Easterlands—though there were actually five. Six, depending on who you asked, though most didn't consider the Wastelands to be anything but what the name suggested. And if you were a Southerlander, you might refer to that same sixth Reach as "our land stolen by the craven ratsbane," which was also not inaccurate.

The fifth Reach, The Hinterlands, had a history beyond the understanding of most men. The inhabitants of these exotic forests first existed in the Time Before Men, and the Medvedev thrived without the complex system of laws and economy those in the Reaches of man enjoyed. They had, many years prior, been assured of peace from the crown and kingdom, when one of the prior Rhiagain kings—Carrick the Dreamer, if Gretchen's memory of the history served—performed the only promise that couldn't be broken, the Sacred Vow. A Sacred Vow made by a father still bound the son.

Gretchen wondered about this, how the Hinterlands had

escaped the scrutiny of not only the neighboring Reaches but the greedy Rhiagain, who had in the past two rules lost any of the honor of their forbears. What did the Sacred Vow mean to men who had no morality? She supposed the reason had something to do with the Medvedev's magic.

Elsewhere in the kingdom, magic was forbidden except under the strict governance of the Consortium of the Sepulchre. So it had been for hundreds, maybe thousands, of years, long before they began recording their reasons in *The Book of All Things.* But magic was a rare and delicate wonder to the men and women of the kingdom, with no understanding of how and where the Guardians chose to leave that blessing. It was given to lowborn and highborn alike; at times several per family, and more often, none. If you had it, it wasn't always seen as a blessing, for your choices were the Sepulchre for training or, if caught using it without training and authorization, a sentence of death. Gretchen herself had witnessed several executions for convicted magic dealers. It was why, when Christian manifested his visions, she didn't hesitate to send him to the Magi of the Sepulchre. Even with the choice he made there, to never return to her, she'd do it again.

But while magic was sparse in the world of men, the Medvedev were magic at their core. Some in the kingdom used the word *druid,* others more disparaging monikers, but none debated that to use the word Medvedev was to imply magical beings that absolutely no one understood. And by product of the treaty of peace, which not only left them in peace but kept men from stepping into their forests, no one had the opportunity to learn.

Gretchen thought if it weren't for their hair, the Medvedev would look like any other man or woman in the kingdom. It was through her grandfather's friendship with Yseult, the chieftainess, that Gretchen learned that their hair color was linked to the Medvedev's familiar, an animal tied to them by both birth and death. Violet hair appeared when their familiar was a creature of flight, where pale blue indicated an animal of the sea, and light green, the earth. They were born with these colors, as they were born linked to their familiars, and she'd never seen anyone who could recreate it with herbs and dyes.

She knew they lived in what they called clahnns, and had no system of law beyond a code of honor binding them to never do harm. If they aged beyond maturity, it was not at the pace of men. They had no spirit for war. They existed in simplicity and sparseness, and both things seemed to bring them joy. Gretchen's knowledge of the Medvedev ended there, and it was more than what most in the kingdom knew.

The trouble with leaving them entirely alone was that The Hinterlands was in the center of their world, and traveling between the Reaches required passing through. For months of the year, the seas were impassible except by the most experienced mariners. The Medvedev agreed to a system of roads bisecting the center of their lands, going both north to south and east to west, as long as men never strayed from the path. They also gifted to men the castle of Termonglen, for brief respites on long journeys across the kingdom. It sat at the crossroads between the Hinterlands, Westerlands, and Easterlands.

Termonglen was a castle, but it was not beautiful. No one knew when or whom had built the derelict structure, as Medvedev dwellings were very different in design, but it had fallen into disrepair over the years. Some kings used it as a neutral ground for meetings involving the Lords of the Reaches, while others never stepped foot inside at all. Because it had no permanent master, there was no one to repair the cracks in the stone, or keep the weeping vines from taking over domicile. Boar and pig roamed the main floor, rutting and shitting as they did, the rats scampering behind to consume what waste their bodies could hold. When guests were expected, they sent servants ahead to ready it for a proper host.

She'd been here only once before, on the day she both discovered she was to be married to Holden Dereham and then, within the hour, was.

Like the last time, she had no desire to be here. Two of her children were lost in the world, and she was tending to kingdom politics. Holden sent the best of his guard in search of them, but that left them vulnerable here. He insisted to her—impervious, for once, to her tears—that the best protection for Lisbet, Drystan, and Eavan was easing the king, and there was no one they could send in their stead.

Ravenna was possibly among the children. Varinya Ravenwood had paid them a visit the day they loaded the caravan for Termonglen. *No, we haven't seen Ravenna in some time,* Holden had said, and Gretchen had simply nodded, dutiful, committing to nothing. Holden wasn't lying; the young priestess had finished her apprenticeship in Wulfsgate a while ago, in preparation for that arcane ceremony that turned Gretchen's stomach. But Holden didn't know what Gretchen knew about her dearest son, her lone wulf. Or perhaps not so alone. She hadn't killed all the spies, only the ones whose loyalty was in question. Most of her children were at an age where they'd stopped talking to her, but she had no intention of losing that insight just because they were inclined to their privacy.

If Ravenna was with the others, this both made them more and less safe from harm. The other Ravenwoods wouldn't dare spread their wings any farther south than Torrin's Pass, but what would the rest of the world do about Ravenna once she was free of the Northerland protection? Like the Medvedev, Ravenwoods could pass for men of the realm at a glance, but with a closer look, their otherness flowed from them in waves.

Gretchen pressed her shawl to her nose when they stepped inside. There'd been no one to send ahead to tend the tidying on their behalf; their clandestine meeting came only two days before the king and his retinue were to arrive, and that meant his own servants would arrive sometime tomorrow. Along with Aiden, whom Holden had intentionally left off the invite, at her request. Holden didn't like to believe the worst in Aiden, but he hadn't grown up with the man. Gretchen had.

"What a foul place," Pieter complained. He held his nose pinned in the air. "Is there not an inn?"

"You should've left him home with the twins," Holden said, marching ahead.

"Yes, you've said that already. It's quite enough." Gretchen stepped carefully through the dusty floor. She didn't reiterate the reason they hadn't left him, because it wounded her heart to even address the fear. If Drystan and Lisbet didn't return home, Pieter was the heir to Wulfsgate and the Northern Reach. An honor he would only gain in exchange for her greatest heartbreak. "And no, Pieter, there is no inn in the Hinterlands. Termonglen is the only place we're allowed rest and refreshment without invitation."

"How long do we have to stay?"

"I don't know, cub," Gretchen replied. "Your father and I have matters to discuss with Lord Warwick and Lady Blackwood, and then in two days we have business with King Eoghan of importance as well. As you know."

"You're plotting against the king," Pieter said, moving ahead of them.

Holden's mouth parted, but Gretchen bade him to let her handle it.

"You're old enough to understand that Lis and Eavan's leaving has created an unfortunate situation for us. When the king arrives, it's important we have an alternative arrangement to offer him. Something he'll be pleased with even without the brides he's expecting." This was only half-true, but so was the part about Pieter being at an age to grasp the enormity.

"Unfortunate for you and Father, you mean," Pieter said. "Lis never wanted to be a queen. I don't know why you're so surprised she ran away. I don't need to see things like Christian to predict something that obvious."

Holden shot her a look that said, *careful.*

"It wasn't our first choice for Lisbet, but it was the one our king commanded, Pieter. When you're older, you'll perhaps understand, in a way that you cannot now, how our duty must come before our desires."

Pieter stopped and turned his head over his shoulder. "You don't believe a word you're saying right now, Mother."

Holden laughed in surprise. Gretchen, after a stunned pause, joined in.

"I believe, cub, that we must always be careful of the language we choose for we never know who might hear our words."

"Not in Wulfsgate. You poisoned them all."

Gretchen blanched. Her husband shook his head at her side. "Don't pay mind to the rumormongers, Pieter. You're a Dereham, not a scullery maid."

Pieter nodded and went back to kicking at animal dung. Ahead was the great hall, where they would break fast with their Westerland and Southerland friends, and, Guardians willing, come to some sort of agreement on how to proceed.

"The king has spies here," Pieter said.

Gretchen flashed a glance of conspiratorial amusement at her husband. "Oh, and how would you know this?"

"Because," Pieter said, entering the dining hall, "it's what I would do."

"And what would you need spies for, cub?"

Pieter's shoulders lifted. "No one likes him. It's easy to make people obey you when they like you. When no one likes you, you have to do other things to make them obey you."

Gretchen ignored the dark flutter of warning in her chest. When she looked at her husband, he was no longer smiling.

KHALLUM BROUGHT AN ENTIRE RETINUE. HE ENJOYED THE STUNNED expressions from his so-called friends from the north and west corners of the kingdom as the endless stream of Southerland soldiers passed by in formation. He read it all in their eyes. The questions, the critical assessments of their own meager litters.

Gwyn's proud face, aged by her grief, put a swell in his belly. He couldn't bring back their girl, but what he could do was show this craven ratsbane king the might of the region that was no longer his for the taking.

It was more than her brother had done. The twelve men Holden Dereham had awaiting orders would bring Khallum to humor if it didn't also bring him to rage.

Asherley Blackwood was no fool, at least. A hundred or more in her camp; a sliver against what Khallum himself brought, but a message to the king that would not go unnoticed. Rush Riders, most of them, with their longbows and pretty hair, but they trained all their lives for the promise of even an hour of eventual battle, and he had a reverent respect for this.

Khallum grinned to himself as they exchanged their greetings. 'Twas more likely the influence of Asherley's Warwick husband, Khallum's brother Byrne, that caused her to see the situation for what it was.

"Twenty years," Gwyn said at his side. In another woman, it might have sounded like nostalgia. In his wife, Khallum instead heard the dripping ache of acceptance.

Twenty years since they'd all been forced into marriage bed with spouses of the king's choosing. Twenty years since all six of them were in one place, under one roof. Since they'd still counted their parents and grandparents among the living.

Khallum had seen Byrne, of course, and Gwyn had visited her brother. This was different.

If Holden made one wise choice, it was excluding Aiden Quinlanden from their convocation. No honest talk would happen with that bootlicker present, and Khallum cringed at the name Quinlanden nearly as much as he did Rhiagain. His sister Yesenia was wed to the cretin's brother, Corin, but Corin was cut from another cloth. If Corin Quinlanden had been the Lord of Whitechurch, the matter of the Right of Choosing would have been settled before it ever took form.

Termonglen was a hall of filth. Khallum and his men were made of salt and sand, and sometimes shit, but the castle looked as if it hadn't seen a woman's touch since the Epoch of the Accordant. They turned their noses and stepped lighter through the heavy, untended grassland that could be home to anything at all.

He ordered a handful of his men to clear out the Great Hall, at least, while the lords and ladies ran through their required formalities. Embraces. Disingenuous declarations of missing one another, that it had been far too long. Only in the fleeting moments where Khallum wrapped his arms around Byrne did he feel the reminder of the great distance separating them all. A distance not one of them had chosen, but had all, in their own ways, fostered.

Asherley snapped at one of the men to find a pail and wipe down the film covering the long slab of oak that passed for a master's dining table. The others settled in, forming inevitable and unsurprising sides. Khallum chose a seat on the bench next to Byrne. Gwyn eased in by her brother Holden, who'd claimed the head of the table with his boot while he stood, holding intentional court as he watched the others take their places. Asherley perched at the very end of the bench. It was unclear whether she did this because of her open disgust for the place, or for the situation. Gretchen sat across from her husband, but was otherwise alone.

Holden cleared his throat. Khallum exchanged a grunt and a hard look with his brother. Gwyn flashed him a warning. So this was how it would be. Fine. Holden had called this meeting. He could have the honor of starting it, but if he couldn't finish it, the Warwick brothers would.

Holden waited for the bumbling footman to finish with the table, and, once he had a nod from Asherley, he pulled his foot from the bench and stepped back.

"Thank you for coming. We've always had differences, but our presence here shows we're in accord on one thing. We have a predicament that requires answer. One best addressed if we are united."

"I have no predicament. My daughter is dead, gone to the Guardians. I have nothing," Khallum said. Byrne nodded in supportive silence at his side.

"We are much aggrieved at your loss, Khallum," Gretchen said. "But we can do naught for the dead. Between the Reaches, we have seven missing children, none of whom have been seen or heard from in nearly a week. All of whom are innocent in any of this."

"*You* are much aggrieved. What of your husband, Lady Dereham? I ask for aid and he sends a cloak."

"You asked for aid for a war," Holden said. "I have no aid of the sort to offer."

Khallum snorted. He pointed his fist toward the front of the castle. "Aye, I see that now, with your finest dozen keeping us safe. How well you must sleep."

Holden leaned forward, hands on the table. "There's been no war in our lifetime, or the lifetimes of our fathers. Men who never see battle grow fat and lazy on their farms, and without a foe to fight, their swords collect blankets of rust in the corners of their barns. Their blades dull. Their reflexes soften. I have men, Khallum, but I don't have men capable of fighting the war you've sought against the king since his father was on the throne. I do not have the men *he* has."

"And what battles has the king's army seen?" Asherley said from the other end of the table. "Or do you suppose they kill themselves for practice and sport?"

"If the Rhiagain Guard don't patrol your Reach, consider yourself among the fortunate," Khallum said to her. "I cannae say how he trains his Guard, or his beloved Knights of Duncarrow, but they're not lacking in size or skill. But while the rest of you lot rests on your laurels, I *have* been sharpening my forces, because I didnae lack the foresight to grasp the utter atrocity awaiting us."

"We came here to negotiate an alternative to present at the Right of Choosing, not to plan a war," Gretchen said. She hadn't looked at her husband at all. She trained her gaze on the others. "While none of us have a bride to present, we cannot come empty-handed. It would be foolish to assume he will leave it at that. If we believed he'd let it be, we wouldn't all be sitting here."

"Gold," Byrne said. "We brought our share. We cannae be the only ones who did, no?"

Khallum laughed. "He'll take the wives, mark my words. Instead of condolences when my Esmerelda died, he sent a reminder that with no other daughter he'd be taking my Gwyn. Gold isnae what glitters in the eyes of the hairless pube, 'tis hatred. What hatred he possesses for me will spread across the rest of the lot of you, and that will be our punishment. Unless we stop him."

"Aiden will offer one of his other daughters. Assana is next oldest." Gretchen's lips twisted in disdain. "If he does find Eavan, it won't be to embrace her. I fear for her life if she falls back into his hands."

"I know the man Aiden Quinlanden is. My sister Maeryn knows it more," Asherley said. "As I know you do, Gretchen." The women exchanged a look. "We excluded him from this convocation for a reason. Whatever nonsense he presents to the king should hold no bearing on our own decisions. As Byrne said, we have gold. More than the king or any of his descendants have ever laid their hands on."

"He'll take your gold, and you," Khallum quipped.

"We also came with gold," Holden said reasonably. "But I suspect it will buy us only time."

Gwyn spoke for the first time. "But if Aiden is the only one with an offering, does that not make Eoghan's wrath upon the rest of us that much greater?"

"We haven't come with our original offering for the Right of Choosing," Holden said, speaking slowly. He paced before the cold hearth, filled with gnarled weeds and discarded nests. "That doesn't mean we have no offering."

"What are you talking about?" Gretchen pivoted, turning toward her husband for the first time.

"Forget the gold. We ask for time," Holden answered. He didn't meet her accusing eyes. "Time to find our children and return them to the original agreement."

Gwyn reached across the table to steady Gretchen, who wore a look of stunned betrayal. "Brother, we came here to save our children, not put them on a path back to our enemy."

"I wouldn't use those words, even here," Holden said.

"Aye, and your words are better? You shit on the watery grave of my Esmerelda with your quickness to sell your own daughters to slavery. You deface her honor. Her memory." Khallum beat his fists into the table. Only Byrne did not jump. "I didnae come here to help you lap at the cock of the craven ratsbane."

"Aye, you came for warfare," Asherley said, with a roll of her eyes.

"Warfare comes in many forms, Lady Blackwood. You married a Warwick, I'd expect you to have learned a few things about it."

"You evidently haven't seen the way your brother frolics with forest animals in my woods these days," she replied with a bored look.

"Surrendering our children is no longer an option," Gretchen said. Her voice rose with each syllable as she fought back tears. "They have made their voices known. They will not be sold."

Murmurs of assent passed through the room. Holden tried to speak, but Gretchen could not be silenced.

"I cannot bear the pain of knowing they're out in the world, alone, scared, and with none of the comforts or safety they've known all their lives. A safety we agreed to surrender on their behalf because we had no fight in us. We had no fight for *them*. Well. It's a fine day when the children are better leaders in this kingdom than the lords and ladies sitting at this table, and when we find them, I will say it once more, make no mistake, they will *not* be sold."

Khallum briefly mused that it was the lady of the Northerlands with the bigger cock.

"For all we know, The Pretender already has them," Gwyn said. "You've had no word? None at all?"

"None," Gretchen said. "Asherley?"

Lady Blackwood shook her head.

Gwyn gasped into her hand. "And why are you here? And not out looking for them with every breath in your body?"

Gretchen went to answer, but Asherley leaned forward over the table. "I raised my kin to be strong. To care for their own selves. They'll come home when we give them reason to."

"You cannot be serious." Gwyn paled. "Your littlest ones are babes, Asherley! You'd leave them to the elements? To all the dangers of this world?"

"There's no danger greater than the one we tried to pass them into. So soon we've all forgotten that Eoghan's father took every-thing, from all of us. Not only our futures, but our pasts. Our beloved mothers, fathers, grandparents. All of them," Gretchen said. "Our children are not blind fools. They know these stories well. They feel the keen absence of ancestors to receive the passing of stories from. They're well aware of who the Rhiagains have shown themselves to be. They told us how they felt, and we plied them with reassurances. Their rebellion is the only way we would listen."

Khallum nodded. His comprehension of his own daughter's agony came too late for them all.

"Lady Blackwood," Holden said. "Your daughter was looking forward to being Eoghan's queen. I remember your note, after we received the invite. Why do you think your children are missing?"

"Yes, Hollyn was excited to be marrying the king," Asherley said with a sigh. "Guardians bless her. But she's been plagued with an illness none of my healers can identify. I suspect her siblings feared for what Eoghan might do if he discovered we supplied him with a frail bride. I feared for the same." She looked at Gretchen, ignoring Holden. "Our situations are different, but our children have each taken control of their own destinies. In that, we are sisters."

Gretchen nodded. Her lower lip quavered, but she held strong.

"The reasons no longer matter," Asherley went on. "Gretchen is right. When our children come home, we will not be shipping them off to Duncarrow. That day is done. That choice is made."

"How did we allow this to happen?" Gwyn asked, passing a desperate look around the table, searching for an ally. "How did not one of us make a stand and say, nay, you cannot take our girls? You cannot take what is not yours!"

"By the reason of Holden, without an army, you lie down like a dog and allow it," Khallum answered with a sharp glare at the subject of his accusation.

"I am on your side," Holden volleyed back, and the others laughed or sneered, to varying degree. "I am," he insisted. "Can we remove emotion long enough to remember how we all felt twenty years past? We came here, to Termonglen, expecting a feast and celebration, and instead every last one of our lives were put on a new course. Some of you were promised to others before. Some of you were in love with others." Khallum noted that Holden avoided landing his intense eyes upon his wife. "We lived with what we were dealt, and we made lives of it. Some of us believed King Khain when he swore to us and our mothers and fathers that he did this not to punish but to unite and end the disputes, even if we didn't agree with his chosen course. We were given a fortnight to respond to King Eoghan's unreasonable demand of our eldest daughters. A fortnight! A fortnight is nay long enough to even consider the request, forget about building an army, or mounting a defense. Sister, you ask this question, but all of us in this room have loved our daughters. And you, dear one, have lost yours." Holden bowed his head as he rested a hand on Gwyn's shoulder. "There perhaps come times in our lives where, no matter the wrong, we have no right for it."

"Do ye even listen to the words before they spill from your mouth like watery shit?" Khallum boomed. "We are not the same! When the raven from Duncarrow arrived, I begged of you!" He turned to Asherley. "And you! I begged of you all. We have but one option and that is to unite against this folly. And ye answered, all right. With the silence of cowards."

"We answered as we felt we had to," Gretchen said, looking again away from her husband. The rift between them deepened before a room of their peers, and Khallum enjoyed it, if not for the hurt it would cause the fool Holden, then for his growing admiration of his peculiar, but strong, wife. "And now we're here, and our answer has changed. Looking back is a fool's errand, and the sun is already slipping into night. What do we do *now* is what we must answer, or we'll lose more than we already have."

Khallum released one of his four blades. The waning light of day passing through an open patch in the roof landed on it as he turned it. "There is but one answer now, lass."

"Children are playing only rooms away," Gwyn hissed. "Lower your voice."

"Children," Asherley mused. "I find myself reassessing the meaning of the word. Seems it is the *children* who've been left to the task the adults failed at."

"Khallum speaks true," Byrne said, raising his voice even louder than his brother. Living in the forest with his beautiful bride and brood had changed Khallum's brother, but it didn't change that he could count on him. "There is one way to end this madness. And only one. We all know it. We dance around it, because the suggestion itself is also madness. But what he has taken from the Southerlands, he will take from all of us. He takes the King's Decree and shits upon its intention, taking and taking and taking, beyond what his forebears would have dared. Eoghan isnae his grandfather. He isnae the men who came before."

"So it is written upon the fates," Gretchen agreed, drawing the shape of the Guardians against her breastbone with one finger.

"What the two of you are suggesting isn't only madness, it's treason," Holden rejoined. "You assume the rest of the kingdom shares in our misery and won't rise against us. Eoghan is not the last Rhiagain. He has two sisters, who will command his knights long after he is cold in the grave."

"But it isnae their kingdom!" Khallum cried. "Our ancestors bowed and bent to the strangers from Beyond, because they believed them to be gods, but they are no gods! We have but six Guardians, and not one of them bears the name Rhiagain."

"It is time to take it back," Byrne agreed. "Take back what is ours."

Asherley laughed and turned her head away from the conversation. Byrne's face fell. Khallum could punt him for how easily he'd acquiesced to a foreign woman who knew nothing.

"We've all lost something to this king and his father," Gretchen said. She ran her hands down her face, red from the same exhaustion they all felt. "Khallum, no one more than you. I recognize this, even if others have failed to. Holden is wrong about many things. I will bear that blade in my own hand before I allow my daughter into his hands now. But time is the one thing we have none of now, and so desperately need."

"And what will time do, lass, but delay relief of agony?" Khallum pressed.

"We are all, all of us, distressed about our children lost in the world without us," she answered. "But what of the other children? The ones we haven't lost?" Gretchen pulled herself from the bench with a weary sigh. "We have no more than twelve ticks of the sun before Aiden arrives. You all fear this king, but I've never known a greater monster than my brother. He wants the one thing he has never had, and that is what Eoghan does. Aiden also has an army, a force that now belongs to Eoghan. Are you following me yet? Do you understand what I would avoid, if we could?"

"You think your brother aims to be king," Asherley said.

"I think we would be doing him great favor if we ended the Right of Choosing Khallum's way."

"He laid Rowanwen at The Pretender's feet. He swore especial fealty. That doesn't sound like a man with intentions of betrayal," Gwyn said.

"Aiden is cunning," Gretchen said. "He is wise. He will understand that an alliance must come first, and that he can gain more by earning the trust and kinship of Eoghan than he can by fighting him with only half the knowledge he needs to defeat him."

"Those are bold assumptions. And distractions. We have a greater enemy that must be dealt with, and we're running out of time," Byrne said.

Holden nodded, centering the room back on his intended command. "Let us find rest and refreshment, and perhaps reflection. Time is running out."

ASHERLEY SLIPPED THROUGH THE DAMP AND DUSTY HALLS ON LIGHT feet. She'd learned this trick from her mother, who learned it from hers. Even with her heaviest boot, she was soundless when she wanted to be, and she very much wanted to be as she followed her husband and brother-in-law at a safe distance.

Khallum was a bloodlusted fool. Nothing had changed. But he was a bloodlusted fool whose losses could not be discounted. She had never felt more distanced from her husband than she did after the two men visited. Byrne was one man with his brother, the salt and sand in his blood growing dense and hardening him. He was another with her. Gentle and kind, and a father unlike any other in the kingdom.

Truth be told, Asherley appreciated the more chiseled version of Byrne Warwick. He was more commanding in the bedroom, and she felt safe with him at her side, a sensation she had never experienced from any other man in all her life. She didn't need this comfort, but she enjoyed it nonetheless. Some days she even thought she'd been the luckiest of all the young lords and ladies at the Epoch. She'd never been miserable, anyway.

But her enjoyment of this rare side of her husband was tempered by the trouble Khallum liked to pull him into. It had always been this way, but never before had the danger been more than fleeting. Khallum's reckless disregard for consequence jeopardized her family and their future. If he was going to drag Byrne into another one of his mad schemes, she would be prepared this time.

"Let them," Khallum was saying. "I dinnae care what the others choose to do. Let them waste their words and breath."

"Holden will never see reason. He'll talk his way into the answer he wanted all along."

"Holden enjoys the sound his words make when they leave his mouth. That doesnae make them interesting."

"Gretchen was on the right path with time, Khallum. We could do so much more with it."

Khallum laughed. "Would that we could if we had it. All time has done to our homeland is give leave to the ratsbane to rape it of men and resources. The others can speak of time like this because they've nae lost what we have." Khallum clapped both hands over his brother's shoulders. "Donnae forget where ye come from. You may have a wife who willnae take your name, but you're no less Warwick."

Asherley tensed, thinking of the vials of poison she carried with her always.

"My wife is a warrior," Byrne answered. "She can have whatever name she likes. I'm no less salt and sand."

"Aye," Khallum said, relenting. "Ye are. Salt and sand come together and form a bond. It does what others cannae. Willnae. Are we brothers?"

"In this. In all things."

"In this. In all things," Khallum repeated. The sound of steel leaving its protective sheath rang through the old stone walls. "In this. In all things."

"In all things," Byrne said once more, and Asherley slinked back into the darkness.

· · ·

Gretchen put her son to bed. Elsewhere in the castle, Gwyn would be doing the same with her son, Ransom. One was an heir, one might be, if the Guardians determined.

Gretchen sometimes loathed the Guardians. Even the very idea of them troubled her. She was taught that all things, all decisions, all outcomes were pre-determined, and that her own will in the matter meant nothing. *It is decided. All you will do you have already done. The Guardians have written it into the fates.* If it was all decided, then what was the point? Of effort? Of joy? Of love? Of sorrow? Why aim anywhere if your destination has been decided already?

She'd struggled with this her whole life, but her questions about this rose to a pique following the Epoch. Even in her darkest memories of that day, she couldn't forget the hopefulness, the anticipation she'd felt as she and Aiden and Corin had bounced around in the back of the wagon on the way to Termonglen. On that day, even Aiden had been all smiles, playing skips with the two of them when the road was smooth, and not even cheating at it. They were the highborn children of the Eastern Reach, and their entire lives awaited them.

A fete for my newborn son, my heir and future of the realm, the invite had said, and no one Gretchen had known had ever been to a party thrown by the king himself. And so few had even been invited! Only the Lords and Ladies of the Reaches, and their three eldest children. How their youngest sister, Saoirse, had cried, and how they'd teased her for not being as important as they were. How later, they'd cried together as Gretchen came home to collect her things and say goodbye to her. She wouldn't know then that this was the last time she'd embrace her baby sister. Saoirse drowned in the Sparkling Beck not a year later.

But that goodbye hadn't been Gretchen's hardest. Drystan Sylvaine, the son of Lord Sylvaine of Rushwood, met her in the poplar grove the day of her return. Her darling Ash. He'd waited for days, he said, without food, without rest. She didn't know if that was true, but she loved when he said such things, because they made her feel like the most important girl in all the world, and not simply a third daughter destined for whatever her father decided for her. Yet as it had turned out, not even the Lord of Whitechurch had a say in her future.

Ash's kisses had done nothing to assuage the grief, and the memory of the king's words lived within her, exactly as he'd said them.

On this day, I present to you new life. And as your king, I understand there can be no new life without new beginnings. Alliances unburdened by the pettiness of squabbles and jealousy.

Lords and Ladies Dereham, Quinlanden, Blackwood, and Warwick, I have brought you here with your children today to right wrongs that have mounted since before I ascended the crown. The fighting, the trade wars, the grudges older than any present. They end today.

Today, we come to celebrate the promise of unity. There will be six blessed unions of marriage on this day, and I will ask all those taking their vows to put aside your quarrels, your sorrows, and step forward in the best interest of all in the realm. Know that the bonds you create today will be the foundation of a united realm for all future generations.

Asherley Blackwood, first daughter of the Westerlands, you will be joined with Byrne Warwick, second son of the Southerlands.

Khallum Warwick, first son of the Southerlands, you will be joined with Gwyn Dereham, third daughter of the Northerlands.

Aiden Quinlanden, first son of the Easterlands, you will be joined with Maeryn Blackwood, second daughter of the Westerlands.

Holden Dereham, second son of the Northerlands, you will be joined with Gretchen Quinlanden, third daughter of the Easterlands.

Corin Quinlanden, second son of the Easterlands, you will be joined with Yesenia Warwick, third daughter of the Southerlands.

Alric Dereham, fourth son of the Northerlands, you will be joined with Earwyn Blackwood, third daughter of the Westerlands.

Ash listened to her recollection of the day with mounting horror. The pure, raw dejection in his eyes haunted her dreams then and now. His dawning realization that she was not only promised to another—after having been most of her life promised to him—but already wed and bedded, sent him to his knees with a sound that shattered whatever resolve she'd built up on the voyage home from Termonglen.

I leave in two days, she told him as he grasped at earth, grass, flowers, tearing, keening.

It cannot be so, Gretchen. The Guardians did not deliver us to one another, only to rip us apart!

It can be, and it is. We are not the only ones suffering.

And what is the suffering of others to me, when I feel nothing but my own soul splintering?

And then she'd made a choice. One that shifted her anger toward the Guardians, for she was certain this was not in their plan. Whatever they'd intended for her, it hadn't been this bold defection of duty and honor.

She'd brought her Drystan, her Ash, to the Northerlands with her, and there he'd lived, in secret, until the day she found his lifeless body on the stone floor of her bedchamber.

"Is he asleep?"

Gretchen blinked her eyes at the sound of her husband's voice. Through varying points in their marriage, she had been both comforted and repelled by the sound. Today it felt like briars against her skin. He had many times angered her with his indecision, but until now, she had never thought him capable of betrayal.

"See for yourself," she said and walked away from the bedroll, where Pieter lay snoring. She approached the flames that licked and snarled in the hearth. They'd started this fire when they arrived, and only now was the room catching up to the warmth. Earlier, she'd collected the moss and sticks littering the chamber floor, and it almost looked tidy in the dim, flickering light of the fire. In daytime, the truth of his Guardian-forsaken place would again be revealed.

"Gretchen—"

"Stop. There's nothing to be said."

Holden's soft brown eyes pleaded with her. "Nothing went as I'd hoped earlier. But what happened between us is worst of all, to me."

Gretchen wrapped the wool blanket around her shoulders, huddling close to the fire. The crackles and snaps dulled the sound of his voice. Brought her away, again, to those first days with Ash in the Wintergarden of Wulfsgate as they, together, learned to love the wonder of snow.

"I love Lisbet as you do."

"Do not say her name again. Not to me. Not after you promised her life to maintain your comfort."

"That's not what happened."

"That's exactly what happened."

"You infer this is easy for me, but that's very unfair."

Gretchen cast a look toward the far wall, where his shadow born of the flame hunkered in cowing retreat. "If I infer this has been easy, is it, maybe, because you've never worked harder toward a better way? Because that, husband, is most unfair. Unfair to her. To Drystan, who's joined her because she's only *fourteen* and he couldn't let her go alone into the world, unprotected. Fourteen, Holden. Did you not think that, if nothing else, could have been your counter to the king? That she was just too young?"

"As if that would've been enough for him?"

"We'll never know. Because you never tried."

"I do know. You know. Everyone here knows, and this is why no one did a thing! Esmerelda Warwick *died* because we had no better answer!"

A surge of pain passed through Gretchen as her teeth clenched together. She released some of the tension in her jaw. "And now we're ready. To do a thing, as you say. And you're not."

"You all talk of war, when everyone knows there won't be one. You have always thought of me as weak, Gretchen, and I can't entirely fault you for this belief, but it is not a weakness to understand the position you're in and find a way to accept it. There was never a way to avoid this, and we can play pretend or we can live in the world we were given."

"Ah, but there was a way. It only took the children to sort it out."

"And when they are found? Have you considered what will happen when they come home to us? To the west, and the east? It all begins again. Just as we didn't fight on the eve of the Epoch, we have no fight here. We have nothing with *which* to fight. Our wishes hold no authority."

Gretchen dropped the blanket at her feet and threw upon him a gaze that would have melted him where he stood had she the power. "Would that the king had given me to a man like Khallum, who will fight even if it costs him everything."

Holden exhaled and closed his eyes. "It will, if he does."

"And what more do you have to lose, Holden Dereham? Nothing, because you have already shown to the world that you possess nothing of value."

"I would do anything for you to better understand me, Gretchen."

"Is that so important to you?"

"I've tried our whole marriage to understand you."

Gretchen threw her head back and laughed. "Understand this, Holden. If Khallum cannot find the mettle to wield that blade, or you cannot find the words to persuade, it will be my hands that end this. Find a better way, or I will provide the answer."

15

WILD HOGS

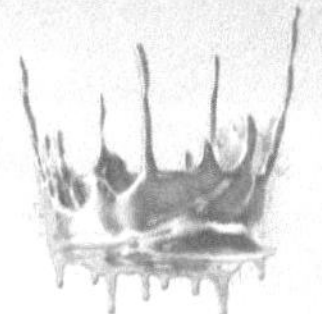

The storm's momentum slowed as they moved farther south. For a boy with Northerland blood coursing through his limbs, Drystan had no fear in traversing a land blanketed in dense, relentless snow. The horses only slowed for obstructions in the path, but seemed unbothered by the knee-deep white up to their knees as they lifted their hooves in and out. Slowly, surely. It wasn't the pace they could have taken on one of the Compass Roads, but they aimed for safety, not speed. And for now, at least, the weather held to their level of comfort. Drystan had lived through far worse.

Ravenna had seen far worse in her castle atop the mountain, too, though when he asked how bad the weather was in the skies, where snowbolts were said to rain down death, she found a way not to answer, as was often true when the conversation veered too close to her own life.

The two of them rode ahead of the girls. Drystan grew weary of listening to Eavan whine about their cold, meager rations and how nothing warmed the chill in her bones. He wasn't cold, but he was hungry, and hearing her drone on about the great banquets her father threw in Whitechurch pulled hard on his half-empty belly.

He also wanted the time with Ravenna. So often she took to the sky with a claim to look out for the path ahead and the trail behind them, but Drystan sensed she had thoughts she wished to keep to herself. This had always been the way between them, but before, she'd been tethered by the worlds separating them, fearful of betraying an extreme set of laws that could see them ripped apart for good. They were free of that now, even if her eyes cast over her shoulder meant her own fears had yet to catch up to reality. She could tell him what plagued her. He could handle it.

Days before, when they'd crossed to the other side of Torrin's Pass, she'd tried very hard to sound unaffected when she announced it was the farthest she'd ever been from Midnight Crest. While the girls laughed and assured her of all the great adventures they'd have as they traversed a world new with every step, Drystan read the contents of his love's heart, through both her clipped words and the light quaver in her hands, and understood there was more than nervous excitement there.

"I thought we'd pass out of the snow by now," Ravenna said. She leaned into him as his mare moved at an easy pace. The trail behind them had gone cold for now, with the search party halted by the storm Drystan and the others had emerged on the other side of. Ravenna continuously retraced their steps in the sky, renewing her distractions born of magic, until she'd spent her vitality and Drystan gently told her to stop. They could afford not to exhaust themselves, or their horses, who needed to preserve their energy for the rest of the voyage. They would be in a world of trouble if one of the horses injured a leg on a fallen tree because they pushed them too hard.

Though, she'd said something quite curious on her last trip back. *I find it odd that we've had not one close encounter with your father's scouts.*

Your magic is that strong.

No. It's not. And even the storm could not halt the experienced men of your realm, Drystan. Ten days we've eluded them, moving at half pace, on paths unfamiliar to us, but familiar to them. It's almost as if...

As if what?

Nothing.

Say it. Tell me.

It's almost as if there are no guards after us at all.

That was indeed odd, but he reminded himself that there were many things with no explanation, and he must be satisfied with that or go mad with questions.

"The snow is a constant in the midwinter, all over the Northerlands, not just where we live," Drystan answered, with the confidence of a young man who had been all over his Reach a hundred times over, traveling at his father's side as they visited the heads of the Great Families. He had one arm draped gently over her belly, the other with a light touch to the reins. "Even longer sometimes. We can pass entire springtides without seeing the ground, all the way into autumnwhile."

"I never gave it much thought until now. In the mountains, we have no seasons," Ravenna said. Her head fell back into the curve of his neck. She seemed relaxed, but he felt the twitch. At any moment, she might take again to the sky, leaving him to his worry.

"This storm is different than most, though," Drystan went on, buying her presence in moments with each word. "It's not only in the Northerlands. The Westerlands will be seeing snow for the first time in decades. Can you imagine what that must be like, seeing snow for the first time?"

Ravenna made a soft sound, resembling a laugh. "The Westerlands! And how would you know this, all the way up here?"

"My father taught me to read the weather."

"Read the weather."

"That's right."

"I've never heard of such a thing," she said lightly. "How does one read the weather?"

"I could try to teach you," Drystan replied, soft chills swirling through him at the thought. "Though it would take years."

"Sounds like magic."

"I wouldn't know about that."

Ravenna sighed. Her eyes drooped closed. "Nor would I."

"Funny."

"I wasn't making a joke." Ravenna looped her fingers through the mare's mane. "I never learned to do much more than heal, or produce gentle persuasions. My mother could shift her shape, rearrange a room, and create fire from her fingers. My father could cause death with a blink of his eyes, speak to the birds, and raise water with his fists. And I..."

Drystan's heart raced at these revelations. Something new. Something *real*, finally. "You're hardly fifteen. They're twice that. You told me when you came to Wulfsgate that even when you're born with magic you need practice to surface it."

"My mother could do all these things at fifteen. More. When they married, their magics were fully formed. Mine should've been as well, and wasn't."

Drystan chose his next step into the conversation with great care. This was often the point where Ravenna would laugh and divert them to something less personal. But he wanted to know more. Now that they were free, he wanted to know everything. Loving her could mean so much more, once he truly knew her. "Were your parents close as children?"

Her eyes opened. She twisted lightly in surprise, as if she'd expected him to ask something she would shut down immediately. But she answered. "They're brother and sister. They don't talk about their childhood. A Ravenwood sees those years as necessary, but unfortunate. But as we've found no magic to skip the first fifteen years of our lives, we focus instead on how to prepare for when they end. We're sent into the realm of men to train once our wings are strong enough to sustain us for the trip down."

"You never played games?"

"I didn't know what they were until I watched Torrin and Nyssa playing that thing they do in the Wintergarden. The one where they pretend to be farmers coming upon a blight."

Drystan's chest ached to hear her verbalize what others had whispered about. *Ravenwoods are heathens. They breed to sustain themselves, for they are at risk of extinction. They know nothing about love or family. No better than animals. They are guarded by their carnal instinct, in the absence of Guardians to steer them. They would murder their own ilk if it suited them. They sometimes do it for sport.* "You were close to Alasyr."

Ravenna's hands stopped moving through the silken mane of his horse. He froze. Had this been it, the wrong question?

"We're raised never to question the rules and laws of the Ravenwood legacy, but Alasyr and I... we spoke freely. We protected one another and found joy in the corners of our fears and duties. I never feared he would share my doubts with Mother or Father. I began to think that, one day when I had no choice but to take up my birth-given role in the Langenacht, that he might be my one comfort. And then he cast his lot."

Drystan didn't bother asking why she didn't fight against the Langenacht. There were no defectors living amongst the Ravenwoods, only the dead who'd dared. He understood the necessity of the tradition, in a practical way. The Ravenwoods had no others outside their blood, and even if they had allowed that, it would have diluted what made them special, and they seemed to cherish their magic above all things. He couldn't, and didn't want to, envision a life where he was bound to his sister, or his aunt, in wedding bed, but Drystan accepted there were other ways than their own.

But his practical view ended where his love for Ravenna began. His worst moments involved imagining her in the orgiastic throes of carnality with the other men sharing her blood. Not one. Not two. Not even five, or six. They didn't limit the lots cast by anything other than men who were still young enough to procreate, and hungry for power. Some, he'd heard, even abandoned their wives to take their chances.

"How many Ravenwoods are there, in Midnight Crest?"

"Five hundred or so, I suppose."

Drystan's eyes widened. "That's more than I thought."

"You like to think about such things?"

"I like to envision your world to understand you better, yes."

"Your world is so much more interesting," she said, but then added, "we live longer than you do. About twice as long, as I understand. Most women will bear seven or more children over their lifetime, though they'll be done before they've experienced thirty years of life. You're required to bear no less than two, and a High Priestess must continue until she has at least three daughters, to ensure continuation in the event of accidents." Ravenna bobbed against his chest as she swallowed hard. "Of course, your first child comes to you by the greenlight fires of the Langenacht. The magic is at play there, and there has never before been a future High Priestess who's not had a child light within her at the ceremony. But as for your second child, you're given three years into your pairing to conceive. If you don't show signs of a quickening by then, you are cast out."

"Cast out?"

"You know what I mean."

Drystan's skin flushed. He was becoming lightheaded, between the learning and the fear of it stopping. "You mean... when they throw you... down the mountain?"

Ravenna nodded. "They bind your wings with magic so you cannot fly away."

"What of the man? The husband?"

"What of him?"

"Could it not also be his fault, if conception doesn't happen?" He thought of his friend Jorin Hardeham of Westport, whose mother had five children with her first husband, and not one with her second. She was still young when she was widowed, so the people blamed Randall Hardeham instead, making jests about what did or did not dangle between his legs. He'd given her kids his name to stop the talk, but it only incited it more.

"That isn't the way we think. And you must remember, your High Priest is chosen because he *did* light within you the spark of new life. If he did it once, he can do it again. So it is assumed that the High Priestess is the one who's become damaged if conception fails a second time."

Drystan was rooted into silence, unsure where to go next.

"I know that sounds ruthless to you, Drystan. But our world is small. Everyone existing within it must contribute to our continued existence or they are but a leech on our limited resources. It isn't all the horrors you're imagining. We have banquets and fetes and even dancing, like you. We laugh, and have our own songs, though they're not nearly as imaginative as yours. We love, in our own ways, even if that love was one you wouldn't recognize."

"What did you sing about?"

"Sorry?"

"Your songs. What do you sing of?"

"Oh, well…" Ravenna tilted her head to the side. "Most are about something none of us have ever seen, except in visions. From when the Ravenwoods lived Beyond. They're only stories, though."

"Sing one for me."

Ravenna laughed. "I will not."

Drystan leaned forward to kiss her. "I want to hear one."

She shook her head. "They remind me of home."

"Are you missing home?" Drystan didn't know where the question had come from. It seemed painfully out of touch with what had come before.

"You think that's what's wrong with me," Ravenna said, leaning forward against the horse's neck. She turned to look at him, and the fire in her eyes burned him.

"I don't think anything is wrong with you."

"You do. Your careful words. You hardly sleep. You're afraid to touch me."

And you touch me almost too much. As if to distract me. "I'm not afraid to touch you. I'm... I... I'm only thinking of how to protect you, and I'm supposed to be your husband, if not in name, least not yet, then—"

"Not yet or ever, Drystan." Ravenna pivoted, rotating her legs so she faced him. "I left with you because there was no other way. I couldn't stay. I couldn't live without you. And now we're embroiled in this journey that your sister and cousin seem to think is so romantic and noble, but where does it end? Don't say the Hinterlands, because you know that's not what I mean. Where does it end for us?"

Drystan resisted the powerful urge to cry. "It doesn't. Isn't that why we left, together?"

"You silly man." Ravenna's pale cheeks flamed in the cold. "We left because time ran out. Not because we had a vision for the future."

Drystan cupped his hand against her cheek and kissed her. "I don't need a vision for the future. I only need to know you're in it."

Ravenna shook her head slowly. "You and your poetry. You see? This is the problem."

Drystan's mouth hung in mid-reply, but she was already gone again, soaring off into the sky, leaving him wondering how he'd failed to be what she needed most.

"AND, OH, THE HOGS! YOU'VE NEVER TASTED SUCH SUCCULENT, SUCH juicy meat, Lis! The crispy skin melting off in delicious peels. Crunching in your mouth, oily and wonderful. We get that first, of course, like a tease. And when it's gone, you have to pretend you're possessed of patience, but you can hardly wait for the carver to sever the meat and place some upon your plate. It takes all your good breeding to sit back and wait for him to carry the dripping, salty perfection, but oh, once it lands before you, there's little stopping yourself, good breeding or no."

"Yes, Eavan, I've had hog in Whitechurch. We have our own, too, you know," Lisbet murmured.

Eavan made a *pfft* sound. "Your boars are wild, and you have to tear their meat with your teeth. I guess that's what the cold does to them."

"Your boars are wild, too."

"Not *as* wild."

Lisbet's toes curled in her heavy boots. All day, Eavan had been colorfully reciting down the list of her favorite meals, with an imagination that was commendable if it wasn't also torturous. If she wasn't fixated on the colorful dishes of her childhood, she was rambling about Kian de Medvedev and his complicated but apparent undying love for her. The more she spoke of their relationship, the less confident Lisbet felt about their eventual encounter with him.

Lisbet could throttle Drystan for going on ahead, but she understood why. She'd noticed the oddness in Ravenna, too, and it had only grown as they moved farther from their known world. They'd all changed, but none more than their rogue priestess, who should be pulling closer to the man she'd given up everything for—for a love strong enough to spur the entire idea for this voyage—but was instead withdrawing.

A shrill caw broke through the quiet woods.

"There she goes again," Eavan quipped. "She's moody, that one."

"Hey. Keep watch on the rear. I'm going to check on Drystan," Lisbet said, readjusting Starcaller's reins.

"I'll come with you."

"No, I won't be long. Keep your ears open."

"For *what*?"

"For anything we can eat tonight." Lisbet tapped the bow at her back. "We may not have the Guardians-blessed hogs with nectar flowing through their blood in the Northerlands, but ours will still fill a belly."

Eavan blanched in disgust, but stayed behind as Lisbet rode ahead.

"You all right?" she asked, as Starcaller drew up beside her brother's mare.

Drystan pulled himself out of his daze. "Where's Eavan?"

"Ruminating on all the things we'll never eat again."

"Don't say that."

"What?"

"Never. You sound like Ravenna."

Lisbet thought to herself that Ravenna was wiser than she'd given her over for, but didn't say that to her brother, who was clearly hurting. She didn't know anything about love, but it seemed to her that joy, not pain, should be the prevailing sensation. Whatever Ravenna was dealing with, whatever Drystan struggled with, they appeared unable to do it together.

"She'll come around," Lisbet said, riding the soft rise and fall of Starcaller's easy gait. "I don't think one of her kind has been this far south since Rhosyn Ravenwood ran off to the Westerlands to form the Blackwoods."

"You think that's really true? What they sing about in the songs of Rhosyn and Thedyn? It's not in *The Book*."

"And who writes the tales in *The Book*? Think of all those ridiculous journals Mother makes you dictate your life into. We spin our own histories. The Blackwoods decided they were never Ravenwoods, and they wrote it so. But if the love of Rhosyn Ravenwood and Thedyn Blackrook can survive to create a new legacy, yours and Ravenna's can too."

"What if they're just songs?"

"What if they are? Does it matter?"

Drystan angled his head toward the sky. The snow had stopped hours ago, but clouds blocked the sun from warming them. "I thought I was doing what she wanted. She said to me, many times, that we had to leave, and until you and Eavan came to my room with a plan, I didn't know... I was..." A long sigh escaped him.

"It's okay to be afraid, Drys," Lisbet said, reaching across their horses. "I was afraid before I told Eavan, but I'm even more afraid now."

"You've never been afraid of anything."

She tried to smile. "That's not true."

"Christian and I, we were in our books. We made every reason not to learn swordplay, or the bow. I only learned to hunt with great reluctance, and Christian, well, he was lucky, you could say, with the magic. He found his way."

"You'll find yours," Lisbet assured him, though she, too, struggled to see the path. Even if they made it in one piece to the Hinterlands, and even if the Medvedev welcomed them with open arms, the world beyond remained hospitable as long as the Rhiagain king held the throne.

Lisbet tried not to think about home too much. Where Eavan dealt with her fears through reminiscing, conjuring up images of her mother's face, or her father's strange humors only put Lisbet's decision into question. Questioning would lead to mistakes. Looking at the dark moods of Eavan and Drystan, Lisbet understood her role was to hold them all together.

But she did wonder what her parents were doing about their absence. If she'd kept track of time well enough, the Right of Choosing would be happening in a day or two, which meant they were likely in Termonglen now. When she'd first realized this, in a panic, Eavan reassured her that Termonglen was days away from where they were headed, but that didn't ease her as well as it should. They were all headed south, parents and children alike. Her parents may have taken the easy path via the Compass Road, and they through the woods, but that didn't mean it was impossible for their paths to intersect. And without a pace slowed by underbrush, their parents had likely passed them days back without ever knowing it.

Even more strange was how none of the Dereham Guard had caught up with them. They'd had not even a whisper of their presence, not one twinge of the fear of a close call. She told herself

Ravenna's magic was holding strong, but there was more to the matter, if she only let herself explore these suspicions, see where they took her. But she couldn't. All her strength was occupied in keeping them pointed forward.

And what would the Right of Choosing be, without three of the brides? Would Uncle Khallum hand over Aunt Gwyn? Would Uncle Aiden present Assana instead? A very dark feeling enveloped Lisbet's heart as she then wondered if the Northerlands, to assuage the king's temper, would present little Nyssa.

If they did, it would be Lisbet's fault.

She retched into the dry air.

"What's wrong?" It was Drystan's turn to reach across.

Lisbet put her hand up. The sickness passed. When he tried to ask after her again, she hissed between her teeth as she went to draw her bow.

Very carefully, she pulled her left leg over the side of Starcaller's back as she eased them to a slow halt. Reaching back into the quiver, she withdrew an arrow and, without making a sound, pulled back the bowstring.

The air whistled as she released. A satisfying thud came next as the animal toppled into the snow.

"Supper," Lisbet said.

She felt Drystan grin behind her. "Warm food. At last."

"Hog, though. Eavan will be so disappointed." She hopped down from Starcaller's back. "He'll be too heavy to carry far on the horses. The sun is passing beyond, anyway. I'll dress the meat, and you and Eavan find a place for us to put up for the night. Get a fire going."

Drystan looked around. "There's nothing here."

"You have one, maybe two ticks of the sun before we lose the light and the Guardians light the sky. Better get to it."

16

TAVERN AT THE MIDDLE OF THE WORLD

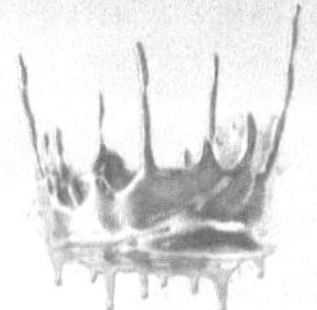

Hollyn moaned against Brandyn's chest. The heavy blanket, shielding her from the deadly sunlight, caused her to break into violent sweats. Her fever had broken in the night, but now she complained of pains in her belly, and the soles of her feet were inexplicably covered in blisters, despite that her feet had seldom set foot upon land. Not long after the complaints left her lips, she fell into a fugue, no longer speaking. Brandyn put his hand against the back of her head and stroked her silken hair, the way their mother would have done, but as the waning figure of his oldest sister shivered in his arms, riding the slow pace of the mule, Brandyn was again reminded that he was the baby, and this wasn't supposed to be the way the world was.

"She hasn't had a hot meal in a week," Storm said, keeping pace beside him. "None of us have, but I don't think our lives depend on it the way hers does."

"We'll be in Briarhaven soon enough." They should've been there already, but Hollyn's state slowed them far beyond even what they'd expected. They weren't even halfway. To avoid the rocky crags of the Seven Sisters, they'd veered north, but then had to take another detour to stay clear of Valleybrooke, because the Bristols were unfailingly loyal to Lady Blackwood and would recognize Brandyn too easily. This path also kept them from crossing the Easterlands straight into Riverchapel, and the Resplendent Reliquary of the Guardians, which would pose even more unique challenges they weren't prepared to face. There'd be no avoiding the mass of Fionn's Pass, and the Gap of Ever, the singular and favored point of crossing, would be too trodden to buck detection. What remained of their journey would be no easier than what had passed already, and that was if they made it.

It was, as his father used to say, the two sharp sides of a sword. *You can be sliced by one side, or severed by another, but sometimes you cannae avoid the cut.* They could race to the Sepulchre, and Hollyn might grow worse. Or they could slow, as they had, and delay her relief. He didn't know what to do. Ember would, but she wasn't here, and hadn't given them more than a rough instruction. She'd only whispered to him, as they left the cave, *just get her there. Do whatever you have to do.*

But Brandyn didn't know what that meant, and he had a lot more faith in his judgment *before* he'd put it to test.

"Another week, and that's if we can move the pace along. You think she has that?"

"She can hear you," Brandyn reminded her with a light hiss at the end. Though he wasn't sure what Hollyn was picking up at all. She'd said nothing for hours. Her language was pain. "And I don't know what she has. That's the problem. No one does."

"We don't have to name it to know she's growing worse, and it's happening fast. She's never been this poor, and you don't know why, which doesn't help us any more than the herbs are helping her. We have another seven days or more until we reach Briarhaven, and help, but if you think she has another seven days you're mad, blind, or both. There's one thing we haven't tried, and it's the only thing available to us right now."

"What?"

"A hot meal. A bath. A night in a soft bed." Storm closed her eyes, apparently imagining these things. "We have the coin, Brandyn. We're doing this for her, so we should do *this* for her."

"You're mad if you think stopping at an inn, while we're still *in* the Western Reach, is a good idea."

"We're at the border, about to cross."

"The sooner we cross, the better."

"As you've reminded me, speed isn't our priority."

Brandyn sighed. Hollyn's limp hand swiped for purchase at his waist and failed, dangling. "Blackwood men will be everywhere. We agreed, no roads."

"And you forget, I know this land better than you. I chose the path. I know precisely where we are."

"You're right, Storm, now is a fair time to boast."

"It's not a boast when it's true," she said. "I've spent my girlhood at my father's side, collecting rents and taxes. Because of that, I know that there's a tavern a quick ride from here that sits off the path. My father said it's the kind of place a man goes when he doesn't want to be found."

Brandyn rolled his eyes. "Does he now?" He grunted as he again adjusted his sister to keep her from falling clear off the mule. The cover over her head to protect against sunlight wasn't helping her labored breathing any.

"I don't mock how you've been reared as a princeling. I won't take your mocking of my family serving yours," Storm returned. All playfulness was gone from her voice. "And I won't temper my words around you or Hollyn. She's dying, Brandyn. Perhaps she's been dying a long time, or the dying part came around recently, but I've tended many, many bedsides with my mother and I know what the time before death looks like. This cold isn't our cold. We're getting the wrath from the North right now, though I can't say I know why. Scraps don't even fill our bellies, you think they do anything for hers?"

"What if we're discovered?"

Storm looked straight ahead. "Then the Guardians have willed it so. For if we take a risk to save a life, then it was a life never meant to be saved."

Jesse didn't know how the princess had talked him into it. He'd learned to filter her out so well, and only occasionally perked up to answer her inane questions. His father told him all good husbands learned to do this at the right times, but this was Ryan's bride, not his. And if this was any indication of what marriage looked like, he failed to see the appeal.

They were so close, now, to the Hinterland border, and yet far enough away from their destination that as Esmerelda dreamily recalled the feeling of her warm bed, and the taste of succulent meat and bread fresh from the oven, Jesse, too, went there with her. He didn't care about the finest things. It was the simplest things that called to him. Food in his belly and a place to rest his head without freezing to death. Had she waxed on about her silks and creams, no doubt her words would've fallen where most of her words did with him.

"One night," she pleaded. "Just one. I can't shake the chill. If I can only get warm..."

"Aye," he said, so low he wondered if he'd meant it for her at all. For days, the snow fell without cessation, and they had no reprieve. By daylight they rode slowly through the substance their horses were so afraid of, and by night, they shivered against it. The storm had eased, and the snow was receding, but the effect lingered upon them both.

"There's a town ahead," Esmerelda said, pointing.

Jesse's lips curled. His forehead knit together. "How could you know that?"

"Look at the ground. The snow. There're tracks."

Jesse dropped the wry expression. There they were. Three sets of them, going different directions. How had he missed this?

"All I mean to say is, it seems that when you see tracks such as these that it must be close to a town, because we haven't seen any before now."

She was rambling. Fearful he'd snap at her, as he'd come to do regularly over their short but unfortunately unforgettable voyage. He wanted to, and the instinct came naturally to him now, but she was right. The foolish, spoiled princess had discovered something he hadn't; something he should've seen long before she noticed.

"Stay close to me," he ordered. "I don't know these lands, and if there is a town, we know nothing about it."

Esmerelda narrowed the gap between them. She tightened her hood, and he resisted the urge to say *good girl*, because though he'd forgotten to remind her to do it, she'd remembered anyway. She was learning. He'd give her that, though where she was concerned he'd never be charitable.

"And will we? Stay? If there is?"

"If there is," Jesse conceded. "I'll assess the risk."

CHRISTIAN SHOT FORWARD IN HIS BED, THE WEIGHT OF HIS DESPERATE breaths rocking him through his motion as he gasped for air. Sweat dripped into his eyes, obscuring the band of moonlight falling across the room into a rough blur. The room stayed out of focus. It shook with his elevated pulse.

Aylen was awake in seconds. "What? What is it?"

"I saw..." Christian reached blindly in the dark for his water. When he felt the cool metal against his palm, he cupped it with a guttural sigh and brought it hungrily to his mouth. He swallowed what remained in several generous gulps.

"It's all right. Take your time." Aylen's hand moved the length of his back.

A deep shiver started at the base of his spine. He fought it back, but it jerked him again forward, and this time she took all of him into her arms and held him tight until the spasm passed.

"It wasn't a dream," she said. "Was it?"

Christian shook his head.

"Who was it? Your mother?"

He shook his head again.

"Drystan? Your father? Your sisters?"

"Brandyn," he managed, and then said it again, intrigued by the strange sound of his voice, which seemed as if it had aged twenty years overnight.

"What did you see?"

"He's in trouble. He's riding. Or will be."

"Riding?"

"Riding. Hard. He has two with him. One is very ill." Christian shook his head. "No, no, do better. Do better, Christian. Like you always tell the others." He opened his mouth and let his breath slowly pass into the air. "Not just anyone. The one who is ill is his sister."

"The one with the disease no one can identify."

"Or cure."

"Why is he riding? Where is he riding?"

"Away," Christian said, and then ran his hands through his hair, wincing. "Away. To. Toward us. He's coming here."

"Here? With her?"

"Yes!"

Aylen paused. "But why?"

Christian turned to look at her. Her soft, thoughtful eyes calmed him some, but there would be no real calm this night. This night was only beginning. "To heal her," he said, and then the next words came to him more clearly than any before. "To protect her."

"From what?"

"From who," Christian said, "seems more the question."

"All right," Aylen said, looking around the room. She slid out of bed and reached for her robe. "Well, she won't be allowed here under any ordinary circumstance, so we'll need to concoct a fair explanation. Sanctuary? If they're on the run, we could make that case."

Christian watched her, both listening and somewhere else. But as he observed his wife spring into action, satisfied that her questions had no answer just yet, he loved her more than he had ever loved another creature in all his life. He loved her so much he wanted to cry.

He had no time for tears. He joined her at the desk. "Ready a room for them, Aylen. Something not in the tower, for they won't be allowed up here. I'm going to meet them."

Her bright blue eyes widened. "Now?"

"Now. They're at least four days' ride from here. Two if I don't stop."

The shock appeared and melted in her face in the same instant. "Very well. I'm coming with you. They won't punish us both."

Christian had been thinking of this, too. Although Magi were free to come and go in a way the Adherents were not, they were still required to apply, and be approved for, leave when they wished to leave the Sepulchre. All magic practitioners in the world had to be accounted for. It was the way.

But there was one exception to this, and that was when called to help another when the danger was discovered by use of magic.

"I wish you wouldn't," he said to her, because there *was* danger. He sensed it, but he already knew her answer.

"If there *is* trouble, a healer may be needed. And it seems to be that since their need of a healer is why they're on their way to us, we may as well get ahead of that," she said reasonably and went to the small bureau to dress, the matter decided.

THE TAVERN AT THE MIDDLE OF THE WORLD SAT AT THE END OF A town, if one could call it that, called Parth. Storm explained to Brandyn that Parth was mostly a waypoint for hunters and trappers, as it was far enough from the Compass Roads to be useless for most travelers. Parth itself was a single road, half stone and half dust from stone that once was, with a straggle of neglected and decayed buildings on either side. Even the ones in use, like the trading post, belonged to another era. There were no lanterns to help them along their way as they moved slowly, cautiously down the untended road; only the moonlight. The only man-made illumination came from the tavern at the end of the way.

He noticed the upper floor first. It was a mess of rotting wood, foggy glass, and a patchy thatched roof. This was the inn, Brandyn supposed as they drew closer, and he hoped Storm knew what she was doing because the feeling in his belly that they were in danger—the one he'd had since they left The Hidden Cave—was becoming something else now. Something Christian and the other Magi had trained him to listen to.

Storm jumped off her mule and knotted the reins around the hitching post. She straightened her riding jacket and threw an impatient look at Brandyn, who was both trying to contend with his sister's dead weight and his own wayward mule.

A faded, rough shape decorated the splintered shingle illuminated by a lantern. Brandyn thought it resembled the kingdom as it appeared on maps, but crudely drawn and even less maintained. Below it, a series of stone arches with milky windows inside them were ablaze with the only signs of life in Parth.

He read the inscription bending around the entryway arch. *All ye who passes beneath these arches passes the bread and the ale.*

"What do you suppose that means?" Brandyn asked as Storm appeared to shift some of Hollyn's burden to her own strong shoulders.

"We're all mates here," Storm said. "My father always checked his sword at the door. That sort of way isn't welcome here. Food and laughs for the belly, women for your other needs, and a bed to fall into after."

"Well, we don't have swords," Brandyn answered, and Storm

diverted her eyes and moved on, easing them all up the short set of steps that brought them inside.

A welcome, overwhelming warmth passed straight through Brandyn's flesh and right to his bones. The flames from the hearth —two hearths, one on each side, underneath arches like the ones outside the tavern—licked at his soul, and he knew right then and there that no power existed in the kingdom that could pull him from what else awaited them inside that night.

A rich scent of some gamey meat was the next enticement. Even Hollyn stirred, lifting her head. Brandyn's eyes traveled the wondrous place. Candlelight danced on tables and at sconces, a thousand lights competing with the flames for the right of illumination. Patrons, with flagons in one hand, and hunks of meat, cheese, and fruits in the other, leaned into benches backed with white furs that reminded Brandyn of the wulves of myth. He'd never seen fur like that come from any animal he'd met with his own eyes. Men pulled wenches into their laps, the women laughing and going right along, no battle of wills here. Garlic and onions hung from the rafters amid dried herbs of all kinds. Swirls of smoke and sizzle appeared from behind another arch, this one quite large, in the center of the tavern, where a barkeep passed mead to patrons while meats and stews cooked behind her.

Brandyn jumped when an orange cat snaked itself around his ankle. Storm laughed, and then he did, too.

The rest of his senses caught up then, and now the din of animated conversation was all around him. Dozens gathered in cheerful, drunken repast, mugs clinking, food passing around tables. Against a far wall, he saw a keg filled with steel. Swords, bows, other weapons, even a scythe. As he started to make sense of that, a genial man with a large belly approached them.

"Aye, weapons for the pot?"

"The pot?" Brandyn repeated.

"Aye, the pot, what yer looking at right now. We leave our trespasses at the door. Ye can collect both yer troubles and yer weapons when ye see fit to leave."

"Right." Brandyn shifted Hollyn to Storm and relinquished his bow and quiver. The man draped it over one arm and looked at Storm. With some reluctance, she passed over hers as well, then nodded to indicate that was it. Brandyn started to remind her about the daggers in her boots, but something stopped him from saying the words.

"Right then. We have boar on the spit, a right good potato stew cooked up only this afternoon, and bread with butter from Una's farm. Ye picked a fair night."

Hollyn came around as the man left, head lolling to the side. "Where are we?"

"The middle of the world," Brandyn said to her.

"Or so they say," Storm said, with a sideways grin. "It's not *really* the middle of the world, if you look at a map. Not even close. But maybe if you stood in the real center you'd be in the river? It's a good name, though."

Brandyn shook his head. "Over there. A table just opened up."

They half-dragged Hollyn, ignoring the curious glances from those slowing their palaver, briefly, to watch the sickly girl. They eased her onto the bench, and she slumped against the fur, a light stream of drool dried at the corner of her mouth.

"You see about the room, I'll get us some food and drink," Storm ordered. She leaned over Hollyn. "You'll be all right here by yourself for a few?"

Hollyn stared at her through empty eyes. Moments passed. Then she nodded.

"We'll eat, sleep a full night, and then be on our way," Storm said to Brandyn. "And in a place like this? We'll blend right in."

Parth seemed to Jesse what Greystone Abbey would look like in another decade, if Easlan James couldn't find the means to turn it around. The James men hadn't mentioned this place at all when they helped them make their safe route. It was both close to the Easterlands border, and yet far from anything else, and Jesse's belly constricted in a mix of anxiousness and eagerness as they made the slow approach toward The Tavern at the Middle of the World.

"Do you believe in ghosts?" Esmerelda asked at his side, and he almost asked her to repeat the question, as strange as it was.

"Ghosts? Like the dead returned?"

"Yes."

"I don't believe in anything I cannae see with my own eyes."

"I don't know what I believe," she answered. "But if there are ghosts, they'll be here."

Jesse shivered. He told himself it was the cold acting up against the promise of warmth. She sounded again like a foolish girl, but he also understood the meaning behind what she'd said. The only words passing through his head as they took in the decaying wooden structures to their right and left were, *once was*. It seemed a place forgotten and also discovered, as there were always men looking to pull themselves further from society. Under another circumstance, Jesse would keep passing through a place like this, for the forgotten and those wanting to be, but in their present state it seemed as if the Guardians had plucked them from their path and set them here intentionally.

By contrast to the rest of Parth, The Tavern at the Middle of the World was inviting. It beckoned, like the comforting arms of a mother. Light and warmth. Bread and meat, and mead, and a roar of conversation that would provide excellent cover for a brother and sister traveling through.

"Can you hear that? My belly? I think it knows we're close to relief."

Jesse shook his head. "Remember. John and Elizabeth Dunn. Greystone Abbey. If anyone asks, but we donnae offer."

"What if they identify our accents? Like the James men did?"

"A place like this won't question. 'Tis what keeps it in existence, why it's the only place full in this dead town. They'll accept what we tell them, if we give no trouble." Jesse would try to cover his own affectations just the same. He sounded like all the salt and sand Southerlanders, whereas Esmerelda's blend of her mother's softer lilted speech and her father's burr turned into something undefinable.

Esmerelda seemed to accept this answer, and she followed his lead as they tethered their horses to the posts. Jesse reached into the satchel and gave them each an apple and a soft pat, and then led them inside. The rush of warmth almost sent him to his knees, and he felt Esmerelda sag at his side. When the man asked for his sword, he passed it without argument, because if it came to it, he had stronger aptitudes elsewhere. And a little something else in his boots.

It wouldn't come to it. Not here. He could see that in the eyes of men from all over the kingdom as they relished in the company of each other and of the strange women in bursting dresses straddling their laps. The boom of laughter and rancor covered everyone's secrets well. It would cover theirs.

Jesse scanned the room, checking each patron off his running list of potential dangers. Most were men of his father's age, some older. Curiously, in the corner, there was a table of children. A young boy of no more than ten or so, and two girls with not many more years than the boy. He saw no ma or pa with them, and wondered how they'd come to be here, in the middle of the world and the middle of nowhere. He had an urge to see if he could help them, but it was quickly replaced by the reminder of their mission, which involved nothing more than a safe delivery of his brother's woman to their mother's people.

There was only one table open, near the bar. He urged Esmerelda into it, passing to her his satchel, and left her to procure food and drink.

The barmaid looked up with a face painted in sweat and grime, but her smile seemed to be the power that kept the establishment running. Jesse sensed in her an authority that went beyond passing drinks to drunken men. He understood at once that she was the proprietor, as well as the barmaid, and the cook. She kept it all running, by herself.

"The boar will please yer wife so much she'll run off with it," she said. "The stew will put her to sleep 'afore she can."

Jesse grinned. "That good, eh?"

"Better," she said, eyes twinkling. "So, both then, and two pints?"

"Ay… yes, thank you," Jesse replied, catching himself as he slid the coin across the bar. He wasn't a Southerlander here, even if there was something about this woman that reminded him very much of home.

Jesse balanced the bowls, mugs, and platters with a hunger that granted him a sudden burst of dexterity. He nearly dropped them on the table and was spooning up the stew before Esmerelda could even arrange everything where it belonged.

"Animal," she whispered, and it almost sounded as if she was teasing him.

The barmaid dropped another platter at the table. They both looked up. "Forgot yer bread. To sop up the stew."

"It smells wonderful," Esmerelda said with a smile.

The barmaid passed Jesse an almost disappointed look that harkened back to her earlier promises of what the food would do. He almost volunteered that this was his sister, not his woman, but he remembered his own advisement. *Only if they ask.*

A round of clapping began, and then boots stomping. Esmerelda looked up, brightening, and then she, too, was clapping in rhythm.

"What is this?"

"*Ah, ice and cold, a history untold, a magic to unfold, this is the house that Rhosyn built,*" she sang, clapping, two dozen voices from all over the kingdom joining in unison. "*Oh, salt and wheat, food so sweet, all kinds of meat, this is the house that Thedyn built.*"

Esmerelda clapped and clapped, urging Jesse to do the same. He picked up the rhythm well enough, but he'd never heard anything so silly.

"Young Rhosyn fell, from her mountain by spell, flew toward love and well, Thedyn surrendered, his kingdom he severed, to join raven to rook, and this is the route they took, this is the route they took, yes, this is the route they took, and this is the house the Blackwoods built."

The rounds went on, and Esmerelda's voice climbed higher, the delight in her face bringing a bright flush to her cheeks. When eventually the song came to a halt, all the singers raised their tankards and tossed a pinch of mead over their shoulders with one last rousing chorus of boots.

Esmerelda giggled as she came back to reality. Jesse stared at her.

"I'm sorry, I couldn't help myself," she said, her pale face still ablaze.

"It's fine. Calls less attention if we go along with it."

"You could've joined in."

"I don't know the song."

"Don't know it!" Esmerelda laughed. "Everyone knows it."

"Not me. I don't care for songs."

"Songs make the world hum," Esmerelda countered. "They tell our stories."

"That's not a real story," Jesse said, licking the boar from his fingers. "No Ravenwood has ever left the Northerlands."

"It is well-known across the kingdom that Rhosyn did that very thing. And why do you look so bothered? I think it's romantic to give up everything for the one you love."

"That is what you're doing. I'll concede to that," Jesse replied. "But I venture you'll not find it so romantic when you live the rest of your days in exile."

"It isn't exile if you're with the one you love."

Jesse shook his head. "You're hanging too much hope on him getting out, Princess. Your father would've taken his head if my own father wasn't so loyal."

Esmerelda frowned. "And where do they think *you* are, these weeks? Taking a stroll?"

"I said I had business in Rushwood. I'll pass through there on the return to remove the lie."

She stopped eating. Her face fell. "On the return. You'll leave me there, then?"

"You expected me to stay?"

She answered with silence. At once, the disappointment faded from her eyes, as if she'd willed it away, and she was again someone he recognized.

"I don't know if it's the hunger talking, but this may be the best food I've ever eaten," Esmerelda said dreamily, trying her hardest to maintain her highborn composure through her desperation to fill her belly.

Jesse swiped his finger along his already empty bowl. "I've had your mother's cooking, so I can see why you might think that."

Esmerelda laughed into her sip of mead. She lowered her voice, though even if they were yelling no one would've heard them. For the first time on their journey, they could speak freely, and it only took surrounding themselves with people to do it. "She never had occasion to cook until she married my father. It was done for her, where... where she came from. And when she arrived to her new home, where she was expected to do it all, she had no one to teach her." She set her mug aside, eyes going glassy as she kept them trained on the misshapen metal. "They weren't welcoming."

Jesse ripped a corner of the bread in his teeth. "She didn't belong there."

"And you think that was her fault? She had no choice. None of them did."

"She didn't try to fit in. She turned her nose at our traditions."

"How would you know? You would've been a bairn."

"My father told me."

"Your father." Esmerelda snorted. "He was angry because your mother and my mother were friends. She told me."

Jesse pushed his empty bowl to the edge of the table and leaned in. "My mother was an outsider as well. They never let her forget it. My dad was only trying to draw less attention to the fact, and your ma was a reminder of it."

Esmerelda picked at the boar. Jesse didn't know what made her act so dainty all of a sudden, but then he remembered how Khallum would spoil her. She never ate what she didn't like. When the rest feasted on deer, he'd have cod prepared for his little princess.

"If you aren't going to eat that, I will."

"I'll eat it."

"I already know you don't like it."

When she looked up, her eyes were wet with tears. "How would you know?"

Jesse curled his lip as he laughed. "I've dined at your table many times."

Esmerelda nodded. She looked away, toward the table of children. Only one was there now. The others had gone elsewhere. "Because my father thought me too delicate to eat like men? Because, when he caught me sneaking the scraps from the cattle feast, he whipped me until I bled and told me I'd never make a good marriage if I was built like the women who ate such foods? I suppose that's where you earned such feelings of me?"

Jesse paused. The sneer in his expression melted away. He pushed her plate closer and nodded. "He's not here now. Eat what you want."

"What if he's right? What if it turns me fat?"

He almost laughed, but her very serious expression curtailed the reaction. "My brother doesnae care about that. He'd love you if he had to roll you to bed every night."

Esmerelda's green eyes widened, and she clapped both hands over her mouth to suppress the laughter. Had she even been to bed with his brother, then? She conveyed the delicacy of one who'd only considered such things in scandalized passing.

"It won't turn you fat," Jesse said with a sigh. "But it will fill your belly. We only have one night here. Make the most of it."

Esmerelda nodded slowly. She pulled the hood, which had fallen back in her bout of laughter, closer around her face and bowed to eat the boar in privacy.

Jesse leaned back against the lush furs and let his eyes flutter closed for only a moment. Belly full, bones warmed. Esmerelda was right. This was what they'd needed at the halfway point in their journey.

Esmerelda's gasp came just ahead of the sudden cessation of conversation. Jesse whipped forward, toward the direction of her shocked gaze, and for a moment he couldn't believe what he was seeing.

The children... one of them, one of the girls, had run two knives into the back of a man's neck. At her feet lay another, blood seeping into the cracks of the uneven wooden floor.

Jesse jumped to his feet, but Esmerelda reached and grasped tight to one of his hands. She shook her head at him. Her emerald eyes implored him from behind the hood. *Don't get involved.*

But he couldn't tear his gaze away from the young girl, standing tall, knives dripping with the blood of two men, daring others to come forth to the same fate.

Esmerelda's hand started to shake. He felt it through his, as she hadn't let go.

He reached into his jacket with his free hand and felt for the two keys, for the rooms he'd secured before ordering their food.

Jesse needed to get Esmerelda out of the dining hall before the break in the din drew the attention they needed to avoid.

Brandyn watched the worst night of his life unfold, frozen to the floorboards.

He didn't see all the things that must have led to the fated moment. He'd been paying for the rooms when he heard Hollyn cry out, and by the time he turned to see the two men with their hands down her dress, one of them was staring lifelessly into the crowd. Blood coursed from his neck, courtesy of the swift, clean cut from Storm's two daggers. She released him, and he flopped to the ground. The sound resonated through the now-silent tavern. It rang in his ears.

The other man, hands still secured at Hollyn's breasts, never saw his fate coming. He didn't even know his friend was dead before Storm jammed both blades through the back of his neck. The tips exited the front, and with them, a geyser of fresh blood, streaming outward into grotesque arcs that rained upon the empty table.

Strangely, Brandyn's first thought was, *we didn't even eat yet.* Storm's chest heaved as she extracted her blades and held them out toward the onlookers, eyes like an animal, regarding the other patrons as if she were challenging them to rise up and try their lot against her.

Guardians help us. Brandyn again looked at his sister, who was now drenched in the blood of the two men who had assaulted her. Wood scraping against wood came next, as the other men nearby slowly reacted to the shocking scene.

"All right now, girl. Put the knives down," one said, inching toward her with his hands out.

Storm waved both daggers in the air. She wiped at the sweat on her brow with her arm.

"Someone grab her!"

"Mother's blood, get the cursed blades before she does it again!"

Brandyn clutched the black keys in his fist, breaths heaving in, out. Storm still hadn't looked this way. It seemed she wasn't there at all, by the look in her eyes. She'd gone elsewhere.

The barmaid appeared from the corner of his vision, moving slowly toward Storm.

"'Tis all right, girl. We saw what they did. You was only protecting yer own."

Storm, eyes nearly shuddering out of her head, they were so

wild, turned toward her. The other men stopped trying to approach and turned their own attentions to the barmaid.

"You'll nae find law here. But you can't stay," the barmaid said, and Brandyn remembered her name was Una. The man at the door, who'd taken their weapons—but not all, not all, and now Brandyn wished with all he had that he'd called Storm to account for keeping those daggers—had told them this. It seemed unimportant and yet a fact that kept him breathing and rooted in reality.

"She's... she's sick," Storm said, struggling through her first words. Her face was stark white. "She's sick. She needs food and rest."

"I can see that," Una said. "But now she'll be finding it elsewhere, girl."

"Where?"

Una pointed. "I can't help you with that. What I can do is keep these other men from slicing you and your friends from ass to neck, if you leave now."

"Aye, and you think you can stop us, old woman?" said a man, from the other end of the tavern. Brandyn noted that for all his big words, he was still seated.

Una said nothing, but the hard look silenced the only man who dared speak against her.

"Gather what you checked at the door, and be gone, or I'll do naught to stop what happens next," Una warned, and the softness, that sense of motherly comfort, was gone entirely. Brandyn now understood it was Una who could have their heads on pikes lining the empty Parth road. She was also the only one who could save them.

"Storm!" Brandyn shouted, and the sound of his own voice freed him from the spot. He moved now through the tables, weaving quickly toward her, and when he reached her, he yanked at her stiff arm, pulling it down so he could take the knife from her. She'd lost the other one in the melee. He slipped it into the back of his trousers and pushed her forward.

Hollyn sobbed as Brandyn yanked her out of the bench, away from the warmth and the promise of a night that might save her life. He tried not to think about that. He couldn't process it right now, just as he couldn't really let sink in that Storm had killed two men. Right now, they had one thing that needed doing. One.

He somehow found the strength to bear Hollyn's weight alone, and, with a hard tug, he launched Storm forward, ejecting her from the daze. She ran to the pot to grab both their bows and then rushed behind them, out the door, toward their horses.

"Forget slow. We have to ride hard now!" Brandyn ordered, tossing his sister over the back of his mule while he worked at freeing it from the pole. "We have to get as far from here as we can, or it's over!"

Storm nodded, tugging furiously at her own reins, mounting the mule as it was riding off. She kicked her heels against the animal and launched out into the night. She disappeared from his view in mere moments.

Brandyn followed, heart racing, beseeching the Guardians to protect them from what Storm had done; to let his sister live long enough for them to lay her at the feet of someone he trusted more than his own family.

Hollyn moaned at the rough ride, but Brandyn, in his fear, had no comfort for her this time.

CHRISTIAN'S BOOTS CRUNCHED IN THE DRY HAY OF THE BARN JUST outside the blacksmith's outfit on the outskirts of Briarhaven. Some Adherents and Magi kept their horses when they left home, but they had to pay the board and care, and accept the reality that they'd so rarely see them because of their duties. Most realized it wasn't worth it. Others did it anyway, only to eventually sell them or send them back home.

Christian and Aylen had been raised their whole life on and around horses, and it was inconceivable to imagine any life that didn't include them. When they were given leave to venture into Briarhaven, it was their favorite outing together. They'd saddle up Sun and Moon, and ride down into the gulch just beyond the perimeter of town. Aylen would remove the bread and cheese from her saddlebag, and he a bottle of wine that some of the Magi produced from a vineyard in Briarhaven, and, together, lay out under the skies. It was a strange thing for those who spent their lives at the Sepulchre in the Skies. While the rest of the world looked up, they looked down, and they cherished these moments when they could return to the way their lives had started.

There was no one looking after the horses at this hour. Christian knew the horse keeper retired at supper and didn't return until the day was fresh, and their next meals were due.

Aylen saddled Sun, and he Moon. The horses were foals when he chose them. Sweet little Lisbet, who'd been so small at the time, didn't understand why he wouldn't take the horse he'd grown up on, but at her age Snowfall deserved more than he could give when he went to pursue his studies in magic. Instead, he'd taken Snowfall's final foal, and purchased another from a nearby farmer, and brought Sun as a gift to Aylen, who'd come to the Sepulchre a year ahead of him and was missing her own horse terribly. He didn't know if it was that which had won her love, or the years intervening, but she sometimes called him the moon in her sky.

"You have a good heart, Christian," she said, checking again Sun's straps. She ran her hand down her chestnut mane. "Others might think you're a fool, for what we're about to do tonight, but it's why I chose you."

Christian nodded, finishing with Moon by laying a kiss at the center of her nose.

"You've treated him differently than the other students."

"Brandyn has been lost since he came to the Consortium. More so than most."

"It's more than that," she said. As she moved toward him, a rush of cool air passed through the open doors and sent a chill straight through him. "You treat him like family."

Christian sometimes felt the shadow of Drystan trailing him through his days. The others had been too young to miss him. When he really wanted to torture himself, he'd remember that he'd left before the twins would ever have recollection of him, and he'd never returned to rectify this. But all of Wulfsgate had been the playground of the two oldest Dereham children, and though Christian had always felt as if he belonged elsewhere—a feeling that had lived with him every day of his life until he stepped through the magic portal into the Sepulchre—Drystan was the only piece of home he'd ever regretted leaving behind.

"I belong here," Christian said. "With you." He reached a gloved hand to the side of her face and she let her cheek fall briefly in his palm. "But I should've belonged in Wulfsgate, with my family. I've never been what they needed. And even knowing that, I never can be. I won't try. There are some things in this world we don't have to like, only accept."

"I understand."

Christian smiled. His breath furled into a small white cloud as he exhaled. "I know you do. I can't go back, Aylen. But I can do for others, in my own way. I can be for Brandyn what I couldn't be for Drystan. I don't know if this rights any of my wrongs, but... if I were a spiritual man, I would say the Guardians put us on this path tonight."

Aylen pressed both hands to the sides of his face and kissed him. "Then we must take it." She released him and mounted Sun, angling herself into position in the saddle. "Do you know where we're going?"

Christian swung himself atop Moon. He checked the silver swinging from his sword belt. Hoping it would not be needed.

"No, but I will."

. . .

THE POWERFUL THUD OF HOOVES POUNDING INTO MUD OVERWHELMED Brandyn's words, even as he shouted them in strained bursts across to Storm. Hollyn lay limp across his lap, flying with every bounce, and he half-wondered if she might get jostled right off. It would kill her. He was certain. But he wasn't entirely sure she wasn't dead already. He was afraid to check.

"Faster!" Storm cried, beating at the side of her mule. But there was no faster. Foam curdled at the mouths of the beasts. They'd chosen them not for speed but durability, and the past hour had pushed them beyond their limits.

"The mules will drop if we push them any harder!" Brandyn cried out over the blur of panic and mud sailing up from the ground. The rain from earlier was now a curtain, blinding them from anything more than a few feet ahead. It ran down his face, soaking his clothing and flesh to the bone. His boots slipped in the stirrups, and he had to yank Hollyn back up every few paces to keep her from sliding clear off.

"We'll drop if those men catch us!"

He wanted to yell back that there was no one coming, but he'd replayed every moment from the tavern in his mind in the bloated seconds that ticked as they pushed harder, harder. Most were jumbled, out of order, but he kept returning to the memory of four men, not two. Four men at a table together. Four men who had been something to one another. Two had died. Two had lived.

There was little hope the two hadn't come to avenge their brethren. Even tough to the bone Una could only pause the inevitable, not stop it.

Brandyn had been trained well with a bow, but his instruction was cut short when he was sent to the Sepulchre. He still remembered his awe of the great archers of Longwood Rush, with their longbows stretched from head to toe, strings pulled back in delicate but precise rhythm. They were even more beautiful in synch, one fluid pass of arrows through the sky, matched in speed and song.

These were no warriors; they were artists. And, as his mother said, there was a place for both in battle.

Some, Brandyn recalled, had additional skills with a standard bow, and these men could shoot from their horses. Horse lords, he called them, but his mother had another name for them, Rush Riders. They'd rotate in the saddle at any speed, arrows flying from their bow in all directions, with the same precision as if on solid ground. He'd heard that they awaited the exact moment the hooves had left the soil, suspended in air, before firing their shot, and that detail stuck with him more than any of the others. How anyone could live in the moments between the seconds was astounding to him. Brandyn imagined himself with such an impressive skill, saving the day as he pivoted backward in his saddle and picked them off, averting the danger that had Storm more terrified than he had ever seen her.

"We can't maintain this pace!" Brandyn called again. "We have nowhere to go."

"And do what?" Storm kept her gaze straight ahead, half standing in her saddle as if on a warhorse. "Stand and fight them when they arrive?"

"You seemed to have no problem with it back in the tavern."

"I did what I had to do."

"You didn't have to kill them!"

"Yes. I did."

"You're the one who insisted Hollyn needed a night in the inn! A hot meal. Remember? Now she's had neither and is worse than she's ever been!"

"Those men would've raped her."

He laughed through the snot and mud caking his face. "There were at least two dozen others in there to stop them. Why'd it have to be you?"

"Bless you, Brandyn, but you're not part of the same world as the rest of us."

"And just what's that supposed to mean?"

"You're not a Blackwood here, is what I'm saying."

"So what?"

"There's no powerful mommy or daddy in the back of these men's minds to stay their hands. No one to answer to, not out here, where a man is no one at all. Men have no names here, no families, no people to identify with or to fear."

"You don't know they would've done it."

Storm cast a furious glance from her peripheral. "And it was enough to me that they'd tried."

"But to kill them, Storm."

"You're very fortunate to never have had to fight for anything. I haven't been as lucky."

Brandyn was too winded to keep sparring with her. He was dizzy from the rush of fear that left him buzzing from toes to ears, and he felt at any moment that it all might catch up and he'd fall to the mud and die there. He wasn't so afraid to die, it surprised him to discover. It was something one could only really know when faced with the possibility. But he was afraid of doing it before he could get Hollyn to safety.

Hollyn. She'd said not a word since he threw her over the back of the mule. He reached to touch the side of her neck, to check for the soft thrum, but removed his hand again. Once he knew, there'd be no going back to a moment where he didn't. And if she was…

"You didn't see this coming?" Storm ripped him from his reverie. "You couldn't have stopped it?"

"What?"

She waved her hand in the air. "All of this! The tavern, what they did to your sister. Me."

"I don't see everything. You know that."

"I hear the lie in your voice, Brandyn Blackwood."

He could hardly hear *her*, so he doubted she could sense such small changes in his voice. Still. He had sensed something. But he lacked the training to go after the vision and see it in its clarity. He was still an Adherent, and a fledgling one at that. Magi Christian had taught him much in a year, but it had taken almost a decade for Magi Christian to learn to harness his own magic. *And even then, Brandyn, it takes a lifetime to know it. A bit of a curse, really, that you could spend eighty years finding the answers only to also discover yourself at the end of the path, your promise fulfilled.*

How he wished Magi Christian were here now. He'd know what to say. What to do. How to fix what had been horribly broken.

And though he couldn't spend the energy on it now, there was something else that had changed in the dim light of the Tavern at the Middle of the World. He'd grown up with Storm. Adored her, looked up to her, as he did Ember. Loved her, though he was still too young really to understand what that might mean.

Tonight he'd seen her take two lives. She'd done it without hesitation, and without the delicacy he ascribed to girls, at least the ones he'd known. She acted with precision and finality. And though she, too, was scared, not once had he sensed in her that she felt conflicted about having done it.

"It doesn't matter," he called back, answering her, answering himself. "None of it matters anymore. Only Hollyn."

Storm pressed her heels into the mule and pulled ahead into the night.

J ESSE UNLACED HIS BOOTS. H E SET THEM IN THE CORNER AND reached for the pillow Esmerelda had left at the end of the bed for him. He regarded it with a hollow look before returning it to her, easing it under her dangling arm.

Two rooms he'd bought, but they'd only use one. After the strange scene in the tavern, Esmerelda, shaking, begged him not to leave her alone. She'd seen, she said, what those men had tried to do to that girl. She'd never seen a man die before.

How sheltered you are, he wanted to say, but he, too, was shaken. He'd never forget the feral look in the young girl's eyes as she waved both daggers in the air, forming a cross above her head. Was it desperation? Anger? Something that called more to the raw core of who they were, as men, as women? Jesse had never seen warfare, but he supposed that was how a man might look in the middle of it.

If he'd gone to check on the children, would the night have ended better for them?

"You need sleep, too," Esmerelda pleaded when she realized he meant to rest in the rickety chair. She gestured toward the bed. "We can both sleep here." When he said nothing, she added, "It's one night."

"It's fine."

"It's not fine. If it wasn't for me, you'd have your own bed."

"What happened down there wasnae your fault," Jesse said, so rattled he didn't realize he'd slipped into his Southerland cadence again.

"I'll take the chair, then," she said, jumping up. "You take the bed."

"Don't be foolish."

"Jesse."

He didn't admonish her for saying his name this time. No one here was looking for them. No one here would talk about anything, for weeks to come, other than the girl child who had killed two men, unaided.

"Get some rest, Esmerelda. I won't quarrel about it."

She nodded, looking miserable, but did as he said. She removed only her cloak before slipping under the quilt, but before she laid her head down, she gave him her second pillow. It was a rather pathetic gesture, but the serious look she wore as she offered it made him think twice about telling her no.

Esmerelda was asleep within moments of her head hitting the pillow. Her soft snores gave her exhaustion away. When he placed the gifted pillow under her arm, she snuggled up into it, making little mumbling sounds that made her seem like a child.

Jesse kicked his feet up onto the table. He leaned his chair back until it touched the wall and closed his eyes, knowing there'd be no sleep to greet him. He pulled his father's dagger from the strap on his ankle and held it against his chest.

Outside, a fresh rain peppered the earth. It was a sound that reminded him of home, of months on the sea.

More importantly, it wasn't fecking snow.

17

THE BOOTLICKER

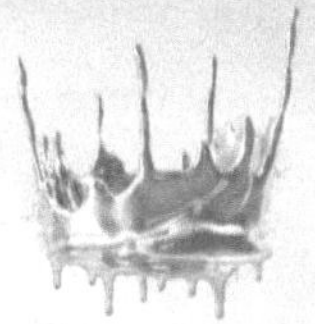

Aiden envied those with the incredible honor to watch him arrive at Termonglen at the head of his glorious cavalry. All men behind him were bedecked in the crimson and gold of the Easterlands. He donned the same colors, but there was no mistaking their rank versus his, not with extravagant plume upon his helmet that stretched so high into the air others joked he might swipe birds from the sky. They were a vision, glimmering in the last sun of the day, which was precisely the time he planned to arrive for this exact reason.

None would offer him the praise he deserved. They loathed him. But he'd see it in their eyes, the dark tendrils of jealousy, and perhaps even fear, at how they'd neglected to melt the fat and rust off their own men while he'd been training something formidable. Something worthy of a king, which even Eoghan had said as he accepted Rowanwen in the spring.

He didn't think it was any great secret that his army was second only to the king's, but he hungered for the looks on their faces as they realized what he'd been doing to raise them to this greatness. As the understanding spread over them that the men and women of the kingdom saw serving a Quinlanden to have honor in the same way as serving a Rhiagain.

Aiden's best men were in the front and rear. Those he considered less than men he placed in the middle, surrounded by others with greater merit, loyalty, and bloodline. There was scant chance of escape. He'd seen to that.

He'd almost waited until the others were sure to arrive, but a scout who'd gone on ahead with the workers sent to tidy the old heap returned to tell him the other Reaches were already *there.* Aiden rushed his men until they were near, then slowed them once more in order to make the memorable entrance he'd intended all along. It wouldn't be the same, but the result, the other Reaches coming to the dawning realization that they were already bested, would be the same regardless of the specifics in the choreography.

His second-in-command, Oakenwell, asked what they could expect from the others in terms of size. Aiden told him he'd appreciate the answer more when he could see it with his own eyes. Aiden knew only the Warwicks had the foresight to fortify their forces, but it wasn't an especial intelligence so much as a race of men with war bred into their blood. Holden had let his farmers and trappers grow fat on their lands, and Asherley was a foolish woman whose crowning military achievement was bowmen.

Gretchen was outside awaiting him, hair caught in the foul east wind. She had one of her sons at her side, though he couldn't remember this one's name. Third or fourth born. The others had left her.

His sister was still exquisite, as all women of the Easterlands were, but the cold of the Northerlands had hardened her features. Her eyes narrowed, and small lines decorated her perfectly shaped mouth. He had no doubt she'd still be his, if he desired it. He didn't, but he might. Better for her to wonder when it was coming.

Aiden dropped to the ground, enjoying the way his cloth of gold cloak swung behind him in the motion. He embraced Gretchen, which she allowed only long enough to recoil at his touch, and then she edged her son behind her with one hand.

"Are you having your moon cycle or something?"

"You always had a way with words, Aiden."

"It's been years, Gretchen, and this is how you greet me? Your brother?"

"Where's Corin?"

"In Whitechurch, seeing after things in my absence. As I'd assume Holden's ineffectual brother Alric is doing for the both of you?" Aiden very nearly made a joke about Holden's two dead brothers, and the fantastical circumstances surrounding *that* debacle, but he'd save it for the man himself, who would appreciate it so much more.

If there weren't so many observing this reunion, Aiden would slap the disappointment from Gretchen's face, and then keep doing it until it pleased him to stop. She wanted to see Corin, did she? She'd always taken to him, coddling him, playing with him, and he'd become a weak man as a result. Where Aiden should have an ally in his brother, he had the makings of an adversary. Corin didn't agree with what he'd done to strengthen their defenses. He claimed to have a moral objection. But he'd also done nothing to stop it.

"And Maeryn? Did you leave her behind as well?"

Aiden laughed. "And hear her whine for the rest of my days about how I kept her from Asherley? She's here, in the back, with Assana. She cried about it until I wearied of the sound. Much like you're crying over Corin now."

"You didn't leave him behind to look after things. He's the last person you'd trust with your land and seat," Gretchen said. She nudged her son—Pieter, that was his name, he remembered it because it was a very Northern-sounding name, and a black mark on Gretchen's heritage—and he reluctantly followed the unspoken command, backing away from her mother and uncle with increasing scrutiny. "He's well-liked. That's a threat to you."

Aiden brushed a hand atop her hair with a placating smile.

"Leave the politics and scheming to the husbands. Stay to what you best know. Poisoning gossips."

Gretchen again recoiled, this time taking several steps back. She crossed her arms over her chest. "You haven't asked about your daughter."

"Assana is in the back with her mother. As I've said."

"You know I mean Eavan."

"Eavan made her choice when she shamed our house by running off. There's no place for her should she return." Aiden enjoyed the horror Gretchen wasn't quick enough to hide. He'd always enjoyed it. One of life's few true pleasures. "A treatment you should adopt if your own wayward children return home, whimpering for the comforts they so carelessly tossed aside because they failed to grasp their place in the world."

"I'll search the ends of the kingdom for Drystan and Lisbet, and I'll continue that search until they're found. If it takes my life," Gretchen said, and her head tilted higher with the words. Even now, trying to impress him with her steely resolve, when her greatest feature had always been her strawberry golden hair. "And Eavan will have a home in Wulfsgate."

"A fool's task. Maeryn speaks like you, but I should stop expecting better from women. Ruled by emotion. Governed by whim."

A pound of heavy steps sounded behind Gretchen. Khallum, Byrne, and some Southerlander men, obvious by their leathered skin and absence of grace, appeared on the drawbridge. They said nothing by way of greeting, each piercing them with their coarse looks and salt and sand breeding.

"I'm not who you remember. I haven't been her for many years," Gretchen said, and then fell back, retreating to these men she had nothing in common with. Khallum reached forward and gently, almost protectively, guided her into the center of his small retinue, never taking his eyes off Aiden.

"I expected to be the first here, and somehow, though I've

arrived early, I'm the last," Aiden called out, loud enough to be heard inside. Where were the others? The craven leaders of the North and West? "None of you wear the mantle of the freshly arrived, either. It seems I'm late, but for what?"

"Your suite is ready. There are tents in the field for your men," Byrne said evenly. "There's a feast underway, as you know, because you sent it ahead. We expect the king in the morning."

"I know precisely when the king will arrive," Aiden replied. "We are in frequent and amicable conversation."

"Hmph," Khallum answered.

"Dearest sister," Aiden called. "I request time alone with Holden to discuss certain matters."

"No," she said, and Khallum grinned. Were they fucking? He wasn't the sort of man Gretchen lusted after. She preferred the pretty ones, who could only be certain to be possessed of cocks if one lifted their skirts to verify.

"Anything said will be said in front of us all," Khallum said. "There willnae be side deals brokered today."

"You mean such as whatever the rest of you discussed prior to my arrival?"

"Our journey was longer. We arrived early so we could be rested for the events," Gretchen attempted.

"Holden," he repeated. "Where is he?"

"He could be deep in the pointless task of sucklin' from the teats of a scullery maid and we'd still say anything you have to say to him, you say to all of us," Khallum said.

Aiden smiled the same smile he gave to the children of his house slaves right before they learned he didn't give a whit how young they were. They were old enough to feel the back of his hand. "With such a command for diplomacy, you wonder why I'd exclude you from a conversation?"

"I'm here," Holden called out from behind the thick of Souther-landers playing tough. "And we can meet, but I won't keep anything said from the others."

"I wouldn't expect you to," Aiden said, winking at his sister as he shoved through the men and followed his brother-in-law inside.

"What's he playing at?" Khallum asked, following Gretchen as she fled the burning memory of her brother's touch. With each step, more of her past peeled away into the wind, and if she ran hard enough, far enough, she could outrun every painful memory.

We could kill him, Gretchen.

Then we'd be no better than he is, Corin.

She picked up her pace, and her skirt, as she entered a place she remembered from the last time she'd been here, hardly a girl: the menagerie. They called it this because someone, no one knew precisely who, had carved the shrubs and bushes into the images of forest animals. Bears, wulves, hawks, and others now impossible to discern. Some said they were meant to represent the familiars of the Medvedev. Whatever their origin, they'd fallen into disrepair, wayward branches twining and obscuring any resemblance to the creatures they once were. The rich bluish emerald grasses, so unique to the Hinterlands, grew wild and dominating as they rose higher and higher around the once-animals, threatening to overtake them if no one intervened.

"Lady Dereham."

She didn't wish to talk about it with anyone, least of all Khallum.

When she leaned into a bush roughly shaped like a deer to catch her breath, Khallum stopped, too. He angled in front of her, but he must have seen it in her face, for he relented some. Byrne appeared a moment later.

"What's the trouble?" he asked, hand tentatively stretched toward her, hovering, as if fearful of actually touching her. She didn't understand his hesitation. He never operated with it under other circumstances. "Did he hurt you?"

"Not today," she answered, gathering within her the wits required to return to the world that needed her. Beseeching the

Guardian of the Warrior's Aim to restore, at least, her breath, before she had to go back and return some order to the day.

"Asherley has told me things. Stories from Maeryn," Byrne offered. "He's less than a man."

"They are no longer stories when you live them," Gretchen said. "And I cannot say. What he's playing at. With Aiden, it could be anything. But it's never nothing."

"You trust your husband will do as he says, and tell us what's spoken?"

Gretchen hesitated. Nodded.

"Why Holden?" Byrne asked. He hovered near her, as if afraid she might melt if not surrounded by a capable man. She almost laughed. It was men who had done this to her. No man could ever undo what another had done.

"Aiden has no respect for my husband. He believes he's easy to manipulate," Gretchen said. It was more than this, but she couldn't put her finger on the rest of the thread. She feared learning the answer too late.

"He made a point to rub our noses in his closeness to The Pretender," Khallum said. "It seems very important to him that we know it."

"He hasn't forgotten that Eoghan is still very young," she said.

"Aye. At least his father had a head about him and pubes on his balls."

"A father is what Eoghan is missing. Or someone to fill a guiding role," Gretchen said. She reached to the sides of her hair, fixing it back into place. A deep breath filled her lungs. "Aiden knows this as well."

"He'll look as foolish and traitorous as the rest of us when he has no daughter to present."

"I told you he'd bring another, and he did. And he'll be the only one unless you intend to hand Gwyn over." She turned to Byrne. "And Asherley."

Khallum pressed his hand to his side, where undoubtedly a knife lay strapped to him. "On my corpse, and even then."

"Even then," Byrne repeated, and Gretchen could see the man living two lives, straddling two worlds, as he sought to impress his brother while remaining tethered to the man his wife loved.

Gretchen shook her head. "That's what he wants. For you to threaten the king. To refuse to acquiesce. Think of what it does for him when he's the only one who comes to the king with an offering? The only one who steps forth as an ally?"

Khallum spat at his feet. It disappeared somewhere in the tall snarls of blue grass. "I dinnae care what he wants. He can choke on his wants."

Gretchen looked toward the castle. It should be her inside negotiating. Holden didn't have the stomach for war, but he also lacked what she'd developed and hardened within herself, living in the shadow of the torture of Aiden Quinlanden. Whatever Aiden had planned, Holden would fail to identify it, and thus fail to counter it. She'd never before wished for magic the way she did now, where she'd do anything to take the form of Holden and hold these negotiations on his behalf.

"Where's Asherley?" she asked Byrne.

"Inside somewhere," he said. "With her seer." From the way he said the word, seer, it was clear he didn't think much of the man.

"If I didnae know better, I'd say she was sucking his cock," Khallum said. "All the time she spends with him, 'hind closed doors."

"He knows I'd cut it off. If he even still has one after tucking it away from Asherley's grasp all these years."

The men laughed together.

Gretchen pointed herself toward the castle. "Unless her seer can stop hearts beating with his mind, he's no weapon against the monster who just landed upon our doorstep."

. . .

"As I've said every time before, Lady Blackwood, I am not a healer. My magic does not work that way."

Asherley stood before her sister Maeryn, who cowered nude at the base of the mirror. She couldn't quite tell if Maeryn's reaction to the assessment was modesty before Joran, or horror at others witnessing the roadmap of violence inflicted upon her body by her husband.

At last, she draped a quilt over her sister and eased her into a chair. "*Now* will you let me kill him?"

Maeryn gratefully accepted a cup of tea from Joran and nursed it near her face, still shivering. "You'd never get close enough. He has too many men. You'd need your own army." After a deep sip, she closed her eyes. "You don't know what he's done."

"I can see it with my own eyes."

"I don't mean to me. I mean to..." Maeryn trailed off and curled further into herself.

"I've seen it," Joran piped up with a helpful smile.

Asherley sighed in exasperation. "Have you? Seen what? What haven't you told me now?"

"It's yet unclear, but I believe I know what Lady Quinlanden speaks of."

"Don't you ever call her that," Asherley snapped. "She's a Blackwood."

Joran affected a light bow.

"Maeryn, I'm not afraid of men. I have no need of them, and they've only one need of me."

Maeryn looked up. "You married a good one. A good man."

Asherley nodded. She paced the room, moving to the window. Outside, Aiden's men milled around in their glittering uniforms, as pretty as their master... and hopefully as useless, though she doubted it. "Byrne *is* a good man. But it will not be a good *man* that saves this world from Aiden, or Eoghan, or any other who would rise up in their pathetic need for adulation."

"I know what's in your mind, Ley, but if you come for him and fail, he will take my children."

"Eavan is safe with the Dereham children, wherever they are. Assana is already lost," Asherley said. When Maeryn gasped a cry into her hand, Asherley remembered her sister was no longer a confident ancestor of the Ravenwoods, but a cowing mouse, fearful of the cat always at her tail. She knelt before the chair and reached for the cup of tea, setting it to the side before taking both her sister's hands in hers. "I know this is difficult to accept, sister. But there is nothing more you can do for Assana. The best to be hoped for is that she is early widowed. As for your sons, they're too valuable to Aiden for him to harm them. Cian will rule the Easterlands one day. This is good for us. He's more Blackwood than Quinlanden."

"Aiden knows this. There are no laws preventing him from passing his oldest son over for one more amenable."

"Sons all raised by their mother. Raised of their mother."

"Not all. He sent Breandan and Dorrin to the Council of Universities. Against my will."

"Aiden may claim the universities are beholden to the Easterlands, but that does not make it so."

Maeryn's wide eyes seemed to tremble. "You don't know what he's capable of."

"Byrne and Khallum will raise an army against him if it comes to it. The Westerlands would not sit idle, either."

"His army would cripple theirs. You don't know what he has done."

Asherley laughed. "I've seen the men who serve Aiden Quinlanden."

Maeryn reached forward and wrapped her swollen fingers around Asherley's cheek. "Ley. You're not listening. Hear me now. They are *not all men.*"

. . .

To hear Holden say the words with such conviction, Khallum could almost believe them. Holden evidently believed them, but that only proved him a greater fool.

Khallum paced the small bedchamber where the Derehams stayed. Holden had ushered them all in after his meeting with Aiden, looking especially pleased with himself. But it was Gretchen the others looked to for the proper read of the situation. She was practically green in the face, though her husband seemed oblivious to this as he ran down what he perceived to be both a successful negotiation and a balm for their problem.

Byrne passed his hands down his face when Holden finished. "And you believed him?"

"I know you all have your suspicions of Aiden, but he no more wants a war with the king than any of us do," Holden said, still riding the rapid excitement of his reveal.

"He already has the means of preventing a war against the East-erlands," Gretchen said. "He brought a bride. We did not."

"And we will use that bride to appease the king, a display of fealty," Holden went on. He could hardly sit still. "To prove we are in accord. We will present Assana and then, together, we'll offer a five percent increase in taxes paid for the next five years, and will give his son and heir, when he comes of age, the choice of any bride in the kingdom."

"So we protect our children only to sell a grandchild?" Gretchen asked, incredulous.

"It will never come to pass, Gretchen. For, there is no 'we'," Asherley said. "Aiden has no reason to ally with us."

"I did what I felt we needed to bring this problem to conclusion. I will not apologize for that," Holden said to Gretchen. Turning to the others, he added, "Aiden said he would, and I'll have him at his word."

"Then you're a fool," Khallum spat. "You cannae take a creature like Aiden at his word. He's no man. Asherley is right. He has no motivation to aid us, and every reason not to. You cannae forget he didnae consult with us when he laid Rowanwen at the ratsbane's feet. He knew what he was doing then, and he knows it now."

"We hardly know him, and yet all here act like you've access to every last of his waking thoughts," Holden said, deflating.

"I ken your wife knows him well enough," Khallum said.

"It isn't hard to see that a war against the North or West or South is still a problem for the East. What happens when Eoghan gets a taste for conquering? This is his kingdom, yes, but we are all, all of us, still in possession of our own customs and ways, as was agreed in the King's Decree. If we force him to come for us, he'll strip us until we're mirrors of himself. And when he is done with the other Reaches, he will come for the Easterlands. Aiden knows this. He won't be exempt from such carnage."

"He played you, husband," Gretchen said, stepping away from the warmth of the hearth. Her hair had fallen from the neat plaits holding it together earlier, and she had the wild look of the wives of the miners of Leecaster Bay. Feral and otherworldly. Something stirred in Khallum's britches. "And none of us will know how much until it's too late to change course. He is the *only* one with something to offer this king, and that works better for him than if things had played out as arranged. Things could not be more fortuitous for Aiden than they are now. He won't let that advantage slip through his fingers."

Holden glared at her from across the chamber. "You cannot see far enough past your own hatred to appreciate that we've narrowly avoided a disaster we were not prepared to rise against." He pointed his finger at her. "I won't ask you to let go of what you feel for him. But, for once, have faith in *me.*"

"I have faith that Aiden now has confirmation of his suspicion that we were all plotting against him before he arrived, which, though you cannot see it, was the reason he chose *you* to talk to and not any of the rest of us, who would have seen through to the truth of it!"

Gretchen wrapped her shawl around her and fled the room. After a moment, Asherley followed.

Khallum nodded at his brother. Byrne returned it. Even now, after all the years and distance, words were extraneous. Byrne understood what Khallum didn't need to say.

There was no sense in staying to argue with a man who had tried, and failed, to slow the tidal force that would fall upon them in the morning. Holden would believe in his own convictions to the grave, and any further breaths spent were breaths wasted.

The Warwick brothers had their own plan, and, when the plans of others failed, they'd see it through.

"WE SHOULDN'T BE DOING THIS HERE," GRETCHEN SAID IN A RUSH, though she was the one who'd summoned him, in her desperation. "I hate myself for this weakness."

Ash held her against his chest, where she breathed in and out to the sound of a heart that had once beat so true, and only for her. "You're so strong, Sparrow. Stronger than you'll ever know."

"If I'm so strong, why can't I do this without you?"

"Strength doesn't mean doing everything alone. Strength is knowing when you cannot."

"You sound like Holden, in all his flowery hog shit."

Ash lifted her face to his. "I am *nothing* like Holden."

Gretchen stretched up to kiss him. "I know this. It's why I returned you to life."

"Holden is a fool, but he is a good man. One trait is hardly without the other," Ash said. "I'm neither a fool, nor a good man."

Gretchen didn't argue the point. Just as there was more than one sort of strength, good was only good in the definer's eye. To her, there was no better man than Drystan Sylvaine. She'd taken that conviction into labor, as she birthed the son Holden would forever believe was his, but was named for his true father.

Now the son was somewhere lost in the world, and the father only bound to it by magic that she feared would have an expiration.

"Something terrible will happen tomorrow morning." Gretchen finally put voice to the fear.

Ash nodded. "I'm sorry, Sparrow. I wish I could disabuse you of this belief." He kissed her. "But I won't lie to you."

"How bad will it be?"

Ash didn't answer.

ASHERLEY PRESSED HERSELF FLAT AGAINST THE STONE, FOCUSED ON conquering her heaving breaths.

Gretchen was the only one she trusted with what Maeryn had told her. Why, she couldn't quite say. She barely knew the woman, but in her she sensed something kindred. Something only another woman who was smarter and more capable than the men they were expected to serve would understand. Asherley served no man, but she never forgot how easily one would take it all from her if she gave them the opportunity.

But what she'd just seen…

Was Gretchen Dereham mad?

What other explanation could there be for a woman who would fall into the arms of the air and call it a man?

The answer was unimportant. The outcome was.

Asherley was alone in this, after all. Khallum and Byrne could scheme until the Guardians saw their promise fulfilled, Holden could hold fast to his idealist dreams of alliances, and Gwyn could wallow in her grief. Gretchen could continue to do whatever it was she did to survive.

Asherley had within her possession the only plan that could counteract Aiden's play for power, and Eoghan's overreach of it. If none were strong enough to join her, let them all be as surprised as the king when the moment arrived.

18

CHERRIES IN THE WINTERGARDEN

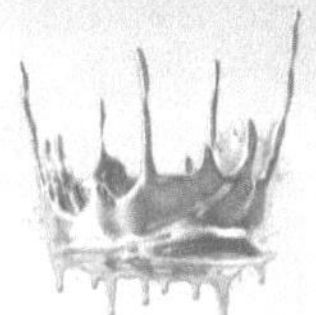

Stefan played with his piles of old driftwood, forming them into castles and warriors that lived solely in his imagination. She laughed as he told her about the battle brewing, through a pale face that had never seen the sunlight except through the thatches in their tiny window, and had no inkling of a castle beyond the words she'd chosen to help him see a world that would never exist for him.

Days since Eoghan had left for Termonglen. He rarely left Duncarrow. Until he departed, she spent her restless nights imagining that this was when they might starve to death, when with him went the knowledge that the two needed food and drink to survive. But at least one other person knew of their existence, for their two meals a day continued, as they always had, and they went on as they always had, except she had a reprieve from his strange demands.

On his day of departure, Eoghan had fallen asleep suckling her tender breast. Stefan had stopped requiring her milk years before, but Eoghan had kept this part of her alive with his inexplicable requests. He'd suckle sometimes for hours, curled up in her lap like a child needing succor. Sometimes he'd reach into his trousers.

Anabella had long overcome her disgust at watching him pleasure himself. She hated this now only because when he climaxed, he would bite down on her nipple hard enough to make it bleed.

He was so unlike Darrick. Darrick was built for strength, tall and sinewy, flesh full of life. Anabella wondered if this was what happened sometimes with twins. One taking all the milk, all their mother's precious resources, while the other suffered, sickly and unfulfilled. Eoghan was no taller than a young boy, and he hunched over when he walked, as if drawing all his strength into the core of him. His sallow cheeks and dark eyes regarded her with the exhaustion of one who looked death in the face each morning and somehow lived on to address another day.

But he was more dangerous than any man she'd ever known. Her father had wisdom about men like this, though until Eoghan, she'd never met one who fit the words. *Keep your eye on the weak ones. They will find their strength any way they can, at any cost.*

When she was certain Stefan was fully lost to his imagination, Anabella again pulled from the stack of vellum and returned to her story.

LIFE AT WEATHERFORD HALL WAS PEACEFUL. I WAS THE LAST OF FOUR daughters, and we were all true children of the Northerlands, joyous in the cold, disordered when the sun spent too much time warming the ground. As the youngest, I had more freedoms than the others, who were promised in marriages to other Great Families before I'd even made my appearance in the world. And what an appearance... to offer my gift of life, my mother forfeit her own, and though I was never made to feel at fault for this, it was a truth that became part of me, just the same.

My father was a good man. An honest man, who had earned his place amongst the Great Families the proper way, by making use of himself. His grandfather had started the business of fur trading, but it was my father who made the Weatherfords the foremost traders in all the Northerlands. His friendship with Holden Dereham, stemming from childhood, helped, no doubt, but my father's merits are what they are, and my sisters and I were raised knowing the trade in the way other girls never would. Without sons, he trained us, and we became his eager apprentices. He once told us that we could be both great ladies and great men, and to this day I count amongst my finest traits my ability to kill and dress an animal with my own hands, and then turn his fur into magic.

The Derehams bought all their furs from my father. Lord Dereham had no trouble coming to us, as he spent over half his time traveling his Reach, meeting with his men, but my father knew how the four of us loved Wulfsgate. In particular, the Wintergarden, which was unlike anywhere else in the kingdom, with cherry trees blooming in the dead of midwinter, and apples and grapes, and fruits that seemed gifted from the Guardians. We believed they were.

Twice, three times a year, we came to Wulfsgate. Even after my sisters made good marriages, my father took me with him, and it was on one of these trips that Darrick Rhiagain made his entrance into my life as well.

My father hadn't known the king's heir would be at Wulfsgate upon our arrival. For certain, he would've prepared especial furs for Prince Darrick, the one all the kingdom held their hopes upon. Already, the rumors said he wasn't like his father. That he was cut from the same mold as Fynne the Good, and that what had been taken from so many might be returned.

I watched from the shadows as my father, hands shaking, presented his furs to Lord Dereham with Darrick observing. And when Darrick remarked at how beautifully they'd been crafted, and asked if there were more, my father cried. Afraid what we'd brought wasn't fit for a future king. Wasn't good enough.

Darrick insisted that the furs were more than exceptional, and then he asked for more. Crestfallen, my father had no more, not in our wagon, but Darrick said he would wait, at Wulfsgate. And would that be all right? This future king asked a mere lord this, and though he didn't know it, not then, I fell in love with Darrick in the tick of a heartbeat.

Never, ever did I envision it could be a love that was returned.

I wasn't yet promised to anyone. My father seemed hesitant to release me to the world, though I was already seventeen, the same age my sisters had left Weatherford Hall for their own new lives and adventures. He'd told me he would keep me forever if he could, but that he understood that to do so would be unfair. He was always in conflict over this. I would have stayed with him forever, too. Would that I were a boy, I often said. And he, in return, promised me he'd never wished for anything more than what the Guardians had given him.

My father left me in Wulfsgate when he returned to Weatherford Hall to procure more furs for Prince Darrick. I liked the Dereham children, though they were younger than I was. The oldest, Christian, was already at the Sepulchre by then, and so I played with Drystan and Lisbet in the Wintergarden, as I once had with my own spirited sisters. Their mother was kind to me, and for the first time in my life, I realized what I'd been missing, having lost my own before I knew her.

And I learned Lord Dereham, too, had a playful side. He was a most unusual man. My father had, of course, told me the tale of Hadden's Bane. Of the fate of Hadden Dereham's true heir, Rinn, and everything that came after. I was, myself, from an unusual family; a great house with no male heirs. It fascinated me to think of Holden Dereham as he realized, once a spare and now an heir, that the fate of his Reach was now settled upon his shoulders. Drystan would experience this, too, I could see. Even then, it was clear Christian didn't intend to return.

Drystan and Lisbet were pulled to their studies during the day, and I spent that time reading from the books in their library. We didn't have a library at Weatherford Hall. Books were too costly, and my father sent me to a local scholar for my own studies. The Dereham children took their instruction at home, and so the books available to me were not unlike the ones the scholar bade me read as a child. Many of them were sections of The Book of All Things, from histories to foods and animals. But there were also several tomes filled with local legends. It wasn't common to find written words that did not further knowledge, but some existed, and I was pleased to find Lord Dereham had several in his possession.

I most liked the ones about the Medvedev and the Ravenwoods. Though the Ravenwoods sent their children into the larger towns to practice their magic—and I had been acquainted with several, however briefly—they betrayed nothing about themselves to anyone outside of their blood. It was said some had defected over the years, like the infamous Rhosyn, and that this is where the stories originated, but no one knew for sure.

I was reading one such story in the Wintergarden when Darrick surprised me. It was less that he'd snuck up on me, though he had, and more that he was there at all! Was he lost? I quickly prepared to offer him instruction back to the keep, but he wanted to know what I was reading. Failing a better response, I answered him.

He confessed that he was also curious about the origins of these creatures, like men, but not. But he asked if I had those same questions about the Rhiagains, who had also come from Beyond. I said that it was not my place to have questions about the royal family, and he said that if I had them, he would answer. I didn't, I said, though I did. My father would be horrified if he'd learned I wasn't only speaking with Prince Darrick, but also questioning his origin. Of all the things!

But Darrick told me anyway.

He was only fifteen, closing in on sixteen, but he seemed more man than boy, and I could see then the king he could become.

He told me first what we were all accustomed to believing. That the Rhiagains had come from a kingdom that made ours pale in comparison. A place so great that there could be no imagining what you could not see with thine own eyes.

And then he told me the truth.

"We do not know," he said. "That is the terribleness of it. Wherever we came from before ceased to be a place where we could live. I don't know the whole story, but some say there was a great fire that ran unabated after a year of no rain. We left in search of something better, became lost, and shipwrecked at sea. Most of us died. Those that lived, rolling to shore, invented a tale of great kings and gods out of fear. We didn't know if whoever greeted us would kill us or imprison us, so we decided instead they should worship us."

"Why are you telling me this?" I asked him.

"Because you are curious," he said.

I slammed the book shut, heart racing. I'd compelled this future king to tell me a terrible secret, and now I was in for a world of trouble.

Darrick kissed me. I think he may have been trying to calm me, but when it was done, he asked if he could do it again and I said yes.

"I'll never tell," I whispered when he pulled away. "I swear to you, Your Grace. I would never tell a soul."

"I know that," he said. "Though I rather wish you would."

I felt the heat rise in my cheeks, and he laughed at my scandalized expression.

"When I am king..." he trailed off. "There are better ways. My grandfather knew this. He tried to put it all to rights, but some things are not so easily changed back."

"About the kiss, either," I went on, in a rush, wondering when I'd lose the courage. "I won't tell tales about it."

Darrick kissed me again. "Which one? That one?" Another kiss. "Or that one?" And yet another. "Or the ones that came before, or after?"

"After?"

"I apologize. I shouldn't be kissing you without your permission. I won't kiss you again unless you give it expressly."

"Why would you kiss me at all, Your Grace?"

"I don't know," he said, with a whimsical look. He reached for a lush pink branch of the cherry tree and pulled it down, inhaling the scent. "Why do the cherries bloom in midwinter in this garden?"

"Persistence," I said before I could stop, again, this terrible tendency of mine to be impertinent.

"Persistence," he said, laughing. "I would name my daughter that."

"What a terrible curse, to be thought of as so unfeminine!"

He was still laughing when he released the branch and took my hand in his. "You're not like the girls chosen for us."

"I don't understand."

"We have no say in the brides we are given. No say in any of it," Darrick said. "The wives of the Rhiagain are chosen from the most unremarkable families intentionally. They picked the young women for their amicability, not their suitability. There can be no uprising without wealth

and power, right? No troubles in marriage with a wife who is nothing but agreeable?"

I realized I didn't know where the queens had come from. None bore any great names. And I realized, too, that I wasn't meant to wonder, and that was the point.

"You have a bride chosen, then?"

"Most likely, yes."

"You'll grow to love her."

"We're all capable of anything when we must," Darrick said. "I'm sorry I've interrupted your quest for discovery." He pointed at the book. "I'll let you return to it..."

I realized he was after my name. "Anabella."

"Anabella. That's not a name I'd forget," he said and instead of kissing me, he gave me a sad smile. Having already scandalized my father, and family name, I almost asked him to stay. He waited, as if I might.

The next morning, I awoke to find a book at my bedside. The title was The Ballad of Rhosyn *and a note sat atop, reading, 'If you finish before I'm to return to Duncarrow, let us discuss even more truths where the cherries blossom in the snow.'*

"Mommy! Look!"

Anabella set aside the quill. Stefan waved a patched together pile of sticks and cloth from the shirts he'd outgrown. She squinted, knowing he expected her to identify this new creation without prompting, but her imagination had died the day she knew she'd never leave this dungeon.

"It's incredible, love."

"Don't you know what it is?"

"Of course. It's your creation."

"It's a ship, Mama! Like the ones outside. Like that one." He ran to the window and pointed.

How she'd been tempted, in those early days, to wave and scream until someone saw her. But these were the king's ships, bearing the Rhiagain crossed swords upon their waving flags. Beyond them, the Isle of Belcarrow, where the Rhiagain Guard and

Knights of Duncarrow lived and trained, reminded them of how far the prison extended.

Their only friends here were the strange comforts of sticks and old threads.

"One day, I'll be on one," Stefan said, and Anabella turned her head so he wouldn't witness her tears.

She wasn't done writing, but her heart was spent. Anabella curled the vellum into the tightest coil and slipped it into the hole in the drain, like she had before. She held her breath until she heard it move down the pipe, away from them, toward the sea.

Anabella wrapped her fingers in the steel bars covering the window. She pressed her face to the rusted metal and whispered her prayers to the Guardian of the Treasured Past.

19

NIGHT

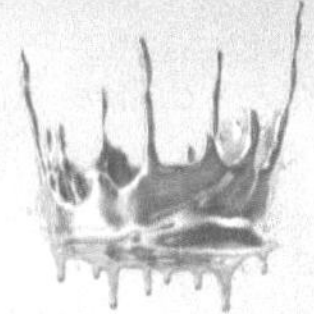

The women swayed to the music, which was not music at all, but the melodies of the wind falling off the mountains. If you listened close enough, Adynora said, you could even hear words.

Ravenna watched, enraptured. She couldn't hear the music or the words. Her mother, Varinya, said the music grew louder and more demanding for those close to their time as High Priestess. Adynora was dying, and this was her last dance. Not death as the men below understood it, but First Death, which meant a passing of the veil of duty. Drystan would call it retirement, but men retired when they were close to their True Death. A Ravenwood could live a hundred years after their First Death.

Ravenna once asked her mother why there was a First Death at all, and it was not Varinya who answered but Ravenna's grandmother, Adynora herself. Our lives are far too long for us to hold such power for more than a season. Once we pass the mantle to our daughters, we rule beside the High Priestess and Priest until their own daughter is five, and has survived the peril present in early days. And then we retreat into our gossamer years, which we have earned by staying true to duty, to blood. For many, the First Death is when the Ravenwood women truly begin to live.

All this talk of death unsettled Ravenna at five years of age. Her grand-mother, dancing to the ethereal song of her First Death, had lived only thirty-seven years. She might survive to two hundred. Some did. Most of her years were ahead, not behind.

Varinya, drunk on her power, laughed at her mother. She told Ravenna not to listen to the old woman. Old. Not a wrinkle, her hair still black as midnight. When Ravenna's own oldest daughter turned five, she would watch her mother dance this dance, and Varinya would be no older than Adynora was now.

Ravenna, too, would dance this dance. And would it be the end, or the beginning, of her life?

Alasyr took her by the hand and pulled her away from the dancing, out into the open balustrades overlooking mountains none but the Ravenwoods could ever see from this vantage point. He showed her the bread he'd snuck from the kitchen and together, giggling, they broke off pieces and hid their faces as they stuffed them. Alasyr could eat as he wished, but she could not. She must, always, wear the dresses of her forbears, which must never be hemmed or altered. Her food, her drink, her play, all was so closely observed, but Alasyr saw she was more than what she must become, and looked for ways, within his means, to provide her these small but important rebellions.

I don't want it, any of it, *Ravenna said, out loud for the first time in her life.*

I don't want you to be killed for that, *Alasyr said then, and between them passed both this truth and another: he couldn't stop what fate had determined for her, but he could make it easier, and he did.*

Later, much later, her mother watched as another Ravenwood brushed Ravenna's long hair, which sprang up in defiant curls at the ends. Varinya frowned at these and cut them off, but as her hair grew again, they returned.

Do you know where you come from, Ravenna?

Midnight Crest, Mother.

But before? Has it come to you yet? The memory of who we were?

Ravenna didn't know what her mother was talking about, and if she should say so, or pretend she did. She'd asked her mother before about the world the Ravenwoods had come from before coming to the kingdom, and the answer had always been the same. No one knew.

No, Mother.

Varinya dropped her eyes, but not before Ravenna sensed the disappointment burning. She'd failed again, at a test or task she'd not even known how to prepare for.

Let us hope you will, before the Langenacht.

You… you do, Mother? You know who we were?

Yes.

Why won't you tell me?

You must discover it for yourself. As all High Priestesses do. Do you know, Ravenna, why it is the women who rule Midnight Crest?

Ravenna shook her head.

Because we and we alone hold these memories within us. There are no males within us who possess anything of who we were. Only us. The women. Is it so surprising, really? That those bred for nurturing and ushering others through the cycles of life would be the ones to protect the truth of it?

Ravenna didn't know this word, nurturing. Later, she'd remember it, when she knew the meaning, and wonder why her mother had used it at all, because there'd been nothing like it in her childhood. Her nightly kisses were perfunctory. The only hug she recalled her mother offering was when Ravenna had nearly fallen from the stone walls as a wee one, and Varinya had crushed her to her chest in gasping relief.

Ravenna's thoughts whirled forward in time, to her fourteenth birthday. One year from the Langenacht. On that day, as with all birthdays, Varinya again asked her daughter if she'd seen their histories. As with all birthdays before, Ravenna contemplated her answer, weighing the lie, settling upon the truth.

Later that night, she overheard her mother and father talking.

Maybe she isn't the one.

Argentyn, she has to be. It has never gone to a second, or third daughter, unless the first perished.

She spends all her time with the Derehams, and yet her magic is still undeveloped.

And how do we know this wasn't the way for others before her? We only know the experiences of the High Priestesses still living among us.

We have but one year. She cannot see the ancestors. She cannot create fire, or ice.

She can heal, Argentyn, and I can think of no better magic than one that preserves. You worry about whether she can destroy?

I worry about whether she is worthy.

On the night of her fifteenth birthday, Varinya again asked Ravenna if she could see their histories and this time Ravenna lied.

Yes, she had said, she could see them all. In all their glories and triumphs.

Heart racing, she waited for her mother to ask her to prove it, to share a story, or a memory to validate Ravenna's claim.

But Varinya did not.

Varinya knew her daughter was lying.

RAVENNA'S FACE AND NECK WERE DRENCHED IN TEARS AND SWEAT when she awoke with a violent start. She looked around the camp at the others, still sleeping. Even Drystan, snoring, oblivious at her side.

She scrambled out of her bedroll and breathed in the cool air, letting the scratches from the broken branches and undergrowth from their ledge above the world bring her back to it.

She looked down, over the valley below, blanketed in snow. They'd still not run far enough to escape who she was, but she didn't think she wanted to escape it. A part of her sensed that there'd be a type of death once she passed that threshold, one Rhosyn Ravenwood surely experienced when she turned her back on everything.

Ravenna closed her eyes and turned to flight, but she didn't immediately change form. It had been like this for days, worsening. She closed her eyes once more and focused. It worked, but the twinge of pain accompanying her internal commands was sharper now.

As she flew off, away, from nowhere, to nowhere, Ravenna thought of all the lies she'd told and been told, and wondered wherein the truth—*her* truth—existed.

Lisbet tried to breathe, but had to force herself to push against this instinct. With every exhale, something sharp greeted her skin, and each sound made in protest deepened the sting. She wasn't asleep anymore. This wasn't a dream. She could see so little in the darkness.

Eavan's screams grounded her. She tried to search for the source, but a hot grunt in her ear was the first tangible truth that surfaced as she put the pieces together. Someone had her pinned in his arms. He had a knife at her throat.

Lisbet opened her mouth again, but the stranger hissed a warning in her ear. They weren't words; it was some incomprehensible sound, without accent or place. She knew only he wasn't from her father's people.

Eavan screamed again, and this time the sound came with another; the rough tear of fabric indelicately ripped away.

Where was Drystan? Ravenna?

Lisbet's eyes adjusted to the darkness. She could see, now, the outline of Eavan and… and another, in jarring movement atop of her. Eavan's head turned to the side and her eyes glowed through the obscurity of night, but a hand now covered her mouth, and her screams died away.

A heavy horror spread through Lisbet. The last of her sleep left her. A sickening tingle traveled through her, limb to limb, and whatever brief respite she'd had, where she didn't yet know what was going on, had passed with the sight of Eavan lying helpless under another dangerous man.

But now she heard Drystan, too. Indistinct echoes of him struggling and being put down, again and again, like a dog under heel. His groans rolled through the camp at the sound of boots swiftly connecting, not once, not twice, but ongoing, past the point where it made sense to count. She heard a crack as something broke. And then Drystan, too, went silent.

Ravenna? Where was Ravenna?

Eavan's cries again pierced the night as the man rolled off her and another took his place. The one who'd assaulted Eavan tramped through the branches and brush and then knelt down before Lisbet. His filthy face filled her vision, obscuring anything else.

"Dinnae worry," he whispered. He licked her cheek. "We'll not leave ye out."

She knew that accent. But from where?

"Leave... her alone," Lisbet managed as the blade this time broke skin. "Leave her alone!"

Both men laughed. The one with Lisbet turned to look at his friend, a third man, now taking his turn with Eavan. "Aye, because ye said so, lass?"

Lisbet struggled against the strong arms binding her. She couldn't bear to think of Eavan, alone, enduring this terrible violence. Worse was her utter helplessness to stop any of it. "I have money. I can give you anything. As much as you want."

"Aye, we'll take that, too."

"Please. Please let her go. Please don't do this."

The man kneeling looked behind her, at his friend. "Aye, we could give that one a break, I reckon, and switch to this one?"

"It's my turn," the one holding Lisbet said. "I always go last."

"We'll all get as many turns as we want, Rolph. Today the Guardians have delivered virgins. Virgins!" the other said. Lisbet didn't know if this name would matter, but she noted it, saying it over and over in her head, committing it to memory in hope of a time where she could exact a revenge a thousand times worse.

"Not that one. Not anymore."

Drystan's soft groans caught the attention of the two men with Lisbet. The one not holding her went to see to it when something stopped him in his tracks. He went still and then fell over. Only after did Lisbet register the whistle passing through the air, and as she heard it again, and the man behind her went stiff and then limp, her confusion shifted, but it wasn't quite relief.

She scrambled away from her attacker, searching the darkness for Drystan. Eavan made a heaving noise, and then what sounded like the man who'd been hurting her landing in a tangle of briar.

A strong arm pulled Lisbet to her feet. Someone new. He asked her something, if she was okay, but now that she was no longer in imminent danger, her ears started ringing, as if delivering her to somewhere that things like this didn't happen. Not to girls like her and Eavan. Not to anyone.

Lisbet nodded, propelled into action by instinct. This new man was beckoning her to come. He reached for Eavan and in one move had her over his shoulder.

"Help me with Drystan," he commanded, and instead of asking the man how he knew any of their names, Lisbet followed his order. Drystan was badly injured. He could hardly stand. But she aided this new stranger as they dragged him toward one of the horses, Starcaller, and draped him over the saddle.

"I need you to lead the horses and follow me," he said to Lisbet. He was looking directly at her. His eyes were gentle, but was he? He'd saved their lives, but that told her nothing else, nothing important. Did she have any other path than to follow him and his word?

Lisbet nodded. Instead of looking into his eyes, she focused on his longbow. She'd only seen one like it in the Westerlands, where they trained their men to be one with their weapons.

"Lisbet, all will be well, but we must be quick. There will be more of them. There are always more."

"Where… where are we going?"

"There is a farm, not thirty minutes by foot, quicker by horse. No one lives there. Not anymore."

"You know the way?"

"I know it," the man said.

"Rav—our other friend. She's not here. She needs to know where we've gone."

"Ravenna will know how to find you. Now come."

THE MAN SAID HIS NAME WAS VALEN. LISBET DIDN'T THINK THIS WAS his real name, but after what he'd done for them, she'd call him anything he wished.

A fire awaited in the hearth, and a rich stew simmered in the cauldron over flames. He asked her to settle the horses into the barn at the back and bring anything of value inside with her. By the time she was done and back in the farmhouse, Valen already had the wounds of Drystan and Eavan dressed, and the two sleeping on the single bed in the corner of the main room.

Valen offered Lisbet a stone bowl, and she accepted it with greedy appreciation, lapping up every last bite before he'd made much progress on his own. She eyed a hunk of bread growing stale on another table with feral hunger.

"Do you live here?" Lisbet asked.

"At present." Valen removed a knife from his vest and went toward the bread Lisbet hadn't taken her gaze from. He cut a generous slice and handed it to her.

"Is that how you found us? You could hear from here?"

"No," Valen said, without elaboration. "I've never seen them so far north."

"Who are they?"

"Others call them the Blackpool Brigands. I don't know what they call themselves."

Lisbet thought that sounded like something made up; like what

Drystan would call them when they played pirates in the Wintergarden. "Blackpool. That's in the Southerlands."

Valen nodded. "You're old enough to have studied the maps."

"I love maps," Lisbet said. "I want to see the whole kingdom one day."

"I imagine you will, then."

"Not unless…" Lisbet stopped herself. This man, Valen, had saved them, tended the wounds of Drystan and Eavan, and filled her belly. The danger she'd sensed earlier was passed, even if the effects would linger on between all of them, for longer than she could know. But she didn't know this man.

And *where* was Ravenna?

"I know who you are," Valen said. "Where you come from."

Lisbet dropped her spoon in the bowl. He'd been using their names all along, so of course… of course he knew. This should have set her hair on end, but it didn't.

He reached a hand across the wooden table but didn't touch her. "Lisbet, I'm not here to return you to a home you ran from."

"How do you know? Who are you?"

"I told you who I am," Valen said. "I know you the way any man of the Northerlands knows his land. I know your father." He took a sip from his mug. "Your mother."

Lisbet cast a glance toward the longbow leaning against the wall. "You're no Northerlander."

"Not always," he said. "But I am now."

"Why are you helping us?"

"Why must someone always have a reason to be kind?"

Lisbet frowned. She looked at the bed, where both Drystan and Eavan remained lost to sleep. Had he given them a draught? Or were the wounds that grievous? Drystan's, of the body, Eavan's, of the soul. Lisbet's mother had a way with nursing and had said before that sleep was the best protection, better than any medicine she could proffer. Gretchen had learned this from her own mother, she said, but of course Lisbet had never met her grandmother.

"All men I've known seek something in return for a favor."

"Then you haven't known the best men."

"Hmm," she said. "Since you say you know everything—"

"I definitely don't know everything, Lisbet." Valen smiled.

"Since you know *so much,* tell me, where are we going?"

"Well, I cannot say I know where you're going, but I can tell you what I suspect."

Lisbet nodded. "Go on, then."

"The Hinterlands," Valen said. "Though you're off course. By a day or so, at the pace you're traveling. Not surprising, as even those experienced with the trails beyond the Compass Roads struggle with keeping true to their path."

"When you say experienced men, you mean like you."

Valen nodded. He cut another slice of bread for her, but she shook her head. There wasn't much left. Drystan and Eavan would need it more, when they woke. And Ravenna, if she hadn't returned to Midnight Crest.

Lisbet didn't think she had, but if not, where was she? Had she run away when she saw the brigands fall upon the camp? *Would* she just leave them, all of them, undefended? Lisbet should know this answer, but in understanding why she didn't, it dawned upon her how little they knew Ravenna at all.

"You think we're safe here, tonight? From the brigands?"

Valen leaned back in his chair. She got her first good look at the stranger who'd saved them all. Pale hair, pale eyes. No older than her father, but this man had seen things her father hadn't, and it was written in every line around his mouth, every blink of his eyes. He was beautiful, in the way Eavan was beautiful, but beauty wasn't the word running through Lisbet's mind as she assessed him.

"They won't come here," he said after a pause.

"How can you be sure?"

"The Blackpool Brigands rely on stealth and surprise. I have this farm rigged with traps, and they know it."

"Traps?"

"Sounds. Tin and wires, stretched across ground and sky. I change the design every few days so they have no proper time to learn it."

Lisbet remembered now that he'd taken them on a strange path to the door, and had told her to follow the same when she was done with the horses. She'd still been in shock and hadn't thought much of the request. Now that her shock was wearing off, there was no telling what else would come back to her, welcome or not.

"Or maybe they're afraid of you and your bow."

Valen grinned. "Could be." He reached for her bowl. "Would you like more?"

Lisbet shook her head. "Save some for when they wake." She looked up at him. "They will... wake?"

"Of course. I gave them some root of Valeria, so their sleep could aid in healing them. But they'll heal so much faster if your friend returns. Ravenna."

Lisbet's heart skipped.

"Your priestess. I saw her in the skies earlier tonight." He read the panicked look on her face and softened his own. "Lisbet, I'm not after a bounty. I don't intend to tell your mother or father we've crossed paths. I have no motivation to harm Ravenna, or any of you. If you know how to bring her back, do it swiftly. Drystan's injuries will take months to heal without the proper care, and I suspect you don't have months to stay here, do you?"

Lisbet shook her head.

"No," he said, nodding. "I'll help you find your way to the Hinterlands, when Drystan is well enough for the voyage. There's nothing more to be done tonight." He pointed toward a ladder and a loft. "You'll find a blanket and some rags up top. Not what you're used to in Wulfsgate Keep, but preferable to sleeping on the cold ground."

"Thank you," Lisbet said. Her voice cracked. "For your kindness."

"Off to bed with you."

. . .

Ravenna found the farm asleep when she arrived. She didn't come upon the place by accident. The pendant Drystan wore around his neck, the one she'd given him, was connected to her own, and because of this she could always find him, anytime, anywhere. She couldn't recall if she'd told him this when she gave him the gift.

But she'd found him too late. Consumed by her own confusion and miserable wallowing, she'd flown away and now he was broken. Eavan was broken—violently ripped into her womanhood. She might never be the same. Now *nothing* was the same.

Ravenna told herself she didn't possess the magic required to have fought off the attack, but though this was true, it left her hollow. She'd surrendered to the vacant call of her own hollow distress while the others experienced *true* suffering. She hadn't seen Drystan beaten almost beyond life, but she felt it now, watching him sleep through his tormented healing. Still, and then thrashing until the moment eased. Calling out for his mother. For Ravenna.

Her hands shook as she held them aloft and, again, tried with all she had within her to heal him. She lost count of how many times she'd pressed her palms to his flesh and commanded him to return to his complete self. Each time, small progresses, but never what she knew she could do. What she'd done the day she saved Gretchen Dereham's life, and bound Drystan to her forever.

"You're far from home," a man said, settling into the chair beside her. They hadn't met yet, but she knew he'd been the one to save them all. But did he know what *she'd* done? How, after finding the dead men at the camp, she had flown through the night to find the others and killed them all, one by one? It hadn't been easy. She'd never learned to destroy, as her parents could. But she rained fire upon them anyway, using the tools of man. Sticks and flame from their own campfire. And then she'd settled upon the high branch of a tree and watched them all burn.

"Thank you for saving them."

He laid a hand upon her shoulder. "Rest for a moment. It isn't your fault. You're separated from the source."

Ravenna shrugged his hand away. "What are you talking about?"

"Your magic, Ravenna."

"How do you know my name?"

"If you'd been here earlier, I would've told you what I told Lisbet. I know all of you. But you don't need to be afraid of me."

"Who are you?"

"My name is Valen."

"The hell it is."

He smiled. "What's a name, anyway? Does it matter if we use the one our mothers gave us, or the one we've chosen for ourselves?"

"You know nothing of our magic," Ravenna said.

"I know what happened to Rhosyn when she went to the Westerlands."

"Rhosyn was a traitor."

Valen laughed. "All of us are traitors when we pursue our own happiness, aren't we? When we go against what others have decided for us?"

"You know nothing of me. Of my magic. My family."

"I know it is strongest at the source, and what you're experiencing now will grow worse as you find yourself farther from home."

"I've healed him," Ravenna shot back. "Look at his arm. It's no longer broken."

"It took one tick of the moon for that, and you still have so far to go," Valen said. "Ravenna, I'm not trying to add to your grief. I can see it in you. We always give up something for love, don't we?"

"What would you know about that?"

"More than some," Valen said. "Rhosyn gave up everything, by the opinions of some, but what she gained was so much greater. All things in life have value, and that value is determined by the beholder. I don't know how Rhosyn perceived the loss of her potent magic, but I know she loved the man she'd given it up for until the end of her days."

Ravenna turned away from him. She loathed that this man, this stranger, was right, and could know something she did not. No one had ever talked about Rhosyn after she left, except to brand her as a defector, never again welcome. And because of this, no one had followed her life or her story. No one knew her fate, except men, and this particular man who knew more than Ravenna ever had.

"You can stay here as long as you need," Valen said. "And when you're ready, I will take you to the Hinterlands, by the most straightforward path."

"We'll find our own way."

"Rest, Ravenna. Try again at sunrise."

He left her. She again looked down at Drystan, eyes bruised shut, mouth split near in half. She'd been the one to say, *we must leave,* and in his beautiful idealism he'd seen a world where they could make it work, all of it, no matter the complications. And even after she failed to see what she'd asked him to do, he held fast, to her, to their love, to whatever future they could make if they stayed true to one another.

But she had not been true. Not to Drystan. Not to herself. Not to her family, her blood, her fate.

Ravenna pressed his broken hand to her mouth and quietly sobbed.

20

THE BEAR

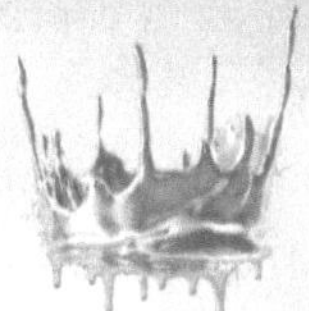

When they'd stepped into the Hinterlands for the first time, Marsh shuddered. She'd ignored his fears and knelt upon the shimmering blue grass, speaking her intentions to the earth, moon, sun, and sky, as her mother had taught her. *We come filled with peace and good intent. We seek only to pass through. The Compass Roads are barred to us, our life forfeit if we traverse them. We will be swift, and aimed true, and will cause no disrupt to your life, which is your own. We come filled with peace and good intent. We ask for safe passage.*

"What are you doing?"

"Protecting us."

His face paled. "You never said a word about going through the Hinterlands."

"Just how did you expect to reach the Northerlands, Marsh? Magic?" She sighed. "Gabi, Brook, and Meadow will be in the Hinterlands as well. If it was so terrible, would I have sent my own sister there?"

"It's forbidden, Ember. They could slaughter us, and no one would raise a hand in defiance, for we would be in the wrong."

"We will be captured, and likely killed, if we travel by road. The Medvedev are peaceful, and we're children in their eyes. We mean them no harm. They will know this."

He'd said nothing more, as she withdrew her map. Asgill was the only clahnn on the western side of the Reach, and it would be easy to circumvent without adding time to their voyage. But all the Hinterlands was sacred ground, and she wouldn't know if her words would be enough to allow them to pass without trouble until they were clear of the Reach, or a captive of it. They had to be, or she'd sent Gabi to her doom.

That was nigh a week ago, and though the Medvedev had left them alone, danger pressed forth into their journey.

First, Marsh's horse fell ill.

The cursed thing was old. Ember had told him to pick one with better range, but he'd insisted the old nag was family, and that he couldn't leave her behind. Ember had intentionally left her own favorite, Prue, back in Longwood Rush, for precisely this reason. She *was* family. And out here, Ember couldn't protect her, or even feed her properly. For all she knew, the flora in the Hinterlands wasn't fit for consumption by the horses of man.

Marsh prayed to the Guardians day and night. He seemed to believe they heard him, too. Ember didn't have the heart to tell him that the weather, and, with it, what would be available to the horses to graze, would grow even more sparse. Susannah—an odd name for a horse, but so was Prue, she supposed—wouldn't last another few days in current conditions, and they couldn't afford to stop.

The day after Susannah stopped eating, they awoke to find half their own remaining food had been stolen in the night by forest creatures. A bear, she thought, but dared not think it for long, for they were no match for a beast of this size.

Marsh cried. Ember looked to the north, toward answers. She ignored the bloody blisters on the bottoms of her feet, the cracks in the skin near her fractured fingernails. Even the pang of hunger, of a stomach never satisfied, she could tune out with other thoughts, which were mostly a trail of questions she'd spent her whole life not asking.

The deeper they went into the Forest of All, the less certain she was that this path was safer. She wondered if the Medvedev had plagued them for this choice after all, sending other horrors to thwart them rather than coming themselves.

"These are signs, Ember. Signs from the Guardians. We shouldn't be here," Marsh pleaded as she single-mindedly adjusted the saddle on her own horse, which had no name. More than likely someone *had* named it, but she preferred the distance created by thinking of it as a creature and not as a friend.

"The Guardians." Ember scoffed. "Would you listen to yourself? You think the Guardians stole the food from Susannah? You think they possessed the bears and deer to come take our food?"

"You shouldn't speak of them that way. Of course they didn't."

She turned. "Then what?"

"They don't care about such trivial things, but they watch us, Ember. They measure us by our decisions. We're being punished for leaving as we did."

"Then go home, if you feel so strongly."

"I would never leave you. Even if I wanted to. They'd judge me ever more harshly for that."

"Do you know how foolish you sound?"

"I'm afraid for you, that you would even say that."

Ember stepped away from her horse. "The Guardians are symbolic, Marsh. They're set in place for us to have comfort and consequences. Nothing more."

Marsh stared at her as if she'd grown a second, third, and then fourth head. "You don't mean that."

"I do."

"Tell me why. How?"

"Tell me first why you believe as you do."

"Because these are the teachings of the Resplendent Reliquary of the Guardians. The words written in *The Great Codex*."

"And who created the Resplendent Reliquary of the Guardians? Who wrote the *Codex*?"

"They did. The Guardians."

"That's wrong, and you know it."

Marsh shuffled in place. "The Guardians chose the Rhiagains. They'd been waiting for the right stewards to come along to usher structure for the reliquary. It was always meant to happen."

"Or," Ember said. "The Rhiagain chose the Guardians. There was a time when worship of the Guardians was personal and pure. And then, these men from Beyond come to our shores and they *tell* us how to worship, and where, and when, and they put so many rules around it that we lose sight of what we believed in the first place."

"You can't know that any more than I can. This all happened years before we were born. Hundreds of years."

"And by making your point you've also proven mine."

Marsh backed away as if afraid of catching whatever plague had diseased her mind. "I thought I knew you, Emberley. How can we have gone our entire lives, and I never knew you were a traitor to The Reliquary?"

"You can't ride Susannah anymore," Ember said evenly. She was weary of Marsh's contrived histrionics. She'd seen enough of the blindly faithful in her life and knew them to be faithful first, reasonable second. Marsh had listened to his father for too long. "You'll have to ride with me."

"We won't leave her!"

"We won't," Ember said. *Not yet.* She didn't relish what she'd have to do in a day or so, when Marsh could not. "But she isn't strong enough to bear your weight."

"I'll walk."

"Then you'll be left behind."

Marsh found yet another incredulous look to level upon her, but she was impervious. They had one goal, just as her other siblings had theirs. If the Guardians *were* watching over them, it would be this, their resolve, that would be judged.

And they were so close to the Northerlands now.

In the end, he climbed on the back of her nameless horse and held to her waist only tight enough to stay on, making his reluctance known in sighs.

Ember pushed forward, deeper into the storm.

Gabi and the Sullen Siblings, as she called them in her head, hadn't left the cave in days.

Following her first burst of courage, they'd made some progress, but she had to face reality. She wasn't Ember. She wasn't even Brandyn, who, though the youngest, seemed propelled forward by the fear that if he didn't take a leap, he'd be still forever. She didn't know where they were going. What to say when they got there. Who to ask for. All Ember had given her were the words to speak to the earth, moon, sun, and sky, so that their intentions were clear and known.

They'd traded one cave for another. The Hidden Cave was what brought them all together. First, Hollyn and Ember had played there with Storm, and later Marsh came along. When Gabi was older, she, too, came. And then the Ashenhurst siblings found their way into the fold, and, because it felt wrong to exclude him, they'd dragged Brandyn along, too.

The Hidden Crew, they called themselves, seldom together all at once, often with months between meeting at all. The other children were from Great Families throughout the Westerlands, and came to Longwood Rush when their parents visited. They were great friends, sometimes lovers—only in their imaginative play—often enemies, and always family. Even when the oldest ones grew out of their need to play, they still came, for The Hidden Crew.

And they'd come together one last time, for this. Ember had convinced every one of them to leave their homes, upon the faith of her vision, on the back of a vow of loyalty they could have never imagined would lead them to this, for a plan that had more chance of failure than success.

Like The Hidden Cave, they had to leave this one, too. Gabi had to find the courage, because the Sullen Siblings looked to her in absence of their own. Their questions only chipped away at her strength. What was happening? Why hadn't they moved from the cave? Should they return home? Would their food run out? Why was Gabi hesitating?

I don't know was her resounding answer for all these queries, if she even bothered to respond at all. Mostly, she preferred the memory of her father singing songs about the great rivers and streams, perfectly nonsensical little numbers, but lively and hilarious when he sang them to her. *Am I a river? Am I a stream? Oh, what body of water carries me into this dream?* And she would really, honestly consider her answer. What was she? A river? A stream? Her answer was always different, and he loved to hear her reasoning.

Sometimes he'd take her with him when he went hunting. He didn't take the others. Hollyn was too proper, and Ember was always off on some adventure or another. Gabi knew her father would have preferred to take his son, but Brandyn was too little, and then one day he was simply gone, sent to the Sepulchre. So Byrne settled for her, though he never, ever made it feel like a consolation.

Ah, look, a stream! He'd cry, and then he'd sing the song, and ask her if she was a river, or a stream, and she'd say, *oh, I'm a stream, I'm right there!* And he'd laugh, and laugh, and then get very serious and tell her that streams struggled to be still, but if they were to catch a deer, she would have to be very much *unlike* a stream in that moment, so they could catch the deer unawares.

"Gabi."

"Gabrianna."

See, Father, I can be a perfectly behaved stream! She'd say as she helped him first find and then dress the deer. She never flinched at the blood or entrails. She wanted to, but it was very important to her that her father see that she was strong and capable.

"Gabi!"

"What?" Gabrianna screamed the words violently as she was ripped from one of her most favorite memories. "What? What is it now? What question can I fail to answer for you now, Meadow?"

Meadow exchanged a look with her brother, Brook. "There's a boy outside."

"There's a *what?*"

"A boy."

"What nonsense is this?"

"A boy, Gabi. Outside the cave. He wants to speak to you."

Ah, so she *had* lost her mind. When? Maybe before they even reached this cave. Maybe this whole voyage had been a product of her imagination. Maybe—

"Gabrianna." Brook this time. He kneeled before her. "I know it seems mad, but there really is a boy outside, and he has the most incredible violet hair—"

Gabi rocked forward. "Did you say violet hair?"

"Yes, violet. Like purple."

"Yes, I know what violet means," Gabi said, but she wasn't paying him any mind. Violet hair. A boy. Outside the cave.

Was this what Ember meant when she said, *Only go, Gabi. Go and reach the point where you will know what comes next.*

"Gabi?"

"He asked for me by name?"

"Yes, only he said Mistress of Longwood Rush."

Gabrianna nearly laughed. Mistress of Longwood Rush! How much nicer that sounded than simply Gabi, unremarkable middle child of Lady Blackwood.

"All right, then. Invite him in."

· · ·

EMBERLEY WAITED UNTIL MARSH WENT TO RELIEVE HIMSELF A FEW paces off the trail. She whispered in Susannah's ear, reminding her she'd been a good and true horse, a dear friend to her master, and then drew the blade over her neck. Ember held her as she died and then laid several long branches over her body.

"I'm sorry, Marsh. She was failing even faster than I thought."

Marsh dropped to his knees by the corpse of his oldest friend. Ember knew she should comfort him, but she needed him strong, at her side, not folded into his own emotions.

They should dress and eat the mare. She'd never liked the sweetness of horseflesh, but it would be the most substantial meal they'd had in days, since before their food was eaten by the forest wildlife. But that, she realized, would be a step too far for Marsh Tyndall.

"Marsh. Go and collect some larger branches. Some still have the needles on them. We'll give her a proper sendoff. To the Guardian of the Unpromised Future. Yeah?"

Marsh nodded, wiping his tears on the back of his jerkin.

MEADOW AND BROOK HAD BEEN TRUE IN THEIR DESCRIPTION OF THE violet-haired boy. He introduced himself as Kael, of the Clahnn Drumain. Medvedev, he clarified, though it hardly seemed necessary.

He wasn't any older than Gabrianna and was dressed unlike any child she'd seen before. His clothing was both made of branches and leaves, but also durable, like it would stop a sword from penetrating. Woven, layer after layer. He wore his violet hair short, and even before she saw his hawk, Gabi remembered that violet meant his familiar was one of flight.

"I've come to take you to your destination, Mistress. You and your mates."

His voice was normal enough, though it came with no accent she recognized, and his words seemed strange somehow. "That's very kind of you, but why?"

Kael recoiled, seemingly offended. "It is where you wish to go."

"How do you know where we wish to go? How do you know who we are?"

"I saw it."

"Saw it?"

"Yes, in a vision. I saw you." He looked at the Sullen Siblings. "And the Ashenhurst children of Windwatch Grove."

Gabrianna had to resist laughter at the way he said *children*, almost derisively, when he was one. He couldn't be older than Emberley. "You saw us in a vision and you came all this way."

"It isn't so far, really. Only around the bend."

Now she did laugh. "Around the bend! We've hardly left our home. Where is it you suppose we're going?"

"To my mother," he said, frowning at her humor. "To Yseult, Chieftainess of the Drumain."

Gabi recognized the honorific. Chieftainess. Yseult sounded familiar as well. That seemed promising. But none of this felt right. "We thank you, Kael of the Drumain, but we'll find our own way."

Meadow gasped. "Gabi! Are you mad?" Brook made some noise or another, in agreement, which no longer surprised her anymore.

"You won't find the way on your own," Kael said. "It is impossible."

"Why?"

"It is." He leaned his head to the side. His soft face was a strange juxtaposition to his hands, which were calloused and well-lived for his age. "It's not a place you'll find without invitation."

"Hogwash," Gabi said. "My mother has been to the Hinterlands many times."

"Twice. She has been twice. And both times, to the ground that's neutral to all, Termonglen."

"How would you know—"

"She was there when her hand was forced to your father's. She is there now, searching for a way to assassinate the king."

"Guardians!" Brook cried. "Don't say such a thing!"

Kael smiled. "He is not *my* king."

"Don't speak such blasphemy about my mother," Gabi said, fuming now. "She is there to seek peace."

"A peace necessary only because all her children ran off. Is that not so?"

Gabi's eyes narrowed. "Why are you really here?"

"To secure safe passage to Yseult, Chieftainess of the Drumain. Or you may stay here, in this cave, contemplating whether it would accommodate your indecision for hours, days, or weeks."

Perhaps he was older than he looked. He talked like the men in her father's circles, in cleverness and riddles. She didn't understand this, but she identified it well enough. "Yes, but why does it matter to you whether we're presented to Yseult, or not?"

"She sent me," Kael replied, now looking utterly exhausted with her. "She said you would not make it on your own and asked me to bring you safely along."

"And we thank you, sir!" Meadow said, now smiling so broadly, as if the past week had never existed. "We are most appreciative of this kindness."

"Yes, please accept our apologies for our friend. She's distressed," Brook added.

Gabi rolled her eyes and turned back to the Medvedev. "Why should we trust you?"

"Guardians, Gabi, would you rather die here?" Meadow asked.

Gabi ignored her and waited for Kael to reply.

"You shouldn't do anything you're not predisposed to," Kael said with a strange twist of his mouth. "No, you shouldn't."

"You're not making any sense."

"I said you should not do anything you're not predisposed to, which is true. You should not, and from what I can see, you have not. You're here because of trust, yes? Because of what your sister, another Mistress of Longwood Rush, said to you? And so I would feel it is fair to presume you are, after all, predisposed to trust."

Gabi's eyes closed as a heavy breath passed through her lips. No, none of this felt right. This child of their destination, showing up in their hour of greatest need, was like the stories she'd read in *The Great Codex of the Reliquary.* It transcended anything that really happened to anyone, because in the real world, which they were now a part of, removed from the shelter of their homes, bad things happened, not good ones. There were no gallant knights or heroic rescues.

But... She sighed again. *What else do we have?*

"Very well, then, Kael of the Drumain. Lead the way."

M arsh was gone ten minutes before E mber heard him scream. Her senses perked. The sound now piercing the sky was unique to a man who was seconds from losing his life.

Ember dropped the pile of brush and jumped into a sprint. She peeled through the woods, dodging logs and branches, running faster than she'd ever run in her life. She launched into a clearing, and there were only two things ahead of her, but they were the only two things that mattered.

Marsh and a large red bear.

The bear had Marsh's arm wedged in its jaw. Blood painted Marsh's jerkin, running down his legs, his face, staining the soil beneath him. They had seconds before it would go too far. If that.

Ember's heart rate escalated into a staccato that blanked even the sound of Marsh's terrified screams from her ears. It thrummed, building, primed to explode. But it didn't explode. It radiated outward, traveling through her shoulders and then down into her arms, lighting her elbow, burning her forearm, and granting new life to her fingers.

Her entire self was aflame as she lifted her arms, and with it, the bear. The shock of leaving the earth caused the creature to release its prey, and Marsh tumbled to the ground, rolling away in agony. Ember hardly noted this. He was free, but she was not. She was bound to this creature that she lifted higher, higher, raising it into the sky with not one thought but a thousand. A million whispers inside her pushed the impossible to possible, and when she finally breathed out, it tasted like fire.

"Ember!" Marsh cried, but he was far away, like the bear, and he wasn't a part of her like this bear was. The bear regarded her and for a moment, she knew him. Enn. That was his name, Enn, or so he told her, and now that she knew him, it would be so much harder to kill him.

With the same power that lifted Enn into the sky, Ember passed her arms to the left and flung him with a grunt that rumbled the earth. Enn hurled through the air, toward certain death, and in his final moments he knew her, and she knew him, and she managed to say, to only him, *I'm sorry, but there is no other way now.*

The thud of Enn's massive body hitting the ground stunned her out of whatever had possessed her. Ember dropped to her knees, drawing in the cool air, absolutely yearning for the icy world around her for the first time on their journey. When Marsh laid a warm palm on her back, she rolled away from him, screaming that she was on fire.

"Emberley, say something!"

"Your arm," she whispered before she left the world for a spell.

WHEN EMBER AWOKE, IT WAS TO DARKNESS. THE FIRST THING SHE noticed was the acute scent of ash from a dead fire. She reached for something, anything, to cover her, to stop the chills, and Marsh appeared with his bedroll. He opened it wide, and she climbed in and let him hold her to quell the shivers.

"I'm sorry… the fire, I tried to start one, but you launched yourself at it and I didn't… so I put it out."

"It's all right," she said, burying her face in the fabric's softness.

"Can we talk about what happened?"

"I'd rather not."

"Ember."

"You were in grave danger. I reacted. That's all."

"That is *not* all. You know that isn't all."

Emberley wound her hands together, pressing palm to palm. Her hands seemed very normal now, not like whatever they had been when she did what she did.

"Do you think the bear was a gift from the Medvedev?" Marsh asked.

"There are bears in every Reach. Except perhaps the Southerlands."

"That's no answer."

"How's your arm?"

"Sore. I've wrapped it. Did you know you could do that, Emberley?"

She nodded.

"How long?"

"I don't quite know… it's not something…" She reached around. "Where's the water?"

He uncapped the skin and handed it to her, watching her take generous sips. She drank as if the fire wasn't yet extinguished and might never be.

"All Blackwoods can do something," she said, returning the water. She had to tell him something. For better, for worse, he knew her secret. "Most of us can do something small, inconsequential. Pick up someone's stray thoughts, heal a minor abrasion."

"What happened here… that was *not* minor."

"It's never been like that before. I think… I think as I come closer to Midnight Crest, perhaps, it grows stronger."

"Stronger?"

"I can only guess. I don't have the answers. It's my hope that I can get some when we arrive." She closed her eyes and leaned into him. They'd been fighting just that afternoon. She was still mad at him. What anger lay between them had gone unresolved. He'd just have to forgive her. She needed another living creature to connect with her now and remind her she was still one herself, and not lost to whatever she'd done. "I need to understand it, Marsh. I *must* understand it."

"I understand why you chose Midnight Crest for yourself," he said. "If you can all do magic, why is only Brandyn at the Sepulchre?"

"He's the heir. He's not safe in this world, except there. Mother is protecting him." This brought Ember's last conversation with her mother—the most important one—to the very front of her mind, though she'd tried so hard to keep it safe. She hadn't told her siblings, but she could tell Marsh, because now they'd been through this terrible thing together, and he would understand in ways others could not.

"Marsh, there's—" No more words escaped.

Marsh stole them with a kiss.

21

WITCHWIND

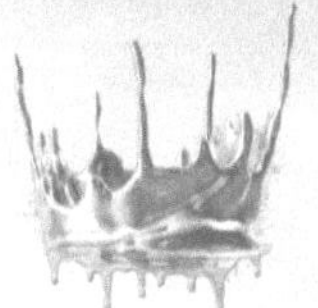

Brandyn guessed they'd been riding at least a day. It had to be longer, but he'd counted one night past the one that had driven them from the Tavern at the Middle of the World, and they were fast approaching another. He supposed that made two. Two days of pushing a pace that should've killed all three nags, and had likely killed Hollyn, if he could find the courage to confirm.

Exhaustion tore at the back of his eyelids. He fought desperately against the urge to roll right off the back of his beast and tumble into the abyss. Even a final sleep would be better than none.

They hadn't eaten. They hadn't slept. Hollyn didn't stir at all. They'd slowed only when the path required more care, but that meant their pursuers had to slow as well. Neither Brandyn nor Storm complained. Whatever awaited them—death at the hands of two mercenaries, death by the elements, death from starvation—had elevated them beyond whatever niggling, needy voices in their heads competed for place. Easing their pace to eat could give purchase to the men who were a mere sun's tick behind them. Sleeping was out of the question. They'd get only a blink of shut eye before the men sliced their throats.

That had its appeals, too, Brandyn thought. To die quickly would be a mercy. He tried to imagine the Brandyn before this voyage, that young man thinking this thought, but he couldn't be this Brandyn any more than that Brandyn could be him.

He wondered why the men didn't narrow the gap. One small push and they'd be upon the kids who had killed their friends. It wouldn't take much. Storm would have a theory, no doubt, but he couldn't talk to her.

Brandyn had just taken a conservative swig from the waterskin when Storm came to a sudden stop ahead. He blinked through his dry eyes. She was looking up, toward a small outcropping that emerged at the edge of the foothills to the west. The stretch of range ran alongside their path, had for hours now, but the sheer face made them more a wall than a hill. Except this outcropping, which had a winding path leading up to what appeared to be a flat crag.

Brandyn's heart flipped. He knew what Storm was thinking before she said it.

"We can't do this for two more days," she said, the adult version of whoever she'd been before Parth. "We have to make a stand."

Brandyn swallowed.

"We have to eat. She needs medicine. Our mules are fading." Storm turned to face him, eyes bloodshot and wild. "We climb up there, we have the high ground. We can pick them off with arrows."

He brightened at the idea of Storm with an actual plan. He'd seen the crag as a trap, and she, an opportunity. He tried to imagine himself sweeping men from their feet, from life, with a bow, but he didn't have to. Storm would do it. She'd do it as she'd done in the tavern—decisively. No place for remorse.

Storm pointed. "And look. A waterfall. We can refill our skins. I can't tell from down here, but it may also come to a pool at the crag, where the mules can drink, too."

"How do we even know they're still behind us?" Brandyn asked, but they knew. Storm flashed him a look that neutered the question.

The path was littered with loose rocks. Brandyn and Storm had to dismount and lead the nervous mules up, but once halfway, all three found new life, practically prancing to the top. Storm was right about the waterfall, and the pool. The mules broke free and made for the relief, but Brandyn and Storm were right behind, almost laughing as they splashed water into their mouths, across their faces. Storm even splashed water at *him*, and he sent it back, narrowing his eyes in playful confusion, as they both aged backward to a time where they'd frolicked in The Hidden Cave without a care.

Storm unloaded Hollyn and set her under a sparse tree near the edge of the crag. The blood in Brandyn's body pooled away, his chest silent as he awaited in excruciating agony the confirmation he'd feared all along.

"She's alive," Storm said. "But her heartbeat is slow. Her breaths are too shallow, my mother would say. See if you can wake her, get her to eat some bread and drink from the cool water." Storm stood, and, covering her eyes with her hand, looked back to the west. "I was right. Only way up or down is the path we took. They can't catch us by surprise then. I'll go await our friends."

"Daylight is nearly spent," Brandyn said. He knelt next to his sister with the confidence of now knowing he hadn't ridden next to her corpse for two days. She was warm, but not hot. No fever, then. She'd gain one if she failed to eat any longer, though.

"They'll be knowing that, too," Storm said and took refuge on a rock, bow at her side. "Bring me some food. I can aim better when my hand isn't shaking from hunger."

Brandyn ground the remainder of their herbs together and waited impatiently for the water to boil over the campfire. Hollyn had risen, briefly, to drink water, and then again succumbed to whatever called her away from them. Maybe the rest was restorative. Maybe she fought away the Guardian of the Unpromised Future. He had no way of knowing. She didn't talk. She *had* smiled, however briefly, before rolling to the side to relieve herself. By the time she returned to the spot under the tree, she was again asleep.

The one thought Brandyn couldn't shake off was that Hollyn had been sick for a long time, but she hadn't been dying until they took her away from her home. He might never know if this was poor timing, the roughness of the journey, or something more sinister, something they should've foreseen if they'd known anything at all. He could fill a whole chapter in *The Book of All Things* with all he didn't know about what was hurting his sister.

They played a game with the men at the base of the outcrop. The men had arrived just as they finished their meager meal, but instead of attempting to make their way closer, up the path, they saw Storm's bow and tucked behind the trees, obscuring all useful views of them. There they'd been, for hours now. The sun was readying to pass into the clearing beyond the mountains. Once it went dark, only their fire would illuminate the standoff.

Hollyn wouldn't wake this time when he went to serve her the paste. Her breathing and pulse were both stronger than they'd been when they ascended the crag, but she wouldn't rouse. He tried to remember what his mother would've done for sleeping patients, and he recalled her once smearing her healing paste upon someone's chest. There were no hard lumps, so he could also press it into the inside of Hollyn's mouth, where it would be absorbed. He knew that, too, from his mother, who told him that the tongue and cheeks were great receivers of medicine.

Poison, too, remember her saying that?

He did both these things, and then went to join Storm, who was now perched behind the tall rock. She hissed at him to get down.

"Don't be a fool, Brandyn. We don't know what their weapons are."

"It'll be dark soon."

"Yes."

"And you don't think that's what they may be waiting for?"

"I know better than to presume what a man is thinking."

Brandyn didn't remind her that she presumed about his own thoughts an awful lot. "If they have enough food and patience, they could besiege us for days. Or more."

"That has occurred to me as well."

"If so, you need to rest."

Storm turned to look at him for the first time. "If I rest, we die."

"We would take turns. You rest, I'll keep watch."

"My point stands, Brandyn."

Brandyn recoiled. "I may not have killed men before, but it doesn't mean I couldn't. If the need arose."

Storm tried to smile. "The difference is, I know what I would do if the need arose. You've yet to discover that for yourself." She reached for his shoulder. "You still can't look at me properly since the tavern. You haven't apologized for the things you said about me. About what I did. I can't know that you wouldn't freeze when trying to pull the string."

Brandyn lifted his chin, loading his defense, but the look in her eyes stopped him. It wasn't judgment, or even anger, but a calm reflection of the facts. She was right. And what was more, his feelings about what she'd done hadn't changed. His feelings for *her* had, and she'd realized it first.

"Then I'll wake you," he said. "If they move. I'll wake you, and you can do what you wish about it."

Storm shook her head. She returned her focus to her peripheral, to the limited view of the hiding spots of their pursuers. "Hollyn needs her brother. Go to her. Rest yourself, if you can. If the Guardians are with us tonight, this will be over soon."

"And if it's not?"

"It'll be over soon, one way or another."

CHRISTIAN'S FACE WAS BRUISED FROM THE WIND. AT THIS PACE, MOST horses would be spent, but not Sun and Moon, who were born and bred as warhorses. Christian and Aylen were more likely to surrender before the horses would, but there'd be respite ahead. They were close.

His steel bounced against Moon's flesh. He didn't know why he hadn't returned Iceborne to its rightful owner. It was meant for the heir of Wulfsgate, not for the son who'd defected to a life of his own choosing. He'd been waiting for his father to come to Briarhaven to retrieve it and deliver a speech shaming Christian for his wanton disobedience, but neither happened, and he couldn't send the sword north in the hands of anyone not meant to wield it. Iceborne was one of only a few, and of them the most significant, symbols of the Northern Reach.

Time held less importance in the Sepulchre, but Christian kept his pulse to the world beyond, often to the point others would chastise him for it. He, who willfully left a legacy behind, should be the last to want to look back. He struggled to explain to other Magi in the Consortium why the world beyond still held so much importance, the same as he would fail to have that conversation with any clergy from the Reliquary. Two institutions meant to serve the kingdom, but preferred the insular halls built to sequester them from it.

Christian knew his mother and father were in Termonglen for the Right of Choosing. He also knew Lisbet wasn't with them. Head Magus Tymagen had shared this news, which had come from an Enchanter in one of the cities of the Great Families up north. He hadn't said which. Had Christian asked, it was impossible to know whether Tymagen would have provided the answer. He was judicious with what he shared, as if he understood how torn Christian was between knowing and not.

Lisbet and your brother, Drystan. They've run off, it seems. To where, no one knows. There are rumors that with them flies a Ravenwood.

Christian doubted this was a rumor. He knew about Ravenna. Drystan had described her in such colorful detail in his letters, which read like poetry. Christian's heart simultaneously rose and sank to read the words. For while he wanted Drystan to be happy, he worried about the world that awaited an heir of Wulfsgate who was all heart, no guts. And was there any world where he and Ravenna could make a life? Even if Holden and Gretchen allowed it, the Ravenwoods held fast to traditions, to the death. This must have been why Drystan felt his only choice was to leave.

To think, had their path veered not an hour north, Christian might have crossed paths with his mother and father, perhaps even Pieter and the twins. He feared for them, arriving without a daughter to offer. Young, tempestuous, and untested, the king wasn't known for his patience or clemency. No one ever had many kind words for Khain, but at least he was a man, and polished by life. He'd died before he could pass this to his son.

Yet, as Aylen would remind him, Christian had given up his concern for these things when he turned his mind to service. And while he could love those of his blood, he couldn't solve for them the problems plaguing them.

The ride from Briarhaven, to where Christian was pulled, was smooth until they reached the Gap of Ever, at Fionn's Pass. Any farther south and they would've been dealing with unpassable peaks, but here, well-trodden paths bisected the foothills.

The terrain ebbed and waned as they crossed. The range bisected the full length of the Easterlands and ran into the Souther-lands, dotting the landscape in hills and valleys. Sun and Moon only slowed enough to adjust, and then returned to their charge, pushing hard enough to make Christian's stomach turn.

"We're close, aren't we?" Aylen called to him from behind her dark green hood. Her silver hair flowed from out the sides. They all had this hair when they emerged as graduates, branded Enchanters and Enchantresses with tresses that would stay forever silver, and a magic-infused silver band wrapped around their upper arms. When out in the world, most wore their silver robes as well, but Christian and Aylen had dressed for a different function today.

"You can feel it, too?"

"I can feel something," she answered. She rested a hand upon her sword, Witchwind. Her father had melted down his own ancestral sword, Witchmar, mixing the liquid metal of this with that of other swords passed down through his ancestry. He then had his black-smith use this amalgamation to craft new swords for each of his children, even the daughters, saying that all Wynters must bear the steel of their blood, man and woman.

Sun and Moon slowed briefly as they eased down toward the valley floor. Ahead, across the tree-covered valley, was another set of hills, these shorter and more erratic in their terrain, as if the results of someone setting an explosion against a wall.

Sun was the first to move on, but Aylen made a clicking sound with her tongue and teeth and both horses came to a stop.

"What is it?" Christian asked. Under the cover of trees, he could no longer see Aylen so clearly, but he felt a certain tension pass across the air.

Her hooded arm rose and pointed. Christian let his gaze follow. At first, he didn't see it. His eyes had hardly adjusted to this new darkness and all he could make out were shapes. Tall coniferous trees with wide trunks, too wide to put your arms around, but just about right to lean against for an afternoon nap.

But trees didn't move. Christian's fist wrapped around the hilt of Iceborne. Two men shifted in anxious steps behind a couple of fir trees. They danced in short formation, never beyond the protection of the trees. Christian looked at Aylen, but her eyes had found something else to piece the situation together. She looked up this time.

A crag. And on top of it... no, he couldn't see up there, but he knew. They'd arrived. His instinct hadn't failed him, after all. Now that they were here, though, Christian didn't quite know what to do about the standoff.

It would be best if they fell upon the men with the element of surprise. If they could subdue them, perhaps an agreement could be reached. Whatever Brandyn and the others had done to anger them, they could assuage it. If it was money they wanted, Christian had on him a cure for that as well. There was no need for violence.

He turned to say as much to Aylen, but she was off like a sudden shot, a blur in the dusky woods, all silver and mare as she and Moon flew toward the men in a dead sprint. Witchwind appeared in her hands, flying high above her head, and it was the moonlight bouncing off her heavy steel that finally spurred him into action.

Witchwind swung again in the air as it arced down and connected with one of the men. Something went flying from his hand—a bow, with an arrow bouncing off and away into the dark woods. Someone howled. Aylen pointed her steel at the throat of the man who'd tried to shoot toward the crag, toward the children, and, loud enough to wake those whose promises were long fulfilled, yelled, "What kind of man hunts a child?"

Christian arrived and quickly surveyed the scene. One of the men clutched his arm to his belly, blood gushing in violent spurts from where his hand had been only moments before. The other man backed away in haphazard steps.

"Who are you?" that man said.

"For all you know, I'm the Guardian of the Unpromised Future, here to claim your promise fulfilled," Aylen answered. "Would you like to find out?"

The man shook his head, eyes wide. He did nothing to help his friend. Christian wondered if Aylen might heal him, but he wouldn't dare suggest it, not when it had been her quick action that had saved Brandyn and the others.

"What do you want with these children?" Christian asked. He'd drawn his own sword at some point. He didn't remember doing it, but Iceborne was a sight to behold, and he saw that now through the eyes of the two men.

"They killed two of ours," said the man who still had both his hands.

Aylen laughed.

"I swear it! The girl. The one with fire in her eyes. Slit their throats without a pause to think of her soul."

"Children," Aylen repeated. "The *children* killed two *men?*"

Christian saw what she was doing, and so did the two men, as she forced them to comprehend the hollow vengeance they'd come to extract. Even if what they said was true, there could be no true revenge if it came as harming a child. There was only shame to be gained here.

"Must have been some friends, for children to feel compelled to take their lives. Mother's blood," Aylen went on, shaking her head. "Well, you'll not be exacting any revenge killings today, men. Those children are sworn to the Sepulchre."

Even the squirming, squirting brigand paused at this.

"The Sepulchre," the unharmed one repeated.

"That's what I said. We've come to return them to the obligation of their studies."

"Can any of you heal?"

"I can," said Aylen.

"Heal him and we'll be even."

"No," she said. "*Even* would be taking one of yours as well." She looked toward the moon. "I suggest you wrap him to ease the bleeding, but he'll need care by morning or he'll be lost. At best, his arm. At worst, his life. *Even* is me allowing you both to leave with your lives. Even is me allowing you to save this friend in the way you couldn't save the others from themselves."

The man on the ground whimpered, rolling himself into a ball. The other sounded several sighs, possibly deciding whether they had any choice, any means of fighting back.

Christian pointed Iceborne at him. "And if you're thinking of going for that knife, you'll not be thinking again about anything."

His hand dropped away from his vest. "But this ain't over. Not even a little. Once I find some law, I'll send them to you, to the Sepulchre. They'll take the runts away in chains for what they did. The girl for killing, the others for harboring her. No one is above the law of King Eoghan."

"You do that," Aylen said. "I look forward to the day."

The man helped his friend to his feet. He didn't take his eyes from Aylen as he led them back to their horses, tethered to a nearby bush.

They waited until both men disappeared into what remained of the dusk before heading toward the path.

BRANDYN FLUNG HIMSELF INTO CHRISTIAN'S ARMS. HE AND STORM had watched, open-mouthed, as Aylen took down the men and drove them off. They ran to greet them halfway down the crag's path.

"I don't understand. Why are you here?" Brandyn asked, as he led them back up the path.

"I sensed you," Christian said. "Sensed you needed help."

"We needed help all right," Storm said.

"Is it true? Did you kill those men?" Aylen asked.

Storm, walking ahead, raised both hands in the air. "It was either take their lives or watch them take Hollyn's. What they intended to do to her would've killed her."

Aylen nodded. "Then you did right."

"I know I did," Storm said. "Brandyn is the one who needs to come round to it."

When they reached the top, Christian moved quickly to gather the children's belongings into their satchels, securing them to the mules. Aylen knelt over Hollyn, working her magic. She was far sicker now than she had been when Brandyn first told the young couple about her, in what seemed a lifetime ago. Christian sniffed the air, and Brandyn wondered if he was smelling death.

Aylen turned her head back. "Brandyn, do you know anything at all about what ails your sister?"

"No, Magi Aylen."

"You still don't know? After all this time?"

He shook his head. "No one knows. No one has ever seen it

before. We've had many come, from all over the Westerlands, trying to work magic or potions, or even prayer. Nothing changes."

Aylen exchanged a look with Christian. Even Brandyn could read it. *I can ease her, but I can't fix her.*

And if Aylen could not...

Christian lifted the unconscious form of Hollyn and draped her over Sun's back. Brandyn stepped forward with a blanket and covered her.

"For the morning," he said. "Sunlight can't touch her."

Christian nodded. "Hollyn will ride with me. Brandyn, you ride on Moon, with Aylen."

"And Storm?"

"Storm," Christian said, with a soft smile at the young rogue, "will follow with the mules. I suspect she will be two days behind us, at the pace they can take. Hollyn needs better than we can give her out here, and we must make haste. Besides, we know Storm can defend herself."

Storm grinned.

Brandyn approached Storm. "Will you be okay without us?"

"'Course."

"You'll come? You won't turn around and go home?"

She shook her head. "I'll be right behind you, Brandyn."

Brandyn launched forward and pulled her into an awkward embrace. "Try not to kill anyone else."

"I will try my very best," Storm promised, landing a kiss on his forehead. "But I make no promises."

He reached into his back pocket and withdrew the dagger he'd retrieved in the tavern. She'd lost the other in the chaos, but she only needed one if trouble came again. "In case you need it again."

She accepted it with a subtle smile, nodding as she slipped it back into her boot.

Brandyn leaned back into Aylen as they disappeared into the night. He didn't turn to make sure Storm followed. He trusted her.

22

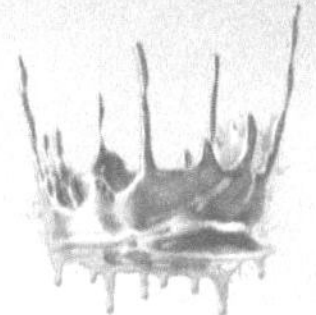

Anabella rose before the sun. Stefan wouldn't come round for a while. They slept more than they didn't in this sky dungeon that had been home since before Stefan was born, because sleeping was a way to pass the time. It dulled the hunger, at least temporarily.

But today… today was the Right of Choosing. The day Eoghan would marry four girls and, soon, bring them home to Duncarrow, where he would have them for his amusements, and if he proved as virile as his father, the mothers of his many children. Anabella experienced a guilt-laden jubilation at the prospect of his attentions turned on others. But these years had been so long. And now that she knew *someone* was still bringing them food and drink, her fears of his lapsed devotions, such as they were, had waned.

Having been raised in abundance and love, she was now much changed. Their needs were so few. Anabella struggled to place herself in the mind of the young woman who had fallen head over heels in love with Darrick Rhiagain. It was a lifetime ago, and she'd long ago shed who she'd been.

So she assumed, anyway, until she'd started the cathartic task of bringing life back into these memories. There was no one to receive them, except the Guardians who had already written them into ethereal record. No one of flesh and blood.

But as the words left the quill and painted themselves across the light tan of the vellum, they *were* alive. *She* was alive, and for more than just keeping her son from the clutches of Eoghan Rhiagain. She was a woman, of full flesh and full blood, and once, she had loved with her whole heart, and been loved more in return.

She was Anabella Weatherford Rhiagain and even when this life was taken from her, no one could deny it had been lived.

Darrick didn't depart Wulfsgate in any rush. He extended his trip again, and then again, until people turned to whispers and speculation. He wasn't yet king. Khain hadn't yet succumbed to that terrible illness. Darrick insisted he could do as he pleased, but the way others spoke about his lingering in the Northern Reach reminded him that he had expectations that would one day become duties. As the days stretched to weeks, his business reasons thinned in the minds of Northerlanders, and rumors spread their tendrils from beyond the Reach, to the edges of the kingdom.

I didn't know this then. I was only aware of the dread I felt over the inevitability of my father's return with the commissioned furs, which had to mean Darrick was finally returning to Duncarrow. Three times my father sent a raven indicating his intention to return, and all three times Darrick returned his own, increasing the size of his order, delaying my father's voyage back, and, thus, his own departure.

Each morning I awoke to a new book at my bedside. I was afraid to ask how he'd gotten them there, flushing deeply as I imagined him sneaking into my bedchamber himself to do it. They were all such a joy to me, something new and wonderful to explore, like jumping into a world unknown. I had never seen books like these. They were of no use to traditional learning, except Darrick had the most unusual belief that learning was about more than memorization of facts, and the skill to put words to vellum. He told me something one day that turned upside down all I'd been raised to believe: that there was nothing of more value, nothing more he could offer the world, than his endlessness of imagination.

I didn't understand that then, though I desperately wanted to. I wanted to know the meaning in order to know Darrick, and this seemed the only key to unlocking this desire. I believe that was his desire, too, and why he kept delivering the fantastical stories to my bedside.

I moved through the stories with voracious zeal, buzzing with anticipation for his daily arrival in the Wintergarden, where we would talk about all I'd read, in a way I'd never talked to anyone in all my life. Even to my father, who encouraged play and make-believe, and indulged both things himself. Darrick talked about beasts beyond comprehension, and magic from other worlds as if they were real, and not words on vellum. He claimed there were other worlds where these things were truth and not legend, and when I asked if he'd seen those worlds, he said with a firm, almost terrifying confidence that he didn't require sight to believe. That imagination required a firmer faith, even than the Guardians demanded.

"I've been all over this kingdom, Anabella. Here in the Wintergarden is the only place where cherries bloom in winter," he said. "That defies our knowledge. Does that mean it isn't real?"

"Perhaps it's magic. A blessing."

"It is a blessing," he said to me, smiling. "But not everything we don't understand is magic."

"Then what would you call it?"

"Not everything has to have a name, does it?"

It seemed to me that everything around me had a name, so I didn't know how to answer this. Not all the explanations I'd been taught were satisfying, but they were accepted.

Darrick wrapped his fingers through mine and held them close to his chest. "Like this. Does this have a name?"

It did, but I was afraid to say it.

"Would you ever consider a life in Duncarrow?"

His question shocked me to the point my face must have paled, because he was immediately alarmed.

"Anabella—"

"Please don't tease me. We both know that's not the future the Guardians have for us."

"And why? Because my father had his wives chosen for him, and his father, for him? And so on, and so back? A king that never challenges tradition is only a steward of rules. I don't want to be king, Bella. I've never wanted it. And yet, I was born into this world minutes before Eoghan, and the only way he would ever be king is if I died. I can't die, because now I have a reason to live." He kissed me. "It's more than that. If Eoghan were king, this kingdom would see a darker time than it's ever known. We share blood, but we share nothing else. I have ideas, Bella... ones my father would call treasonous. But there will come a day where I won't answer to him."

I dared not ask him what treasonous ideas loomed in his mind, and I also didn't press him about his idealistic promises of marriage.

By this time we had been meeting for weeks. I wanted to spend time with him elsewhere, but the Wintergarden was reserved for the children and guests of Lord Dereham, and therefore afforded the most privacy anywhere in Wulfsgate. It didn't stop the rumors, and eventually Lady Dereham pulled me to the side.

"You're a wise and honorable girl, Anabella. And Prince Darrick is an honorable man. But neither of those things matter against the wagging of tongues that would seek to destroy reputations."

How naïve I was. I protested that Prince Darrick was my friend, and, however unexpected that was, it was also a gift from the Guardians. Lady Dereham wore a strange sheen in her eyes, then, and said, "I've had men look upon me the way Prince Darrick looks upon you, and their intention was not friendship."

Her caution didn't have the intended effect. Instead of being warned away, I was invigorated by something that was both dangerous and oh so painfully real. I'd fallen in love with the future king, all while discussing books upon a bench in a garden while cherry blossoms rained around us.

We soon ventured deeper into the Forest of Lycana, Darrick's idea. I never learned if someone, perhaps Lord Dereham, had given him a similar talk that Lady Dereham had given me, but he seemed to understand the necessity of privacy. By this time, he had sent my father his third request, and we both knew time was growing thin.

We no longer talked about books once we left the magic of the Wintergarden. We made our own magic, beneath the firs and pines of Lycana, and we wasted not a second of the time we were given.

And then, when his return to Duncarrow was imminent, he brought into his counsel his most trusted confidante, Wyat Edevane. Wyat was a monk, a scholar of the Reliquary, but his training as a minister gave him leave to perform ceremonies. Darrick asked him to perform a most especial one, and, beneath the last pale moon of autumnwhile, Darrick and I were joined in handfast. A secret held by only the three of us.

He departed for Duncarrow the following day, promising to send for me when the time was right. Months passed. Stefan quickened in my womb, but I dared not share the joyful news with my husband, the future king, in any written letter that might fall into the wrong hands.

At last, I received a letter from him. His words were harried and desperate, so unlike the still lake I knew him to be. He beseeched me in haggard writing to go into hiding at once, for he suspected something terrible was about to happen.

I didn't listen. If I wasn't awaiting him at Weatherford Hall, how would he find me again?

The next raven to arrive announced his death.

Hands shaking, terrified, heartsick, I did as he originally bade me and prepared to leave. I didn't know where to go. What to do when I got there.

I never had to make that decision, for Eoghan's men came for me before I could finish packing a bag. They ripped me from my ancestral home, under cover of night, and the next time I witnessed light it was through the tiny window overlooking the White Sea. The same window Stefan uses to create the world he will never experience beyond the beloved, invaluable imagination his father gifted him.

My heart had been ripped from my chest with the notice of Darrick's death, and then trod upon with the loss of my freedom. Finally, it was Eoghan, in his infinite cruelty, who shredded the remnants with his teeth, and then fed upon them.

I haven't the heart to talk about that part. Not after losing Darrick all over again.

But I will.

Because, though I have bared my heart this morning, this is not the end of this story. It is not even the most important part.

And though it was never my intent for any of this to be read by eyes not mine, if the Guardians were fair and just, there would be someone, nonetheless, patiently awaiting my harried scrolls where the gutter meets the sea.

23

HADDEN'S BANE

The ceremony was scheduled to begin at the halfway point between dawn and noon. They'd expected King Eoghan to arrive in the night. When midnight passed, they all retired to their individual chambers, accepting that he'd been delayed. While they all lay in their beds, pretending to sleep, men the king sent ahead worked diligently outside to prepare for the morning's festivities. They built a simple scaffold, adorning it with flowers native only to the Hinterlands; striking arrangements of violet and evergreen, colors most wouldn't see again until springtide and, she guessed, may have been plucked from deep within the forests beyond Termonglen. The moon's illumination gave them an ethereal glow, Gretchen thought as she watched from her window.

Holden slept soundly, snoring so loud he rattled the bed. For a man who may have sealed their fates in ways they couldn't anticipate, he was certainly satisfied with himself and his showing with Aiden. Gretchen occasionally turned to watch the shuddering rise and fall of his animated but peaceful sleep. As always, she wondered how she could both love and hate a man with equal veracity. Holden *was* a good man. But goodness did not save lives, or protect kingdoms. A man like Khallum understood that, but Gretchen couldn't imagine herself loving a man like Khallum.

It wasn't all Holden's fault. He'd lived under the shadow of the curse of Hadden's Bane since before she was forced into marriage with him. Rinn was the brother who should have been the first to be married off at the Epoch. Rinn was the one who would have known how to deal with men like Aiden and Eoghan.

They'd called him Rinn, but his name was Torrin. Rinn chose the nickname himself, to distinguish himself from his forebears, and there was something playful in it, just as there was in the young man who was Hadden's spectacular heir. Gretchen's father and Hadden had an important alliance, having negotiated trade agreements outside the purview of the crown, and Wulfsgate was the only capital beyond Whitechurch she'd seen in her youth. Even all the way in the Easterlands, Rinn's rumored perfection was legend. There was no man handsomer, stronger, more capable, more skilled in the art of courtly love. That was the reputation preceding him all over the kingdom, and when she met him, she could see it all come to life. He stood taller than most men, even amongst the Northerlanders, and his dark hair and emerald eyes stole hearts, even hers. Hadden and his wife, Mylannie, were working through the details of Rinn's betrothal when Gretchen laid eyes upon him for the first, and last, time.

He was set to wed one of the Haddenfoot girls of Dunwoode when everything turned to chaos.

Rinn's reckless, messy affair with Mina Wynter paved the path to the end. Mina was the wife of Gooden Wynter, one of Hadden's top men. Everyone knew about the affair. Everyone except Gooden, who, upon finally discovering the deception, along with the understanding he was the last to know, locked Mina away in a turret of his castle at Dunwoode. Rinn foolishly camped outside the castle, screaming her name, yelling for Gooden to step aside, but this only inflamed the rage burning inside Steward Wynter, and he commanded his men to drive Rinn away and off his lands.

When Gooden's temper finally cooled, in two days' time, he went to the tower to forgive Mina, and found her dead by her own hand.

Gooden's rage now flamed higher than ever before, but this time, there was only one person at the other end of it.

Later, Gooden would swear upon all the Guardians that he didn't know Rinn wasn't alone in the armory. He would fall to his knees in tears at Hadden's feet and beg him to believe that he didn't know little Hughie, Hadden and Mylannie's seven-year-old son, was in there with his older brother.

But Hughie *was* with Rinn when Gooden barred the doors and set fire to the armory. It was Hughie's screams that drew the crowd that would try in futile desperation to extinguish the fire and save his life. When at last the damp smolder allowed them in, they found Hughie wrapped in Rinn's arms, their forms carved in ash. It was an image folks all over the kingdom would recite when reminding others of the goodness of Rinn Dereham. It set the full and immeasurable weight of Hadden's great loss.

Gooden was sentenced to prison in the Wastelands, but before he could be sent away, men from many of the Great Families of the Northern Reach banded together and found their own justice, dragging him in the night away from where he was being held and exacting their own revenge. They gave his lands and titles to his brother, Grafton. His name, erased from *The Book of All Things*.

It was whispered that Mina died with a child in her womb, and while no one could ever know truly, everyone believed that child was Rinn's, thus worsening the crime against the Lord of Wulfsgate, who had now been denied not one but two heirs.

This was what they now referred to as Hadden's First Bane. But he was not so fortunate as to only have one.

The second involved Holden directly. Like many second sons, Holden never expected his life to be remarkable. He'd communicated his intentions to join the Reliquary, a man of faith, forswearing having a family. Hadden put up no argument to this when Rinn was alive, for there was also little Hughie. Alric, too, though no one thought of him when they recited the names of Hadden's sons.

Following the tragic loss of Rinn, Holden was ripped forward into a position he'd never prepared for, and wasn't born for. Holden, the shy one. The tender one.

This was Hadden's Second Bane.

Hadden's Third Bane was the lord's own death following the Epoch of the Accordant, and having to witness his own bloodline tainted. He hadn't suffered from any longtime illness. They found him in his bed, cold, and it was said he died of a broken heart.

Gretchen thought of these things often, because she believed deeply that within these truths of the path lay the key to her husband. Like Drystan, he wasn't meant for the world the Guardians thrust him into, and like Drystan, he was bound to falter.

But her love for him ended, turned to hatred, where her understanding that this absence of mettle in Holden might also cause them unspeakable loss.

She turned her attentions back to the evening construction, and let her mind drift back to a place where her thoughts didn't trouble her so.

An east wind carried across the Termonglen plain. It was an odd stretch of land, a grassland valley surrounded by forests upon hills. The earth around the castle was dead, as if a poison lived there and the bordering trees kept it from seeping beyond the plain. Termonglen sat just off the intersection of two Compass Roads, and if one stood at just the right place, only a few paces south of the derelict castle, they could conceivably be in the Hinterlands, Easterlands, and Westerlands at the same time.

But it wasn't the way the Medvedev had chosen a location the Reaches could swallow in a land grab that perked Khallum's curiosity, but how that exact spot seemed untouched by anything sacred.

To venture deeper into the Hinterlands would, so he'd heard, leave one ensconced in flora unseen anywhere else in the kingdom. Vines like ropes, streams that ran so clear you could use the water to drink and bathe your children in the same breath. Forestland that was as unforgiving as it was inviting. But not here. Here, the dead grass of the plain flew across the hard wind, bouncing off the border of trees. The scents carried were not ones reminiscent of life.

The Medvedev were clever, wily folk, he decided, putting the men of the kingdom in their place when they dared step foot on their lands. Hanging an "unwelcome" sign may have had a more direct message, but they still felt the sentiment as they hovered in small packs, awaiting the arrival of the one who had summoned them.

Khallum had within him many choice names for Eoghan, The Pretender, but for all the imagery he brought forth in conversation to others around him, he had never met the man.

Man was too generous a moniker, he saw now, as The Pretender approached the large scaffold built in the night, flanked by two women old enough to be his mothers. The women were tall, striking, and in possession of a raw strength that was familiar to Khallum, because he knew it from the fishwives of the Southerlands. They'd not take what you had to give unless you intended to receive it tenfold in return.

Eoghan was only two decades into his life. The joint birth of Darrick and Eoghan, the crown jewels of the Rhiagains, had been the ruse for bringing the four Reaches together for the Epoch of the Accordant. They all assumed they knew his intentions now, but Khallum feared that, like the last time, what the crown truly had planned was far worse.

Unlike Darrick, who had spent his youth on progress around the kingdom he would one day rule, Eoghan looked as if he'd never seen a full afternoon of daylight. He was hunched, gnarled, as if shaped by the elements in a terrible storm. His pale, mealy face looked down, eyes never addressing the gathered crowd, as his elder sisters, Correen and Assyria, all but lifted him up the short flight of stairs, a living bundle of feathers. They each had at least a foot of height on him.

Eoghan turned toward them both, as if waiting for their command for what would come next. He faltered when another hard wind gusted through the crowd. Correen sneered, fixed straight ahead, but Assyria bowed, whispering in his ear.

"Quite arresting, aren't they?" Gwyn said quietly.

"Your meaning?"

"The Rhiagain sisters. Isn't it as if they were the two sides of the king?"

"I donnae follow ye, Gwyn."

"Correen, the shriveling darkness, Assyria, the beckoning light?"

Khallum hadn't made such an observation. He'd been too concerned with drawing the measure of The Pretender himself. But it seemed that Correen, glowering to his left, was cut from a cloth different than Assyria, towering proudly at Eoghan's right. The women were from Khain's first marriage, but there had also, once, been a son from this union, Dain. Dain died not long past his release from swaddling. King Khain, left with only two daughters, refused to turn them over into marriages, fearing any man wed to them might attempt to usurp the Rhiagains. But then Khain remarried, and his wife died giving birth to the twins, Darrick and Eoghan. While this should have freed his older daughters to marry, instead Khain assigned them to the job of raising their infant brothers. And they did exactly that. Even now, they were still hard at the task, though Eoghan was grown and Darrick was dead.

Khallum decided this was the difference between how men and women responded to oppression. Had his life been stolen away, he would've smothered those infants in their cradle.

Dain. Darrick. Two sons had to die to make room for The Pretender. Khallum didn't believe this was any coincidence.

"There is no light in The Pretender," Khallum said, without taking his eyes off the weakling king.

"There is light in everyone. For some, you have to mine to the depths to crack through," Gwyn replied. Before Khallum could correct her once more, The Pretender spoke.

His high-pitched voice strained to cut through the hum of conversation. Khallum couldn't make out words. Holden leaned forward, cupping his ear. Others exchanged confused glances.

"We shall begin!" Correen boomed through the din, her joyless expression holding strong. "First, your king has words for you all."

"How zealously we await what dreg the ratsbane has for us," Khallum muttered. He twitched, awaiting the rough nudge from his wife, but it never came.

"Silence!" Correen called when Eoghan attempted, a second time, to be heard over the whispers.

Even the wind ceased for a moment. Eoghan coughed into his arm, and then, blinking into the blinding noonday sun, said, "Thank you for joining me on my most blessed day, my wedding day."

Those gathered looked around, attempting to gauge the expected reaction. Were they to clap? To cheer? To nod?

Khallum grunted a laugh.

"And you have provided me with the brides who will bring our kingdom together, a vision my father foresaw before I drew breath," Eoghan went on. He was still hard to hear, and Khallum only strained for the words because he must fully know his enemy. Others did the same. "Perhaps you had other grooms intended for some of them. If this is so, please provide their names to my steward and we will ensure they are gifted with the same bountiful dowries they lost with my command to make them queens. And all of you will receive riches for your offering. I've brought them with us, so you know I'm a man of my word."

"*Man,*" Khallum rumbled. "He reaches beyond himself."

"You've all traveled far to be here. I won't squander more of your time. Shall we bring up the brides and begin the vows?"

"What? No music? No festivities? No feast?" Gwyn asked. "What kind of wedding is this?"

Khallum shook his head. "You decry a lack of decorum for a wedding that willnae even happen?"

"Aye, but he doesn't know this, does he? What kind of king..." Gwyn trailed off. "I won't waste more words on what is known."

"There isnae a thing kingly about the boy," Khallum said, lifting his palm and pointing. "You were right the first time. He would disgrace us with an alehouse wedding. One only given in shame. If Esmerelda had lived to see this, it might have put her in her grave just the same."

Holden brushed past, making for the steps. He knelt, and then took a single step. "Your Grace, we have a situation we would all like to discuss with you. As four Reaches united, in this, but also, in our reverence of you, our king."

Eoghan's mealy face twitched. A sneer appeared at the corners of his mouth, traveling left to right as if fighting off constipation pains. His eyes glinted as he reached his hand toward Holden, offering his ring to kiss. And Holden complied. Khallum felt a chill pass across his chest.

"He already knows."

"What?"

"Gwyn, he..." Khallum didn't finish the thought. Instead, he looked for Byrne. His brother stood at Asherley's side, an arm around her waist.

Byrne's attention was fixed on the scaffold, like all the others.

HOLDEN'S PERFORMANCE WAS OF THE CALIBER ASHERLEY REMEMBERED from the public plays the local artists in Longwood Rush would put on at springtide, sometimes running all the way into autumnwhile, if the weather held. As children, she and Maeryn would go to the market with the Mistress of Kitchens, an excursion their younger sister, Earwyn, was still too young for. It seemed a consistent truth with Earwyn, that she was always too young for something. Too young to play. To adventure. Too young when she was forced into marriage with Alric Dereham, who, no matter how he aged, always seemed too young for anything, too.

As Asherley watched Holden lay out the sum of things to the young king, using beautiful words and carefully chosen affectations, she remembered Hadden's Bane. Though there were three banes, according to the tales, if Hadden were here today he might think upon the scene unfolding as Hadden's Fourth Bane. And the Fifth, the real tragedy, was that Holden was too blinded by his own beliefs to understand he'd been bested before the first word dropped from his mouth.

But Gretchen knew it. Crazy Gretchen Dereham and her invisible entourage. Crazy, maybe, but no fool. Gretchen had been right to caution him, and now they would all see why.

Asherley had kept her own counsel with the others, because she'd already seen this day, lived its outcome. First seen it courtesy of Joran, yes, but a Blackwood had her own gifts, however precarious and unpredictable, and she'd had a vision that almost too closely matched Joran's. So while she could look down upon Holden Dereham for his foolish and shortsighted plan, his fateful speech was the catalyst for what was to come; what could not be stopped. He must make this fool's speech, just as the events following must play out.

Events she'd done all she could to prepare for.

Emberley, I need to speak with you, child.

I promised to help in the kitchens tonight, Mother. Calla is making tarts.

Calla will still make tarts, come sit.

Asherley noted Aiden's position, off to the left of the scaffold as if imagining himself there in some official duty. Maeryn cowered at his side. One day, Asherley *would* kill this man. She would address the task slowly, and with every limb she tore from his body, every finger and tooth and nail she extracted, Aiden Quinlanden would know, in the horror of these seconds turned to minutes, turned to hours, that all his cruelty and machinations had been for that moment. For that pitiful coward's ending.

But not today.

Today, Asherley prepared to break her husband's heart.

Mother?

Ember, have I always spoken to you like an equal? Not as a child?

Yes, of course, Mother. You never wanted us to be weak.

And you are not weak, child. Not even a hint of it. But what I am about to tell you will require you to be a much different kind of strong than I've ever asked of you before. A strength more than what you have ever needed.

"Lord Dereham is a traitor!" Aiden was the first to break the thickness left in the air from Holden's reveal. Perfectly in position, he marched up the stairs, appearing truly now at the king's side. "Your Grace." He bowed, slow enough to break up the tension. "A traitor who stirred the lords and ladies of the Western and Southern Reaches to his cause, and then encouraged them, nay, *beckoned* them here, days early, so that they might plot against you!"

"Aiden!" Holden cried out. Guardians bless him. He really *hadn't* seen Aiden's treachery coming. "Why would you say such things? We're all, all of us, beholden to King Eoghan, and have made this offer in earnest, that we may serve him even with this unfortunate circumstance."

"Unfortunate, and yet, you brought no other daughter to assuage the slight," Aiden said. "I came not with useless offers of taxes and feigned fealty, but a replacement for the child who has forsaken the Quinlanden name. Where is yours?"

"I have only one other daughter. My Nyssa is but ten."

"Ah, so it is her comfort you put before our king's wishes?"

Eoghan held a bony hand to the side, toward Aiden, a soft silencing. "Lord Dereham, is it true what Lord Quinlanden says? That you entreated the others to conspire against me?"

"No, Your Grace," Holden said quickly. "I wished only for us all to come to an accord that would please you." He spun toward Aiden.

"You were the one who asked that it be me to represent for all of us, Aiden, so I ask again, what are you doing here? What is your aim?"

"I'm revealing you for what you are, before you can do more harm to this kingdom."

"Khallum, Asherley," Holden pleaded. "You can confirm Aiden is playing the king false!"

Khallum looked away. He whispered something to his wife, and she disappeared.

Asherley again looked at Gretchen, but she, too, had disappeared. Asherley knew where the women had gone, but it would be too late. And had she not swallowed her fears and put her own calculated plan into play, it would be too late for her own children, too.

I don't understand, Mother.

Ember, Hollyn is dying. No... there's no time for tears. Save them, for you will need them when this is over. I don't know if she can survive this. She may, she may not. Her fate is beyond my power now. But I have four children, not one. And I would save as many as I could.

Mother—

Ember, hush. And listen.

"And yet, they say nothing," Aiden went on, grinning. "They say nothing, because they will not lay their heads on the block for you, and why should they? You were the one who called them here."

"He'll kill him," Byrne whispered. "To make an example."

"No," Asherley replied. "He has something else in mind. This was over before Holden opened his mouth."

Holden whipped his head around, searching for an ally, for anyone at all who would cut through the lies of the afternoon. His entire understanding of the world changed in seconds before a crowd of his peers, each moment ticking by some new revelation, some new regret, where he began to piece together how his foolhardy plan never had a chance for anything but failure. Eoghan didn't want more in taxes, or a promise for the future. This defection of three of the four Reaches was an assault on his name, his honor, his pride. There was nothing capable of repairing this slight. It would not go unanswered.

Byrne fidgeted at her side. He was anxious, likely thinking of the plan he and his brother had concocted in the shadows. Whether they could do what was needed of them in time to save Holden. Save all of them.

He would not need to.

She'd kept her counsel on this matter, even from him.

Child, the four of you must leave Longwood Rush, just as Lisbet, Drystan, and Eavan have done.

Leave? But, Mother—

Hush, Ember. We haven't much time. Brandyn is on his way from Briarhaven as we speak, which you must know, since it was your face he saw in his vision bidding his return. Brandyn must go one way. You another. Gabi yet another. Hollyn will come with one of you, but you mustn't share with me who she goes with. You mustn't share with me where any of you will go, none of it! I see the questions in your eyes, daughter, and yet I know of all my blood you're the only one who will do as I say even without the answers. I cannot tell you everything. But know this: all four of you are in the gravest of dangers. The only way I can protect you, and protect the bloodline of the Blackwoods of Longwood Rush, is to send you away. You must be long gone before the Right of Choosing.

For how long?

I do not know. But it will be no small thing that brings you home, Emberley.

Ahh, and here it was, the future, unfolding before her eyes. The screams of Gretchen and Gwyn ringing across the dusty blue grass of the plain as their sons, Pieter and Ransom, kidnapped from their rooms while the Great Families were distracted, were dragged from the castle in chains. Eoghan's raspy voice rang to the top of its insufficient ability as he told them he did not come to Termonglen only to leave empty-handed. If they denied him the daughters, he would take the sons. Only when he had his brides, he said, would he return the sons. But he wouldn't wait for long.

Not my Brandyn, Asherley thought, exhaling with relief. *He is somewhere in the world, away from us, but he is safer there.*

And now it was time for the Westerlands to provide their consolation. Now the time was upon them where Byrne would never understand, and possibly, never forgive.

Khallum's feral howl broke her from the suspended review of the situation at hand.

"I'll have your heart in my hand before you leave with my son!"

Eoghan's oily grin would have lasted a half second had he not brought the full force of the Rhiagain Guard, and a select sampling of his Knights of Duncarrow. But Khallum's retinue, though impressive, held a candle in the breeze next to those standing tall with the king. Aiden's men flanked the Rhiagain Guard in perfect accord. Not only men, either, though Asherley wondered how many, in all the panic, and the horror, bothered to notice that.

"And from the Western Reach, where their children are being too clever, I will also not leave with my hands empty," Eoghan called out. Correen repeated each of his words across the screams. "Guards, Lady Blackwood will join us on our voyage back to Duncarrow!"

Finally. Byrne's heated animation beside her was expected. Her own pattering heart at the thought of leaving this man, whom she'd never anticipated loving but did nonetheless, was not.

She reached forward to stay his hand, which lay on the hilt of his knife. She shook her head. "I know what I'm doing, husband."

"Ash, he'll cut me down where I stand before I let him—"

Asherley silenced her husband with a firm kiss, and between his lips, she whispered, "I've known this moment was coming. It is the only way. Trust me now, as you always have." And then, embracing him, for his ears only, she added, "You have my love."

She backed away, willingly surrendering herself to the guards without fight. The horror in Byrne's eyes nearly sapped her strength, and she had the sudden, powerful feeling she'd never see him again.

"This wasn't supposed to happen," Byrne said, tearing at his mail as guards pinned him back. Khallum appeared beside him, wavering between drawing his own steel and reassuring his brother. "We shouldnae have come. We shouldnae have come here, it's just like the last time. It's just like the last time, Khallum, only now they've taken everything from us."

Asherley turned away then, unwilling to observe her husband lose control. Just as she'd bade Emberley, not quite a fortnight past, this would require a different sort of strength than she'd ever known before.

She bit back a smile as the men clamped their hard gloves down upon her arms.

GRETCHEN SCRATCHED AT HER HUSBAND'S CLOYING EMBRACE SO HARD she drew blood. The red stained his face as he gaped at her, in sorrow and disbelief, but what could he expect? She had told him. She had *told* him! She rolled away from him and it was Gwyn whose arms she craved, and the two women held one another, hiding away from the others a pain only the two understood.

She didn't watch the wedding of poor Assana. From the reactions heard rippling through the crowd, Eoghan put on quite a show with the poor girl. Gretchen didn't have the stomach to turn and watch, to confirm her suspicion that the terrible, fumbling sounds heard were his failed attempt at a public consummation. Assana's howl told a story Gretchen's heart couldn't hear, not today when her own heart was in tatters. Her poor niece. Aiden would burn one day. Eoghan would burn. They would all burn, and she, the holder of the flame.

The blur of activity around her faded into a dull, distant heartbeat. People were screaming. Cheering. Running. Leaving. Only Khallum's voice stirred her, and she, blankly, heard him running after Byrne, and Gretchen needed to be where they were, the only two among them who understood their enemy and had the courage to face him.

She left Gwyn with Holden and ran to catch up with the Warwick brothers. Byrne was fast. He sprinted his grief, pounding his heels into the dry grassland, picking up speed with every step. Khallum matched his pace, but didn't close the distance. Gretchen narrowed the gap, until she was shoulder to shoulder with him.

Byrne came to a stop in The Menagerie. He raised his fists to the sky and screamed his fury to the wind.

"Stand and fight!" Khallum yelled. "We do this now, or we lose the chance!"

Byrne's chest heaved with unsteady breaths, and as he turned, his entire body radiated with his fury. "We lost the chance when he took our blood! When he took my wife!"

"You mean to kill him," Gretchen said, more to herself. How she only saw it now was more a mystery than their intentions. What else had their whispers been for? Why else had they given up on persuading Holden from his fool's errand?

"Aye, and not only once, either," Khallum spat, pacing the ground before his brother. "We cannae let the ratsbane slip away, not when he's here, within our grasp!"

"I *love* her, Khallum. If we even attempt it, he'll kill her."

Khallum stopped. "And you donnae think I love my son? My eldest son? My dearest son? You donnae think Gretchen loves her own boy? We do what we must, or he will take, and take, and take! You think he will stop at your wife? Our children? And now, with Aiden at his side, aye, he will take until we're no longer governing our own."

Gretchen stepped forward. She placed a hand on Byrne's back. It felt like fire. "You're both right. He will kill them if we rebel here, where he has the full force of his guard with him. And he will take and continue to take. This is another test. He's gained ground, and he won't be satisfied until he takes it all." She trained her eyes on Khallum's, meeting his gaze equally. "It won't be solved here. But it *will* be solved. And it will take those of us with the strength to see it done."

Khallum stared back at her, stoic. Byrne's tormented breaths ceased. He was the first to nod, and then Khallum, with reluctance, followed.

"We go home. We protect what the bastard hasn't taken. We ready ourselves," she said. "Byrne, you're now the master of Longwood Rush, and there will be temptation to push the search parties harder toward finding your children."

"Asherley was… she was in charge of that."

"Yes, and now it falls to you." She touched his face. His tears tickled her palm. She wanted to close her eyes, to rid herself of the image of Pieter in chains, of the empty keep awaiting them in Wulfsgate. She could not. They would find their strength not in the forgetting but the remembering. The rolling anger, pushing past all else. "If we love our children who are lost to us, we will let them remain lost."

Byrne balked. "What? Why would you say that?"

"As long as they're gone, they cannot be his." Gretchen looked at Khallum. "You understand me, don't you?"

"Aye."

"Help your brother to understand. If you do find them, keep your distance. Do not turn his eyes to them. Do not return them to the place where Eoghan's men will be on alert for their return. Expect the Rhiagain Guard and the Knights of Duncarrow to be residents in all the capitals, from here until the end. This is our life now, until we reclaim it."

She turned back toward the castle. Holden stared in her direction, unreadable.

THE MOON ALONE
HEARING OUR
TREASON

24

THE WASTELANDS

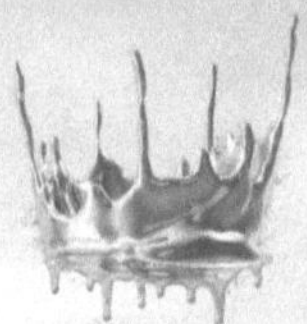

Cap strained against the blinding sun rising beyond the eastern crest. Once, he'd enjoyed the sunrise. No one had ever had to tell him to wake before light. He could see the world best when fewer eyes were upon it.

Now, with the morning ebb of the sun, came the hunger. In the early days here, he told himself he'd eventually grow used to the pang that ripped through his belly, stabbing straight to his soul. He never did. The ache never lessened. While he'd forgotten many of his needs, never this one, the most basic need of all.

They were on day three of no food. Anywhere else, this would've been an annoyance, but here, where men went to be forgotten, to be something other than men, it was life or death. The guards relished granting the news on the first day. They'd always derived a sick pleasure from the suffering of the prisoners, though Cap understood that they, too, were suffering. This was no job anyone sought. It was their prison, too.

If Hill hadn't died weeks before, this would have topped him off.

"They say the Warwicks have blocked exports from the Southern Reach," Andy whispered. They'd gathered to hear that food would elude them a third day. On the first, men had more sense than hunger, and even on the second, but today, the hunger was stronger. A foul energy rippled through the skin and bones hunkered to hear the announcement. It carried across the air, bounced from man to man.

"Couldn't blame them."

"Aye, but they're saying they ran the blockade even before the Right of Choosing."

"Are they." They received scant news of the outside world, but the egregious slight from three of the four Reaches at the Right of Choosing the day prior was gossip too delicious even for the guards to keep to themselves. A disaster everyone would speak of for years to come.

"Aye, and what do ye made of that, Cap? Eh? That they knew? That they were ready?"

Cap warily observed the subtle shifts in the gathered prisoners. The surrounding men began falling into smaller, tighter groups, like mobs. *No, not* like *mobs. You know where this is going.*

He did. He hadn't the energy to stop it.

"I've learned not to make anything of anything that doesn't get me fed and help me live to see another day," Cap said.

Andy flashed him an incredulous look. "The South are fighting back. Can ye not see that? That someone is *finally* standing tall to the ratsbane?"

Cap spun on him and hissed, "Your mouth will get you killed one day, Andy."

Andy scoffed. He pointed at the guards. "They just told two hundred men they willnae eat another day. I ken my words are not among their worries."

Cap tried not to imagine the truth in Andy's supposition about Lord Warwick, for with it might come hope. Hope was more dangerous than hunger in this cursed place.

He had no more time to think on it then, for what had been brewing around them finally boiled over.

He didn't see who slung the first ball of mud at the guards, but others followed, and soon there was an amassing pressure on their backs from the crowd pushing, momentum carrying them inescapably forward into the melee. Cap pushed out through the sides of the throng, squeezing through small openings in filth and shoulders to extricate himself, but Andy thrust himself forward, his own bloodlust ignited by the shared anger of the others.

Cap grasped his forearm and ripped sideways. "Look at the blood in their eyes, Andy! Look at the guards, how they wait for a chance! Don't let them take more from you."

Andy roared with the others and spat at his feet in defiance, but he let Cap lead him away. He made a show of his anger with every step, and when the shouting devolved to a rolling chant of, "Death to the King! Death to The Pretender!" Andy rolled his head to the sky and shouted it to the heavens.

They stumbled away from the mass just in time to see the guards run their swords through four men. Cap dropped his grip on Andy, who turned to him, eyes wide. Cap lowered his own to the side.

"Cap, they're murdering them. 'fore the Guardians and all!"

Cap nodded. "They are."

"We have to do something!"

"And what would you have us do? Find our own selves at the end of a sword?" Cap shook his head. "Andy, there is no justice in a place like this. The Guardians have forsaken the Wastelands. There will be no accounting for the lives lost today. No one to save us but ourselves, and none to help us decide whether it is today, or another day, that we meet the inevitable reckoning."

"That's a right speech from you, Cap. Is tha' what it takes to stir ye, a mass execution?"

Cap again looked to the front of the flank, where bodies dropped right and left. Still, they all pushed forward, into the inexorable evil yawning them forth. Many of these men had never wielded a sword, and yet now died upon them. One, two, three dozen. There was no way to keep count in the confusion, but the blood would stain the dead earth for weeks to come. The gravediggers would be happy in their flood of work, and Cap wondered how large of a hole must be dug for so many men, for surely not all would have kin at the gates to retrieve them.

"Nothing stirs me," Cap said with a heavy sigh. "I don't know why I said the words."

"I do," Andy said. He stepped in front of Cap, blocking his view of the carnage. "Ye do have hope, Cap. I see it. Ye can't be any older than I am, even if your eyes have seen a thing or two."

His eyes had seen more than a thing or two. They'd seen the whole of it all, of everything, both real and not. But that was then. *Then* may as well be the worlds beyond the White Sea, for as tangible as they were to a man of the Wastelands.

THREE DOZEN MEN HAD BEEN KILLED. THAT WAS THE NUMBER THAT passed across what accounted for gossip, and while he'd made few friends in the prison camp, he noticed the absence of certain faces.

There'd been food, after all. Not enough to feed an entire unit, but with the losses, it was enough to spread around those who remained. The rations were more meager, even, than what they were used to, but it gave some ease to the pangs in their bellies. There were whispers that perhaps more should die... that they should pick off those weakest to leave even more food for those who were yet strong. Cap ignored this talk. It was the last of their humanity leaving them.

Cap was assigned to cleaning the filthy rags that night. Andy volunteered as his helper, and the guards, having spent all the fight in them earlier that day, let him go.

The stench was atrocious. Cap turned his head as he dipped the fabrics into the river, soaked them with lye. Andy took the washed ones and placed them in the other basket, where they'd later hang them to dry, catching dust and other filth, before being returned to the clean basket.

"What was life like in Weathercap?" Andy asked.

Cap grunted.

"I know ye don't like to speak about the old life. But I've nae been that far north. Is it cold?"

"Of course it's cold."

"And Wulfsgate? You've seen the capital?"

Cap didn't answer. He'd hoped by now that Andy's dangerous curiosity would've waned.

"I haven't, in event you were wondering," Andy said.

"Can't say I was."

"My family's business is freebooting. Some would say piracy, but there's no truth in the word, as we donnae take what isnae ours. We jus' know how to keep the money silent so the king cannae take more than he already does, ye ken? I saw some of the north, but wasnae invited to dine with the Great Families, though I hail from one m'self."

Cap scrubbed harder.

"Would ye like to know which?"

"No."

"Not even curious?"

Cap looked up. He brushed the grime from his face with his forearm. "I thought you'd grasp it by now. There *is* no kingdom for us. No Great Families. That ended when our lives began here."

"You say that as if you believe it."

"The sooner you begin to do the same, your life here will get easier."

Andy laughed, shoving wet cloths deep into the basket. The sickening squish they made turned Cap's stomach. "You've never tried to get out, then?"

"There *is* no way out. The Wastelands are bordered by gates taller than any castle. The shores are lined with guards, and even if a man slipped past, he'd die in the current." Cap returned to his task. "Only a fool would consider it."

"Would a man still be a fool if he succeeded?"

"Fool or no, he'd be a dead man. That's the only way out of here."

"And if he weren't dead, but was still free?"

"Let's focus on the work before the guards have a go at you again."

But Andy would be heard. He pushed his basket to the side and leaned in. "You say there is no way. But if there was, and it didnae involve death?"

"I told you. There's no hope here."

"Forget hope and answer me. If there was a way out, a true way, would ye take it?"

"But there is not!"

Andy reached for Cap's shoulders and shook him. "Would you? If there was?"

Cap let his wash come to rest at the bank.

"No," he lied.

25

ARCANE TRADITIONS

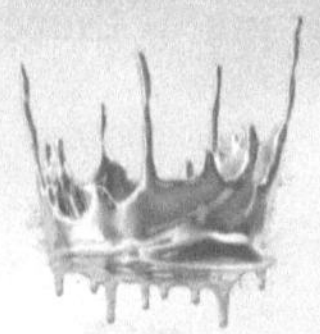

Varinya Ravenwood was a vision. Gretchen, who had been told all her life that her key accomplishment was her Quinlanden beauty, shifted around in her seat, inexplicably thinking, suddenly, of her waistline, and whether her hair was looking especially dull that day.

The Ravenwoods' visit to Wulfsgate as Gretchen and Holden were departing for Termonglen had been brief and hurried, her mind fixed on what was ahead. Now, they had no excuse to turn them away, and it seemed this time they'd expect her to play the role of gracious host.

She'd met the priestess before recent events, though there'd been many years between their last meeting and these. Gretchen was chasing Christian and Drystan around the keep, and Varinya was preparing for her Langenacht, which, though she didn't know at the time, would lead to marrying her own brother, Argentyn. Varinya had been a great beauty even then, roaming the halls of Wulfsgate Keep as she worked to hone her magic skills through training upon men. Age, though, had not dulled her beauty but refined it, as if she'd come into her full, glorious form at an age hardly over thirty. Her black hair sparkled under the candlelight as she regarded Gretchen and Holden from behind her glowing, guarded eyes.

Argentyn and their oldest son, Alasyr, had also come on the unannounced visit to Wulfsgate. They both deferred to the High Priestess, waiting for her to speak, to direct the course of things. It was their way. Had it been the way of the Northerlands, Gretchen thought, they might not be in this mess. Their children would be home. There'd be no looming war.

Holden moved to the great hearth to stoke the fire, which roared so high it needed no attention, and the small smirk playing at the corner of Argentyn's mouth revealed this nervous tic hadn't gone unnoticed by their guests.

A pitcher of their finest wine was laid upon the table. Everyone waited until the glasses were poured and the kitchen maid returned to her post before speaking.

"It's been many years, Varinya," Gretchen said, raising a glass. Varinya didn't touch her own. "Too many. You look well."

"High Priestess," Varinya corrected. She spoke slowly, enunciating her Ss with subtle zeal. "It *has* been some years, but our place is in Midnight Crest. There's little for us here, in the world of men, beyond those years of invaluable training."

Alasyr, the son, pushed his glass away and moved to the corner of the room, studying the portraits of the prior Lords of Wulfsgate. His foot twitched, pounding the stone, creating an acoustic hum that reverberated around the large hall.

"High Priestess," Gretchen conceded. She tugged at the decolletage of her dress. "And yes, while your place is in the mountains, you are always welcome here, in Wulfsgate. The Ravenwoods and Derehams remain friends and allies."

Holden held his post at the hearth. He'd undoubtedly claim that he acquiesced in appreciation of the High Priestess of Midnight Crest being more comfortable speaking with the Lady of Wulfsgate, but Gretchen could feel his relief pass across the warm air.

Varinya smiled thinly. "I come to you now as an ally. For your aid."

Gretchen sipped her wine. "Oh? Has Ravenna not returned?"

"No, she has not," Varinya replied. She met Gretchen's gaze, boring holes in her with the sharpness in her viridian eyes. "As you know, she left us in a storm. It's been over a fortnight since her departure."

"Mother's blood," Gretchen whispered, praying to the Guardians that she might sound convincing enough for Varinya's keen detection of her escalating heart rate as simply that of a mother sharing concern with another mother. "And nothing at all? No sightings?"

"This is why we've come to you, Lady Dereham. To see if you or any of your people have had sight of her. Upon our last visit, you were otherwise occupied, and we now hope you are free to converse with us."

"Of course. That's what we're doing."

"As you know, our raven forms are quite distinct from other birds native to your lands, and if someone *had* seen her, they'd certainly know it." Varinya's porcelain face seemed frozen, devoid of emotion. "I know you have been away, but others may have laid eyes upon her."

"Yes," Gretchen said, exhaling. "Attending to one of our own traditions."

"I know the one of which you speak. Your king has arcane views on unity."

"Regarding Ravenna, no, no one has reported anything on her whereabouts," Gretchen replied. She didn't wish to speak with this sorceress, who thought nothing of bedding her own brother, about arcane traditions. "I will, however, put the call out to all our men, and all the Great Families, to report at once if someone sees her."

"We are grateful," Varinya said. She affected a light bow in her seat. "And your son, Drystan. We have reason to believe they formed a friendship while she was in her training here."

Holden kicked at the grate. Sparks fizzled into the air.

"Though we frown upon such things, if a friendship were to have developed, we would wish to inquire with Drystan if he has any knowledge of her whereabouts." Varinya fingered the wine glass, still full. "However unlikely."

Gretchen wondered if sharing her suspicions would cause more harm or good. She had no doubt of where Ravenna was, and it brought her comfort to know her son wasn't alone; that he had a dealer of magic with him.

Looking into the icy eyes of the High Priestess, she didn't detect the same warmth for her own children. Her love was practical. Ravenna's absence, on the eve of their most sacred of nights, had caused an undue inconvenience upon the traditions that lay at the backbone of their tenuous existence.

"Drystan is visiting his brother, Christian, at the Sepulchre," Gretchen said, surprised with the ease at which the lie slipped from her tongue.

Varinya cocked her head to the side. "Indeed?"

"I would be happy to send word by raven, if you like."

Argentyn coughed into his satin sleeve. "The Sepulchre allows visitors now?"

Gretchen's face flushed at the skipping of her heart. "They always have, for family, and the Magi are free to leave and visit with them in Briarhaven, if they wish. Christian teaches there now. He's no longer an Adherent."

"He's done well for himself," Argentyn replied. "He honors your clan. To wield magic is an honor greater than any other."

Gretchen had never thought well of magic. She'd seen it tear apart families, including her own. Witnessed others executed for the illicit use of it. She'd lost her son and heir to the allure of it. Though it had given her back her lover, she sometimes regretted that, too, for he wasn't the same man she remembered. "We are proud of Christian," she said. "And have much to do in order to prepare Drystan for the void he's left in our succession."

"The raven," Varinya said shortly. "Please do send it. You can send your own to Midnight Crest when you have received his answer."

"You have my word. We will do so," Gretchen replied.

Across the room, Alasyr hummed with a nervous energy. He seemed no longer interested in his survey of the lords of Wulfsgate past, but instead focusing intently on repressing the strange vigor surrounding him. Gretchen herself could not read auras, but she could feel his, so strong it was, and it bordered on malevolent.

"You have our gratitude." Varinya stood, and only after a quick nod from her did Argentyn join her. "We've postponed the Langenacht for now, but if Ravenna does not appear soon, we will consider her lost to the storm that assailed us the night she left." She tugged at her sleeves, snapping them back into neat formation. "Ryandyr has yet two years before the men can cast their lot for her. We have much work to do to prepare her." Varinya sighed. "We put all our energies into Ravenna. Now wasted."

"Ravenna may yet find her way home."

"There seems little likelihood in that eventuality, would you not say?" Varinya made her way back toward the main hall. "She's either perished in the storm, or has run off on some whim, and if that *was* her unfortunate choice, she'd not be welcomed home without grave consequence." Varinya paused.

Gretchen followed her to the door. Varinya shifted into her raven form without goodbye. Argentyn thanked them for their time and followed, soaring high into the air behind her. They disappeared into the fresh snow falling upon the evening.

Alasyr lingered. He looked as if he had something important to tell them, but was fighting with himself about it.

"It was so nice to meet you, Alasyr. We so seldom have the opportunity to meet the men of Midnight Crest," Holden said, reaching a hand to the young man. Alasyr regarded it with disgust.

"If Ravenna had perished, I would know it," Alasyr said, turning his accusing eyes on Gretchen, and then back to Holden. "*I* would know it."

He shifted and flew away.

Holden turned to her as soon as their guests had flown off. "You lied to them."

"How did I lie?"

"I heard it in your voice. I know you. You knew more than you told them." He shifted. "Whatever you kept from them, you keep from me as well."

Gretchen pushed past him and stormed back to the hall. "Your judgment is amusing, for someone who offered nothing to the conversation."

"The Ravenwoods are a matriarchy, Gretchen. High Priestess Varinya had no interest in speaking with a lord. I had nothing *to* offer a woman who sees men as her second."

Gretchen saw her own husband this way, but didn't say so. "Varinya Ravenwood doesn't love her daughter. She *needs* her daughter, to fulfill an ancient tradition."

"What does that have to do with your lying to her?"

Gretchen gathered the glasses. Hers, empty. The Ravenwoods', untouched. "I cannot lie if I don't possess the truth, Holden." She tried to grasp the pitcher, but had no free hands or fingers. Holden rushed to help. "It's only a suspicion."

"A suspicion of what?"

"Do you really not know? Have you really paid so little attention to your son that you've not noticed the changes in him?"

"Gretchen, it's as if talking down to me brings you some great joy."

Gretchen moved toward the kitchen, Holden on her heels. "Your son is in love with Ravenna Ravenwood. It's quite likely she's with him, wherever he is."

Holden grabbed her arm. "Do you take me for a fool?"

"You'll prefer I not answer that," she said, tugging to retrieve her arm. She set the glasses on the wooden slab at the center of the main kitchen, the one from which her family was served. "Drystan believes he's been clever. It's that belief that often gets a man in trouble, wouldn't you say?"

"Gretchen."

"No," she replied, answering the unasked question. "I'm not having one over on you, Holden. Drystan and Ravenna have been involved in an affair now for months, and it cannot be coincidence that they disappear on the same night. Can it?"

Holden pressed himself against the wall. "Is he mad? Why would he pursue such a foolish endeavor?" He dragged both hands down his face. "He's always been a sensitive boy, but he's not addlebrained."

"They've left in search of a better ending than the one promised them here," Gretchen said. "I presume, anyway. Drystan's been hinting at taking dire measures to prevent Lisbet's departure for weeks. Now he had two very good reasons for leaving."

"If the Ravenwoods discover this, they'll have her executed. They may try the same with Drystan, you know. They'll blame him."

"They wouldn't dare touch our son," Gretchen answered. "We're the only barrier between The Rookery and Eoghan's greedy wrath. You've supposed right about Ravenna, however, and Drystan will know this, too. He'll look to keep her safe in any way he knows how."

"Well, we cannot ask them ourselves, now, can we, when you've called off the search party?"

Gretchen tensed. So he knew. She'd made this move in the shadows, hoping word would never make it back to Holden. But of course it would. She had so few allies here that weren't also her husband's. "They did what we could not, Holden. They left for a reason."

"You cannot possibly believe they're capable of fending for themselves!"

"I believe we failed to protect them, and now they've taken the matter into their own hands."

"Gretchen! They're children!"

"Children or no, they're safer out there than they are here. We *have* failed them. Can't you see that?"

"Out in the kingdom, where there are any number of unknown dangers? Off by themselves? With no protection?"

"Protection from those who would barter their lives to appease a tyrant king is no protection at all," Gretchen hissed. "And no, I see in your eyes what you wish to discuss, and I will *not* negotiate the bartering of one child for another. We will not trade Lisbet for Pieter. There's nothing for us to talk about until we find a way to protect them *all.*" She pressed a finger to his chest. "Leave them be, Holden. When I've discovered the means to get us out of these horrors plaguing us, I'll send for you."

Holden parted his mouth. When the words failed him, he turned and left her.

GRETCHEN FOUND HERSELF IN DRYSTAN'S CHAMBERS. SHE HADN'T stepped within the stone walls of her son's room since she found his letter. To her husband, she portrayed a confidence about what her children and niece had done that she spent every waking moment cultivating so that she herself could be convinced of it as well. What Holden saw when he looked into her cool eyes was not what she felt deep within. Calling off the search party went against the very marrow in her bones; the darkest corners of her heart warmed in agony at even the most minute chance someone might find them and bring them back to her, where they belonged.

His chronicle lay open upon his desk. His quill rolled lazily to the side, as if abandoned upon an interruption that had drawn his attention elsewhere.

Ravenna, Gretchen thought, glancing toward the window as she pieced together her son's final evening in Wulfsgate Keep.

Gretchen gripped the wooden table as she eased herself into his chair. She let her hands spread out over the old wood, wondering if he, too, ever did this. If his hands had explored the same grooves in the oak. Her fingers slid over the vellum, drawing down over the final words he'd write. Words she'd *made* him write, and nothing was a more acute reminder of this than the scratched out verse about Ravenna, and her lingering scent upon his pillow.

Beneath that:

Slept fair, awoke just after dawn and broke fast with the family. Boar, quail egg, and bread fresh from the oven. Father was indisposed, so I sat for two ticks of the sun in the Hall of Hearing, considering the petitions from the working class and guilds of Wulfsgate. Resolved two border disputes and granted aid to a farmer whose crops were lost to a rare run of blight. Approved a tanner's solicitation for new business, along the market quarter bordering the southern gates. Collected monthly rents.

The former, the real and true Drystan; the latter, who she'd commanded he be.

Suddenly, without understanding what drove her to do it, Gretchen ran the quill's sharp edge over the words he'd written just for her, tearing the vellum, shredding the center as if mauled by a snowcat. As her fist dragged the jagged marks down the words, cutting deep grooves into the wood of the desk, tears she couldn't cry in the presence of anyone else leapt from her eyes, blossoming into stains on what remained of the vellum. The great, heaving sorrow clawing its way from the center of her chest burst forth and she sounded it into the room that had been vacant for far too long now.

Soft hands fell upon her shoulders. She hadn't heard the steps announcing them. Gretchen looked up. It was her sister-in-law, Alric's wife. Earwyn. Earwyn, who had come to Wulfsgate far too young and had married a man ill-equipped for that, or for anything. Earwyn, who was really not so like her sister, Asherley, but may have been, had she been afforded more time as a Blackwood, and not the mere thirteen years she'd been granted.

Gretchen rolled her head to the side and laid it upon the back of Earwyn's hand.

"If something terrible had befallen them, you would know it," Earwyn said gently, voice hardly dropping above a whisper. "As would Asherley. And Maeryn."

"I know," Gretchen managed to say through her tears. "I know that. It's all I know anymore."

Earwyn planted a kiss atop her head. "It is all you need to know, Gretchen."

It wasn't all she needed to know. She could fill her own chapter in *The Book of All Things* with what she didn't know, but desperately wanted to. But the purity in Earwyn's comfort, a kind which could be born only from the simple but immutably powerful love of one who was a mother herself, served the present need.

Gretchen's tears dried up. Her grief, she would once more bottle and store upon a shelf, not to be accessed so easily again. She wouldn't return to this room until she could do so at her son's side.

But first, she needed to reshape the world in such a way that he would wish to find himself home, once again.

GRETCHEN WAITED UNTIL SHE HEARD HER HUSBAND ASCEND TO THE bedchamber. First checking, as always, to ensure she wasn't followed by any of the keep's busybodies, she darted down the stairs to the Dereham crypt, with featherlight steps, catching the torch from the wall halfway down. Deeper, darker she went, picking up speed as she drew nearer, both running from and to.

Ash was there. He was always wherever she needed him to be. She pressed her hand to her bosom, where the letter was cosseted, unopened.

Ash's gaze followed. "You have something to show me."

"I haven't read it yet."

"A letter, then?"

Gretchen nodded. The damp air burned her lungs today. She'd never liked it down here, but there was nowhere else for them.

"From Khallum Warwick. Addressed only to me. Sent by raven with a scrap of my dress for scent, so as not to fall into the wrong hands."

Ash tilted his head. "And how did Lord Warwick come upon a scrap of your dress?"

"Oh, don't feign jealousy with me, Drystan Sylvaine. Pieter tore his arm on briars. I had nothing to dress the wound, so I tore my skirts and bound him with the cloth. I left what remained. I suppose he found it after Holden and I departed Termonglen."

Ash pointed at her bosom. "You'd like us to read it together?"

Gretchen reached into her gown. The vellum was peppered with the sweat from her breasts. She'd always perspired in the crypts, despite the chill to her bones that never left until she escaped for fresher air. "Before we left Termonglen, we agreed that it would fall upon us, those of us with courage, to put an end to what's happened to our families. As you know."

"Go on, then, Sparrow. Only one way to ease your curiosity."

Gretchen half-smiled and then unrolled the vellum. She read aloud. "There is but one way this ends, and only I know it. I dare not speak it into writing. Our time is imminent. I will send for you." She read it again, this time to herself. Breathless. "I will send for you," she whispered. "What do you suppose he means?"

"I presume he was intentionally vague, for both your sakes."

"But only he knows it? What does he know? Why did he not tell me in Termonglen?"

"You're asking the wrong man, Sparrow."

Gretchen sighed. She read the letter once more. *There is but one way this ends, and only I know it.* "He's a vainglorious man. He enjoys the feel of his own importance. Perhaps that's all there is to it."

"You don't believe that," Ash said. "Or it wouldn't trouble you so."

"No," she agreed. She pressed back against a mossy tomb. "Holden discovered I called off the search party. He's cross with me."

"Holden has a right to his feelings. That doesn't make your decision wrong."

"Hmph." Gretchen read the letter one final time and then dropped the torch upon it. As it burned, she repeated the words in her head, where they'd have to live now. "And you? Do you think I was wrong?"

Ash kissed her. "I don't think you were wrong. And if you need further confirmation, look to Asherley Blackwood. You saw how little fear she had of her own children's fates. It's possible she even sent them away herself. Did you consider that?"

Gretchen gasped. "Do you think?"

"Was it necessary, Sparrow, for all four children to leave to save one? Perhaps, perhaps not, but one thing is certainly true. None of them are in Eoghan's hands."

Gretchen had thought Asherley's reaction to the situation unusual, but to have sent them away, of her own command? "And if she did?"

"Then she knew what you now know all too well. There is only one way to protect the children now."

"But she is now herself a captive of the king."

Ash laughed softly. "She went quite willingly, though, wouldn't you say?"

"You aren't suggesting…"

"I am," Ash said. "And in your heart, you already knew it."

Gretchen settled the torch in the sconce. "Every second of every hour of every day, this is all I think about." She slid her arms around his waist and looked up into the eyes that made the world melt into a place where nothing and everything swirled into the abyss. "Help me forget, for a little while."

26

THE LUTE

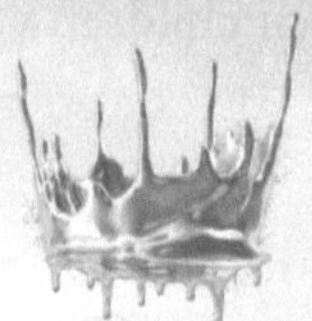

Jesse didn't know the true length of the Westerlands. It was the longest Reach, north to south, and the most verdant and lush. The Easterlands liked to boast about their own green land, Jesse's father said, with castles in the trees and flowers the size of your hand, but it was the Westerlands that looked as if it had been carved by the careful hands of the Guardians, at the dawn of time itself. The freshness of the Easterlands reminded Hamish Strong of an overly tended garden, but when you were in the Western Reach, you knew you were where it had all begun.

Easlan and Kaslan James had given them a fistful of waypoints that might help indicate their progress north and offer some directional certainty. But after the events at the tavern in Parth, they'd ducked even farther from the roads, falling deeper into the Whitewood. For days, Jesse had been uncertain of their course, a fact he kept to himself.

The sign, then, was as much a surprise as a relief.

"Notice to travelers," he read aloud, to rouse Esmerelda. In the early days of their voyage, which now seemed a whole lifetime prior, he couldn't shut her up. Since the tavern, she'd been going elsewhere, slipping further into herself. After a few days of it, he started to worry. He still had no great wish to hear her speak, but he feared the sight of two men killed before her eyes may have had lasting damage. "Notice to travelers," he repeated. "A hundred paces north, you will come upon a Compass Road. If you…" Jesse strained to read the fading letters, carved long ago by a small hunting knife. "If you wish to continue to the Northerlands, your journey must henceforth be by the main road. If you stray, you are subject to the capricious mercy of the clahnns of the Hinterlands. May the Guardians be with you."

Jesse turned to look at Esmerelda. Her emerald eyes stared back, glassy.

They continued on, slower now. He'd known an approach and cross over the Compass Road was unavoidable for their voyage into the Hinterlands. It still gave him chilling pause.

"Princess," he said, without turning. "I'll go ahead. If the road is clear, I'll whistle for you to come. If it isnae safe, I'll return and we'll wait until it is."

There came no response, but he heard her shift in the saddle and took that as the needed confirmation. The trees thinned as he moved on ahead, drawing closer to the roads by which most travel and trade were conducted within the kingdom. They only needed to clear them without detection. A notion that was simpler than reality.

The earth beneath him turned into a path, softly trodden. Likely used by travelers who needed a quick respite along the way. Few dared venture into the Hinterlands without proper invite.

Jesse tethered his horse and took the last few paces on foot. The sun burned bright at its highest point of the day, and he had to shield his eyes to cut the glare. When he reached the road, there was no one upon it, but the ruts made by the earlier rain conveyed the unlikelihood it would remain so for long. He looked left, in the direction of the sea, and then right, toward the east. Just as he was readying a whistle for Esmerelda, he caught something tall through the cool haze.

A tower. No, a castle. Termonglen. If they were at the farthest eastern point in the Westerlands, having met the Compass Road to the north, then they were, at most, a few miles from Termonglen, and the mid-world intersection of the Compass Roads known as The Great Crossing.

So they were still on course.

He turned to look behind him. Esmerelda, for once, had done as he'd asked her. If there was any strong sign something was amiss, it was her easy obedience.

Jesse sighed. Their trek into the Hinterlands would be wrought with challenges, and it would be no easy feat to find the entrance to the Drumain Clahnn. From their father, Jesse and his brother later learned more about Yanna Medvedev, including some of her ramblings about entering the tribal lands. It was a matter of finding the right tree, Hamish had reiterated, failing at anything resembling more useful explanation. *In the trees, you will find a door. No mere man will see it.* Jesse remembered his mother saying these things, absent of context. Knowing where they fit didn't make them any less unclear.

Esmerelda needed a reprieve. He figured he needed one as well. Termonglen was not well appointed, but it was sturdy, built to resist the changing of time and weather. If his telling of time wasn't too far off, it would have been recently vacated, too, which could mean there was food to be heated and blankets not yet gone to rot. Anytime The Pretender was a guest somewhere, there were pickings to be had in his wake.

Jesse sighed again. They'd wait until dusk, and then make their way to Termonglen.

Valen pointed the sword toward the dirt, tapping it as he demonstrated the proper grip. "Look closely, Drystan. The position of not only my hand, but thumb. See? It's as if I'm greeting the hilt. My thumb should be able to touch the pad of my palm, if there weren't a sword in the way. Come."

Drystan moved in slowly. His limp was easing, and he could almost remove the sling from his left arm. But it was his right Valen was asking for.

Valen pressed the hilt against Drystan's palm and released. Drystan grasped at it quickly, before it could slip away. He wished for the use of his left arm to guide the sword into proper place, but he reminded himself, as he had each morning he awoke still among the living, that he'd rather be injured than a tally on the rolls of the Guardian of the Unpromised Future.

"Strengthen your grip with the two end fingers, Drystan. Let your index finger and the middle go loose. Yes, like that. Good."

Drystan's arm quavered as he lifted the sword in the air. Such a weakling next to the grand Valen, who had wielded the steel with such little effort. Somehow, where he lacked in mettle and makeup hadn't felt so egregiously like a sin until now, when he'd failed to save Eavan from terrible cruelty.

He didn't know how to help her even now, a week past the attack. She strolled around the farm, preening and laughing, going out of her way to act as if nothing had happened. As she had before, she colorfully recalled her favorite meals in Whitechurch and bemoaned her limited wardrobe choices. She spoke in whimsical memories of Kian, and all that awaited them in the Hinterlands.

"She's handling this in her own way," Lisbet said, but Lisbet, too, had been changed that night. They all had. It had taken his observation of her practicing her swordplay in the barn that led Drystan to seek Valen for his own instruction. He wouldn't let his failings leave the protection of their group to his younger sister.

"You're distracted," Valen said, taking the sword back. "I understand your reasons. But you must clear your mind if any training is to hold, Drystan."

Drystan leaned against the damp, rotting wood of the barn. It hadn't been treated in years, so the protection against the elements had diminished beyond usefulness. He wondered how long the farm had been abandoned. "If you think training me to be skillful with a sword is a task, try training my mind to go still."

Valen smiled. He leaned the sword against a nearby table. "You aren't unique in that."

"My mother always said my restless mind would carry me to the worst places."

"A mind that never stops can also carry you to the best places," Valen said. "You were right to leave your home, for one."

Drystan kicked at moldy hay. "Even that was Lisbet's idea."

"She looks to you for leadership. She may have conceived the idea, but it was to you she brought it and looked for to see it given life. She would not have left without you."

"I'm not so certain."

"Not all heirs are warriors. Some lead from the heart."

Drystan scoffed. "And some die that way."

Valen approached him. "But you didn't die. Nor did Eavan, or Lisbet. Or Ravenna."

Drystan resisted a sudden, unflattering urge to cry. "My cousin and sister are not the same. As for Ravenna…" It was strange to him how easily he opened up to a stranger, though Valen didn't really seem as such. He'd had so few mentors in his life that understood him. Even his own father had abandoned any efforts when Drystan demonstrated his inability to be like the men before him. "I think she regrets her choice to leave."

"Ravenna's choice was a complicated one. It doesn't mean her regret can be tied to you."

"She can hardly look me in the eye. That is, when she's even here."

"Perhaps you're not the only one feeling inadequate right now."

"How could Ravenna ever feel inadequate? She's perfect."

Valen laughed. "No one, not even your extraordinary Ravenna, is perfect. Her struggles are not the same as yours. Have you seen her try, and fail, to heal you properly? She grows weaker the farther she finds herself from Midnight Crest. She's beginning to understand this truth. Coming to terms with it will be another trial."

"She hasn't said a word of that to me."

"She isn't the only one fearing a dulling love from another."

"From me? She has nothing to fear from me!"

Valen reached a hand out, touching his shoulder. He was a striking man, with pale, penetrating eyes and a face both youthful and also full of hard memories. But there was nothing in him that produced a sense of fear, or danger, in Drystan. "Every man and woman alive is possessed of insecurities that make sense only to them. She fears your love for her is tied to the mystique of magic that the Ravenwoods uniquely possess."

Drystan balked. "But that's foolish! I love Ravenna for who she is... I... I *fought* loving her, understanding the barriers facing us, because of her magic, and who she is. But I loved her. I will love her until the day the Guardians take me."

"Communication begins relationships, and the absence of it ends them. It's not me you should tell, but her."

"I might if she'd come back. She spends her days in the skies, and only sneaks in beside me when I'm already asleep."

"You're well enough to ride now, Drystan. It's time to continue on."

A rush of blood surged forward and left him dizzy. He feared admitting, even to himself, how much he'd enjoyed hiding out in the abandoned farm. Spending nights in front of a warm fire, basking in the safety of their unexpected, unusual new friend. From the time Drystan had been able to sit on his own again, he'd passed the evenings talking well into the night with Valen, who had so many stories and adventures under his belt that Drystan guessed they could spend years in palaver and never reach the end.

Lisbet cautioned him over his closeness to the helpful stranger. *He appears, as if by magic, in the hour of our greatest need? Does that not strike you as overly convenient?*

Fortuitous, Lisbet. He saved all of our lives. He's done nothing to forsake the trust earned.

Nothing yet.

"Drystan. Did I lose you?"

"No, I…" Drystan rubbed the ache forming near his elbow. Earlier, Valen told him he might never regain full use of his left arm. "I suppose you're right. It's time."

"It will be best to ride by night now that we know the brigands have ventured this far north," Valen said. "Let's practice your swordsmanship a while longer and then rest up."

Drystan nodded. He warily eyed the sword. It wasn't their ancestral sword; Christian still had that. It wasn't much of anything, only what he'd had time to swipe from the armory. But it was still more than he had the skill to control.

And now, he finally had someone to teach him.

Drystan slid his hand down the leather hilt and attempted to clear his mind.

THE LAST OF THE SUN SLIPPED BEHIND THE EASTERN EDGE OF THE Forest of All. The men of the kingdom didn't know it that way. They'd contrived various other names for the dense woodlands so unique to the Hinterlands. But the Medvedev thought of the trees as their kingdom, and within the kingdom of the Medvedev, there was no king, no Great Families. The chieftainesses existed as equalizers and upholders of tradition and order, but were not worshipped. Only the land and skies were given those honors, and it was said only a Medvedev understood how to pass through the forests unencumbered.

All this Jesse knew only from the sharing of tales from his mother. She shared these things by whisper, by candlelight, to both children and husband, and until she was dying, he didn't understand she wasn't sharing tales at all, but memories. Knowledge. How

Hamish had kept her secret all those years spoke to her careful nature.

What would she say now, Jesse wondered, as he gazed across the expanse, toward the land of her people? Would she encourage him in his quest to protect his brother's love, having left her own home for a love of her own? Or would she think him foolish for fighting a battle not meant for him?

Jesse uncapped the skin of water and drained what was left. Not enough to slake his thirst, but his expectations of satisfaction in such things had become much adjusted over the weeks on the road. He spotted a stream running along the backside of Termonglen, which was either a sign that taking a night there was the right decision or a reminder that his base needs had been only on rare occasion met since leaving Sandycove.

Satisfied that the passing traders were clear for a spell, Jesse returned to Esmerelda and asked her to follow him. He almost told her where they were going, but he thought a surprise might be good for her spirits. Wondering after her spirits left him perplexed, but soon he wouldn't have to wonder about her at all.

Esmerelda followed, dutifully. No silver tongue tonight. She asked no questions as they moved first to the border of the Westerlands and then, exposing themselves, moved not north but east, down the Compass Road, as any traveler might.

She fell to his rear flank, following but no longer in eyesight. His mother would do this when her eyes were full of tears, and Jesse's curiosity wasn't greater than his desire to keep on moving toward what may be a night of true rest.

Termonglen was an eyesore, sitting at the center of a field that was barren of life or love. Tufts of bluish grass threatened to break through the dearth, but made little purchase against the decay. Beyond, the Forest of All glowed, beckoning those who belonged, warning those who did not.

He veered off the Compass Road and on to the narrow path that led toward the keep. Both horses pushed their pace, sensing their own relief lay ahead. Still, Esmerelda said nothing.

Jesse lifted a hand in the air. As ordered, Esmerelda issued the soft sound to her horse to be still.

"I'm going on ahead, to be sure no one is here." She didn't answer him, so he added, "Stay, until I know it's safe. If fortune smiles our way, greeting us may be soft beds and perchance a meal heated over a real stove. Doesnae that sound nice?"

"Yes," she said.

That was when Jesse understood that something had changed inside Esmerelda Warwick, something not fleeting but lasting. And though it defied explanation, he found within himself a desire to see some of her old self restored. Ryan deserved as much, when at last he joined his bride in the Clahnn of Drumain.

"If you discover we're not alone before I do, make for the Forest of All. At speed."

"The what?"

"The forest," Jesse said quickly, waving into the distance. Now wasn't the time to explain his mother's world. "Make for the forest, and dinnae stop until you're safely inside. Wait for me there, and if it happens a Medvedev finds you before I do, tell them you're the wife of the son of Yanna Medvedev. You understand?"

"Yes, Jesse."

Jesse didn't chastise her for using his true name. He left her, and, with one hand settled against his sword hilt, went to secure the keep.

LISBET FELL TO THE REAR OF THE GROUP, SLOWLY ENOUGH TO KEEP everyone's attentions forward. Drystan and Valen were in the front, riding apace, laughing like old friends. Lisbet's stomach curdled. She had no one with which to share her suspicions, for Ravenna had again grown wings and Eavan existed in a world where nothing bad had ever happened to her. If they ever reached the Medvedevs, her first ask would be for them to ease whatever had taken control of Eavan's troubled mind.

Valen had saved them. She couldn't deny that. He'd fed them, seen them healed, and given them warmth after many days exposed to the cold. But anyone could have known they would crave such things. These were easy temptations to dangle, because they so easily bit upon the bait, desperate for salvation and comforts. Even now she couldn't help but look behind her, at what they'd left, wishing for it as fresh snow fell down around her shoulders.

At first, she thought he was an agent of the king. It hadn't only been the Dereham men they had to fear discovery from, and there'd be nothing worse than falling into the king's hands as exiles. They'd be fingered for treason, no doubt. Even for those hailing from the Great Families, that was a crime worthy of execution. Equal only to the use of magic without license.

But there was no sense in the following days at the farm if Valen worked for King Eoghan. The king would have had them to Duncarrow, or perhaps the Wastelands, in swift order. His men wouldn't have fed and spoiled them, and let them rest.

So then she wondered, was Valen from that same band of foul men that had attacked them? The Blackpool Brigands? It would be a sly move to "save" them, only to gain their trust, and then turn them over to the marauders in the end. But Valen had killed some of them, with Ravenna finishing the remains of the group.

But he was *not* who he claimed to be, and that he couldn't persuade her from. If Drystan couldn't see it, then it was left to her to find the truth.

"I wonder what Assana is doing right now. Do you think she's being fitted for velvet?" Eavan eased back to join Lisbet, giving no pause before launching into her frenzied attempt at erasure. "I'll be so aggrieved if they didn't wait for me this time. Mother says Assana looks better in velvet, but to that I say, who looks bad in velvet? Truly?"

"No one," Lisbet muttered, afraid to goad her, afraid to do

anything to rip her back to a reality she wasn't prepared to confront.

"That's right, Lisbet. No one. Not even you, who's much more favored by fur," Eavan replied. "I suspect emerald would be your color. You know, colors present differently in velvet. Or did you know? Do you even trade for velvet in the north?"

"My mother wears it on occasion," Lisbet said. Or perhaps Valen was an agent of Eavan's father? Lisbet had overheard her mother confiding in her father about the foul things Aiden Quinlanden had done, and hinted at more besides.

"Ah, yes, well, *that* makes sense, for she'll always be a true woman of the Easterlands, won't she? No matter where she goes."

"She says so herself," Lisbet replied. Yes, perhaps Aiden sent Valen. Even Eavan had said, at some point along their journey, that if her father discovered she'd abandoned her duty of her own will, he'd find some terrible fate to send her to. This Valen could lull them into a sense of safety and then dispatch of them when their suspicions ebbed, and Aiden Quinlanden would not be tied to it by deed or word.

"And thinks it all the more, I suspect," Eavan cooed. "She's not lost a whit of her beauty, though they say the Quinlanden women are a vision even as the Guardian of the Unpromised Future arrives to usher them to finality, their promise spent."

"Lisbet!" Valen's voice pierced through the night. "You've traveled this Reach with your father. Tell me, what is this we come upon?"

Goading her? Searching for common ground with which to bring her to his friendship? She reluctantly caught up to where he and Drystan had stopped and strained to see.

Ahead, a Compass Road. The southerly one, and to the left... "Salthill. And the border to the Hinterlands."

"And do you know your way from here?"

"Why? You abandoning us now?"

Valen flinched slightly. "No, Mistress Dereham, only curious what your senses are telling you."

Mistress Dereham. He dared. "I thought you knew the way?"

"Aye, I do. I know a way you'll not have considered, because it's a path not known to your father and his mapmakers. Not known to most men."

Lisbet snickered. "But known to you."

Valen stared back, stone-faced. "Known to me, yes. A story I'd happily share, but we have more pressing matters at hand."

Lisbet rolled her eyes. She pulled the cloak tighter about her, letting the fur obscure her expression. She didn't know the right way to spar with such an unusual man. He always seemed to know how to best respond and leave her unmoored. The wulf pelt muffled her voice, giving her some pretense of upper hand, at least in her mind. She pointed. "Take the path to the west of Salthill, avoiding it and the Compass Road entirely, and then dip back east, crossing at least an hour's ride from the road."

"Very good. But it isn't a road or a path that'll take you to a chieftainess of the Medvedev. You could ride all the years of your life, covering every inch of the Hinterlands, and still not find them."

"You make no sense."

"Not by the reason of man. But the Medvedev, though they may look similar to us, are not men."

Lisbet reached into her cloak and withdrew a well-worn piece of vellum. "I have here a map, Valen, of where to find all four clahnns of the Medvedev."

"And you could stand upon the precise spot and still not see it. Not know it."

"Drystan, we don't need this sellsword. This huckster."

"Lisbet—"

"Drystan, I know the way."

"What if he's right? We know almost nothing about the Medvedev. Mother, Father, knew nothing. Or, they told us nothing. How do we know this map is of use?"

Valen held up his hands. "I only wish to help."

"But why?" Lisbet demanded. Beneath her, her horse snuffled, growing uneasy. "Why do you want to help us? Children you've never met? Have no loyalty toward?"

"Lisbet, don't be cross with him," Eavan said lightly.

Valen's face fell. "I feel very sad for you that you've never known a man whose kindness comes without price." He pulled his cloak back. His intense eyes regarded her with a softness that unsettled her. "If you get nothing else from having me along on this journey, perhaps the discovery that there is more than treachery and deceit in this world will be among the most treasured. I will see you to where the Drumain settle within the Forest of All, and from there you can decide if you still wish me to leave or continue on with you."

Lisbet avoided looking directly at Drystan, but she could feel his gentle pleading with her to let it go. To let them move on, in peace. She sighed. "On one condition."

"Yes?"

"When we arrive, you'll disclose these stories, this *knowledge* you hold so close to your chest. And should you refuse, you'll be parted of us, and we you, and that will be the end of it."

Valen bowed upon his horse. "Fealty, and secrecy, the breaking of which means my untimely death."

Lisbet nodded. She waited for Valen and Drystan to ride on, but Drystan lingered, wearing a look of relief. Her heart sank in her chest. With Valen, he'd found the mentor their father had never been to him. She wished she could be happy for him.

When they moved on, she wound her hand around the hilt of her sword. While Eavan resumed her chipper diatribe about Whitechurch fashion, Lisbet looked up and got a sighting of the fallen princess, Ravenna, before her raven form again swooped out of sight.

Ravenna. She needed to speak to her. Ravenna was the only one who shared her suspicions of Valen, even if Ravenna's was more akin to jealousy.

If she could pull the priestess from her maudlin brooding, Ravenna might know exactly what to do.

JESSE KNELT BY THE FIRE, WHICH NOW ROARED HIGH IN THE HEARTH, flames licking hungrily at the darkened stone. At first, gazing across the dead grass of the plain surrounding Termonglen, he'd worried he might have to venture to The Forest of All and take what wasn't his, to keep them warm for the night, but then he'd come across the logs and kindling near the barn. He wondered where they'd come from; who had left them. He supposed if they were wise they'd ventured down into either the Westerlands or Easterlands for their firewood. Perhaps they were even leftovers from The Pretender's recent visit.

Esmerelda sat sideways in a tall wooden chair, cupping the mug of tea he'd made her after finding a few blessings in the kitchen. Her bare legs dangled over the side from beneath her cloak, which had hitched up to her thighs. Dried mud and forest detritus covered her limbs and feet, swollen and red from the tight lacing of boots meant more for fashion than fleeing.

She leaned back against the design of the chair, carefully crafted roses and lilies on intricate vines. Her eyes closed, but her grip remained firm on the mug. Her legs went still.

"Three, perhaps four days have passed since the Right of Choosing," Jesse said. It was a cut through a long silence between them. She'd said nothing since affirming her understanding of his request outside, to run if accosted.

"Since the day I was supposed to have been made queen," she muttered, more to herself.

He thought it best not to follow that path with her. "Some stale bread, tubers, and dried meats. An herb as well. Rosemary, I think. Enough for a stew."

Esmerelda's eyes opened. She turned them on him. "You know how to make a stew?"

Jesse twisted his mouth. "How else do you expect we eat when out trading? You dinnae think we cart along the women to feed us, do you?"

"Trading? Is that what you call it now?"

He scoffed. Folded his arms over his chest. "Nice to have you back, Princess."

Esmerelda winced and pulled herself to a more upright position. "I make no illusions of the man I love, Jesse. Ryan is a marauder, like his father, and him before. Work that has benefited the Warwicks a great deal, so who am I to judge? I'm no Guardian."

"It's more trading than marauding these days. We've too many alliances to shatter them with piracy. We've only a mind to keep our money in the Southerlands, not the king's hands."

"A stew sounds lovely," she whispered, and then in seconds was asleep.

ESMERELDA AWOKE TO THE SMELL OF WARMTH. EVERYTHING HAD A smell. Some things were sharper than others, or softer. Some evoked a sense of safety, others peril. Some still brought her back to a joyous memory, while others pushed her down into the depths of despair.

This stew, made by the man who regretted his charge of her across each second of every day, smelled like peace. It would taste as foul as a handful of ferns, but would fill her torturously empty belly. It amazed her how her world had changed, how she had come to see each thing within it in such different ways. This stew. Weeks ago, she would've laughed and quipped to her father about not letting their cook have the day off again. Now… now, she spooned it into her mouth in hungry slurps, desperate both to finish and savor every last drop. The tough meat she swallowed whole. She let the starchy blocks of tubers melt in her mouth, drenched in bland broth.

She watched how Jesse ate and followed his lead. Across the old wooden table, the only accoutrement in what passed for a dining room, he sopped the stale bread in the broth until it was as soggy as the tubers, and then scooped it into his mouth in slobbery flourish. She nearly smiled. Ryan had, in the early days at least, attempted to change his ways to please her, to fit himself more neatly into the world in which she belonged. She was relieved when he stopped. Part of his appeal had been the distance between them.

Jesse had no such concern for her opinion. She'd ceased wondering why he'd agreed to sequester her to the land of their mother. The Strongs were headstrong men who didn't know when to give up. This attitude first brought Ryan to her, and then, though reluctantly, Jesse.

The Strongs had been childhood playmates of hers, same as it was for most children of the Great Families. But even within the Great Families there were hierarchies, spoken and unspoken, and the greatness defining them slid across a scale. For a daughter of the Lord of the Southerlands, there'd be nothing less than a Law of Port Worthing, or a Rutland of Whitecliffe. She'd played with the Law and Rutland children, too, but she'd not fallen for them. And then the king took that, too, out of their hands, forcing her and Ryan to act upon their own foolhardy plan.

Ryan had teased her. Provoked her into speechless frustration. He had no fear of her standing, and made that abundantly clear, never addressing her with her proper titles or affording her the respect deserved of a Warwick. She couldn't remember when her ire for him changed to something else. Somewhere along the way, what fell from her mouth were no longer harsh barbs but flushed whispers. Confrontations turned to kisses. More.

I love ye more than salt and sand.

Well, Esmerelda loved neither of those things, but she loved Ryan Strong.

The empty bowls lay sprawled on the wooden table. Jesse paced the fire, checking its vigor every few steps, regarding it as if it were a thing to be watched at all times. He looked so much like his brother they could be twins, all but their hair. Ryan's light as sand, Jesse's dark as night. Where Ryan befriended all, Jesse kept to himself, preferring his own company to others. Especially when that other was her.

But he'd been kind. In the inn and now. This night in the castle was for her, though he'd never admit it aloud. He was worried for her, unsure of how to address the change in her since that evening in Parth. Afraid, perhaps, that he'd broken his brother's fiancée. Esmerelda wanted to reassure him, but anytime she tried to open her mouth, the right words failed her. She very much doubted he wanted a report on the contents of her thoughts, so much as a sign she wasn't entirely lost to the horror of watching two men killed before her eyes. So she said nothing.

Esmerelda Warwick wasn't lost, but she was feeling poorly. So poorly that the absence of her moon flow couldn't so easily be explained by the stress she was under.

"What the..." Jesse knelt at the base of a tapestry depicting a scene from the Epoch of the Accordant. He reached behind it and withdrew a lute. He held it aloft with a strange grin. "Of all things to leave behind."

"Do you play?"

"Me?"

"Yes, you."

Jesse laughed. "No, Princess. I don't play."

Esmerelda unfurled herself from the chair and moved toward him. "What a shame. Give it to me."

Jesse looked uncertain as he reluctantly passed it to her. He often looked at her this way, as if expecting something from her he couldn't anticipate.

It took a moment to find the right position, but then she fell into the rhythm of her gentle strumming right away. *"Ah, ice and cold, a history untold, a magic to unfold..."*

Jesse, arms crossed, merely stared at her until he seemed aware the pause was for him to recite the next verse. "Me? No, I dinnae sing either."

Esmerelda sighed and then leaned into the refrain with flourish. *"This is the house that Rhosyn built."*

"Maybe I accidentally put mead in your tea."

Esmerelda moved around him, enjoying how desperate he seemed to extricate himself from whatever was happening. *"Oh, salt and wheat, food so sweet, all kiiiiinds of meat, this is the house that Thedyn built."*

"All right. We should put it back."

"You think someone will come back for it? All the way to Termonglen?"

"It's nice to see you're feeling better, but we should rest."

Esmerelda's smile faded. He wasn't Ryan, who would have sung louder, who would have slapped his knees in time with the music. He wasn't Ryan, because Ryan was serving a prison sentence in the Wastelands, courtesy of her father.

Jesse sensed the shift in her. He reached forward and awkwardly adjusted her cloak around her shoulders. "Come on. I'll get a fire going in your room."

She didn't argue. She replaced the lute in its hiding spot and followed Jesse down the hall. The air was cooler here without the help from the tapestries and she shivered as her bare feet connected with icy stone.

They wound up the narrow staircase, lit only by the candlestick Jesse found amongst the wreckage in the kitchen. The flicker of flame made a show of light and shadow upon the walls, but did little in the way of keeping her steady. Without turning, Jesse reached out his arm, and she stepped forward to take it. They may not be friends, but, like Ryan, Jesse was well named. Strong. They both made her feel safe. If there was something or someone out there who could best him, then their demise was fated by the Guardians.

They stepped onto the second level. Three doors to three rooms appeared around the edge of the tower's inner circle. He opened the first door and nodded at her to step through.

Like the rest of Termonglen, the room was meagerly appointed. A large bed at the center was the only furnishing, other than a tall lantern holder to the left of the bed. Jesse wasted no time getting the fire started.

Atop the bed was a cattle pelt, and covering that, a quilt filled with holes from moth bites. Holes or no, it was thick and would keep her warm through the night. Even thinking of winding her body across the dense fur gave her shivers. She'd heard tales of the neglect of Termonglen all her life, but she'd never been happier to be anywhere than she was to be there, right then.

Jesse pulled more dried bark peels from the pile next to the hearth, waving his hand to fan the flame. Esmerelda was ashamed to realize she wouldn't have known how to do any of this without him. Something so simple as starting a fire may as well have been naming the stars that sat amongst the Guardians, for all her experience in it.

She climbed onto the bed. Back in Warwicktown, she had lived without ever knowing what it was to go without. She'd forgotten the softness of her own bed. Here, in the neglected tower of Termonglen, was the softest, most inviting bed she'd ever known.

Jesse sat on the edge. "You have all you need?"

"Stay a while."

"We should both rest. If we push, we may make it to our destination in a few days."

"I don't ask for long. Please."

Jesse, with a sigh, eased in enough to get comfortable. "You want us to sit in silence, regarding the shadows dancing upon walls?"

"I want to know about your mother's people."

Jesse tensed. "Ask Ryan."

"Ryan isn't here. You are."

He was turned away from her. Even without seeing his face, Esmerelda knew he was engaged in a battle with himself. He could never decide how he felt about her and her questions. He vacillated between annoyance, anger, and, occasionally, kindness. She imagined him spinning a wheel in his head, never knowing where the pointer might land so he could settle on how to handle her. She was almost grateful not to bear witness to this, except in her imagination.

"I know nothing. I've never been to the Hinterlands until now."

"Surely your mother told you about her life there?"

"Her life was a mystery until her death. We're still putting the pieces together."

"Tell me some, then, if you don't know all."

"Esmerelda—"

"I only wish to know what lies ahead for us. When you leave me to return to Sandycove."

Jesse half turned. "I willnae leave you until I know you're settled and safe."

"You can't tell me anything? Anything at all."

Jesse's sigh pushed him back. Then he surprised her by falling upon the pillow next to her. He stared up at the satin tester topping the bed. It had been long ago torn by time, but it would still be soft to the touch, if she could reach it.

"I dinnae know as much as you think I do. But I know this. There was only one man who could've taken you on this voyage, princess. Only one with the blood of the Medvedev flowing within them can find the doors to each of the four clahnns," Jesse said. His head rested upon his arms, folded behind it. He kept his eyes trained above. "You asked me why I agreed to take you. Because there was no one else who could."

Esmerelda rolled to her side, enthralled already. "What do you mean, see the door?"

"I've never seen one myself. Our ma said the doors weren't doors, really, but entrances, and they'd be invisible to men."

"How will we find it, then?"

Jesse removed a hand from behind his head and tapped his chest. "I'll know." But she caught the fear in his eyes.

"What are they like? The Medvedev?"

He shrugged against the pillow. "I never met any but my ma. And she was... well, she was my ma. She was foremost a Strong. She took care not to forget tha', not in the Southerlands where everyone wants what we have and were too feared of outsiders because of it."

Esmerelda watched him closely. Outside, the wind whipped across the plain, shaking the brittle windows. She pulled the quilt tighter. "Surely there's something you recall."

"You have to remember. Ryan and I, we didnae know. Until the day she died, we thought she was Yanna Rosewood, from Greenfen. All her stories, to us, they were fables. Not memories. And so we forgot most of them." He looked at her from the corner of his eye. "Though... some things made more sense, when we learned the truth. I was telling Kaslan and Easlan how she colored her hair, and she had this pet fox..." Jesse smiled in the darkness. "Fen. That was his name. Fen. Strange little creature, he was. Died the same night as she, but none of us realized it until the next morning when we found him curled up under her bed, stiff and cold."

"Her familiar."

"Aye. I suppose that's what he was. My father caught foul for heaping the little thing on the pyre with her, but we all knew he belonged there."

"Your father loved her."

Jesse nodded. He closed his eyes. "You talk for a spell."

"Me?" Esmerelda considered this. "About what?"

Jesse adjusted, settling further into the pillow. He didn't open his eyes. "Tell me about how you met Ryan."

"Ryan never told you?"

"Something about besting a monster primed to tear you limb from limb."

Esmerelda laughed. "Aye. That's Ryan. I regret to say, there was no monster. Only a man whose quick, sharp tongue aided me from a precarious situation at the market in Warwicktown. I'd traveled without my nanny that day. My father would've been enraged if he knew, but he always treated me like I was overly delicate. Ryan..." Esmerelda paused at the sound of Jesse's snores.

She sighed in the darkness, the sound turning to a soft laugh. Then, with a grin, she rested her head into the crook of his elbow and closed her own eyes.

27

MY HUSBAND, MOST BELOVED

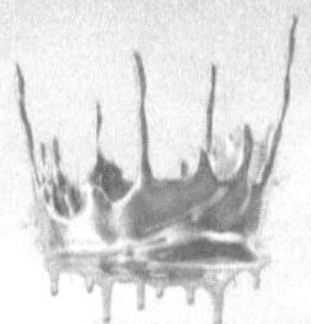

Byrne kept thinking he should burn the letter. This feeling came as instinct, from his upbringing in the Southerlands, where anything put to writing had the potential to destroy their volatile world. Even books were scarce in the land of salt and sand. Reading had been Byrne's first honest joy when forced to leave his boyhood behind, landing upon the doorstep of The Halls of Longwood's library with a twinkle in his eyes.

Anger drove him as well. Anger at her. Asherley had kept *all* this from him. She'd been scheming for weeks, behind his back and under his nose, and he'd never been the wiser. He, a Warwick by blood, a Blackwood by fate, had seen not a sign. Of course, Asherley was always scheming *something*. She couldn't help herself. Her mind, so unlike that of most women, lived in a perpetually tactical state, anticipating moves long before they came to fruition. To most, living this way would be exhausting, but Asherley was built for it. She was most anxious in the stillness.

Yet, when her plotting involved him, his wife included him. *My husband, most beloved.* She called him this in tender moments; Byrne only when she trained her ire his way. Warwick men weren't taught to love their wives, only to protect them and the bairns born of their loins. The irony of this was that most Southerland women needed nothing of the sort. Asherley had never required his protection, either. But she'd earned his love.

Joran must have known it all. But the craven mage had fled, tail tucked, when Asherley was taken to Duncarrow. He thought of sending his men after him, but there was little point. What was done was done.

Asherley had left the note next to a pot of foxglove beset by lilies. A frequent jest between them, though it was hardly funny now. Ash was the lilies, and the foxglove either the death of a man or the means to save his life. She'd sent the same bouquet to many of her enemies over the years, men and women who never understood or appreciated the message until it was far too late. But when meant for Byrne, the message was something else.

You saved me, my wife. I didnae know I needed saving.

And I will, my husband, most beloved, until there's no breath to draw to find the strength.

Once again, she was protecting him.

Khallum would say she'd emasculated him. The Byrne who felt the pull to his roots, to salt and sand, lost many nights of sleep to this fear. But the Byrne—*my husband, most beloved*—who devoured books and played in the gardens and streams with his children, this Byrne understood there was more to the world than Khallum would ever discover.

Byrne paced the empty Halls of Longwood. No wife. None of the familiar, welcoming sounds of little feet running to whatever mischief awaited. He ached for them all. For the woman who drove him mad and had his heart in a vice; for his children, who had softened him most of all. Khallum blamed Asherley for this, but he was wrong. It was Hollyn. Ember. Gabi. Brandyn. The four faces, each of them mirrors, each of them reflecting the hope of the future.

"You witch," he whispered to his wife's portrait, the one she most loved, where she looked more Ravenwood than Blackwood as she lorded over them all, in her emerald cloak, eyes ablaze.

Byrne buried his face in his hands and cried.

KHALLUM FINISHED HIS ALE AND TURNED AROUND TO FACE THE hysterical wife of Hamish Strong.

Hamish's second wife was not like the women Khallum was used to. Andrija was a miner's daughter from Blackpool, a place so devoid of color or joy that those with any means at all thought themselves on par with royalty. Andrija had come into Hamish's life upon the harsh heels of his loss of Yanna, who Khallum himself had been somewhat in love with. It was hard not to love Yanna. She never asked and gave all.

Andrija was a poor replacement, but a man like Hamish needed a woman. He hardly knew what to do with this one. She preened before cracked mirrors. Whined of the loss of fine fabrics with the trade blockades, while others starved because of the same.

Hamish stood behind her with a helpless look. He was breathless from chasing her. His large hands fanned out to the sides. As if to say, *I tried. I'm sorry.*

"Stewardess Strong. Sit," Khallum commanded. "Mind the table edges, unless you dinnae fancy your limbs."

Andrija glared at him, but was careful as she eased into a chair few women had ever sat in. He forbade women in the Hall of Warring. They were a distraction. Histrionics, emotion, had no place amongst the politics of the Reach. But he could see there was only one path to ridding himself of this needless distraction.

"You will tell me!" she boomed, her high, tiny voice almost eliciting a laugh from Khallum.

Khallum exchanged a look with Hamish. Hamish's pink cheeks flushed with shame. His strong man, all heart... and no capacity with which to deal with his unwieldy wife.

"Tell you what?" Khallum demanded, as if he didn't know.

"My son. My Ryan. Where is he?"

"He isnae your son, madam," Khallum said. "And you know where he is."

Hamish grunted. It faded to a sigh, a garbled exhale through his nostrils.

"Oh, aye, I know *where* he is, but you're going to tell me why, Lord Warwick, or Guardians help me—"

"I dinnae advise you finish your threat, cheeky or no," Khallum said. "He willnae be in prison long. His crime was petty. There's no sense in this fuss, as I'm sure Hamish has told you."

"No one leaves the Wastelands! No one! Not thieves, not murderers!"

"Wife, it's as I've said," Hamish attempted, but he was a man beaten. "Lord Warwick takes care 'f us. He'll care fer our Ryan. Sure as the tides."

"Hamish, you fish scale, you say, say, say, and I'll nae hear more of yer lies. For you *said* Ryan'd be home by now. So it'll be Sir Khallum Warwick I'll be getting my truth from here on out."

Hamish gazed at his boots.

Khallum settled against the salt-laden wall of the Hall of Warring. So here it was. Hamish hadn't come browbeaten to Warwicktown for Khallum to repeat his white lies. He'd come seeking permission to tell his wife the truth. A truth few knew, and for the better, for a truth such as this in the wrong hands could spell the end of everything they'd clipped their anchor to.

"Hamish," Khallum said. "What are we doing here?"

"Sir... Khallum." Hamish stumbled. His flush deepened. "My wife, Stewardess Strong, is in thrall to her emotion, as ye see, but she's no fishwife, gossiping in the markets."

"You've already told her, then."

"No, no, I swear to ye I haven't, but, as ye ken, she's... well, as ye can see."

"Yes. I can see," Khallum muttered. Hamish. Ryan. Jesse. That made five Southerlanders in possession of the biggest secret in the kingdom. That it should be this woman to increase that number, widen their risk, was too much to be borne.

But if Khallum had wanted no risk, he would've sent his own son into the Wastelands. His fury pushed him down another course when Ryan set his sights on Esmerelda. Would that he'd sent Ransom instead and swallowed his pride. "He'd be better there than in the clutches of the ratsbane," he mumbled.

"Beggin' yer pardon," Hamish said.

"Nothing," Khallum said. "You'll swear for her, will ye? It will be yer head lining the pikes outside the keep if she runs her pretty mouth."

Hamish nodded furiously. "I will. I do. Andrija puts up a mean fuss, but she's been a good ma to the boys, since Yanna. It comes from the right place, ye ken."

"Yeah. I ken," Khallum said. He inhaled a full breath of sea air. It burned. He relished in the pain. Held it in, preserving in his lungs the hardening he'd yet to experience; the one man in the Souther-lands lacking the constitution for it, and the only one for which this was untenable. "Then we best go into this with our whistles wet. I'll send for a jug of ale."

BYRNE OPENED A BOTTLE OF ASHERLEY'S FAVORITE WINE. SHE WASN'T here to scold him, or share in a glass. He'd drink the bottle whole and leave the empty remains in her solarium. He looked forward to the day she'd let him have it.

He'd dismissed all the housemaids but one. Maye would see to his meals, he could see to the rest. His own needs were minimal.

"Lord Warwick... Lady Wakesell called again." Maye hovered in the doorway. She wasn't afraid of him, but she was afraid. "The Ashenhurts sent another raven. And the Tyndalls—"

Byrne waved her away. "Better they not have answers that will be far from satisfying."

"What shall I tell them?"

"That we have our best men searching for their children."

"Lie, then?"

"Aye. Convincingly, if you have it in you."

Maye nodded and left.

This time, he read his wife's words through the eyes of a man drunk.

My Husband, Most Beloved,

Ahh, I regret our goodbye was not proper. Not ours. How do I know we did not get one? That, husband, is what I wish you to know, and if you are reading this, then what should have come to pass, has.

Do you remember how we talked, long into the late nights, the moon alone hearing our treason, of how we could find ourselves a way out of the terrible fate awaiting Hollyn? She and the other three young women soon to discover themselves wives of a vindictive child king.

We found none, because there was none.

Are you yet drunk on a bottle of my elderwine? If not, this is not permission, you know. You'll prefer the punishment, should I be gifted the occasion to bring it down upon you in the future. I think of it now with a smile, as I write this.

If I had told you... is it not you I do not trust. You know this. Khallum's influence is not as strong as he would like to believe, but it is strong enough. And I love you enough to carry this burden alone, all the way to the bitter end.

It was I who sent the children away. To Emberley alone, I entrusted the plan, to spread them to the corners of the kingdom. I whispered suggestions but told her not to tell me. Who knows what foul magic Eoghan has in his employ. What could be pulled from a mind. And so they left, our babies. To where, I know not, but in my heart I know they thrive in ways they would not if they had stayed.

I have seen the future. Joran has seen it, has seen the sons of the Reaches taken in chains. Brandyn is but a baby. If we'd sent Hollyn, Eoghan would have discarded her in her weakness. I did not see it, but I know it in my heart. By not sending her, we leave Brandyn at his whim. And the others will not be collateral to his unending cruelty.

There is no future that ensures their survival other than the one I have put into life.

And there is more, most beloved. For I have also seen that in the absence of a child to sacrifice to the king, it will be me who returns to Duncarrow at his side on behalf of the Westerlands.

Are you angry with me now? Yes, you are. And you are hurt. And it is my one regret that I cannot ease this from you.

If I can leave you with one parting bit of strength, here it is. There is knowledge, which I have yet to discover, that can take down this entire kingdom, wall by wall. Which I can only discover from Duncarrow. And I will use this, my darling. I can use this best from the inside, and I will, of that I assure you. Eoghan only believes his power is limitless because no one has ever shown him the limits. This I, Asherley Blackwood, great-granddaughter of Rhosyn Ravenwood, will do, and he will not know the walls are crumbling until he is standing along amongst the rubble.

You should burn this. Your brother would. But I can see you now, holding it, stained by one or two of your judicious tears. If this is so, then keep it where none can find it.

I asked Joran not to show me my own days ahead. We find strength in the unknown as much as the known. For me, anyway. Do not take your anger out on the poor man, either. You know he is weak against my will.

Know that it will have taken me weeks to summon the strength to leave you. I beseech my ancestors to give the same to you.

We must protect the Westerlands. With me gone, and the children safely off on their own voyages, it falls to you, Byrne Warwick Blackwood. My husband. The only man I would ever trust my birthright and heritage to.

Be as me until I can return.

Be with me in spirit until we can be united in body.

Be at ease and trust in me.

Also Khallum. It may seem as if I loathe the man, but he may be the only one in the kingdom who will do what is needed when the time comes.

With love,
    Asherley

Byrne fell back in Asherley's chair. Her favorite, the one carved of mahogany and that white stone that was the crown jewel of the Westerlands. He leaned his head to the side and didn't fight the urge for his eyes to close. In moments, the bottle fell from one hand, rolling across the soft dirt toward the patch of camelias.

The letter remained firmly clutched in his fist.

"Drink," Khallum commanded.

Andrija fell back in her chair and crossed her arms. "I willnae be plied with spirits and silenced. Not even by you, Lord Warwick."

"Isnae as if I intend to have my way with ye," he muttered, rolling his eyes at Hamish. "Drink. Dinnae drink. 'Tis none to me."

Andrija pushed her drink across the table. The foam splashed over the sides.

Khallum took a generous gulp of his own. "Ryan isnae in prison for a crime. He committed none."

Andrija spun on her husband. "I told ye! I told ye, Hamish, our boy is innocent!"

"Hush," Hamish warned. "Listen, will ye? Isnae tha' what ye came for?"

Andrija *hmphed* but leaned back and hushed.

"The charges against Ryan were but a ploy to get him into the Wastelands," Khallum went on. "He isnae the first I've sent to dig around, uncover what the ratsbane is up to with our stolen lands. But I didnae send him for that, Stewardess Strong." He poured more ale into his mug. Like all things there, the taste of salt overwhelmed the more welcoming flavors, but, like all other men of the Souther-lands, there was pride in consuming that which was not as well made as the fancies of the Westerlands and Easterlands. "I willnae disclose my source, so asking will be a waste of your breath. But my source, and 'tis a good one, a reliable one, tells me there is a prisoner of interest in the camp. That none knows who he is, 'cept us now, and others with a special interest in seeing him extracted."

"Who?" Andrija asked.

Sharing this was a leap too far. Hamish's almost imperceptible shake of the head confirmed this. "I cannae say. But know I wouldnae have sent your son into the Wastelands for a mere blacksmith."

Andrija looked up at her husband. Then back at Khallum. "And he finds him, and then what? There's only one way in the Wastelands, and it's in. Forever."

"You're wrong, madam. There is one way out. Death."

Andrija gasped. Hamish put a steadying hand on her shoulder.

"Ryan has with him some carefully bundled herbs. Herbs that, when taken, leave a man as if dead. Dead as far as th' world knows. Ryan and our prisoner of interest will take these herbs, and then be brought out on carts, where our men will collect them for their 'dead-given rites,' and bring them back to Warwicktown."

"Tha' sounds like the most outlandish plan I ever heard," Andrija said, but the fire had waned from her face. "Leave it to the two of you to come up with *tha'.*"

Hamish glowered at her. "Ye satisfied, wench?"

"I willnae be satisfied until our boy is home, Hamish."

"Leave that to me. Something ye should've done all along, 'stead of carrying on like a fishwife to our lord of the land."

"And Jesse? What of 'im?"

Khallum shrugged. "What of him?"

"Jesse is running trade. Ain't nothing to do with Ryan, and don't go making it more than it is. Guardians bless." Hamish had regained some of his upper hand in the marriage, however briefly. He brushed a thick arm through the air. "Back to the cart. Ye got what ye wanted. Lord Warwick and I 'ave some business to tend that isnae fit for a woman."

Khallum took a half step back, expecting the tempestuous Stewardess Strong to swing a fist, but she demurred, apparently pleased with her show, and did as asked.

"Ye have your balls back, mate?" Khallum asked when she was gone.

Hamish grunted.

"We do what we must, to keep peace burning in our hearths," Khallum acknowledged. "Little harm in her knowing what I told her, but ye see why I cannae share it all?"

"Aye," Hamish said quickly. He held his large, swollen fingers together over his big belly. "Aye, Khallum. I dinnae want to tell her a whit, but it's as ye said…"

"Aye, aye," Khallum said quickly. "I meant what I said, about her running her mouth."

"I know."

"Good. Because I need your head on its shoulders, Hamish. I need it focused on seeing this through. All the way through."

Hamish shuffled in place and chose his next words nervously. "Why, do ye think, it's taking so long? They should be, would ye now say, 'dead' by now?"

Khallum turned toward the open window facing the sea, and the Golden Coast. He leaned into the shit-covered stone, again hoping there'd be a time when it didn't make him cringe. When he would be truly one with his men. The good ones never let him know he wasn't already. "Nay, not yet," he said. He'd been thinking it, too. It was *all* he could think about, which was something to be said when his son and heir was a prisoner of The Pretender, and he hadn't yet adequately mourned his daughter. "Ryan has his orders. He knows the time he has left, to see it through. He'll get it done. He's a persuasive lad. But our prisoner may not be quick to trust. Guardians know what he's been through."

"I worry, only, that we may be running out of time."

"I ken you'll have to trust me we are not, and I'll be telling ye when the time is nigh."

"But Ransom—"

Khallum raised a hand. "We willnae speak of it. Ransom is worth more to the ratsbane alive than dead. For now. And Lady Blackwood is there with him."

"You trust her?"

Khallum hesitated, but his answer was true. "Aye. I do, Hamish. She's more salt in her than some of the best of us."

"A woman."

"Aye, I know it. Lady Dereham, too. But I dinnae care what's between the legs of what saves this kingdom, do you?"

"No, my lord."

"We look to Lady Blackwood to read the whispers in the halls of The Pretender. We could have no truer ally in Duncarrow. Save yer prayers for her, for much rests on what she can and cannae deliver."

"We have to deliver first."

"Aye." Khallum filled his lungs with another gulp of burning air. "We will."

28

ELVES WEAVING PURE SILVER AT THE LOOM

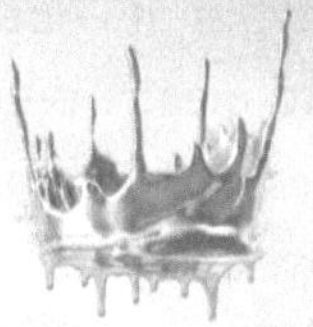

Aylen Wynter fascinated Storm. Or, as she learned, Aylen Dereham. They'd quietly married in a small ceremony at the Sepulchre. They'd yet to notify their families. Even at the Sepulchre, Aylen carried on with the name her father gave her.

One of the defining truths of Storm's life was the pride she felt in the way the world saw her. To her father, she was a fair replacement for the son who had been lost in the world and presumed dead, strong and capable. To her friends, especially The Hidden Crew, she was a natural leader, and always the first to exemplify bravery. Before Brandyn had witnessed her kill two men, he'd been mesmerized by her, in all the ways that made her feel whole.

Storm didn't know if she was pretty. She'd never given it more than a passing thought, as she was possessed of qualities more pressing to the situations she found herself in. She was fifteen now, coming into the period of her youth where her father would make a good marriage for her. A Wakesell bride would be a prize to any groom, even a rough and tumble one like herself. Marriage would dull that in her, she supposed. Her mother said as much, though she declared it as less a happy inevitability, and more a minor tragedy.

Both her parents had encouraged who she was, and Storm knew that to be the woman of your own choosing was rare indeed. Her future husband might have something to say about it. Something she might not like.

Aylen Dereham wasn't pretty. She was beautiful. She was the young woman all mothers dreamed of, possessed with a subtle kindness and a care for all creatures. Her long silver hair, the embossed mark of a true Magi, cascaded down her back, swinging with every soft step, to a rhythm no one but Aylen understood. Her skill at healing went beyond magic. When Aylen moved her hands, it was like watching the elves weaving pure silver at the loom, as her mother would have said. Elves weren't real, but Storm's imagination had conjured the image of Jasmine Wakesell's words with no problem, and she wished she could share this now with her mother. That she'd seen the closest thing to it with her own eyes.

It was no wonder Christian Dereham had given up the whole of the Northerland realm to be with her.

Storm wasn't supposed to be at the Sepulchre. What protected her was the declaration of magical sanctuary. She didn't quite understand the rules. Magi Christian did, and after hours behind closed doors with his superiors, he'd, looking much wearier than when he'd entered, told them they could stay in the chambers of their master falconer, who was home in the Southerlands tending to an unwell relative. His rooms were at the base of the Sepulchre, removed from where the Magi and Adherents went about their days. There was a bedroom, a small sitting room, a privy, and a large barn where the birds lived. It smelled of shit and mold. But it was better than anything they'd had since leaving home.

Christian had secured another bed, and so Storm had her own. Hollyn, on the other, did rarely more than sleep. Aylen came to her before she taught her classes for the day and returned when her duties were done. She moved her hands over Hollyn, elves weaving pure silver at the loom. Hollyn would wake long enough to take a drink of water, or swallow some bread. Aylen would lean back, defeated. But Storm knew Hollyn would be with the Guardians now, if not for Aylen. However ineffective her magic was against whatever plagued Hollyn, it kept breath moving through her.

"Aylen," Storm said, as the Magi tidied the area next to Hollyn's bed. "When you leave here, and go back to the tower, are you truly… as they say… in the clouds?"

Aylen finished wiping her hands on a cloth and turned. "The clouds?"

"Sepulchre in the Skies. My father said you call it that because the magic pulls you into the sky, where the rest of us can't go."

Aylen smiled. "I don't know of any magic that works in quite that way, Storm. They call it this because the Sepulchre is the highest tower in all the kingdom. To some, it *feels* as if we're in the skies, but we're actually quite far from being able to touch the clouds."

"Oh."

The Magi touched her arm. "Many think that. And you know? I think the Sepulchre likes the mystique that comes with such a presumption. Why do you think they never disavow it?"

Storm slowly nodded. "I'd lie too, I guess."

"They wouldn't see it that way. More like a sculpted truth. When I came here as a girl, I remember my disappointment at not being slingshot into the sky by their mysterious magic."

Storm laughed. "What's it like, up there?"

"Have you ever been to a university, Storm?"

She shook her head.

"Ah. Well, it isn't very unlike being in one of those, I'd suppose. Though I've never been, either. Not to a university, or to Oldcastle, where all the ones which matter are found. When I leave here, it is only to visit my father. Or," Aylen added with a grin, "to save you."

Storm grinned back. "I would've broken those brigands eventually, Magi Wynter."

"I don't doubt it." Aylen looked around the sparse room,

searching for something. Her brows moved together. "Storm, I require your aid."

"How can I help?"

She again passed a look at the door. "Brandyn did a brave thing, coming here for the sake of his sister. But my magic does little but ease her temporarily. Whatever ails her is beyond my ability, and I suspect even a stronger Magi could not assuage it." Her voice lowered further, and as she stepped into the light, Storm could now see the worry behind her eyes. "I remind myself there are still things in this kingdom we have yet to define or understand. But until I laid my hands on Hollyn, I'd never met an ailment I couldn't ease or cure. There exists knowledge here, at the Sepulchre, that exists nowhere else in the kingdom. I need to get to it."

"Can you?"

Aylen looked down. "I don't know. Only the elder Magi are allowed in to see the Scrolls of Olde."

Storm balked. "That's foolish. If there's information there that can help others, why hide it?"

"Because there are things in this world that most cannot know," Aylen said with a sigh. "Men are quick to temper, slow to reason. Whatever sits in the scrolls of these archives must bring out the worst of this. Neither Christian nor I have access. None but a few do."

"Then how will you get in?"

Aylen inhaled and looked around once more. "Oh, Christian is a clever man. He may not have been keen to lord over the Northerlands, but he'll make a fine future here, among the greatest secrets known to man. He'll find a way."

Storm thought Aylen looked even more beautiful when she was troubled. She was overcome with a strange but powerful urge to lean in and kiss her.

She swallowed away the impulse. "And me? How can I help?"

Aylen turned to her at the door. "Be their leader, as you have been all this time. Buy me the time I need to either save Hollyn, or deliver, with confidence, the terrible truth that no one can."

ESTHER ELBOWED BRANDYN. HE WAS SO STARTLED HE JUMPED CLEAR out of his seat, catching Magi Christian's attention. Christian paused his instruction, and as he did, the handful of others in the classroom turned their concentration his way as well.

"Excellent restraint," Brandyn accused his friend. "You are the mistress of subtlety."

She shrugged. "I'm not the one catching a nap during instruction."

"Adherent Brandyn, is there something I can help you with?" Magi Christian asked, crossing his arms.

Brandyn blinked at his mentor. As if Christian didn't know that inside himself he was engaged in a great battle, of which there were too many participants. He wanted to be with Hollyn, as Aylen tended her. To pretend as if he'd never seen Storm kill two men, so he could take comfort in her friendship. He wanted news of the Right of Choosing, news of his sisters. He wanted *anything* but to be sitting in a classroom, learning to focus, when he was capable of anything but.

"No, Magi."

"Good." Christian returned to the lectern. "I know this portion of our syllabus is far from fun, Adherents. You'd rather be in the gymnasium practicing your magic, on some unsuspecting beast. Or each other." This garnered the expected laughter. "But magic is a gift that comes with some prerequisites. Anyone with this gift can attempt magic without mastering the prerequisites, but you will master *nothing* if you're unable to be still. To focus." Christian smiled. "Here's where I offer my confession, as your instructor. I failed utterly at this in the beginning."

The Adherents laughed. Brandyn tried to smile. Esther shot him a look.

"I did. As you will. Because to be still isn't natural for men or women. We're taught from a very young age that to be still is to go without. Stillness doesn't tend our crops or feed our children. But you've all been chosen because you're meant for another life, where stillness is essential. To be who you were meant to be, you must be intentional in all things, Adherents. Every word, every thought. You must learn control, in order to be still."

"Magi Christian?"

"Yes, Adherent Esther?"

"What does reading from *The Book of All Things* have to do with being still?"

Magi Christian scanned the room as a few Adherents tittered in agreement. "Do you find what you're reading interesting?"

"Not especially, Magi."

"Then you have learned your first lesson about focus!" Christian's silver cloak caught the air as he swept around the small stone room. "Magic isn't about waving your hands and having thy will be done." He grinned as he watched his Adherents. "Sorry to be the bearer of such disappointment. Magic requires control of the world around you, yes, but more so, of yourself. There is no better way to master your own self than to master your thoughts. To discover what it means to surrender to a moment, even if that moment isn't the one you find most desirable. Reading is a simple but effective means of controlling that impulse to do something more enjoyable. Reading requires all of you at once, and if you cannot offer all of yourself to devouring the dry contents of the catalogue of the four-legged creatures of the kingdom, you'll be ineffective at producing consistent, powerful magic."

Brandyn didn't know how he was doing this. Acting as if everything was *normal*. As if Brandyn's oldest sister wasn't dying in the wings of the basement apartment of their falconer. That he would choose focus as their lesson! Now!

Magi Christian's appearance at his side startled him. Christian knelt by his wooden desk and looked up at Brandyn. "It's time to start your assignment, Adherent Brandyn."

Tears suddenly sprang to Brandyn's eyes. "I can't," he whispered.

Christian briefly touched his hand. "You can." His voice dropped lower. "I know you wonder why I would ask you to focus at a time like this. But I can't think of a better time, Brandyn, than now, for you to learn this. Hollyn. Your other sisters. Your mother and father. They want nothing more than your safety and happiness. Do it for them, and later you may see that you've also done it for yourself."

"Dunwoode. 20 miles ahead." Marsh read the sign. "Great. I told you we've been on the Compass Road too long."

"I was tiring of the woods. Weren't you?"

"I've been tired of the woods since we left home, but that doesn't mean I look forward to capture."

"At least we're in the Northerlands now." Ember pulled out the map and set it against the back of her horse's head. "Not terribly far from Wulfsgate, either. We'll need to dip into the mountains before then, to avoid the Dereham men from sighting us."

"Ember, but can we talk about Dunwoode? If we don't veer east, we'll find ourselves in the center of this town by tomorrow."

"Not simply a town." Ember read the map. "One of the biggest in the Northerlands. Seat of the Haddenfoots." She folded it and pressed it back into her jerkin. "It would be a terrible idea to pass through."

Marsh eyed her. "But you intend to do it, anyway."

"Aye," Ember replied, in her father's familiar burr. She adjusted in her saddle. "Sometimes the best place to hide is in plain sight."

Christian's smile faded as soon as his students dispersed. All but Brandyn, who'd been waiting for this moment all day.

He really had structured this lesson for his benefit. He hadn't expected it to work, but it was worth the attempt. Christian expected the news from Aylen wouldn't be what any of them wanted to hear. Perhaps there was no preparing for it, but it didn't mean he couldn't try.

"Yes, it's time to visit your sister," Christian said. "Go, and I'll meet you there."

"I'll wait and come with you."

"I've some business to tend to first. Go. I'll not be far behind."

Brandyn looked at him with distrust in his eyes. It felt like a dagger to Christian's belly. He needed time with Aylen before facing the children, though. He needed her to speak honestly and boldly, and without fear of the young ones' reaction.

"I promise, Brandyn. Go."

Brandyn went.

Aylen would be finishing her own instruction. It was that time of year where the infirm of Briarhaven were brought to the Sepulchre in hopes of a miracle from the Adherents. The Magi weren't allowed to intervene; if the Adherent couldn't perform the healing magic, then they must also live with having to tell the poor person they would die, anyway. It was a tactic to help them take seriously the responsibility that came with such a rare and powerful gift. But the exercise left Aylen drained of her own energy, as, inevitably, one or two did die, and nothing could persuade her from the belief she'd been partly to blame.

He found her at her desk, staring into nothing.

"How did it go?"

"We saved five. Four will die. Not our best year."

Christian sighed. "I'm sorry, Aylen."

"I only hope my own distractions didn't contribute."

Christian stood over her and let his hands roll over her tense shoulders. "Nonsense. You could have taught my lesson today on focus."

Aylen shook her head. "Focus. Today? Only you."

He lifted his shoulders. "I thought it may help him. I was wrong." He stopped massaging her. "You don't have good news for me, do you?"

"I need access to the Sacred Halls, Christian."

Christian moved around to the front of her desk. He knelt down. "You know that isn't possible."

Aylen lifted her head and met his eyes. "Then saving her isn't possible."

"Perhaps you only need more time—"

Her hand snaked forward and grasped his forearm. "Would that this were true, but it is not. What ails her is not from our world."

"Careful, Aylen, what you say borders upon blasphemy," he hissed, quickly checking the classroom again to be sure they were alone.

"Is it? Isn't that why the scrolls exist? For that which is beyond the knowledge of most?"

"It is for the elders, to spend their twilight years keeping busy."

She shook her head. "No. You know better. If that were true, they would be open to all, not forbidden and locked away."

"What is it you expect to find?"

"I don't know. I will if I see it. But it *is* her last hope, husband." Aylen rolled her hands down over his. Her light eyes sparkled with tears. "You know how magic works. If the illness is known, we can conjure the cure. This is why we study, here, where the knowledge of all things exists. I've completed all my courses on diseases, both infectious and generational. And when we returned, I went back through all my studies, checking again, and again. It isn't there, and if it isn't there, then it isn't a knowledge we're meant to possess."

Christian watched his wife, torn between love and fear. He blamed himself for the impossible situation she now found herself in. "My love, I don't know what's written upon the scrolls in the Sacred Halls, but if there were knowledge of other worlds, don't you think we'd know?"

"No, Christian, I do not. Truly. Why do you think education is only for the very wealthy? The universities have half-empty class-rooms, because so few can afford to send their young. Education is a power few possess, and for those *in* power, that's intentional. What would the average man in this kingdom do with such knowl-edge, do you think?"

"It doesn't matter. No ships are strong enough to stray far from our ports."

"So we've been told." She shook her head. "I don't want to argue a point bigger than you and I. But do you really struggle to believe there are some truths kept from us?"

Christian pulled himself to his feet, using her desk to hold himself. He looked away, breathing in, out. "Even if you're right... why would you think the answer to what ails Hollyn would be in there?"

"I don't know that it is. But I know where it isn't. Here, in the world we know."

Christian didn't argue with her because he doubted her. He never doubted Aylen. She was cleverer than he was, and a force that drew him in and also terrified him at times. But what she was asking... even the suggestion might bring them both under stern reprimand. They were already under a watchful eye for their midnight escape to bring the daughter of the Blackwood lords under protection.

He argued with her because he hoped she'd say there was another way.

"This is it, Christian," Aylen said softly. "The last hope I have of reversing what's killing Hollyn Blackwood. And even this may do naught more than confirm her inevitable death."

Christian nodded slowly. "I will do whatever I can to get you in."

Brandyn sponged the cool water over Hollyn's forehead. He moved the cloth between the basin and his sister's face with mechanical precision, performing the task without thinking much about the steps or the necessity. He'd seen Aylen do it that morning, and in the absence of anything meaningful to contribute to his sister's recovery, he did this.

Storm sat several feet away, sharpening her knife. She'd cleaned it at some point, but a dark crimson stain colored the wooden handle. It always would, at least until time faded it away, but there were many years between now and that happening.

He was so mesmerized by his confused anger at her nonchalant whittling that he didn't at first hear his sister speak.

"Brandyn." The voice was gravelly; old, unused.

At last, his mind caught up to his ears. He whipped back toward Hollyn, and her eyes were open. "You're awake!"

Hollyn rolled her head to the side. "I know."

"How do you feel? What can I get for you?" Brandyn searched around, wide-eyed, looking for the answer to a question she wouldn't know how to answer. Aylen would know. Where were they?

"I know why."

"Why what?"

"Why I suffer." Hollyn's thin skin flexed over her face as she grimaced. "I know now."

Brandyn looked at Storm, who shook her head.

"Okay. No need to talk. Aylen will be here soon."

Hollyn reached for his hand. She grabbed blindly and when it connected with his, he realized there was naught but a wisp of flesh separating skin from bone. "I suffer because I loved him."

Storm stopped playing with her knife and leaned forward. "What did you say?"

"I loved him." Hollyn erupted in a light coughing fit. Brandyn brought the cloth to her mouth, and when he withdrew it, he gasped inwardly. Blood.

Storm moved to the end of the bed. "Hollyn, we're listening."

"It's nonsense. The fever makes her this way," Brandyn said, but Storm pressed a hand out.

"Maybe not," she said. "Tell me about your love, Hollyn. I'd love to hear about him."

"There *isn't* one," Brandyn muttered. "I would know. My sisters would know."

"Women cannot be so easily parted from their secrets," Storm said. "Unless they so choose. Hollyn wants to share hers now. Don't you, Hollyn?"

"I wasn't supposed to tell anyone." Hollyn licked at her dry lips, smudging around the remaining blood. "He said he'd make it so we could be together."

"Who did?" Storm pressed.

Brandyn grunted. They were wasting precious time. Hollyn would be asleep again in no time. They needed Aylen here before that happened.

"Eoghan," Hollyn whispered, croaking the name. She said it a second time with perfect clarity.

"I don't know that I heard—" Storm attempted.

"Eoghan. The king."

Brandyn's jaw dropped. Storm tried to speak again, but failed.

Hollyn's head lolled back to the side, and she slipped away, back to wherever she'd come from.

"Guardians," Storm whispered. "You don't suppose?"

"No," Brandyn said. "There's no way. She's in her delusions. That's all."

"But—"

Brandyn's tears broke through. "She's sick, Storm. She's dying."

Storm reached a hand out to touch him, but withdrew it before connecting. "If she knows this, then you must consider the possibility she is giving you, her beloved brother, the most sacred gift one can give."

Brandyn looked up.

"Her deathbed confession."

29

LADY OF WHISPERS, LADY OF SHADOWS

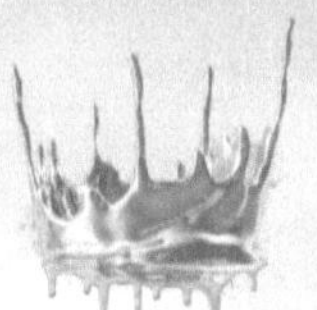

Duncarrow was the name of the island, not the castle. Most used the name to describe both the small island and the keep housing the Rhiagain family interchangeably, but the formal name for the keep, which had been abandoned until the interlopers washed up upon its shore, was Whitesea. Most didn't know, or had forgotten, this. They struggled to recall a history where the word Duncarrow existed nowhere within their known world until Carrow Rhiagain arrived and changed everything with his tall tales of gods and other worlds.

Whitesea once belonged to the Easterlands, but most forgot this, as well.

Asherley remembered. She made it her point to know things. Most of what she knew she'd learned the same way as others, through reading or receiving stories via ancestral storytelling. This is how she came to commit to memory the history of Duncarrow, such as it was. Useless or not, there came a time where most things existing in the annals of her mind came to be tried before the invisible judge deeming whether the retention of such things had been a good use of her resources. Now that she was a resident of

Duncarrow, it seemed more likely she'd be confronted with the matter of whether what she knew about the place had its usefulness.

Most useful to Asherley, though, was what she learned in the way unique to her. All Blackwoods possessed a sort of usefulness and kept this to themselves, to be employed quietly and to their advantage. All her children had usefulness, though it was only Brandyn she'd sent to be taught at the Sepulchre, to protect him from things known and not.

Asherley was a reader of whispers.

As she moved through the dark halls of Duncarrow, decorated in rich tapestries of violet and gold that would be lovely to look upon if anyone bothered to light the torches, she smiled and curtsied, behaving as others would expect a demurred lady of the realm to act. Eoghan hadn't locked her away like he had the Warwick and Dereham boys, nor had he exploited her for sex as he had her poor niece, Assana. He had his reasons. The most obvious, she thought, being that she scared him.

This was nothing new to Asherley. Her whole life, men had alternately been threatened or afraid of her.

Asherley was always on the move. There were naturally better whispers to be read in dark corners, but most were free with their thoughts when they suspected no one of reading them. This was the way of whispers. It was not a free reading of the mind, but the dusting of the corners where the worst of a person lingered. The words that, if spoken, could only be spoken as whispers.

Most living at court were related to the king, either by blood or marriage. Because his sisters had been forbidden families of their own, most Rhiagains roaming the halls were cousins, generations removed from Eoghan. Men and women of all ages, children with no claim to the throne but too close in bloodline to be let to roam free. The outsider brides and grooms of Rhiagain all came from inconsequential families. Daughters and sons of millers or black-smiths. So threatened they were, by their thin veneer of power, that they understood placing within their ranks someone of substance put them at mortal risk.

Which made the business of the Right of Choosing curious to Asherley. While the intent was to take a bride from each of the Reaches to subdue them, it instead strengthened the claims of each Reach, who were united only in their belief that life was better when they ruled unto themselves.

And now Eoghan was the most vulnerable he'd ever been, with a single bride from the strongest Reach. The most ambitious. The others had underestimated Aiden Quinlanden for years, and soon, they'd come to understand this. If she couldn't learn what she came for soon, they'd be bowing to the man and calling him king before the year was up. Duncarrow's proximity, only a mile off the coast of the Easterlands, across from Whitechurch itself, would be more than symbolic. The nearby Isle of Belcarrow, where the Rhiagain Guard and its precious hall of knights were housed and trained, would be absorbed into Aiden's designs, strengthening his ambitions beyond what the other Reaches could answer.

Asherley hadn't met a whisper she didn't love. From them, she learned most of Eoghan's own people loathed him. They still mourned Darrick, what he represented; what the loss of him dug into the empty, lifeless halls. Some had sought leave from Duncarrow, to make their own lives in the kingdom, and been denied.

From Correen, she picked up her regret at not smothering Eoghan in his cradle, as she'd nearly done so many times. Now that he no longer needed her services in his chamber, he'd placed her in charge of the kitchens, a position even Asherley pitied her for, despite her unpleasantness. Eoghan refused to release her, but would not even make staying amenable to her.

From Assyria, Asherley uncovered that Eoghan was deformed in parts of his body that weren't visible when he wore clothing. His spine, for one. His manhood, another. She didn't know the extent of either, but the latter might explain Assana's pitiful crying well into the night.

There was little she could do for Assana now, but one day she would avenge her niece, as she would avenge her sister.

She wasn't remiss with news of Ransom or Pieter, either. She was a mother herself, and if it were her Brandyn locked up, and another lady of the realm walking these halls, she'd hope they would do the same for her. She had no authority in this part of the world, but was satisfied to learn they'd been fed well and had experienced no torture. They were prisoners but were not suffering. This was good, for she wasn't yet ready to sever the king's balls from his crooked body.

There were other prisoners in the tower dungeon. So far, she'd learned nothing about any of them to suggest they deserved her interest.

Asherley didn't let her mind wander to Byrne, or the children. She'd sorted those matters as best she could, and her focus belonged here, in the present.

"Lady Blackwood."

Asherley quickly smiled and performed the required homages. "Princess Correen."

Correen scowled. "Have you lost your way?"

"Not at all."

"You're nearing the king's apartments."

"So I am."

"Where you are not welcome without invite."

"I'm, of course, still learning my way here."

Correen didn't seem especially convinced. What other doubts lived in her head? "You cannot be here."

"So it seems," Asherley said. "I'll see myself back."

Correen hovered, glowering. Asherley intentionally moved her eyes over the woman who wasn't that much older than she was, but looked as if she could be tending to grandchildren. Thinning hair that was half white. Dark, beady eyes beset with wrinkles that folded over the corners. Whatever foul things had come from her mouth over the years had turned it into a prune.

Asherley curtsied and moved back the way she came. After a pause, she heard the heavy clogged steps of Eoghan's favorite sister.

She heard other things, too.

MAERYN LIMPED DOWN THE BRIDGE CONNECTING THE DRAWING ROOM from her husband's chancery. It swayed with the wind, branches whistling in the majestic trees set against the song of a thousand birds. As she fought to maintain control, the tension in her limbs called attention to her fresh bruises. She winced, pushing on.

She never learned. That's what Aiden said. She always had to ask questions she didn't deserve answers to. Always had to *push*. To push *him*. And he said this, always, with an insatiable hunger in his eyes, starving for another excuse to throw her across a room or connect his fist to her pliant flesh.

Aiden wasn't wrong. She had to ask. To push. She had to continuously demonstrate that she was a foolish woman, with nothing to add but silly notions and fears. She had to do this so that he wouldn't concern himself with his cowing wife lingering in the shadows. The silly, foolish woman who was a threat to no one.

Maeryn was used to the beatings after twenty years. She even looked forward to them, in a way. They were like armor. Her tolerance grew with each fresh assault. Sometimes, she even had to fake the pain to satisfy his cruelty. Even though she was used to it, it didn't mean she wanted him to ramp up his beatings to a new level. Her tolerance was hard earned.

She only wished her children could see, that within the shell of a broken body, she was a warrior.

It was only her eldest son now, Cian. Breandan and Dorrin were at university. Eavan was off in the world on an adventure, one Maeryn endorsed in her heart and would one day directly say so to her daughter, Guardians willing. And Assana...

No. Not now.

Maeryn used the ropes to pull herself forward. It was mostly theater, but Aiden had eyes everywhere. It wouldn't do to have her sashay through the world with ease.

And anyway, it *did* hurt. She didn't need to completely pretend, only to exaggerate.

When she reached the platform, she stumbled forward, affecting a series of gasps to convey the monumental effort required of her. Satisfied with her performance, she moved into the room where her husband was addressing an officer in his guard.

Maeryn slinked into a corner, cowering, conveying clearly the absence of threat she presented.

"Mads. I will have more. And I will not have my own man laying before me a list of denials."

"Lord Quinlanden, you chose me because of my experience with the clahnns. I'm offering you the benefit of this experience when I say—"

"What I do not wish to hear!" Aiden's neck throbbed. "Your experience. What is that to me, when you use it to deny me?"

Mads Waters tried his best not to show he thought his lord was a fool. Maeryn recognized the effort. She appreciated it. It was familiar.

"We've taken too many from Saleen. They don't have armies, but they are not without defense. The other clahnns have taken notice."

"Subdued. We have subdued them, Mads."

Subjugated. Enslaved. Maeryn silently corrected them both.

"We take for granted that the four clahnns are disconnected, my lord. But Drumain is already whispering of joining with Asgill and Mayke to put an end to this. If they do, we cannot assume Mortain is enough. The clahnns have different strengths. They are one race, but they are not the same."

"He is more than enough. We will do to them what they did to Saleen. Why do you fight me on this?"

"My words aren't intended to provoke fight, my lord."

Aiden narrowed his eyes. "Any time you come to me with news that limits my desires you provoke fight."

"Our guard is the largest in the kingdom, next to the king's own, my lord."

"And?"

"It will do what you intend it to. Ten times over."

Aiden leaned over the cypress railing. A bird landed on his head, and he swatted it with an open fist, without looking up. The creature sailed into the sea of branches. "It will do so better when we grow it. And we *will* grow it. You possess no objection capable of changing my mind and to continue presenting them will only cause me to question whether I have at my side the right man."

Mads grimaced. Bowed to his lord's back. "My lord," he said and stormed from the room without even a glance her way. He didn't even see her.

Aiden reached for the carafe of wine on the desk and launched it into the trees beyond.

"Scamper, dog," he commanded. "Go beg for scraps elsewhere."

Maeryn smiled to herself. So he had seen her.

She crawled from the room on all fours, knowing it would please him.

Asherley said they could trust Khallum Warwick, and if there was anyone more competent to run this kingdom than Maeryn's sister, she hadn't met them yet.

Tell him what you told me. But wait. You can do it but once. That's all the risk we can afford. Wait until you know what he plans next.

Her foolish, ambitious husband had already abducted and enslaved over ten thousand Medvedev from the nearby Saleen Clahnn. A fact he'd managed to somehow keep sequestered within the treetop kingdom of Whitechurch, through the strange and foreign magic of Mortain, until now, when the separate clahnns of the Hinterlands were talking unification, in order to fight back. And when the Reaches discovered this foul treachery, there was no telling what force they might bring to stand tall against Aiden's untenable overreach.

We have an unexpected ally, who shares with us a common foe.

Yes, she would start with that. That sounded ubiquitous. Elusive. She had more reading to do to learn even more words, but she liked having more ways to describe herself and the world now. If Aiden properly feared her, he'd put a stop to her sessions with their scholar, but Maeryn had done her job well, and so he allowed her these distractions. He seemed to understand there was some point to satisfying her still, and that killing her would be hard to wash over to the outside world. She'd outgrown her usefulness, delivering him five children, but disposing of her would create more problems than it solved.

Maeryn, moving through the shadows, went to share her news with the man her sister told her to trust.

With the dowdy Correen safely handed off to someone requiring her presence, Asherley turned back around and moved in the direction she'd come.

Eoghan hadn't spoken a word to her since she arrived. He assigned his sisters to looking after her, pausing just short of ordering her locked up like the boys. Correen and Assyria both seemed just as confused by the lack of swift dealings on the matter of Lady Blackwood, but it was Assyria who first came to the understanding. Asherley recognized a secret smile from another powerful woman when she saw one.

It was Assyria she hoped to converse with, privately. This tall, proud warrior woman who was the opposite of her sister in every visible way. Hair rich in color, flowing with life, matched the fire in her eyes. In another life, Assyria would rule a kingdom, not be pressed into the corners by an ineffective, deformed child who had no master of his own emotions, let alone his subjects. It seemed fitting that she'd been the one he placed in charge of security at Duncarrow.

Asherley needed time with Eoghan first. To get close to him.

Closer than her desires would let her, but she'd fight them, as she fought any of her limitations.

He spent his days and nights in his chambers. From what she gleaned through the whispers, he even took his meals there. There were rooms in the keep for entertaining, for banquets and masques, but they'd remained unused since the death of King Khain. No ships approached the port; the king's own hovered in the western dock, collecting cobwebs.

Asherley never called him The Pretender, like others did. It was what he was, but to think words was to risk speaking them. A moniker that called attention to Eoghan's dark truth was a name born of emotion, and emotion was a weakness. Khallum could spittle off his cache of insults, but she would stay grounded in the emotions that served her best.

The hall to the king's chamber was empty. So empty she had to lighten her steps to kill the echo. But as she approached the double doors, she realized she was wrong. Another figure, one comfortable enough in the shadows to meld into them, stepped out in front of his door.

Asherley quickly fell into a curtsey. "Princess Assyria."

Assyria nodded. "Lady Blackwood. Here to beg an audience with my brother?"

She saw no point in lying. Not to this one. "I was hoping to catch a word with the king."

Desperate cries sounded from within the chamber. Assyria drew a tight smile across her face. "If only you'd come earlier. They were screams, then."

Asherley knew to be careful with this woman. Whether she recognized kin in her, they were on opposite sides. "Assana is learning, as all women must, how to be a wife. The transition from girl to woman isn't always easy."

"Lady Assana. She is the wife of your king," Assyria corrected. "And I hardly think my brother has made her a woman."

Asherley had been straining to read the princess' whispers since approaching her, but the princess was locked down. She'd come across few in her life who possessed such control over themselves. "Oh?"

"You haven't spent your days wandering these halls for nothing, Lady Blackwood. My brother was born in Prince Darrick's shadow, and he can't escape it now. Their mother was strong enough for one, but two she brought into this world. Only one was ready."

Asherley had met Darrick Rhiagain a year or so before Eoghan had him pitched off the cliffs of Duncarrow. Even as a prince, he'd seen the importance of taking progress around the kingdom. Not only to be seen by his subjects, but to see them. To hear their words and know their needs. When he'd arrived for his spell in Longwood Rush, she'd been possessed of a hope she'd never known before. The Reaches belonged to themselves, and this man would see it and restore what was taken from them. Some of his words suggested he'd concluded this on his own.

Physically, intellectually, Darrick was twice the man Eoghan was. Perhaps this did have something to do with their time in the womb, but it hadn't stopped there.

"Despite his... limitations..." Asherley tread carefully. "The queen has no choice but to submit to her duty."

"The queen cannot submit to what cannot be delivered. And so, if that cannot be delivered, then upon her he delivers instead his frustration at the failed task," Assyria said. And then... then her whispers opened up. And Asherley couldn't know for certain—not certain enough to ever address it—but she could've sworn the woman was doing it on purpose. Delivering them to her, like gifts. *The parts are there. The desires are not. What he most longs for is not a young wife in his bed, but a mother.*

Asherley and the princess locked eyes. An understanding passed between them.

What Assyria suggested was repulsive, but useful.

The doors to the chamber flung wide. Assana, covered in bruises and cuts, decked in a tattered shift, glanced at her without recognition before darting down the hall. Her sobs echoed long after she disappeared.

Assyria nodded at the doors. "Seems you may catch a word with my brother, after all."

"Mama?"

Maeryn froze. She'd left the palace of trees behind for the comfort of the stables, where no one but she went. Their horseman died in a vat of wine, which was fitting. For that was how he'd spent all his hours. It certainly wasn't tending to horses. Aiden never replaced him, because Aiden had no use for horses. He traveled by litter only and expected things to be as they should be, putting no effort in himself.

The stables were her place now. She'd taken over tending the horses. Yet another harmless pastime Aiden said nothing about.

No one else came here but her. She didn't take that for granted. *Fortuitous. Serendipitous.* She'd learned those words, too, and thought of them when considering her privacy here, but she hadn't yet learned the right word for too good to be true. So Maeryn was *cautious, vigilant, heedful.*

She'd been preparing to remove the loose board hiding the box with her quill, ink, and vellum, when Cian's voice stopped her.

Carefully, making extra sure he could see her wince, Maeryn groaned as she stood. Cian was more her than Aiden, but Aiden had taken everything else from her. He would take her son, too.

"My dove," she said. Cian's mouth twisted in sadness as he took in her fresh new battered look. He was used to it after all these years, enough that he no longer gasped or cried at the sight of her. He was also older. Sixteen. Old enough to be the lord of Whitechurch if some accident were to befall his father.

"I… I heard something today."

"Did you?" Maeryn eased herself onto a nearby stool. Behind her, a horse, one of her favorites—a mare named Ayla—made a soft chuffing sound. She never rode Ayla, much as she was desperate to. If Aiden knew she had a favorite, he'd have her slaughtered and fed to the pigs.

"I want to know if I should talk to Father about it."

Maeryn nodded to the stool on the other side of the barn. Cian grabbed it and moved it closer to her before sitting. He leaned forward, dropping his voice.

"I heard Father is involved in some bad business with the Saleen Clahnn."

Maeryn inhaled. It was only a matter of time before the children knew of their father's machinations. Mortain's glamours could only hold so well.

It had started as a partnership with Chieftainess Ohsmha. Aiden wanted an army, bigger than anything else in the kingdom. More numerous than the king's knights. The Easterlands had never been under forced conscription, and there were some demands even a lord from a long, respected lineage could not make. He increased bonuses for voluntary service, but it wasn't enough.

Mads might regret the suggestion now, but it had been his own words that stirred Aiden's idea to life. Chieftainess Ohsmha was a woman of industry. Unlike the chieftainesses of the other three clahnns, she recognized there could be benefits in alliances with men. They first met in Whitechurch, secreting her in under the cover of night.

And then Ohsmha made a terrible miscalculation. She allowed Aiden and Mads, along with a third man, known to most simply as Mortain, to enter the Saleen lands through the sacred entrance.

Mortain was a man from no place, with no name. Maeryn didn't know if Mortain was his first name, or a family name, but it didn't come from the Easterlands. She heard Mads tell Aiden he was from where the Rhiagains were from, but Mads, back then, would have said anything to please his lord and gain favor. Such a suggestion played neatly into Aiden's delusions.

Mortain was a great sorcerer. Maeryn was no stranger to magic, as a Blackwood, but his was unlike any she'd seen. It wasn't the type taught at the Sepulchre, and practiced under their watchful eye. He promised Aiden he could put the Saleen under his sway, and that was exactly what he did. When they left the Saleen lands, they brought with them a thousand Medvedev, each with a hollow look in their eyes and a will to do their master's bidding.

She wouldn't have thought it possible if she hadn't seen it with her own eyes.

Aiden built his army from the subjugated Medvedev of the Saleen Clahnn, taking a thousand and multiplying this by ten. He cleared the working men and women of the lands around Whitechurch and housed his slave army there. He built no wall to lock them in. It wasn't needed. They'd go nowhere their master didn't command.

Maeryn didn't know exactly how many Saleen lived beyond their palace in the trees, but she feared it was more than what still lived in the Saleen lands.

Only to Corin, Aiden's brother, had Maeryn ever spoken of any of this. Corin would make a fine ruler. Corin was everything Aiden was not. Maeryn loved Corin, but Corin was married to Yesenia Warwick. Just as fate had given the wrong brother power in the Easterlands, so had the wrong marriages been made two decades past.

How different her life would have been, as the wife of Corin.

"Mama?"

"What have you heard, dove?"

"That he's in some bad—"

"No, specifically, Cian."

Cian's hands shook. He tried to hide it from her. "I see them, beyond the trees. I knew something wasn't right, but Father always said they were our allies. But that's not exactly right, is it?"

Maeryn had always eased the fears and suspicions of her babies. It did nothing for her or them to have them in her court. She wished to protect them, not draw a target on their backs.

But Cian was nearly a man now. He came to her not with the wide eyes of a child, but the concerned, knowing gaze of one grown and becoming more intimate with the realities of the world.

"No, it isn't exactly right. None of it is right," she said. "But you would do well to keep your concerns to yourself, son. There can be nothing gained in confronting a man with the power your father has. You do know this?"

Cian's lips pressed so tight they were white. His shaking hands turned to fists. Tears of anger burned at his bottom lids. "It isn't right, Mama. What he's doing goes against nature."

"It goes against all," Maeryn said. She wanted to comfort him, but that was what a mother would do to a child. Cian came to her as a man, and she would treat him accordingly. "And there will be a day of reckoning to come, where he will be taken to answer for his crimes. But, Cian…"

Cian looked up. He fought with himself, a tangle between child and man. Between the emotional insistence that something unfair must be made right, and the understanding that things rarely were. "Yes?"

"It isn't you who can take this on. Who can take him on." Maeryn rose and decided she didn't care if he was a man. She needed to feel him pressed to her, as she did when he was a baby. She pulled him to his feet and held him. "I have a more important job for you, dove."

Cian pulled back and looked at her.

"When that day comes, and it will come, Whitechurch will need a real leader. One both untainted by the stain of your father's handiwork, and above his suspicion. Do you understand me?"

It was the man, not the boy, who looked her in the eye and answered. "Yes. I understand."

EOGHAN SLUMPED OVER IN A TALL VELVET CHAIR, DRESSED ONLY IN HIS nightshirt. He clutched a glass of wine in one hand. The other lay limply over the side of the chair arm, bent unnaturally.

"I didn't send for you, Lady Blackwood."

"No, Your Grace."

"And yet, you are here."

"I am."

The bed chamber was a mess. The blankets on the bed were strewn half on the floor. Blood stained the sheets and pillows. More than one glass lay shattered in pieces. Assana had suffered here. She would suffer more. But Asherley could not let her heart rush her.

She approached the king slowly. The dim light obscured the specifics of the man, but couldn't hide how he swam in the fabric covering him. How his thin and gnarled limbs bent inelegantly.

Eoghan grunted. "I've no use of you."

"Begging your pardon, Your Grace, but you cannot know all of my uses. We've only just met."

"I should have you locked in the sky dungeon with the others."

"You should."

Eoghan tilted his head to look up at her. "You think I should?"

"It's what I would do."

He laughed, a high-pitched, childlike sound. "I was told you were an unusual woman."

"All women are unusual to men. They never know what to do with us."

"And tell me, what's that supposed to mean?"

Asherley leaned over his chair, dropping her hands to wrap around the arms of the oak. The panic in his eyes energized her. The stirring under his nightshirt emboldened her. "Only that, once they understand what we can offer—truly offer, that is—they often find it was precisely what they'd been searching for all along."

Eoghan squirmed in his chair. His erection pressed against the thin fabric. She sucked in her stomach, pressing her breasts higher. "I have everything I need," he said, voice cracking.

Asherley reached her hand toward his head. He flinched and a small sound, like a moan, escaped. She knelt down and slid the fingers of her other hand inside of her dress, cupping her breast.

She was close enough now to feel his cock, throbbing with his escalating heartbeat, against her belly. He couldn't take his eyes off the breast in her hand. "Do you?"

Eoghan closed his eyes tight. "Go. Begone!"

Asherley slowly backed away. She'd done what she came to do. She hadn't expected his acquiescence in their first encounter, only for him to receive the message she needed to send.

A small stain appeared on his shirt.

Message received.

Asherley curtsied. "Your Grace."

30

THE DARK CONTENTS OF HIS HEART

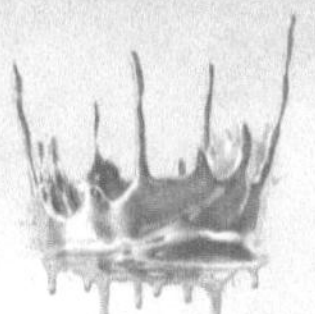

Darrick hadn't always been the heir apparent. And, depending on which version of the truth one believed, he wasn't the first son Khain had killed.

Anabella repeated this thought as she tried, failing, to listen to Stefan's colorful story about pirates circling in the White Sea. She repeated it because her memory wasn't all that was sliding away from her in the sky dungeon, but it was the one thing connecting her to the world she'd come from.

Her hands shook, so she buried them in her tattered gown, smiling through her tears at Stefan's animated joy.

Anabella rarely heard news of the outside world. She strained to hear the guards engage in their light gossip of the day, but what came from their mouths was a mix of facts and tall tales. She tuned it out, unless it was useful, and several days ago, what she heard suddenly became useful again.

The Right of Choosing, to hear them speak of it, words excited and hurried as if there was a prize for being the first to say them, had been a disaster. He'd left with one bride, not four. But that wasn't all. Two sons of the realm, and a wife. From there, the animated guards competed to out-shock the other, and it was evident whatever details came from then on would be whatever made the best story.

But if any of it was true, Eoghan would be in the throes of terrible anger.

Anabella thought the part about the sons was likely true, because she'd heard young men howling for their mothers being dragged through the stone halls days past. The cells were spaced far enough apart that their screams faded once they passed.

She wondered if they would rot there.

This was the sort of thing Eoghan might have talked to her about when he still visited her regularly. He found many uses for her, not all of them physical. She was a safe place to share the dark contents of his heart as well.

Eoghan didn't always talk to her when he came to her cell. Most often it was for the nursing, and this activity came with no words at all. The intensity of his day would melt into the soft, soothing ritual where he would draw milk that her body should no longer be producing, but did, for him. When he left, lids drowsy, drunk on her body's precious resource, he was like a child turning down for a nap.

As humiliating as that was for Anabella, she preferred those visits. He would do what he came to do—sometimes a small stain would appear near the groin of his tunic, but she pretended not to notice this, for both their sakes—and leave her. No threats spewed. No mind games.

Today, he was beside himself. His first visit to her in so long she'd allowed hope to seep into the cracks and let light in. She should've known he'd be back.

"Darling, finish your broth."

Stefan never complained about the food they were served, if one could call it that. He couldn't see the dark circles beneath his eyes, or how he was too small for his age. He knew nothing else. "I want to play, Mama."

"Finish, so you can be strong for the pirate invasion."

He brightened. "Yes, ma'am."

"Mama will be at the desk." She didn't know why she still bothered to tell him things like this. The room had only a bed, a desk, and a privy pot. All separated by no more than ten feet. She didn't dare hope for a day where she might call to him from another room. From the other side of Weatherford Hall.

"Writing your story?"

"It's not a story. It's..." Anabella paused. What was it? Memoirs? Confessions?

No, it's what you need to do before you pass from this world. For him. For yourself. For Darrick. You tell yourself the words are seen by no one, but they are seen through the eyes of the blessed Guardians, and when your promise is spent, they will deliver to you a new one. For all you've suffered. Both of you.

"Yes, darling. My story."

"You know too much, Anabella. You won't ever leave here."

He'd never said it to me before.

I did know too much. I knew more than even he did.

But before I recall what he told me today, I must go back, returning to what he told me in the beginning.

He tended to me more frequently in my first days as his prisoner. Have I mentioned I almost lost Stefan? I was roughly handled on the journey, and my grief for Darrick had not yet taken wings. I had no time to consider the meaning of his loss before I was in Eoghan's grasp.

Eoghan's own physician attended my lying in, and then Stefan's birth. He told the man I was his mistress, and the doctor was paid well enough to believe anything he was told.

While I lay swimming in my own delirium, Eoghan told me the history of his people. As I've written, he spoke of the storm, the crash, the washing upon shores foreign. He started this by regaling me with tales of their old gods, and of riches beyond reason. Gold falling from trees, and rain that renewed not only the earth, but the men walking it.

Like many in the kingdom, I possessed a natural curiosity about the land the Rhiagains had come from, but it was Darrick who had satisfied mine. I listened to Eoghan, because I had nowhere to go, naught else to do. I knew most of it was lies. One day, in a fit of anger at his father, he even admitted to me none of the stories they told were true. That the Rhiagains, including Carrow himself, had struggled for survival and employed quick thinking to appeal to the simplistic nature that sits at the base of all folk: the need to believe in something bigger than them. They lied in silent appeal for their lives and turned those lies into a kingdom.

"We made ourselves from nothing, and I won't have a tired old man preach of gods to me! His time is over, Anabella. I will not be made to take orders from the dying."

Darrick had already told me about the Rhiagain dishonesties, but it was the first time Eoghan hadn't lied to me.

It was that day he commanded me to write him daily love letters spelling out my desires for him and only him.

When Stefan turned two, I said nothing of the anniversary. But Eoghan remembered. How or why, I do not know, but he did. And to commemorate this, he bade me let them both feed from me, Eoghan from one breast, Stefan the other. Like brothers, he said, for he had no other brother. I did as he commanded, tears landing upon both their heads, and swore I would kill him one day with my own hands.

I eventually lost that desire, as I lost many others.

Through the years he offered pieces of his own history. His jealousy of Darrick, which he never directly articulated or admitted but couldn't hide. How his sister, Correen, had been charged with raising him but loathed him. Assyria, his other sister, the more delightful one, doted on Darrick... yet another divide marking the gulf between the twin brothers.

Minutes separated their birth. Another lie that Eoghan liked to tell was that he had been born first, but the midwife had mixed things up. The story grew even more involved when he mentioned his father's sorcerer, Oldwin, had paid her off, for he had seen a future where Eoghan stepped to the throne after Darrick's fall.

Oldwin is a Rhiagain, too. Some distant relation of the king's line. Eoghan sometimes said Oldwin was immortal, and had been with them from the days before the shipwreck, which, if true, made him the only living man who knew the truth of where they'd come from. I'll never know his truth, but I do know the magic they brought from wherever they came is not our magic. It is not the same at all. It is a magic to be feared.

It may be I knew of their plans for the Right of Choosing before anyone beyond Duncarrow. The Epoch of the Accordant had not led to war because, at the core of it, Khain was not wrong. The kingdom was in chaos. Trade agreements severed, borderland skirmishes threatening to turn to full-on battles. Eoghan told me one night that Khain hadn't cared about wars or peace, but submission. "Father would let them all kill one another if it didn't mean the end of the kingdom." By the time he had the elder lords and ladies assassinated, the Reaches were too consumed with fear of him to retaliate.

Though it is often hard for me to separate lies from the truth, when Eoghan told me it had been his idea, and not his father's, to concoct the Right of Choosing ceremony, I believed him. It would have been easy not to. In some ways, the Right of Choosing was the inevitable conclusion of the Epoch. First, unite the Reaches, then make them Rhiagains.

But then, on a night where the rain hadn't stopped for weeks, Eoghan told me he'd met a girl. He never named her, and I never asked. To ask was to break his stream of thought, and to invite something worse. All he would say was that she was from a Great Family. One of the most great, in fact, and before I could wonder how he'd even met such a girl, he confessed also that his absence from my chambers for the past weeks had been because he'd been away.

"I heard tell of a family who had taken in my brother. I had to see for myself."

My heart skipped. His brother. Only now do I know he didn't mean Darrick.

"I will wed her," he said. "I will find a way."

I knew what he spoke of when he suggested a way must be found. As Darrick had told me, the Rhiagains had long married nobodies, or sometimes within their own bloodline. Their hold on the kingdom was tenuous enough without introducing powerful outsiders.

He told me a few nights later about the Right of Choosing. How he had positioned it to his father just as one should if attempting to persuade... a conclusion to Khain's own vision. A kingdom truly united, not only with one another, but the Rhiagains. A bride from each Reach.

Eoghan asked me what I thought. He so seldom did, and I feared the question because I knew he didn't really want to know what I thought about anything. But I was not only his whipping post, but the echoes of his greatest desires. I knew this when I said, "If you love her, then you must find a way."

"Love," he said with a sneer, without elaboration.

Tonight I learned his plan had been for naught.

He returned with a bride, but not the one he'd concocted this mad scheme for.

And then he told me about the other son.

ANABELLA, BREATHLESS, ROLLED THE SCROLL TIGHT AND PRESSED IT into the small opening of the pipe. She should pause there for the night, but she had more to say, and she didn't know how much time she had left with which to say it. She had never seen Eoghan so angry, and if he couldn't inflict his punishments upon those who wronged him, he would deliver them upon those available.

As it had been for the past five years, that outlet was Anabella.

She pressed her tender, bruised breasts against the cool stone. A bubble of relief groaned up from within her.

Anabella glanced over at Stefan, who was properly distracted by the illusion of his pirate invasion.

The last of the day's light was dying. The moon wouldn't be enough tonight to light her desk.

She had no time to waste.

. . .

Tonight Eoghan told me the story of Khain's first son, Dain.

Most in the kingdom forget about Khain's first wife, Decima, or that Decima's first child was not Correen but a little boy named Dain.

Dain died when he was very young of a swift illness—too swift to engage their healers. It was a great tragedy for the Rhiagains, but in this they were not unlike common families. Some mothers did not even name their children until they were two, and then held their breath until they were five.

From Decima, Khain next received Correen and Assyria, but when Decima died without producing another son, Khain did not immediately remarry. When he did, to a Southerland fisherman's daughter named Florian, he finally got his heir, two times over, when twins Darrick and Eoghan came into the world. The tragedy of Dain faded to distant memory.

I know now this is not what happened.

I believe what Eoghan confessed to me tonight is the truth. I know I have said that Eoghan lies. Eoghan has the menace to lie well, but not the imagination. His lies are designed to bolster his image. His truths often threaten it.

And I must make no mistake. Eoghan is threatened. And a threatened man, especially one lacking courage, is one ready to implode.

Dain was beloved as the son and heir of a dynasty many viewed in decline after the death of Fynne the Good. The kingdom had no such nickname for Khain. They had names for him, though.

Understand all this I will convey was passed to Eoghan, from his father. I have said I believe this to be the truth, but I believe it to be Eoghan's truth. What really transpired between Khain and Oldwin, and the others, may never be fully known. It matters not. Stefan and my lives depend only upon what Eoghan believes.

From the time Dain was in swaddling, Khain brought in a bevy of staff to tend to him at all hours. He was taken from his mother and fed by four different wet nurses. Khain's wife was pregnant again soon, this time with Correen, but Correen did not receive the same attentions from her father. It was said Decima prayed for a daughter, so this child could be hers. One for the kingdom, one for the mother.

All was well, until Oldwin came to his master with a terrible vision.

Oldwin's magic, as I have said, is not our magic. But among his many gifts is believed to be the power of clear foresight.

And so he said this to Khain:

From Khain's loins would spring a son who would undo the Rhiagain legacy. He would restore the Reaches to their own rule and burn Duncarrow to the rocks, leaving only salt and ash resting upon the ruins of their legacy.

Khain loved his son. Knowing he may have had a role in what happened to Darrick later, I struggle to write those words, but even terrible men have light in them somewhere. Whether it was a filial love or one born of knowing his kingdom was secure, only Khain and the Guardians will ever know.

Oldwin advised Khain he must dispose of the child or lose the kingdom. It took him half a year before he could bring himself to heed the advice of his most trusted councilor. He gave Dain to his Lord Chancellor to perform the terrible deed and looked to the future.

Khain had his two daughters, and time moved on. He was desperate for a son, but afraid of bringing one into the world, until Oldwin assured him the risk to his kingdom had passed.

When Correen and Assyria were nearly grown, Oldwin advised Khain it was again safe to have sons. Khain remarried, to Florian, and soon after, Darrick and Eoghan were born. All again was well.

Until the Lord Chancellor died. Upon his deathbed, he confessed to his wife that he could not bring himself to murder an innocent child. He told her instead he found a home for the little one, placing him with a couple who had struggled for a family of their own. Before he could say where little Dain went, his heart stopped. The words died with him.

His wife, terrified for her life in possession of such a secret, took her husband's deathbed confession to Khain. Darrick and Eoghan were thirteen or fourteen by then. Khain, however, was old, having lived two lives.

He was already unwell by then. He was stunned by the confession of the Lord Chancellor, whom he trusted like a brother.

He shared the Lord Chancellor's words with Oldwin. Oldwin assured him he had not seen this, and therefore it could not be true, but it wasn't enough for Khain. Khain had the Lord Chancellor's widow executed and Oldwin committed to the sky dungeon.

I've heard Oldwin, from time to time. He speaks from his cell in a language unfamiliar to me. He does not sound as old as he should. Perhaps the rumors about him are true, after all.

Khain's paranoia took over from there. If he could not trust his closest advisors, that left only his sons.

Darrick had already shown signs of breaking with the Rhiagain way. So Khain sent Eoghan into the world, in disguise, in search of the son whose promise should have been long ago spent.

Eoghan did not find his brother, but he did find a young woman worthy of his attentions. His adoration for this young woman launched the nightmare that would become the Right of Choosing. It brought us to the here and the now.

If Dain Rhiagain does live, he'd be nearing forty years of age. A father, perhaps, even a grandfather.

If he does live, Eoghan is not the rightful king.

If he does live, many will die.

As for me, Anabella Weatherford Rhiagain, I never expected to step foot on soft ground again. I long ago accepted my son's life would be so much shorter than he deserved.

I expected our death would come at the hand of Eoghan's neglect, but instead, I now see it may come in the flames of his wrath, which soars high in his many defeats. The failed Right of Choosing. His love—who must be either Eavan Quinlanden, Hollyn Blackwood, Esmerelda Warwick, or Lisbet Dereham—torn from his grasp. His constant reminder of a brother with a greater throne claim, whose existence is only made more sinister but Eoghan's inability to confirm or deny it.

And Stefan.

The son of Darrick.

If he cannot find Dain and his descendants, then he will turn to the heir he does have within his grasp.

Guardians, I no longer beseech you to protect us. I am not so foolish.

Oh, Guardian of the Treasured Past, I ask of you to remember what no one else will know, and that is that Darrick Rhiagain had a son, and his name was Stefan.

Oh, Guardian of Anguish and Tribulation, I beseech you to see how much we have already suffered and make the ending swift.

Oh, Guardian of the Warrior's Aim, I beseech you to sponsor the strength of the one who will end this tyranny, where I, and my beloved Darrick, have failed.

Darrick. I love thee.

31

CIRCLING THE SKIES

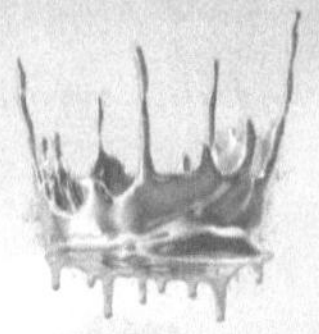

They'd entered the Hinterlands.

Undoubtedly, this man, Valen, was telling the rest of Ravenna's party this very thing. She was too far away to hear. It was better for her, for them all, for her to remain where she was, circling the skies. But she knew the moment they'd entered this strange land. No one had to tell her.

There was powerful magic here. Ravenna herself was experiencing it for the first time, as everything south of Torrin's Pass had been a world beyond her known one. When she was younger—old enough to understand, too young yet to relate—her mother began her training with the histories of the kingdom. She was to experience her own histories later, and of course, she never did. Yet one more failure for Ravenna to add to her growing list. But although the Ravenwoods of The Rookery were never to venture beyond the protections of the Northerland lords, Varinya impressed upon her daughter that knowing your threats was as important as avoiding them.

The Medvedev, and not man, were the threat her mother was most concerned about. *The Medvedev are the only creatures truly native to this kingdom, Ravenna. Men think of Rhiagains as outsiders, but men are too, they just do not know it. Their arrival, from Beyond, happened long before anyone possessed the ability to create records, or write down the histories. But there was no arrival for the Medvedev. They were always here.*

Alasyr says Medvedev look like men.

Alasyr has never met one any more than I have. He knows only what I have told him, and I, what my mother before me. Yes, they look like you or me. You would know them by their eyes and hair, both of which are colors unnatural to us. They have with them beastly familiars, whose souls are linked to theirs. They call them familiars, but they are also guards, protecting them from land, sea, and sky.

Why are they a threat, Mother?

When you one day are sent to Wulfsgate for your training, if you listen too much to man you may hear the lies that the Medvedev were driven into the Hinterlands when man expanded their realms. But that is not true. The Westerlands, Easterlands, they were overgrown with forests. The Norther-lands, ice, and the Southerlands, salt and sand. Intentionally untouched. The Medvedev chose the lands of the Hinterlands and infused them with their magic. Every tree. Every flora, fauna. They all respond to the Medvedev. Serve them. When man arrived, they were massacred by the dozens. Hundreds. Thousands. And then, eventually, they came to a truce. Men asked for roads, and the Medvedev, graciously, allowed them only where travel between the Reaches was necessary.

Why did they allow them? When they could drive men away?

The Medvedev are peaceful, mostly. They wish to be left alone, to live without turmoil or war. It is only when threatened that they turn to violence. And you, Ravenna, are a threat to them.

Why us? When we cannot travel beyond the ice?

Unlike man, who came from another world, with their sticks and stones, you, Ravenna, come from pure magic. A man could not best a Medvedev, but a Ravenwood? They could not so easily dispatch of us. They know this. As long as they remain there, and we here, then we are both safe. If that were to ever change, nothing would ever be the same.

Ravenna had put up no argument when Lisbet declared their intentions to venture to the Hinterlands. Never shared these concerns with Drystan. Nothing. She'd done nothing.

She braced against a northerly wind that threatened to tear her from the sky. She'd let herself become too lax as they traveled farther south, and now east. Was that why her magic was fading away?

It felt stronger here, in these lands, but she dared not test it. She didn't truly think herself a threat to the Medvedev... not her, one lowly Ravenwood who had failed her destiny in all the ways that mattered. But they might not know this, and so she wouldn't risk drawing attention to herself. She didn't care as much about her own life now, but she would not be the cause of harm to the others. Not after she'd failed to prevent what happened to them with the brigands.

But these were pointless mental exercises, guessing, hypothesizing. They were already at risk. The Medvedev knew the moment anyone foreign stepped upon their lands. Their skies as well. If they remained unmolested, that was no accident, either.

Ravenna should tell them. Perhaps Valen, their mysterious, opportune protector, knew these risks and had already shared them. Valen seemed to know about a lot of things that didn't concern him, and these he fed to Drystan like they were his favorite foods. Drystan ate it all up, desperate for something resembling paternal mentoring.

She could think of her love in these gradually reducing terms because she herself was receding. Thinking of him as less than would weaken the damage to her heart when the time came. She wasn't only a priestess losing her power, but a woman who had taken lives. Worthy of no one.

Ravenna was ripped between two conflicting feelings on her actions against the brigands. She wasn't sorry they were dead, these horrid men who had abused Eavan so horribly and nearly murdered

Drystan. They deserved a fate worse than death, but delivering one was beyond her power.

The memory of their screams assaulted her nights. The first one to die sometimes spoke to her in these animalistic echoes. He was the only one to look up... to see her, and to understand that it was she who had rained the fire down upon him. As flames licked at the thin fabric, threads melting into flesh that no longer looked like skin, he never dropped his eyes. Full of questions. That he could die not understanding the action was born of vengeance made it all even worse. The man believed he'd been wronged. By her.

The others flailed around, as if dancing. Their burning limbs formed orange arcs across the air, spelling out their unavoidable doom. And still she swooped in, collecting even more fire, raining it down until the dancing stopped. She waited still until all that was left was the acrid, gamey scent emanating from singed piles of dark ash.

They deserved death, but she could not reconcile her horror that she'd been capable of delivering it.

There was no solve for what she was experiencing. If she returned to Midnight Crest, she'd be killed. Their laws demanded it. Nor could she stay. She didn't belong here. She didn't belong anywhere anymore.

Ravenna did the only thing she could do. She circled the skies in hopes the answer would eventually clarify itself. Just as it had been with the delayed memories of her people, and their history, perhaps her purpose in this world too, was only waiting for the right moment.

DRYSTAN QUICKENED HIS PACE SO HE AND VALEN COULD PULL AHEAD. He wished Lisbet would stop inserting her distrust into everything Valen shared. She might not want to hear what he had to say, but Drystan did. Valen was the first adult in his life who had ever spoken so plainly to him. Who did not look upon him and see all that was missing.

Eventually, they were far enough ahead where even Eavan's nonstop talk of ball gowns and how Kian Medvedev would be so happy and surprised to see her was drowned out. Lisbet would stay with Eavan, because someone had to. Likely she'd pick up on the reason for the distance he created, but she could yell at him later.

"I'm sorry about my sister," Drystan said.

"Don't apologize for her. She wouldn't want you to."

"She doesn't understand."

Valen bobbed with his horse's pace, looking straight ahead. He was more alert now, fearful of losing the path. The woods had closed in on them, as if alive and fully aware of their presence. Drystan didn't think these woods looked very different than the ones close to home, save the more vibrant flora, but they *felt* different. If his better sense wasn't pushing this feeling back, he would've said they were in another world. A world of *more*.

"She is doing what family should do, Drystan. She is protecting you."

"From you? You saved us! We would be dead if—"

Valen held up a hand. "There is nothing more pointless in life than ruminating on the path you could have taken. You'll learn that, and not because of any words said to you."

Drystan didn't respond. Valen was such an enigma. And he, too young to know the questions appropriate to solve the riddle of the man.

"You pulled us ahead to ask me questions. Ask them."

Drystan flushed. He enjoyed Valen's intuitive nature more when it wasn't turned on him. "You've been here before?"

"Aye."

"When? Why?"

"The story of how I came to be in the Hinterlands is long, and I'm not sure it would be as satisfying as what came after." Valen's face clouded over. "I nearly died, when I was not so much older than you are now. I was a man without a house, without a name. I wandered, and those wanderings brought me to these lands." The corner of Valen's mouth twitched. "I had, of course, heard tale of what a poor idea it would be to find myself uninvited in Hinterland territory, but I was beyond such fears. I was dead to everyone who had once cared about me. What would death be to a man like that?"

"How did you nearly die?"

"Betrayal," Valen said, so firmly Drystan knew he'd say no more on this matter.

"You really thought they would kill you? The Medvedev?"

"Is that not what you were also taught?"

"I was, but..." Drystan paused.

"But you, too, question that which seems strange, don't you?"

Drystan nodded. "I struggled to understand how the Medvedev could be peaceful and also cruel."

"Men can be both."

"Yes, but our reputations are not held to the idea of our peacefulness. Or our cruelty."

"Do you believe it is still cruelty if the act is done in defense of oneself and one's survival?"

Drystan considered this. "Cruelty seems defined by the perspective of the one wielding the word. The one with the perceived advantage of morality."

Valen smiled. "So it is. The Medvedev are not cruel. But they don't suffer outsiders with ill intentions. One who could call that cruelty would likely be one with ill intentions of their own."

"They didn't kill you," Drystan said. "So what did they do?"

"They invited me into their homeland. They fed me and helped restore me to health."

"Did you learn anything about them?"

Valen's head fell to the side. "Only that they were both like and unlike anyone or anything I've ever known. I know that's not an answer, but you'll understand, when you meet them yourself. They're both familiar and foreign. When you witness them in their world, their actions will seem like ones you know, but they are not. The foods they cook seem like ours, but they are not. When they speak, their language is universal. They are not fixed words, but sounds upon the air that can be delivered to the one receiving them however they choose. They can speak those same words to themselves later, and you'll understand none of it."

Drystan laughed. He couldn't help himself. "That makes no sense."

Valen didn't return the humor. "Many things are like this. This is why I say you must see for yourself."

"What made you decide to leave?"

"They released me back into the world. They saw my purpose was yet to be realized."

"And what purpose was that?"

Valen continued to look straight ahead. "To find you, Drystan. To aid you toward your own purpose, which is so much more than you know."

RAVENNA WAITED UNTIL NIGHTFALL TO SAY HER GOODBYE.

Swooping, gliding down upon the earth, she gently unfolded into her erect form. She tiptoed across the underbrush until she came upon where Drystan slept in his bedroll. His sleep was anything but restful. He murmured his worries into the night, fingers twitching against the moonlight. He dreamed of her. She could only read his thoughts when his mind was vulnerable and bare, like it was when he slipped away from the day. He wanted to understand what was happening to her. He couldn't.

She had to be cautious. The girls were sound sleepers, but Ravenna didn't trust Valen not to rest wide awake. She didn't trust him at all, though for very different reasons than Lisbet. She didn't suspect him of wanting to do harm to Drystan, or any of them, but in wanting to take Drystan away from them, to use him toward his own purpose. Even as confused as she was about her own value to the world, Ravenna didn't take kindly to outside threats further confusing matters.

Her love for Drystan had always been confusing. It was unnatural, and she'd fought it for longer than he had, even if her efforts had been just as futile. Drystan was easy to love. He was unutterably kind. His heart was too big for his own body, but that didn't make him blind to the foibles of others. His mother talked to a dead man as if he was alive, and his father was a soft man who struggled to lead and hadn't been born to it. Neither of them had prepared Drystan to be the next Lord of Wulfsgate. They'd ignored his eventual fate, and ignored him, and so he'd become the man he wanted to be.

The man she wanted.

Ravenna conjured her favorite memory of Drystan as she prepared to whisper to him her final words.

She had just entered her second month of training in Wulfsgate. Although she was expected to return to The Rookery every evening, they made exceptions when snowbolts were prevalent in especially heavy storms. A single snowbolt could kill a Ravenwood in flight. This, a fact they knew from experience.

They'd been enmeshed in a brutal storm. Banks of snow brushed twenty to thirty feet high over the gates of Wulfsgate. Ravenna was on her third day of staying with the Derehams and knew she should be eager to get back to Midnight Crest, but strangely, wasn't. She drank in the joy of Nyssa and Torrin as they played around the fire, their imaginations transporting them to places Ravenna could never go. She guiltily enjoyed letting Lisbet braid her midnight hair in a series of extravagant plaits, as they talked by candlelight well into the early hours of the morning.

Drystan, she avoided. More and more, she listened carefully when he spoke; her eyes followed him no matter how many others were in a room. This wasn't the innocence of her casual friendship with Lisbet. The deep flutter in her belly warned her of something forbidden.

She was about to retire for the evening when she crossed paths with Drystan. He was covered in blood. It stained his shirt, pants, and ran in streaks up his forearms. He froze when he saw her, the dark red dripping into stains upon the floor as he gaped at her.

"What happened?" As a healer, Ravenna's instinct to repair whatever had befallen him took precedence over any internal warnings about her developing feelings.

"It isn't how it looks, Ravenna. You should go to bed before I get this on you."

"Tell me," she demanded.

"It isn't my blood."

Her eyes shot wide. "Then whose blood is it, Drystan Dereham?"

"Not a who. I came looking for the physician. To see if he could spare that powder he uses to stem wounds." He looked away, ashamed. "I was coming back from the stables when I saw a small hare. She was covered in blood, but she was still alive. Still trying to run." He gestured to the evidence painting him. "Even pressing my hand upon the wound, the blood refused to stop. I don't know what else to do."

Ravenna almost told him the kitchen staff would love a fresh hare to spare them the hassle, but she could see in his eyes how he agonized over the fate of the small beast. "I haven't seen the physician, but I could try to help."

Drystan's shame deepened. His face was near purple. "I couldn't ask that of you."

"You didn't," Ravenna said. "Show me your little friend."

They arrived at the makeshift nest Drystan had fashioned from his jacket, with no time to spare. Whatever had attacked the little bunny, it knew where to bite, and would look for the spent kill later. Without wasting a second, Ravenna laid her hands upon the stained white fur and focused on seeing her healed.

The hare stopped thrashing. There was a moment of fear, and then understanding in the creature's eyes. Ever briefly, a third look, relief, and then she sprang to her feet and darted away, disappearing in the snowdrifts.

"I'm sorry, Ravenna. I shouldn't have involved you. I feel so foolish now." He pressed his lips tight into a bashful smile. "Thank you, though."

Drystan told her later that he'd loved her the day he met her, after she saved his mother, but she first loved him then in the snow, as his soft heart skipped around at the sight of a little hare running back to whatever life remained.

"You are pure light, Drystan Dereham," Ravenna whispered as he slept. "Your light is bigger than me. Bigger than all the kingdom. You're too good for this world." She brushed his lips with hers. "I have to find my own light. I cannot steal yours to create my own. But the love you've given me has shown me the beauty of such a thing."

She eased back, but hesitated. She needed to say the words directly; the ones he would need to hear, and would remember, when he woke at morning light.

"If you never see me again, Drystan, know that it is not the absence of my love keeping me from you, but the utter enormity of it."

Ravenna shifted into her raven form before the tears could blind her.

32

THE WARWICK THRONE

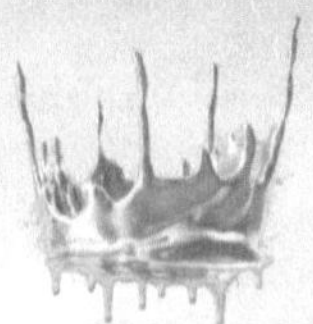

Gwyn found Khallum standing on what he liked to call The Warwick Throne. The Southerlands were known for their jagged, rocky cliffs, but most of Warwicktown sat at sea level. Farther inland, or even down the shore, the rise in elevation made mining their most lucrative asset, but Warwicktown looked more like a shore side hamlet where the very wealthy took residence in the cold season. His grandfather had rebuilt their keep here because he said one needed to be close enough for the salt to settle in their chest and demand residency. Khallum's father had moved the keep further inland, but when he died, Khallum moved it back to Warwicktown, drawing on the same reasons as his grandfather. Khallum didn't know if either his grandfather or father had felt successful in their choices. A Warwick never laid voice to their insecurities, not even with another Warwick.

The Warwick Throne was the only place where the shoreline crested upward in Warwicktown. It wasn't high enough to be considered a cliff, but a fall would break the bones of even a sturdy man. Khallum went there when he needed the space to be reflective, and to think upon the land that had been his by right of birth. and would stay his, by his promise to defend it. The arc of wind whipping northward as it slapped the cliffs; the slightest chance of danger promised in a single misstep. Khallum's men were not soft. He couldn't be soft.

Time moved slowly, but he never forgot that it was within his grandfather's memory that the Rhiagains had begun their quest to steal from the Warwicks. For a time, Karsein Rhiagain, the father of Fynne the Good, had even usurped the Warwicks to place one of his own men at the seat of Warwicktown. If a coup, involving the men of the Great Families who would not suffer to serve a Rhiagain as the Lord of the Southerlands, hadn't been enough to supplant that particular pretender, there would've been war in the kingdom.

The Rhiagains collecting taxes, and fashioning themselves as kings, was tolerable. The Rhiagains overstepping and seeking more was untenable. From time to time, they forgot how tenuous their hold on the kingdom was. They would again find out.

After their lackey was unseated, Karsein then endeavored to requisition the southeastern peninsula, a land where nothing grew and no man would live, and turned it into the crown prison. They named it the Wastelands, either a nod to how it was seen or a diversion from the real reason they wanted it for themselves. There was no purchase made, no currency exchanged to the Warwicks, to whom the land belonged. Khallum's grandfather suspected there was more to the stolen land than needing a place for prisoners. He regretted never exploring the scorched, red earth, never uncovering its hidden value.

The Rhiagain assault on the Southerlands had been personal to the Warwicks. But what Eoghan did now was personal to them all. The Warwicks had been done with the crown for years. The Derehams and Blackwoods were late to the cause.

"A raven came for you," Gwyn said. He read the angst behind her words. She'd read the message already. She wanted him to ask about it.

Khallum bit back annoyance. "From?"

"Lady Quinlanden."

The name jarred him until his mind caught up. "Maeryn, you mean. The sister of Asherley."

"Aye."

"So. Hand it over."

Gwyn regarded him with wary eyes. Her crimson hair caught the sea breeze, and it whipped around her flushed cheeks. He spent little time thinking about his wife's beauty, but he was reminded of it now. She was perhaps the greatest beauty in the kingdom.

"We have to tell Holden."

He grunted. "I donnae even know what it says yet."

Gwyn clutched the crumpled vellum in her fist. "We have to burn it. What she shares is treason, and even knowing makes us complicit."

"I'll decide what we do with it once I read it." Khallum tensed. His jaw ground around the tops of his teeth. He rarely kept his temper checked for his men, but he made the effort with his wife. She had given him everything. He'd offered so little in return. "Gwyn. Come now. You wear down my patience."

Gwyn thrust the paper into his hand. She gathered closer, shielding him from prying eyes, though they were alone.

My sister bade me to send to you the truths of the Easterlands Guard, Khallum began, and when he finished the rest of the message, moments later, he stared at his wife in disbelief. Was this true? How could this have gone on with no one the wiser? How had not a single spy uncovered this? Thousands of Medvedev. Thousands!

"It cannot be borne," Gwyn said. "It must be answered for."

"It will be," Khallum said, thinking, thinking. Remembering how Aiden's guard had seemed disbelievingly large. How had it been this? How had it never occurred to Khallum that a man aligned with a Rhiagain was capable of such treachery?

"How? How will it be?" Gwyn positioned herself so it was impossible for him to look away. "You must have a plan. You always do."

Khallum tucked the vellum inside his shirt. "I will send ravens. One to my brother. The other to Gretchen. Donnae look at me like that, wife. It is Gretchen who runs the Northerlands, as ye well know."

"Holden is a good man."

"Aye, and ineffective at that."

Gwyn's eyes burned with a fire he missed in her. How wild she was, when she'd come to him all those years ago. They'd tamed one another. "It isn't his fault. It was Rinn the Guardians chose, and then an evil, jealous man took that away."

"Nay," Khallum said. "The Guardians donnae make mistakes. Rinn's spent promise wasnae an accident, nor was Holden's ascendance. It was Holden who was meant to marry Gretchen, who is more man than your brother, and will ally with us to see the end of the Rhiagains. We are where we are meant to be. Never forget that."

Gwyn's anger pulsed through her gaze, but she presented no further argument. She was loyal to her brother, but knew Khallum wasn't wrong. Khallum once believed he couldn't break her loyalty to the Northerlands, but she was his now, and always would be. If forced to choose, he knew her choice. "And will Gretchen Dereham get our son back? Our Ransom?"

Khallum softened. He pressed his hand to the side of his wife's face. "We must prepare ourselves. Ransom maynae return to us." Gwyn sagged, and he swiftly caught her, looping both arms around her waist. He felt the sob rise from her chest before she released it. "Niall is our heir, should the worst come to pass. Our hopes live with him. He isnae safe in Blackpool. Too many know of his mining apprenticeship. Garrick requires protection as well. We will send them both to Stewardess Strong."

"Andrija Strong? But why her?"

"There isnae another in the Southerlands with more incentive to protect our sons."

"I don't suppose you'll tell me why."

"I would prefer not to."

"You keep too much from me."

"To ease you. To protect you."

"Do you not see keeping me in the dark does neither?"

Khallum exhaled. "Ryan Strong willnae be in prison much longer. Hamish prepares to retrieve him. And another."

"Another? I don't understand. Who?"

Khallum kissed the tops of her eyelids. "Someone who will turn the tides of fortune away from The Pretender."

Erran Rutland arrived after dusk. Samuel Law shortly after. Hamish had been there since the early morning hours, quietly pacing the Hall of Warring. Hamish had never been a man of many words, but he kept his counsel as he awaited the men who would join him on the most important thing Khallum had ever asked of them.

They may think his choices in men for this mission to be odd, but they hadn't been chosen accidentally.

None of Khallum's men liked Samuel Law. He was aptly named, a true enthusiast of rules, of taking the path most expected and safe. But he was also a man who, due to his overabundance of caution, was well placed to consider all outcomes, both desirable and not. He would foresee danger the others could not. If Hamish Strong was Khallum's errant muscle, and Erran Rutland made of decisive action, Law was the balance to them both, but they were also the counterweights to his fears. None of these men were entirely capable, alone, of what Khallum would ask of them, but together, he could think of no better combination of men.

Khallum took his place at the table. The other men fell into their usual positions. It felt like any council meeting, except the low, nervous energy bouncing from man to man. The absence of the others normally present made this sensation keener.

He said what he needed to say. He didn't dress his words, nor did he drag them out. He said what was necessary, and when he was done, he waited for the inevitable questions. For the objections.

But there were no questions from Strong or Rutland.

From Law, the expected objections died without being given life.

Khallum passed a hard look upon all three men. "I need to know you all understand what I've told you. What I ask of you, and what may come if you succeed."

"Ye know I do, my lord," Hamish said, the first, always.

"I have all the clarity I require," Erran said next. "I thank you for confidence in me, my lord. I'll not let you down."

Khallum nodded and turned to his resident naysayer. "And you, Law? What say you?"

Law's jaw was set tight. He turned his hands over atop the table, ruminating.

Then he looked up. "I would see this land set to rights, same as you. You have gifted us with a path forward." He nodded his head low in reverence. "Thy will be done."

Khallum's relief buoyed him from his chair. He rose, and the others followed.

"There can be no mistakes. No hesitation. No second chances."

The men sounded their understanding.

Khallum reached for each of them, one by one, laying hands upon their shoulders. "The future of the Southerlands, of this entire kingdom, is now in your hands."

33

THE VIRULENT SPINDLE

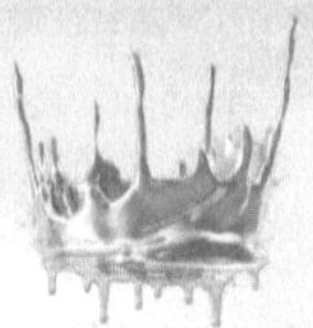

Christian didn't say how he gained access to the Sacred Halls for Aylen. It was not a request the Head Magus would grant under any circumstance, and it was only the elders granted access at all.

Aylen didn't ask him for the truth, because she was already asking too much. She had decided upon the answer anyhow, for whatever that was worth. Christian wasn't the only Dereham at the Sepulchre. There were three, but one, in particular, was especially notable to the tenure and order of things at the Consortium. Rorric Dereham was the brother of Christian's esteemed grandfather, Hadden. He'd spent every year of his life since his twelfth within the Sepulchre, and when he entered the yawn of his twilight years, they made him an elder.

The position of elder wasn't a guarantee with age. Age was only one qualifier. They gave the coveted title to those who had demonstrated such a commitment and aptitude to not only the magic itself but also to their histories that their acquired wisdom was an invaluable and irreplaceable boon to the world of magic. Rorric Dereham had devoted his life to the instruction of other Magi and now enjoyed his later years performing vital research for the Consortium.

With old age came the inevitable wearying of the body, and most elders retired before their supper had moved through their frail systems. The Sacred Halls were empty in the midnight hours. Christian was insistent on this, that she couldn't enter a moment sooner. He needn't have wasted his breath, for Aylen had no interest in being apprehended and excommunicated.

Years before, when she'd arrived at the Sepulchre as an Adherent, they'd whisked her through the Sacred Halls in the briefest of tours. That was the first and last time any Adherent or Magi were allowed within its walls, unless selected later in life for the role of elder.

The shelves and shelves of rolled vellum took her breath away. It was as if seeing the sight for the first time. Hundreds of thousands of scrolls, all written by the hands of the Magi of past. These were not works from *The Book of All Things*. The Consortium made their contributions to that vast tome of the kingdom, but there were things for them and them alone. Discoveries and observations that had no place outside their dense, confined world of wonder.

Aylen closed her eyes and pictured her hands running down the long line of precious paper. How it would respond to her fingertips. Would the knowledge written within flow through her, its own form of magic?

The moment passed. Somewhere in this room, the answer she needed awaited her. As she scanned the signs lining the tops of the long shelves, she put together the system that the elders had created. The first few rows were sorted by time periods, until the point where efficient record keeping became a way of life in the kingdom. That time corresponded with the arrival of the Rhiagains. The very next section was dedicated entirely to them.

A chill passed over her. What mysteries were written here? How many questions, questions long lingering over the kingdom, could be answered within the scrawled swirls of ink? What would it change?

She wasn't here for that. Oh, how she wished... one day. She would earn her place here, perhaps long after the answers mattered.

But she was in the right section. *I loved him,* Hollyn said. *Eoghan. The king.*

It seemed impossible, but Aylen had no other inkling to follow. She again scanned the headings until she came upon what she was after. *Diseases and Maladies.*

There had long been rumors that the Rhiagain had brought rare illnesses with them when they arrived to the kingdom. The naysayers insisted if that were so, then it would have wiped out the population, but the Rhiagain had always stayed tucked away on Duncarrow. Few kings ever progressed throughout the kingdom, and when they did, many kept their distance. This helped preserve their mystery, which was both essential to their survival and also anathema to it.

A single death ascribed to a rare illness would generate no broader concern. With their insistence upon marrying beneath them, this kept their exposure to populations that were less notable to the public. Minor houses, with unforgettable names.

Until Hollyn.

If. If Hollyn. She's abed with fever. Dying. Delirious.

And yet.

Aylen slipped on her gloves and unrolled the first of four scrolls. She scanned the sharp scrawl, surprised to see she recognized much of what was written, even if the names were different than the ones she'd come to know. What she knew as the feverbane, the Rhiagains, wherever they'd come from, called the sweating sickness. What she called a case of the chilblains, the Rhiagains called the pox. On and on it went, Aylen nodding in new understanding of old learnings.

The second and third scroll were the same. Common ailments, uncommon names.

The fourth contained something else entirely.

Diseases and Other Maladies Unseen Before the Arrival of the Rhiagain Kings.

The scribe articulated the reasons they believed the diseases stayed undiscovered until that time. There were three diseases listed, and beneath them the citations for cases studied and documented.

Two were minor ailments that resembled the chills or other transient disorders with high recovery rates.

The last left her numb.

The Virulent Spindle.

She read on.

A most aggressive and egregious affliction, it has been documented less than a dozen times in the kingdom, and only among the poor of our society. It can only be passed by a male of Rhiagain blood, and through the excretion produced during copulation. It is assumed that it is passed unwittingly, and that the males are mostly asymptomatic. It is also not passed along in all cases. Thus, given its rather limited means of spread, and the Rhiagain preference to remain upon Duncarrow and have their wives and husbands delivered from the hovels and hamlets of the kingdom, it has not sparked notice from the populous.

The symptoms match no other illness we have on record. One begins with a fever, and from there it might be assumed they have a bad case of the sniffles, or even feverbane. Then the fever recedes, though it will return, repeatedly, sometimes daily, throughout the course of the disease. Other strange things then begin to occur. A sometimes mortal sensitivity to sunlight. Loss of short-term memory. A tendency to slip into a comatose state, for days on end. Loss of appetite, or the craving of things not intended for consumption, such as wood chips or soil. A loss of body mass that cannot be replenished with an increase in nutrients. In the final days, a fever that melts the body from within, and crazed madness takes over the mind.

Thus far, all known afflicted have been women. There is a belief that it cannot affect men, or if it does, not to the same extremes. It is the women who inevitably perish, and often in painful ways.

No cures known to this kingdom can allay this disease.

There is, it is said, a cure, but it is known only by the Rhiagain clever man, Oldwin. There are whispers he brought with him the seeds of a plant from the kingdom from which they hailed, and that he alone controls their growth. Or perhaps the same rules of magic apply, and as the disease is known to him, he can thereby cure it, where we cannot.

As of this writing, we have yet to witness a cure for ourselves, and so we must lay it to account as speculation.

Aylen quietly re-rolled the scroll. Her hands were steady, though only through great restraint. She then gathered her borrowed reading and replaced all five to their rightful place on the endless shelves of the Sacred Hall. She slipped her gloves into the pocket of her robe.

When at last the heavy oaken doors whispered closed behind her, Aylen exhaled.

CHRISTIAN'S CRAZED HEART RATE DIDN'T SUBSIDE UNTIL HIS WIFE SLID safely into the bed next to him.

She'd only gently probed about his means in securing her access. Likely, she knew. The Consortium knew he was the great-nephew of Rorric Dereham, and to Aylen, who had grown up around the Derehams, and was now Christian's wife, the old man was family.

But it had been no familial nepotism that swayed his great-uncle to allow the forbidden access. And thinking about the conversation in hindsight made Christian so ill he'd lost his dinner in the privy twice that evening.

Christian had, years ago, learned why Rorric Dereham had so easily given up a life of prestige as a Dereham of Wulfsgate. Why he'd never married. It was a crime for a man to love other men, and it was safer for Rorric Dereham in the sequestered life of an elder Magi in the Consortium. Where such laws didn't touch them and were less important than the laws they had for their magic dealers.

Important or no, it was still a secret Rorric had kept for over seventy years.

Is this really what you want? Rorric regarded him not with anger, but a disappointed sadness. *We cannot return from this, nephew. Our relationship cannot be the same after a threat has been laid upon it.*

Uncle Rorric, please forgive me. I didn't know what else to do. There's something in there we need, and you're the only one—

Spare the breath, Christian. I already know of your Blackwood patient living in the falconer's quarters. I suspect I know what ails her. Aye, you'll find your answers in the Sacred Halls, but you'll find no satisfaction in this transaction.

Where is the balance, uncle? Between doing what is right and turning your back on those who need you?

I suspect you just found out.

Rorric had been so good to him when he arrived, green and fearful, only eleven years old. He'd helped him get settled, subtly but effectively making sure others knew Christian wasn't one to mess about with. When Christian showed signs of promise, Rorric mentored him, a rare honor bestowed by the elders upon those they predicted one day would become one themselves. He was the comfort of home, but the reminder that home could be many places.

What choice did I have? Let an innocent child die because our knowledge ends where the doors to the Sacred Halls begin?

You know, Christian, even high-born children aren't exempted from early death. Would you have gone to such lengths for a pauper's bairn?

He didn't like how the question made him feel, because he knew the answer. He would not have. But he didn't destroy his lifelong friendship with his great-uncle for a high-born child. He'd done it for Brandyn, because like Rorric had been to Christian, so he was to this young man thrust into a world unknown and forced to learn a new way, a new home. One day Brandyn might face such a choice, and he would remember this. His occasion to be the mentor was a day yet to come.

"I don't believe Hollyn lied to us."

Christian's stomach turned. "So you found it."

Aylen nodded. The moonlight caught the fine edges of her silver hair, but her face was obscured to him. "They call it the Virulent Spindle. The Rhiagains brought it from wherever they came from, and they can only pass it one way. Through… through a joining of man and woman. This is perhaps why it hasn't become prevalent, or even known to us."

"And the cure?"

Aylen shook her head against the pillow. "If there is one, the knowledge and the means exist upon Duncarrow alone. No one here has found another way."

"Duncarrow."

"Yes. The king may not even have known that he passed this to her. There are inadequate notes on this, but the scribe who documented this seems to believe it either only afflicts women or in men it is mild and recoverable."

"There's no other explanation for what's wrong with her?"

"I cannot see how. Everything matches what the notes say."

"Only a Rhiagain can pass it?"

"They seem to be blood carriers, though this is so frustrating, Christian, because we know next to nothing! In all the years the elders have been exploring the inexplicable, they still know so little. And yet, it makes sense. No healers could assuage her, because no healer had seen this disease. All the physicians Lady Blackwood called upon were helpless, because nothing in their arsenal of herbs and tinctures held sway upon this awful affliction. It came from where the Rhiagains came from, and thus, so does the cure."

"How do you suppose…" Christian didn't even know if his question was important, but he asked it anyway, to avoid reaching the conclusion he knew was coming. "The king never leaves Duncarrow. How would the two of them even have been acquainted?"

"You could ask that question a thousand ways and we'd be no closer to an answer. There's a story there, and we may never learn it. Hollyn knows the answer, but it isn't our place to ask."

Christian sighed. They were nearing the point now. "And without a cure?"

"Without a cure, Hollyn will surely die." Aylen inhaled. "She is dying now. Even had we access to a cure, it may be too late."

Christian reached for her hand atop the blanket. He twined his fingers through hers. "No one can know, Aylen. Not anyone here. Not Brandyn, or Storm. No one."

Aylen sniffled in the darkness. Nodded.

"We cannot have the king's eye turned toward the Sepulchre."

"I know."

"Even if we could get her to Duncarrow..." He closed his eyes. "She wouldn't make the journey. And there's so much we don't know. What if he intends to do her harm? If whatever passed between them wasn't consensual?"

"Christian, I know. I knew before I told you what I learned. I know." Her face turned toward his. Tears sparkled in her eyes, but he could see they were born of frustration more than sadness. "We cannot save Hollyn. Her life is in the hands of the Guardians now, who will determine when her promise is spent. This may be days. Perhaps hours. But the control is no longer ours."

She pulled their twined hands to her lips. "And King Eoghan must *never* know she was here, or Hollyn's will not be the only Blackwood blood on our hands."

34

DUNWOODE

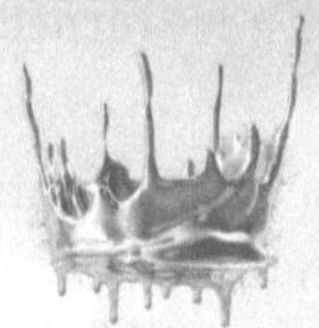

The road to Dunwoode widened, increasing in both horse and wagon traffic as they neared the town gates. Smaller roads, intersecting from tiny villages, and a larger road, with travelers from Westport, brought Ember and Marsh back to a sense of community that neither had known for weeks. Marsh grew ever more tense as more people appeared, filling in the spaces of the once empty road. His fingers gripped the curves of her waist, which disappeared behind layers of bulky travel clothes. Clothes she couldn't wait to shed in favor of a long-needed bath.

He stopped asking why they were returning to civilization. Instead, he conveyed his questions and fears through nervous groans, and the occasional jump against her back. His paranoia amused her. He had nothing to fear; a home in which to return when this was over. If her mother's premonitions were at all true, Emberley Blackwood wouldn't know the meaning of home again for a long time. If she failed...

But she wouldn't. Everything she'd done, that her siblings had done, was to save the Blackwood line. One of them must prevail. She hated to think of her siblings falling along the way, but Lady

Blackwood had chosen her second daughter for her pragmatism, not idealism. Of all of them, Ember had the highest chance of success. Brandyn may find safety with his Magi, but the Sepulchre would never ally with any of the four houses. It wasn't their way. And Gabi... through some reflection, Ember realized she'd not sent Gabi to a place that would help her but shield her.

No, this was incumbent upon Ember to solve. Her mother had her role, and Ember had hers.

It was her father she most missed. That gentle, intelligent bear of a man who was not hard enough to be a Warwick, not shrewd enough to be a Blackwood, but balanced just right for taking them on treks through the Whitewood, or pretending to be errant forest animals they could chase around for hours. It was Byrne who taught his children to read, and then later, to love doing it.

Ember desperately hoped her mother had a plan to protect him, too.

"Do you know anyone in Dunwoode?" Marsh asked from behind her. His grip had lessened, but his tone warbled. He was unsteady because she kept truths from him, and she might feel the same if roles were reversed. She decided she'd tell him everything before they left this town.

"No," Ember said. She pulled her hood back. Reaching so high the sun blocked the balustrades were the town walls, and before them, the gate, open to travelers and locals. "I'll tell you something I do know. The Haddenfoots are known for their blacksmithing. They craft some of the best swords in the northern half of the kingdom."

"Are you after one? A sword?"

Ember laughed. "Something wrong with mine?"

"I don't think you need metal to lay waste should you mean to."

"Best to keep that to yourself," Ember said as they passed easily through the gates, mixing in with the throngs of traders and locals milling about. All at once, scents both rich and foul assaulted every sense; a veneer of smoke from various sources burned their eyes.

Vendors set up shop along the entrance road, calling out to the visitors to sell them leather goods, vegetables, or dried meats. The recent rains had rendered the dirt into thick mud. Splatters painted the booths, horses, the dresses of women as they moved about. Ember felt it paint her own legs as they moved through the bustle.

A young boy, no more than four, tugged at her boots, begging for coin. His thin face was obscured by filth that had started, likely, on the day of his birth and had never been wiped clean. Ember pushed on, but Marsh reached behind and slipped the lad a piece of silver.

"You're a fool to be parted so easily with your money. There will be a thousand more just like him."

"He's only a boy, Ember. I don't want him to starve."

"He'll still starve, Marsh. Only his mother or father will be in the cups while they watch him do it."

"For someone raised like a princess you sure have a hardened view of the world."

"I was raised by a queen," Ember said, as she angled them toward an inn at the center of the melee. "I see the world more clearly than I'd like."

GRETCHEN NURSED THE STEAMING MUG OF CIDER BETWEEN HER chilled palms. It was the thing she appreciated most in her life as a Northern lady. Mulled cider was a staple all throughout the Reach, but it was only in Wulfsgate you would find one crafted by the Derehams themselves—and only Derehams.

The crisp, sweet apples came from the private grove at the back of the Wintergarden. Twice a season, Holden, along with his sons, his brother Alric, and any other Dereham men eager for some laboring in the cold for the sake of tradition, picked, crushed, and pressed them until they were ready for the kitchens. There the Dereham women took over, transferring them into the cauldrons with the leftover wine from springtide, and there they'd stir and press, sweat pouring from their brows and into the vats. They transferred the sacred liquid to jars and placed them in rows by the hundreds in the cool pantry, a supply fit for a season. Enough to last even the harshest winter.

The steam rolled from the stoneware, mixing with Gretchen's breath, becoming one. She let her lips linger on the warmth as her eyes followed the raven circling in deliberate trails, dancing intentional arcs over the keep. A message.

Holden announced his presence with boots crunching through snow. She knew his step. It wasn't as heavy as that of most men, and there was a reticence in each lift of his feet, as if unsure of his destination, or his intentions, when he arrived.

"You'll catch a chill," he said. More hesitance followed as he let his gloved hands hover above her shoulders, an instinctual tenderness that no longer felt welcome to either of them.

"He's been up there for days."

Holden looked toward where her attentions were fixed. "He? A Ravenwood then?"

"The son. Alasyr."

"Are you certain?"

"Fairly."

"Why would he be circling Wulfsgate?"

Gretchen was too cold to laugh. "You were perhaps too enchanted with the High Priestess to notice the son. He struggles with his sister's defection. He believes we have something to do with it."

Holden reached for her mug and took a sip. He handed it back. "As we told his mother and father, we don't."

She scoffed. "And they didn't believe us any more than he did. But where they're willing to sacrifice her, replace her with another, isn't."

Holden shook his head. "We have no time for the silliness of angry children. Let him spin around in circles for the rest of his days if he wishes. It doesn't concern us."

He touched her shoulder, briefly, and then returned to the warmth of the keep.

Gretchen looked up at the raven, Alasyr. Nodded.

Holden had forgotten that it was the children who had changed the course of the kingdom.

EMBER PICKED A TABLE IN THE CENTER OF THE ACTION. THE TABLES to their left and right were filled with merchants, locals, and just behind them, a prostitute working her best sales pitch on travelers with accents that sounded like the ones she'd heard from Southerlanders. Ember wanted to tell her not to work too hard; there was a certain hunger in their eyes. They'd buy no matter the price.

She knew hunger. Marsh's eyes darted around the room, taking inventory of his options. The only thing bigger than his fear was the promise of food. Real food. Warm enough to fill their bellies, and, if Ember was feeling generous—and she was—a night in a bed softer than the ground.

Tearing into a hunk of fresh but tough bread, Ember asked, "Why'd you come with me?"

Marsh finished several generous spoonfuls of stew before answering. "Huh?"

"When you received the raven calling you to The Hidden Cave, telling you to bring anything you'd need for a long journey, what made you say yes after I told you what we would be doing?"

Marsh sopped up the dark sludge at the bottom of the bowl. "Did I have a choice?"

"Of course you had a choice. There are no guards come to drag you to your death for the sundering of the Sacred Vow, no matter what the others may think."

The way he looked at her before he spoke made Ember regret asking. "You asked for me. There wasn't a choice."

A strange silence settled between them. They each finished their food and refilled their ales.

"And yet…" Marsh sat up straight on his bench. "You keep me intentionally in the dark, Emberley. It took me nearly dying to learn about your…" He lowered his voice and leaned in. "Magic. I understand why you would want to go to Midnight Crest. I would too, if I were you, and knew nothing about where I came from."

Emberley glanced around at the patrons nearby, but the other tables were immersed in their own conversations. "That's not what you want to say. Or to ask me."

"We're not going to Midnight Crest, though, are we?"

Emberley wrapped her fingers around the metal of the empty stein. She wished the barmaid would refill them again, but her head was already tipsy. Any more and she might do—or say—things not fit for their large audience. "Not at first, no."

"Will you make me guess?"

"You seem to want to."

"All right." Marsh lifted his hands in the air. His palms landed on the table. "If I had to guess, we're here in Dunwoode because you want to be seen. Seen by those who will report your presence to someone specific."

Emberley said nothing, waiting for him to continue.

"Lord Dereham."

"Okay."

"Am I on the correct path?"

She nodded.

"But not Lord Dereham himself," Marsh went on. He tapped his fingers against the table in a light staccato. "Lady Dereham. No… not her. But I'm closer, aren't I? You have an aunt in Wulfsgate. One who married Lord Dereham's brother, right?"

"Aunt Earwyn," Emberley said. "But you were right when you guessed Lady Dereham. While you were securing our room for the night, I told three different people that we were traveling on business with the Derehams. I didn't ask for them to send that news north, but they will, and because I declined to tell anyone who I was, they'll make assumptions. Seeing as I'm only fifteen, and a girl, I'm not a threat to Lord Dereham and his family. It's safer to assume I'm seeking refuge."

"Guardians," Marsh whispered. "And how... why? No, *why* is what I want to know, Ember? Why are we doing all of this?" A dark look passed over his face. "It wasn't for Hollyn at all, was it?"

"No," she said quickly. She'd wanted to be seen, but there was some business suitable only for quiet rooms and whispers. "Let's go upstairs."

MARSH TURNED HIS BACK WHILE EMBERLEY PEELED HER OUTER LAYERS away. The thick fabric stuck to her skin and the thinner layers beneath. She hadn't thought much about how grimy she was until the clothes were off, and then it was all she could think about. She pushed open the window and laid them along the windowsill. It wouldn't be enough to distill the rotting stench, and in the morning she'd struggle to make herself put them back on, but if everything went to plan, she'd be in a warm bath by week's end.

She returned the courtesy and let him do the same. She caught a brief sight of his bare ass in a cracked corner mirror and quickly looked away, wondering if he'd seen her, and if he'd looked away, too, when she was changing, or let his gaze linger a moment too long.

Marsh leaned against the table. He'd stripped down to his wool hosen, throwing his shirt and all else over the sill with her travel clothes. Week-old dirt caked between the muscular lines defining his abdomen. Emberley saw him as not a boy, but a man, and it caused a realization within her that she herself was more woman than girl.

"Tell me what you wouldn't down there."

Emberley bit back a wave of vulnerability. She drew her knees to her chest and leaned back into the meager bedpost. "My mother came to me just before I sent the ravens to you and the others. She and her seer, Joran, had both, independently, seen terrible things ahead for the Blackwood house if we didn't work to correct the course of the future."

"What did they see?"

"Children of all the Reaches taken back to Duncarrow in chains."

Marsh's mouth dropped. "And from the Westerlands?"

"Me."

"Not Brandyn?"

"Brandyn is safe at the Sepulchre. He is protected. The rules of asylum cover Adherents and Magi, too."

"Then why'd you bring him back to Longwood Rush?"

Emberley sighed. "I almost didn't. But the story my mother and I came up with, that we all fled in separate directions in order to find succor for Hollyn's ailments, only worked if we all did it. And if there did exist knowledge of a cure, that knowledge would belong to the Sepulchre. He's the only one who could bring her there." She paused. "I knew he would sense the trouble brewing. So did my mother. We were right."

Marsh nursed his wounded arm. He flinched at his own touch, at the wound that might never quite heal. She would find him a healer. "What about Gabi and the twins?"

"I sent them to a place where the king has no authority. Don't ask me if the Hinterlands are friendly to us... I don't know. But they're safer there than any place the king's men have free rein. They're children. I have to believe they will protect them, or at least do no harm."

"And..." Marsh blew out a breath. "I hate to even ask. Hollyn?"

Ember looked down at her hands. "Mother told me it would be a miracle if Hollyn survived this. That, if the Guardians are kind, she'll wait to expire until she's somewhere safe, and with one of us."

"I'm so sorry, Ember."

She nodded. "I accepted that when I embraced Hollyn in the cave, it would be for the last time."

"This was your mother's idea?"

Emberley shook her head. "She left it in my hands. She didn't want to know where we would go. She was afraid someone might pull this from her mind and find us. She would've said she sent search parties after us. All her best. And that would've been a lie to buy us time to get as far from home as we could before the Right of Choosing."

Marsh watched her. His eyes, one green, one purple, twinkled in the dim light. "You didn't choose the north for Midnight Crest at all."

"I'm pulled to Midnight Crest. My blood directs me there. There are things I *must* know. But whatever I can learn there will matter to no one but me if my house ends with my mother. My aunt Earwyn is blood. And Lady Gretchen… Mother said she can be trusted. That she's the real power in the Northerlands."

Marsh moved to the end of the bed. He kept his distance from her; for the same reason, she thought, that she was now suddenly afraid to be close to him, too. "Do you think there will be war, Ember?"

"I don't know," she said, sighing. "My mother has a role to play. Just as I couldn't tell her my plan, she couldn't tell me hers. I heard her and my father talking not long before we left. Something involving Lord Warwick, and the Southerlands." She looked up. His eyes burned through her, and she had to force herself not to turn away. "There's something bigger than us brewing, Marsh. We have our part, but it is only one piece. Although my mother couldn't tell me where she wanted me to go, in my heart I know she needs me with our allies, where I can be of use."

"And me?"

Ember rolled forward. She reached a hand out toward his, and he slid his fingers through hers. His skin was on fire. "You are of use to me. This voyage would've been so much harder without you."

"That's not what I'm asking, Emberley. I don't want to be merely useful. I want to be needed."

Emberley's heart throbbed in her chest. She could take down bears with her magic, use her knife and press it over the throat of a beloved dying horse. She would rather do either of those things a hundred times over before talking about her feelings in such a raw, exposed way. But he had given over his life to help her, and only the barest truth would do.

"*I* need you," she whispered.

Marsh crawled up the bed toward her. He wrapped a hand around her head, through her matted, filthy hair, and kissed her for the second time.

35

MOTHER'S MILK

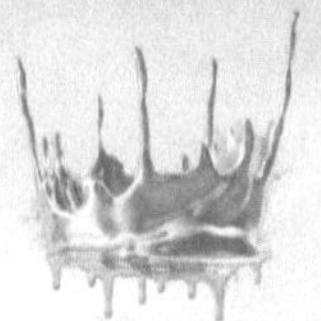

Asherley hadn't been certain, until the precise moment the pearled liquid left the tips of her nipples, that she'd still be able to produce milk on command.

The year before, she'd birthed a baby boy who died weeks later in his sleep. Her breasts screamed at her afterward, aching for expression, and Byrne had helped ease the physical pain for her. This went on for months, until at last, mercifully, the need waned, and with it, her grief for the child lost. He'd died before she could even have his naming ceremony.

She'd expected none of her plans to fall so neatly in line. Eoghan, known for his artless cruelty, known for his irrational temper, surely possessed some cunning. But showing him what she had to offer had been a straight line toward her goal. She hadn't needed to work at it at all. Eoghan called for her just after breakfast, not two days after she'd teased her potential to him. She rushed to find a suitable dress from the collection granted her by the crown for her stay, when the pageboy handed her a matronly sack to wear. King's orders. It wasn't fit for a woman of any decent station, let alone of royal blood. It resembled something a lowborn wet nurse would wear, and never if her betters were present. But she was beginning to see how the young man's fantasies came together. She noted all these small details, each one contributing to the fantasy, to be certain she was playing the part he'd cast:

A nameless mother whose love and nurturing was meant for one man, and one man alone.

Asherley moved in slow rhythm atop the peculiar, bony man-child. He suckled hungrily, already milk drunk and growing harder within her with every ravenous drink. Every few strides she made soft, comforting sounds, whispering what a good boy he was, a growing boy. Getting so big. So *strong*. His guttural moans in response, the damp heat of breath burning against her bruised flesh, betrayed how desperate he was for precisely this.

At last, she whispered the magic words: "You did so well. It's time for your nap." A new, stinging heat accompanied his awkward shudders, ungainly limbs jerking against her like sticks. He sounded his release through a series of stunted words and cries. Asherley gently extracted what was left of his erection, offering a soft, motherly pat as she returned it to his trousers, where the throbbing continued with less enthusiasm. His eyes rolled back in his head as he slumped into the chair.

Asherley frowned. She couldn't leave him like this. That wasn't what his fantasy mother would do. With an inward sigh, she slipped an arm behind him and, with a light tsk, told him to come now; naps happen in beds. He grinned in his half-sleep, eager to comply, and when she had him settled, he blinked at her through hazy eyes.

"I'll want to eat again after my nap," he said.

"Of course, darling," Asherley said sweetly, and planted a soft kiss at his brow before tucking the blanket around him. Just right.

His soft snores followed her as she marched out of the room.

THERE WERE THE WHISPERS ASHERLEY PICKED UP INADVERTENTLY; THE ones that, in a fair world, would be charged as an assault of the mind if such a court existed to try her. Little intrusions with big, sometimes devastating results. Most believed that pressing their darkest thoughts into the tiniest corners protected them, but these were the places most exposed, to those who knew where and how to look.

Then there were the whispers people sent her. She believed this was mostly unintentional. A way of expelling the worst of their secrets into the world, without realizing they were flinging them straight to her. But there were those who knew. Who knew, or at least suspected, what she was, and what she might do with certain knowledge.

She distrusted this last method. She could never be certain of the motivations of one sending her information in this manner, and often had trouble discerning precisely where the whispers had come from. It was a gap in control, with uncertain results.

This was how she picked up the whispers that told her she needed to find her way to the guard posted near the waste runoff at the rear of the castle. That the guard had something she would be very, very interested in. This guard stood sentry just below the sky dungeon, the tallest point of the keep. It was the only place where there weren't multiple guards assigned to the same spot, for there was nothing to guard. Any prisoner attempting escape would not need to be accosted, because they'd be dead.

Asherley played it careful, passing her eyes around the dozen gathered in the hall. Women huddled in circles. Men passing through. A servant girl saw her and then, eyes filled with panic, turned, lifting her skirts, and darting in the other direction.

She could follow, but it would draw attention she didn't need. Many had already seen her leave the king's chambers, flushed and out of sorts. Let them remember that, and not whatever this attendant wished for her to know.

She made her way toward the rear of the keep, passing faces that were growing familiar to her. Assyria nodded. Assana moved down the corridor with her head down, spirit broken. The poor girl wasn't strong enough for this world, let alone a dangerous marriage. Even if Asherley could save her from this, she couldn't save her from herself. She'd do what she could, for Maeryn, but it wouldn't be enough.

The briny air hit her on the wave of a southerly wind. She stepped out through the side entrance and followed the unsteady path toward the back. Duncarrow was no typical royal court. There were no ornate gardens, only the herb garden kept by the kitchens just beyond their doors. No courtly beauty. No trellises or court-yards. Only rocks of various shapes and different degrees of serrated sharpness. It seemed to her more a place to withstand a siege from sea vessels than one you would use as your showpiece to the kingdom.

Waves lapped at the outer barrier stones. She could already feel the salt sinking into her skin. *Salt and sand,* as the Southerland men would say, with such swelling pride. As if being further burdened by the world gave you unique strength and not simply one more tether to the past.

Asherley pulled her cloak tighter, burying her face. This was more than a practical move. As she neared the spot where the whis-pers had drawn her, she had to exercise even greater caution. She sensed no danger, but she was not foolish enough to rely entirely on senses that worked only inconsistently.

There were few men outside the keep. Only the guards, huddled into their armor, heads down in a futile attempt to preserve warmth. Duncarrow wasn't a large enough island to provide cover from the elements, and there were no trees to slow the wind. She nodded as she passed the guard stations, but kept her face obscured under the woolen cloth of her hood.

As she rounded the back of the keep, she came upon the man she'd been urged to seek out. He bent at the base of a drain of some sort. She followed the path of the metal pipe and saw that it reached up into the sky dungeons. For the prisoner waste, then. She wondered how fortune had landed this job upon this man, and what he'd done to displease the Guardians.

He pulled something from the end of the pipe, and then jumped back as she came into view. He stumbled, shoving whatever he'd retrieved into a pocket, and then attempted to return himself into formation.

"Who are you?"

"John Cantwell, of the second guardhouse. Ma'am."

"You know what I mean. Who are you to me?"

"Pardon my ignorance, ma'am, but I don't understand. Are you lost? Can I help you?"

"Someone sent me to you."

The man's armor clinked together as he quivered in fear, but he looked up, slowly. She let her hood fall slightly back. His eyes brightened in recognition. Something else. "Lady Blackwood." After a harried glance to confirm they were alone, he affected a light but reverent bow.

Well, now. *This* was interesting.

"Who are you?" she demanded. "Not your name."

"No one," he said. He stumbled over the next words. "That is… no one important."

Asherley stepped closer, carefully navigating the unsteady rocks. "Then you must work for someone important."

"His Grace, the king," he said quickly. "As we all do."

"No," Asherley said. "That is not who you work for, or I wouldn't be here."

The guard looked up. He squinted through the glare. "You're fortunate, my lady, that you're not in their company. They don't live according to their station."

"The prisoners, you mean."

"Aye. The prisoners. Important, all of them. The ones who aren't are shipped off to the Wastelands." He dropped his eyes. "Some more important than others."

"I know of the children of the Northern and Southern Reaches already."

"Some Rhiagains, too," he said. "Not all of them born into the family."

Asherley withheld her growing impatience. "Say what you mean to say, John Cantwell. Before we draw attention upon ourselves."

The guard shook his head. "It isn't for me to say. You should hear it from her instead."

"Her?" Asherley asked, but the man was digging around in a top hole of his armor.

When he withdrew his hand, he had what looked like scrolls of vellum in his fist. Tiny and badly re-rolled. He sighed and then thrust them toward her. "I have been told you are the one to read these. I came upon them by accident myself. One day I discovered a scroll in a puddle where the drain empties into the waste runoff. And then another. And on it continued." When she reached for them, he pulled his hand back slightly. "My lady, they cannot find these on you, or you will find yourself in the sky dungeon yourself. They cannot be found by anyone. By..."

Asherley's heartbeat found a quicker pace. What was this? What secrets did this lonely guard hold, and who had he shared them with? Who had sent her to find him? "Right. I understand."

The guard laid the scrolls in her palm, sealing her fingers around them. "No, my lady. But you will."

THE GIRL RACED THROUGH THE STONE HALLS, DODGING MEN AND women of the court. She should slow down. Her master would scold her. She shouldn't draw such attention to herself. She was to be a mouse, quiet, unnoticed. But if the cat caught the mouse, then she would be no more.

Breathless, she pushed the chamber doors open, forgetting to pause, to announce. Her master would be angry. Her master preached discipline, in all things. Especially emotion. And she, the mouse, had emotion to spare.

Her master turned toward her. Yes, the master was angry. She'd disappointed again, which was a shame because she had also done exactly what her master asked.

"And, mouse? What news have you to tell me?"

The mouse clutched her midsection, gasping for breath. Her ability to cause disappointment was endless. "I sent the message. Just as you asked, master."

"And was it received, mouse?"

"Yes, master."

"How can you be certain?"

The mouse stood straighter. She fought with her breath, which still betrayed her race through the halls. "She looked me straight in the eyes, master. As if I'd spoken aloud, though I had said nothing. Only in my head, as you instructed."

"And then?"

"I ran..." The mouse groaned. Another failure. Her master would punish her now, and she'd deserve it. "I did not see."

"Did she follow you?"

The mouse furiously shook her head back and forth. "No, no. But I ran, just to be sure, master."

Her master approached. The mouse winced, bracing for the slap. It didn't come. Instead, her master laid a soft hand at her cheek.

"You did very well, little mouse. Very well indeed."

THE KING HAD SENT FOR ASHERLEY FOR HIS EVENING MEAL. SHE gambled with her response; to make him wait. He was an irrational man, so she couldn't guess at his response, but part of the role he'd crafted for her was one of authority. She couldn't agree to his every ask. She must instill in him a sense of patience, as part of her discipline.

She had more pressing matters. The scrolls she'd hidden in the gap of her bosom until she was safely in her own chambers. She had a fire roaring before she removed them, and even then, something kept her from immediately consuming the contents. She poured one, then two glasses of wine, standing by the fire, regarding the scrolls with a confusion that would end as soon as she unrolled and read them.

Whatever was written inside, it had been enough for a guard to risk his life. For whoever he worked for to risk theirs. And why her? Why seek her out at all? She had no power here. Not even her fleeting dalliances with the demented king were enough to grant her anything of importance outside the bedchamber. It bought her time, and access, but not command.

Why her?

You know the only path to the answer.

Blood dripped onto her tongue. She'd been chewing her lip so hard she'd split the skin.

You are not one to deliberate. Hesitation does not become you.

Ah, but what if this is a trap, and I am walking right into it?

You will sense it. You will know, once the words become embossed in your mind. And then you will do what you have always done.

Asherley approached the silver tray, her second glass of wine dwindling and needing replenishment. After filling the goblet once more, she reached for the first of the scrolls. The one that looked the most weatherworn. *I found it in the waste runoff.*

After one last glance toward the chamber doors, she slowly unrolled it and read.

I begin this in the fifth year of my captivity, though I long ago ceased to count the days, or the hours. I know the time only by my son's growth, which is both a joy and the sun ticking down toward the end.

An hour later, Asherley stood before the fire, scrolls in hand. She'd stopped drinking the wine halfway through her reading, despite the dry scorching heat forming in the back of her throat.

Burn them. They cannot find them on you.

She stretched her palm flat, scrolls atop her flesh. Tilted it ever to the side; pretended to let them fall into the flame.

She couldn't.

Within these scrolls lay the story of Darrick Rhiagain's wife. Of his son.

A story very few people knew, and she was now among them. A secret that would change everything.

The secret she'd come to Duncarrow for.

She couldn't fathom why Eoghan hadn't killed them both already. She would have. Stefan Rhiagain stood between Eoghan and the throne. He was real, and he was on this very island.

Perhaps the sniveling, weak boy who had been second all his life kept his brother's wife and son around in order to deceive himself and regain the power he'd seen but never had.

But where Eoghan was weak, Asherley was wise.

She would find who sent this knowledge into her hands. She would find out why.

And then she would bring Eoghan Rhiagain's world crashing down around him.

WHERE ALL THE UNASKED QUESTIONS LIVE

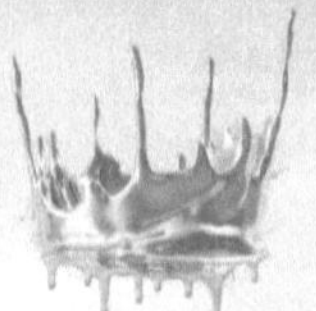

Andy hadn't experienced a restful night of sleep since arriving in the Wastelands, but there was, even now, a special sort of terror in being woken in the middle of the night by harried whispers.

Lake knelt between the hard cots of Andy and Cap. "Wake up. Wake up!"

Cap was the first to come around to the intrusion. He was up and alert with an attentiveness that made Andy wonder if the man truly slept at all. He was always at the ready. "Lake," he said calmly, "is there a matter of urgency, or do you gather enjoyment from frightening sleeping men?"

Andy bit back a grin. And there again was the extraordinary duality of Cap; both predictable and also surprising.

"Come, both of you," Lake said. He was unfazed by the uncharacteristic teasing from Cap, and that alone was cause for concern.

"Come where?" Andy asked. "'Tis the middle of the feckin' night, Lake."

"I found something." A hint of moonlight hit the young man's crazed expression. He looked as if he hadn't seen a moment's peace in days. "Something you need to see."

"Right now?"

"Right now. We cannot go there in the day. We'll be stopped."

"Where?" Andy asked.

Lake turned away from him. Looked directly at Cap. "You have to come, Cap. Someone has to see this, before we all end up the same way."

"End up?" Andy said. "You see why we donnae want to come, my friend? You cannae speak plainly and we've a few good hours left 'fore they'll have us working to our bones again."

Lake grimaced. "Bones are all that'll be left of you if we do nothing."

Andy didn't like where this was going. Not at all. It wouldn't do to get them killed before he could convince Cap to exit the Wastelands a better way. "Aye? We'll take our chances."

Lake, flabbergasted, turned again to Cap, who laid a hand on his arm. "We're both very tired, Lake. You know how hard they work us these days. Now that our numbers have reduced."

Lake's eyes stretched wider in his sockets, almost to bursting. "Aye, and you think you know why, don't you? But do the math! We've lost four times as many men as we saw butchered in the revolt. I know why. I know where they've gone. I've seen it."

"Shut yer mouth!" another prisoner yelled from the other side of the tent. "Sun's comin'!"

"It willnae be coming at all for you if ye donnae feckin' mind yourself," hissed Andy. He turned back to Lake and said, "And you're gonna withhold the info unless we come with. Tha' about right?"

"You won't believe me if you don't see it with your own eyes."

Cap, with a small but weary sigh, peeled back the stitch of fabric that passed for a blanket and nodded at Andy. "The sooner we go, the sooner we return to whatever sleep still awaits us."

Andy decided that if Lake was funnin' with them, he'd snap the kid's neck before he returned to whatever sleep still awaited him.

. . .

ANDY HADN'T BEEN IN THE WASTELANDS LONG ENOUGH TO understand. The ones fresh from their mothers threw around their bravado until it was kicked and beaten from them. But as Cap, and many others, had come to learn, a man didn't take risks in the Wastelands. You did what you were told. That was all you did. No more, unless you wanted to draw attention and be singled out. No less, unless you had a mind to die of starvation.

For Lake to take a risk, he had to fear something worse than a slow death from the pangs of hunger.

The Wastelands was a peninsula. Most of the borders dipped into the White Sea. Unless you were near the northern end, closer to shore, the seas were too choppy to make it more than a hundred meters before being pulled under by the tide's power. Where the Reach met the mainland, a narrow strip at its northernmost border, iron walls stretched into the skies, a functional and symbolic reminder of the futility in attempting escape.

The bulk of the guards in the Wastelands were the ones assigned to the camps. They were supposed to take shifts, but there was no system of laws governing the guards in the Wastelands. Had there been, the prisoner massacre at Camp Atonement would have stopped at first blood. After midnight, snores replaced small talk, and the reality of the unforgiving terrain became the barrier preventing prisoners from attempting anything foolish.

Cap had heard a rumor the guards weren't there any more willingly than the prisoners. Although their food rations were a square larger, and their beds decked with a single pillow, they were trapped here, products of a similar misery. Most turned their anger toward the prisoners, whose existence demanded theirs, and not at the regime who had ripped them from their lives and sent them to a place devoid of hope.

Even though the guards were useless in the midnight hours, few ever dared chance it. There was no reason to be out at night stronger than the desire to garner what little sleep they were granted.

Yet there were also places that were never, at any hour, available to them, and as they navigated the rough terrain and moved beyond the camps, toward the volcano that lay beyond a short, jagged mountain range, Cap understood Lake was leading them to one of such places.

"Quicker! We have to be back by sunrise!" Lake called, scampering along ahead. Andy cursed plagues at the man under his breath, but livened his pace. Cap was too busy taking in the details of his unfamiliar surroundings to feel any emotion other than vague wonder. None of them had ever ventured this far. There was a reason they were confined to the camps and mines. Curiosity was the first to die in the Wastelands, and he'd eventually given up wondering. What was an answer, next to food? Survival? What did it matter?

It did matter to some. To those who profited off their labors and used incarceration as a tool to slake greed, not fine tune punishment. Men came here to die, and they died by working themselves to death or starving when they failed to. But before they died, they would line the coffers of those receiving the shipments of that elusive gemstone more valuable than gold.

They climbed over a graveyard of rocks. It took some time doing, as they had no light to guide them through the serrated edges. One wrong move would lead to an injury with no ending but death.

As they scaled to the other side, they came upon a valley. The vast dead land stretched all the way to the base of the volcano, untarnished by the hands of men.

Lake pointed. "Over there. Careful. Almost there, but it gets steep."

Now between two rock ranges, a hard, sulfuric wind whipped through them. Andy faltered and almost took Cap with him, but Cap steadied them both, planting his tattered boots. He did this while searching through the haze of reddish dust for whatever Lake had been so motivated to show them.

As the foul air moved, a gap appeared. Cap caught a fleeting glimpse of it, and then it was gone. What he'd seen… had he seen it? His fatigue and hunger worked in tandem, always, and it was possible he was simply confused. But this was no accidental sighting. Lake had brought them here, for a reason, high on his own very real terror.

He kept pace with Lake, but with a different, duller enthusiasm, easing quickly toward dread. But he hadn't felt genuine fear in so long that he didn't recognize this acrid burn in the back of his throat. The tingling that started from his shoulders and radiated into his hands, which he clenched and unclenched to restore feeling to, and his fingers, now swollen.

Lake came to an abrupt stop. He faced ahead. "What were we always told, about our deaths here?"

"That they were inevitable?" Andy quipped.

Cap understood the question. "That in death we were again free. Returned to our families when our promise was spent, if there was a family to see us returned to. Those with no one to meet them are sent to the flame, their ashes buried."

"Aye," Lake said. "We know this is true. We've watched good men drop from hunger or insubordination. We've seen their carts pass through the gates. But these men died before our eyes. They died in the open, for others to see. What of the men dragged from their beds and murdered in the shadows?"

"Lake, tha's only nonsense from the tongue waggers—" Andy interjected, but Lake would not be silenced.

"There's no more food. No new shipments have come. There is only one way we don't all starve to death, and that's if the camps have fewer mouths to feed." Lake stepped aside, and what he'd come to show them passed into full view.

Andy stepped down another couple of rocks for a better look. Cap didn't need to. He could see it all plainly enough. The rows and rows of dugout earth. The tangle of flesh that no longer resembled men, more closely resembling piles of discarded dolls.

"But their clothes…" Andy's hands were atop his head, tugging at his hair.

"More to go around now," Lake muttered. "Where do you think your new jumper came from?"

Cap swallowed. Nothing went down. He was dry from mouth to belly. "How many?"

"Hundreds, the first time I came. When I began to suspect," Lake said. "Thousands now."

"Tha's not possible," Andy whispered.

"I don't possess the power to conjure such an image," Lake said. "Or to persuade you it isn't hunger creating it." He turned to Cap. "You understand?"

Cap slowly nodded. "Tell me what else you know, before we have to turn back."

"After the riot, I noticed more men dying. Men who were sick, aye, but not dying. Not on the verge of a promise spent, you hear? I had to know. For bad or worse, I had to know. I started listening to the guards. Mostly nonsense, as you know. They'll talk about anything."

Cap's mouth twitched into a smile.

"Then I heard it. I heard them talk about the pit. That's what they called it, Cap, the pit. Not something respecting the dead, even. Just the pit. I went out, night after night, until I found it. Then I started paying more mind to the disappearing men. I slept with an eye open, and that's when I saw the guards dragging men from their beds. Men who they told us later had expired of hunger. But I saw… I *saw* them strangle the life from their bodies and take them away. Before that, I could guess, but I *saw* it."

Cap touched his shoulder. "You're free of the burden of carrying this alone, Lake."

Lake visibly sagged. Clutching his jaw, he again fixed his gaze on the mass grave. His head shook with his sighs.

"What do we do?" Lake asked.

"I don't understand," Cap said. "Do? There's nothing to do, Lake.

All the power belongs to others here. It's never been ours. If they've taken to murdering men in their beds, we're already lost." He looked again at the mountains of bodies, rotting in a poorly dug hole in the red earth. "We've always been lost. Even when we claimed we didn't cling to hope, we must have clung to some, or this would not be the kick to the gut it feels now."

Andy was uncharacteristically quiet.

"But there's more of us, Cap! There's more of us than them. If we all rise together, and remind them of that—"

Cap shook his head slowly. "Look at us. We're among the strongest men here and our clothes hang from our bones. Our eyes retreat into our sockets. The voyage here took what little energy we had, and we'll pay for that tomorrow when we starve for our poor production." He drew closer to Lake. "I know you came to me for direction. I cannot say what I've done to earn that faith from you, but I'm dearly sorry for not being able to give what you seek. I can give you only my advisement to take peace in what you've seen. Perhaps some can be found in knowing what's coming, rather than being taken from this world unawares. Send your requests of the Guardians before that time is taken from you."

Lake bowed his head. His shoulders shook. Cap looked at Andy for aid in supporting the despairing man, but Andy had gone elsewhere. As he looked out upon the horrors awaiting all of them, he was no longer present.

"Go back to bed," Cap said, issuing his words with the comforting authority of a command. "You'll do yourself no favor if you cannot complete tomorrow's work. Go on."

He hadn't expected such easy compliance from Lake. But Lake, he saw, as the man shuffled away, all the fire in him died to embers, had never intended to lead a resistance. He had only the energy to pass the flame to Cap, and when Cap denied him, there was no more fuel in his fight. Cap almost felt a sense of failure within himself for not being what Lake needed him to be, but his survival these past years had been predicated upon the moment he accepted his only power was in acquiescence. In rising with the sun, working as hard as he could but not so hard he dropped from the effort, eating a meager meal to sustain what was left of him, and letting his worries go when his head dropped to the cot at sundown.

Somewhere within Cap still burned that old fire. There was a world that had been his. There had been love.

But if the Guardians willed these things to remain his past, and not his future, then he must surrender that flame and approach the hour of his promise spent, not with the regret of how it all came to an end, but with gratitude for the sliver of joy he'd once known in a garden of winter.

"You got quiet," Cap said, as the two men made the wearying trek back to their camp.

"Aye? It's okay for you to hold yer tongue, but not me? That it?"

Cap held up his hands in retreat. "I'm not looking for quarrel, Andy."

"And why should ye? You're ready to lie down like a dog and die."

"I can be ready and go in peace. Or I can die resisting, in agony."

Andy cackled. "I dinnae know why they all think you're so wise when all ye do is blubber such nonsense!"

"Thank you," Cap said.

"Tha's it, then? You're burying the pick-axe and surrendering to tyranny?"

Cap stopped walking. "You think you know tyranny, Andy," he said, and then found his pause before he could say too much.

"Oh, aye. I do. I'm a man of the Southerlands, and *no one* knows tyranny like those bred of salt and sand. Look around ye, Cap. Over half the men, nay more, ripped from their homes along the southern shores for their names and allegiances, naught more."

"Like you?"

Andy huffed under his breath. Then he said, "I wasnae ripped from anything. I was sent here. I've a purpose to fulfill."

"Then I hope you're close to fulfilling it. Something has happened in the kingdom. We may never learn what. But the trade lines to the Wastelands have been halted. It would be a fool who wishes for better days when the worst ones have just fallen upon us."

"You're not going to ask? Aren't ye even curious when a man says he wasn't sent as a prisoner, but as a spy?"

"Does it matter?"

Andy stopped and yanked Cap's arm until both men nearly fell back against the rocks. "Yes! It feckin' matters, ye fool! Do ye really want to die here?"

Cap exhaled. "What did I tell you, when you arrived? What advice did I give you?"

"Some bollocks about leaving hope at the door. And tha's all it is, Cap, bollocks. Utter ratshit. Yer so keen to die, well, why not try it my way, then?"

"What are you talking about?"

"I asked ye, Cap. Ye remember? When I asked ye if you'd leave if there was a way out."

"And I said there wasn't."

"Aye, ye did. And while yer right about much, Cap, yer dead wrong about this one." Although it was clear they were alone, Andy looked around him to be sure of it. A strange energy radiated off the young man. "I came in here with two bundles of herbs. One for me, one for you."

"You're not making sense, Andy. Me?"

"The herbs, they put you to rest. A deep rest. The kind where most folks assume yer promise is spent and the dead-given rights are read. Ye understand now?"

Cap's mouth was as dry as the surrounding land.

"Yer heartbeat becomes so weak they stop tryin'a find it. Then ye find yourself on one of those carts, the ones meant for yer family. And, slowly, yer heartbeat returns to where it's meant to, and by that time, the Wastelands is a distant memory."

Cap found his words. They were thick and tacky, filling his mouth. "I've never heard of such a thing."

"Aye, I've never heard of things, too, but that donnae mean they aren't real. This? I know it's real. I've seen it used on men. I've seen them, like dead, return to life."

"And what if you didn't? Return to life?"

Andy laughed and gestured around him. "I cannae imagine a worse death than one I didnae choose. Can you? At least if I take this herb, and die by it, I've done it on my own terms. I've nay given the satisfaction of stealing my last breath to these men beholden to the ratsbane."

Cap tried to inhale, but the dust was repressive. It all was. Andy. The mass grave. Lake, and his expectations, hanging them upon Cap's shoulders. It was all wrong. All of it. From the day he was thrown into the camp, nothing had been right, and he'd, Guardians help him, tried so very hard to accept this lot of his. To not dream of cherries in the Wintergarden, or of her hair; her beautiful smile. How she responded to his touch. Oh, how he'd tried, and the audacity of men like Lake, like Andy, to take that from him?

"Cap." Andy said the name with a firm command. And then he said it again. "Cap. My friend. I know who ye are. My da' knows who ye are. Lord Khallum Warwick knows who ye are. And when I say I was sent here with two bundles of herbs, Guardians know if I don't return with none and a crownless king, then I may as well let these heathen guards ha' their way with me."

The numbness started in Cap's toes and swiftly traveled upward, breathing the whisper of new life into limbs that had long ago surrendered to the monotony of labor. After it spread throughout all of him, it exploded into a blaze of fire, bringing him again to life.

"Cap?" Andy cleared his throat. "Your Grace?"

Cap dropped to his knees, and five long years rolled to the surface as he sobbed.

37

GATES OF THE NORTH

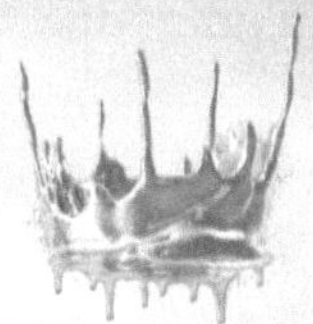

"You seem less tense here. In the Forest of All Things."

"The Forest of All. No 'things,'" Jesse gently corrected.

"If I seem less tense, it's because this is the first time I've felt safe since we left Warwicktown."

"And are we? Safe?"

"Safer than anywhere else in the kingdom." Jesse guided his horse over tree roots and dense underbrush. They had to move slowly here. One wrong move and they'd lose a beast to a broken limb. There were no paths in the Forest of All. One knew their way, or they did not. Jesse did not, but… yet… he felt compelled. Aimed true. That scared him as much as it encouraged him, for he'd only know for certain if this instinct was real if he arrived unmolested to a place he'd only heard tales of.

"Because men won't venture here?"

"Correct."

"It's dangerous for them?"

"Yes."

"Can we talk more about these dangers?"

Jesse grunted.

"Jesse." Esmerelda pulled her horse up and brought her to a halt. "I don't wish to return to when you could hardly stand to be near me."

"Come on," Jesse called back without stopping.

"Not until you look at me."

"We're not children, Esmerelda."

"Aye, and I'm not the one acting as one."

Jesse dropped his hood and looked back over his shoulder. "Not being keen to converse isn't unkindness. I donnae feel as you… as you said. All right?"

Esmerelda peeled back her own hood. Her green eyes glowed among the bold emerald leaves and mossy preternatural flora flanking her. "Yet you do think something of me. Something that's wrong, and unfair. And I cannot finish this journey until I have disabused you of such beliefs."

Reluctantly, Jesse angled his horse sideways. He looked at her more directly. "If you could do it mindful of how little sunlight we have remaining."

"I'm grateful you've stopped calling me princess."

"You are a princess."

"I cannot help the circumstances of my birth any more than you. Yes, I'm a princess of the Southerlands, or would be, if my father had his way and would see us again govern ourselves. I didn't ask for this."

Jesse tried not to groan. "Make your point."

"I am spoiled and enjoy the finer things. I shall not deny it. But to my father, I am a mere woman, whose sole contribution to this world is to bring more Warwicks into it. My value is tied to my beauty, and not my abilities. You and Ryan, you've learned an invaluable trade that makes you useful to this world. I know little about piracy or trade, but I hear the Strongs are the best at what they do. Do you know what I'm good at?"

Jesse shook his head.

"No, you wouldn't know. Because it doesnae matter." She took on her father's accent. "It doesnae matter what a *wee lass* can do, as long as she's pliant and can lie back and do her duty. When a man meets another, he's asked about his trade. When a woman is introduced, she's asked how many bairns she's birthed, and whether she thinks there'll be more in the coming seasons."

"Women are the only ones who can bring life into the world. The Guardians honor you," Jesse said, but he'd seen her point, and it was one he'd never considered before. That a woman might have a will beyond motherhood, or joys that reached further than seeing her bairns thrive. He was at once ashamed for this, because though he'd not had experiences with the fairer sex that left him satisfied beyond the immediate need, he hadn't realized that he'd so poorly regarded them until now.

Esmerelda laughed. "Spoken like a man who will never know what it's like to not be one."

Jesse gestured behind him, to what was ahead before she'd pulled them to a stop. "Maybe not, but have ye not chosen this new life for yourself, running away? Where you can be anything you want? And donnae have to be anything ye don't wish?"

"I have. And you still look at me as if I'm an invasive critter better dealt with than addressed as an equal."

"No. That isnae what I think of you."

"Then tell me."

Jesse sighed. The sun was cresting, and they'd need to find cover soon. "I think my brother must love you a great deal to risk spending the rest of his days in a prison camp where men go to die."

"You didn't answer my question."

"I did."

"I asked what *you* think of me. Not what your brother does."

"I have no opinion of you."

"Liar."

Jesse laughed. "Why is this so important to you?"

"Because I'm trusting you to see me safely to the land of my beloved's people. I have a right to know."

"Weeks we've been on the road already. You're still drawing breath. Your safety has never been at risk, least not from me."

Esmerelda shook her head. Her expression changed, fading to a blank and unreadable canvas. "It doesn't matter. I already know the answer. You think I'm a princess. You'll always think that. You'll never be capable of seeing beyond your prejudice of me."

Jesse sighed and then pressed his lips tight.

"But do you know why I chose Ryan? Why I chose your brother?" Esmerelda moved her horse slowly closer. "Because Ryan Strong was the first man in my life who treated me like I *wasn't* a princess. I grew to love him, because I saw him differently, too. To me, he wasn't just a trader, fit neatly into the mold the kingdom created for him. He was so much more. And I will wait a hundred years for him, if that's what it takes, but I will never return to the land of men like you who are incapable of seeing the world beyond what you've been told and taught. And I will raise his child, be it a son or a daughter, to be whatever *they* choose."

GRETCHEN SLID THE HEAVY GLOVES OVER HER HANDS. THE DENSITY OF fabric made moving her fingers a fantasy of the past. She never wore them when milling about the keep, but when amongst the public, the Derehams must be seen as practicing the habits they expected of others. For those with less fortunate circumstances, even an hour without gloves in the Northerlands could cause a loss of fingers or hands.

Nyssa, standing on a chair, pulled the fur hood tight around her mother's face, securing it with a quick tie of the leather straps. Gretchen smiled at her youngest daughter. She'd taken them all for granted, until she was left with only the twins. Nyssa, sweet and always eager to please. Torrin, a ball of fire, the true baby of the Derehams. The last of her babies.

"Would you like to go?"

Nyssa's face flushed bright pink. Her blue eyes betrayed the excitement of being asked. "To the important meeting?"

"Are you not important, my little wulfling?"

"What about Torrin?"

Gretchen winked. "What about him?"

Nyssa hummed with enthusiasm. She jumped down off the chair with a haphazard look, as if she had a thousand important tasks to complete before she would be allowed to join.

"Your parka, boots, gloves," Gretchen said to help focus her sweet girl. "And throw on your wool jumper. There's a fresh storm afoot, and the ride to the gates will take longer than usual with the checkpoints in place."

"Yes, Mama," Nyssa said and scampered off to do as asked.

Holden's steps, heavier in his boots and mail, sounded as Gretchen finished the last of her cider. "Are you certain this is a good idea? Bringing her?"

"How can it be a bad one?"

"We don't yet know what we'll find. Who's coming here. What they want of us."

Gretchen scoffed. "I know precisely who's about to enter the Gates of the North. And if I've made any error in choosing companions to greet them, it is that I should have invited Earwyn. But she'll appreciate the surprise when I return with someone she loves. She's been agonizing since she received her sister's raven. She'll be so relieved to know at least one of Asherley's children made it to us."

"A Blackwood child?"

"Yes. Asherley's favorite. Emberley. Her second eldest."

"And she's alone?"

"She's the only Blackwood, but she isn't alone." Gretchen straightened his parka. "Don't ask me where the remaining Blackwood children are. I cannot answer, any more than I know the whereabouts of our own."

Holden regarded her with suspicion. "How is it you know, and I do not?"

"That's a question you should ask of yourself, husband," Gretchen said. She patted his cheek with a gloved hand. "But we have nothing to fear. We're about to do Lady Blackwood a great service. One which, I can only hope, she will return, if she can, for our Pieter."

Esmerelda was right. Jesse did think of her as a spoiled princess, with the entire world in her hands and the audacity to be ungrateful about it. A little girl who only needed to follow the plush life set out for her, and she'd never want for anything. She would've been married off to one of Law's sons, more than like, and the Laws lived better than anyone in the Southerlands, even the Warwicks. Her children would further strengthen the Warwick stronghold, and she would do great honor to her house.

It had never occurred to Jesse that Esmerelda's choice of Ryan Strong was anything more than the tantrum of a petulant child.

He'd been angry to be dragged into this mess that Ryan created when he ventured beyond his station. They needed him in the Southerlands, where the Strong men had been singularly pulled into protecting the greatest secret—and weapon—of the resistance against The Pretender. Not here, playing chaperone to a whim.

And I will raise his child. Jesse hadn't consciously noted the changes in Esmerelda since they started their journey, but as he thought of them now, the buoyant, vibrant sparkle, the quick defiance, had faded to a soft-hearted curiosity. She'd not understood his acrimony, but had come to, and had put a finer point on it than he could have done on his own. He didn't think her mention of a child was figurative, and if she was carrying a Strong, then Jesse would die protecting both of them, if that's what the Guardians demanded.

He didn't hate Esmerelda Warwick. He understood that now. He'd been raised to fear women like her, for they were both out of his reach and from a world with no clear tie to his. Esmerelda wasn't the first noble to play beneath their rank, but past examples proved the only one to suffer was the one lower on the rung. The Strongs were respected, a Great Family, thanks to Khallum, but their greatness came in what they could offer the Warwicks, not who they were. Their bloodline could only dilute what Khallum and his forbears had built. A man who knew his place could go as far as the limits allowed.

"Esmerelda," Jesse said. He fell back to where she'd been riding, a pace behind him.

"Are we close?"

"I'm sorry."

He felt her frown from inside her hood. "You're what?"

"I'm sorry. For having made you feel as if the problem is you and not myself."

Esmerelda stared straight ahead as she rode apace with him. "I wasn't expecting you to say that."

"Nor was I."

"Why did you?"

"You. Your words." Jesse pulled the waterskin from the holster on his saddle and handed it to her first. "I'd never had cause to think that way. You say you've been given a role to play, but so have Ryan and I. We have more freedom than you do, but we still know our place in the world. It's simple to blame those of you who've set those limits, but that takes away our power more than any system could."

"I hadn't thought of that."

"We're accustomed to see the world through our own eyes, not the eyes of others."

"You've done me a great service, protecting me, ushering me to a place where Ryan and I can be together, and be safe," Esmerelda said. "I hope one day you can look upon me fondly. As a sister."

Jesse reached a hand across the space between them. She looked at it and then took it. "And I hope you'll one day call me brother."

· · ·

THE ROAD WIDENED, AND WITH IT, MORE TRAVELERS FELL IN BESIDE and behind them. Horses, wagons, and even carriages; young, old, and everything in between. Wulfsgate was the lively center of the Northerlander's world, just as Longwood Rush had been theirs.

As they drew closer, the line of men and women vying to enter became more densely packed. Ember and Marsh strained to see ahead. All she could make sense of was the mammoth Gates of the North, but they were not open. Nor were they closed. A small opening allowed travelers in, in what seemed to be one at a time.

Ember called to a man heading in the other direction, away from the town. "Hi there! What's the situation ahead? Why are we stopped?"

"Ayuh, the gates have been closed since the Derehams returned from Termonglen. Since that nasty business at the Right of Choosing. They're checking everyone who goes in, everyone who goes out."

Ember felt a knot forming in her belly. "Right. Of course."

"Hope your ma and pa aren't in a hurry. I expect you've another half day before you reach the gates."

Ember nodded and thanked the man. She didn't correct him.

"I don't like this, Ember," Marsh said.

"Don't get to worrying. They're probably doing the same in Longwood Rush."

"But we're welcome at the Rush. That's your home. We're outlanders here. We don't belong."

"We don't, but they know we're coming. They'll see to it we make it through without trouble."

"What if you're wrong?"

"Have I been wrong about very much, Marsh?"

Marsh slid his arms tighter around her. It wasn't for purchase. They were hardly moving now. Since the night in Dunwoode, he'd made a point to be closer to her, and she couldn't say she minded it.

"You think I worry too much," he said.

"You do," she teased. "If we were a little older, people might think you were my henpecked husband."

Marsh laughed against her back. "You and me? Married?"

"Only if fortune smiled upon you, Steward Tyndall."

"Don't get excited about one night in an inn, Lady Blackwood."

She was quite happy he was behind her, so he couldn't see the scarlet flush she felt fill her face all the way to her neck. She now had a much better appreciation for the madness that filled men and women alike where each other were concerned. "My mother is Lady Blackwood," Ember said, as they moved forward another inch. "Ember suits me fine."

"Or Stewardess Tyndall, as your fantasies seem to suggest."

Ember scoffed and slapped his hands, which were wrapped fully around her. "I wouldn't deign to take a name not my own."

Marsh leaned in and whispered, "Give me another night, in another inn, and I might change your mind."

A hubbub ahead silenced their playful volley. A heavy, wooden creak ripped through the crisp winter air as the gates moved slowly, opening wider. Guards appeared and urged the crowd to move back, back. Ember and Marsh were shoved to the side in the wave of gatherers struggling to comply. Ember fought to keep her horse calm as they were first pushed left, then right, and then back. An undulating wave of confusion.

Ahead, the crowd parted, forming a V shape, starting at the gates. Guards charged through the center, creating a gap, leaving some behind to maintain it.

"What's happening?" Marsh asked.

"I don't know. Something important, I suspect."

"The gates are all the way open, but the guards are six flanks deep."

"Yeah. Oh, here more come. Hang on, I'm going to angle us off into the snow so we aren't crushed."

The guards continued on until there was an empty center of road stretching from the gates to the end of the line. The guards themselves lined the two sides to keep them from folding back inward.

Three horses came through the guard flank at the gates. Their riders were two adults and a child, but more than that, Ember couldn't see. All around her were men taller, and she found her vision through small gaps, catching only glimpses of the three riders. Their lavish furs signaled their importance, if the show with the guards had not.

The riders came to a halt at the center of the gap. The one in the center, the tallest one, pulled back his hood. From the happy reactions of those gathered, he was someone they were eager to see. Ember didn't recognize him, though she felt she should.

"There's no cause for worry!" he called out. "All will enter before nightfall. My wife, daughter, and I come to greet our guests, who've been lost in the throngs of those eager to return to their homes, or to secure trade." He nodded to the woman at his left, and her hood came back as well.

"Child with the name of fire!" the woman cried out. "And your companion! Please make your way to us, so that we may properly greet you."

"Does she mean us?" Marsh asked.

"She must."

"What do we do? Do we go?"

"We have to." Ember cleared her throat. "It's why we're here. For this."

"How do we know they don't mean us harm?"

Ember didn't answer with words. She nudged her mare forward, calling out for others to make room for her as she pushed through. Some did; others cursed her for trying to skip the line. But with one final push, she was back on the clearing of the road, about thirty paces from where the trio sat atop their own horses.

The woman opened her arms. "Come child. We heard your plea."

Marsh tensed behind her as Emberley narrowed the gap. All

around her, curious, accusing eyes burned holes in her, but she ignored them. She wasn't here for them.

When at last they were all close enough to touch, the woman smiled. "Lady Gretchen Dereham. And my husband, Lord Holden Dereham." She gestured to her side. "And my youngest, Nyssa."

"Welcome!" Nyssa cried out. Ember couldn't help but smile at the sweet girl, who reminded her of Gabi.

"We got your message," Holden said. "Which I assume was sent with intention."

Ember nodded. "I thought it might be… easier to make our way here if you were expecting us."

Gretchen moved her horse next to Ember's. She reached a gloved hand toward her face. "You've grown so much. I last saw you when you'd hardly found your legs, but I would recognize the fire in your eyes at any age. It's where your mother found your name."

"Forgive me, Lady Dereham. I don't remember."

"No, you wouldn't. It was a lifetime ago." She waved a hand behind her. "You and your friend are our most welcome guests. For as long as you desire, or your purposes allow."

Ember nodded. "We thank you, and Lord Dereham. And thank you also for not using my name." Her whisper was almost lost on the wind. "No one can know we're here."

Gretchen nodded. "The whereabouts of you and your siblings are a topic much discussed in the kingdom. Many would wish to be the one to say they've located you."

"Have you news? Of the others?" Ember despised the hopefulness in her voice. It was weakness, and her mother had chosen her for her strength. But for the briefest of moments she thought Lady Dereham might offer words of optimism, and in that moment, Ember came alive.

"I'm sorry, dear. No one here has had word of any until your message reached us. As you may know, two of my own children are missing. My niece as well."

Ember closed her eyes and sighed. "Mother was right. We'll never be safe."

"Not out there, Ember. But you're safe here, with us." Lady Gretchen held out her arms. Ember leaned across and allowed the embrace, and when it felt good and warm and wonderful, she extricated herself before she was forever lost.

"Come home, now," Lady Gretchen said, again smiling. "You and your friend. We'll get you a warm bath, a hot meal, and then a long night by the fire where we'll listen to the stories of your adventures, and tell you what we know that you may not. Your aunt will be so pleased to have you by her side."

Holden nodded. "You're safe with us. And we long for whatever news you bring that might help us prepare for what comes next."

38

A MAN MORE LOYAL

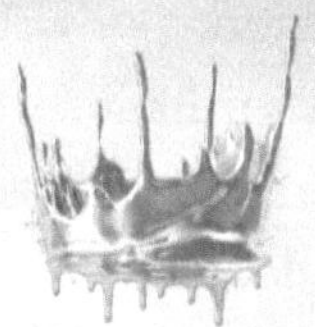

Hamish's belly hadn't ceased its incessant gurgling since they set off from Warwicktown. Law and Rutland kept their thoughts and words to themselves as they made for the seaside village of Whitecliffe. He didn't have many words himself, but he rather wished for something to break the silence, which might distract him from the persistent need to empty his bowels.

A greater man might question why Khallum Warwick had chosen *him* to shoulder the burden of protecting the kingdom's future. Hamish Strong had asked that question, but he'd posed it to the lord himself, and the answer was simple, though not satisfying. *There isnae a man more loyal.* Nothing to speak of his capabilities, the probability of his success. Hamish was proud of his loyalty to Khallum, and it puffed him up to hear his lord say the words. But it did little to boost his confidence.

Nor did the addition of Law and Rutland, two men that, together, were ten times the man Hamish was. Law, even without the grand regalia of Port Worthing, looked almost a king himself, his righteousness radiating like a banner of pride. Rutland was less serious, but Whitecliffe was his territory, and it made Hamish a little less raw to think *that* had to be the reason Khallum chose him. What they planned couldn't happen under his nose and watch unless he was read in, and part of making it happen. Khallum hadn't said that, but Hamish knew that was to protect the man's pride.

And Law, well, *Law* was the opposite of a man like Hamish. He was learned. Sure, Strong couldn't string letters together into coherent thoughts, but when had he needed to? The men he traded with didn't put their transactions in writing. Law, and his libraries filled with scrolls by his own hand, would die one day, same as Hamish, and be read the same dead-given rites. Their bodies, if not put upon the pyre, would decay at the same rate, though Hamish, with a swell of pride, imagined his might take a touch longer with all the extra meat on his bones. Leave a little more for the vultures.

His sons came from different stock. Neither had inherited the ruddy, saltworn roughness of Hamish and his forbears. Hamish had spent his entire marriage to Yanna protecting her secret, but there was no hiding that these young men were more Medvedev than Strong, in the ways that mattered in a place like the Southerlands. Jamesan—his Jesse—was a handsome, talented lad, though serious, and Ryan had a playfulness that Hamish couldn't guess where he'd picked up. They were both capable men, like all the Strong line, but Jesse was the first of them to learn his letters, and even read books, when he thought his father wasn't looking.

And Ryan… ahh, this is where Hamish's feelings about the whole situation went fuzzy. He couldn't fathom what the boy had been thinking, or Esmerelda. She was a pretty lass, but there were pretty lasses in Sandycove, or Iron Hill, or places where women were bred to marry a man like Ryan. When he confronted the boy, Ryan would only say, "I didnae choose to love her, but I cannae stop that love, nor can I return to a time where I didnae know what it was to love her."

Hamish had been the first to learn of Ryan's dallying with Esmerelda, and it was his duty to tell his lord what he'd discovered.

He never saw himself as having a choice, and sharing what he knew before the so-called love between Ryan and Esmeralda swelled to a point that couldn't be returned from.

That loyalty was rewarded by two sides of Khallum's sword. First, in Khallum's choice to bring Hamish into his plot regarding the prisoner of interest. And then, punching him in the gut with the same hand that once lifted him, choosing Ryan to complete the task, knowing full well no men came out of the Wastelands unless on the backs of a spent promise.

Khallum may fill him with compliments, may declare there *wasnae a man more loyal,* but had Hamish not exercised that loyalty at the expense of his son, Khallum would have chosen elsewhere.

Hamish rarely let his thoughts wander too far down that path. Khallum *had* chosen him. For months, there'd been none but the Strongs brought in on this, the most important plot the kingdom had ever known. The Strongs. Not the Laws. Not the Rutlands. Khallum assured him Ryan would survive this, and would be revered as an especial favorite of Khallum himself; his sins with the lord's daughter washed away with the low tide. That he'd tender a fine bride, perhaps one of Law's young daughters, or another who would equally buoy the Strong name to even greater heights.

Jesse was the one who worried Hamish now. His claim to have a lead on a trade partner in Rushwood felt strange when he'd said it, but, weeks gone without a raven or word from other traders who might have crossed his path, and Hamish, for the first time, doubted his son's honesty. Jesse knew well what important work awaited him in the Southerlands, of which the Strongs' role was the greatest honor they'd ever known. What could be more important?

Mercifully, Khallum hadn't asked after him. Had he, Hamish didn't trust his own ability to lie so smoothly.

THEY'D BYPASSED STRONG'S TERRITORY, SANDYCOVE, AND MOVED ON to the village of Leecaster Bay, but their path ventured clear of the town, away from the scent of Leecaster's men. The bay was the main trade port in the Southerlands, greater, even, than Hamish's own Sandycove, a fact that stuck hard in his craw when he spent much thought on it. Khallum was explicit: no one else could know. Not a man. Not so much as a beaten and starving mongrel. Not even a man like Leecaster, who had a seat at Khallum's great table.

The strong winds carried off the water, chilling all three men to their bones as they huddled around the fireless camp. Winter in the Southerlands was a phenomenon without prediction, with some days so hot a man could hardly stand the clothes on his back, and others, like this, where the leather felt like silk as the hostile coast wind ate at their marrow.

Law passed around the bitter root and one of the last portions of dried rabbit. His barely veiled disgust wasn't unnoticed. Even Rutland, face lowered to his food, shook his head at the way Law picked at the meal like a princess sent to live in poverty. Guardians help him if he ever truly had to fend for himself.

Hamish consumed his own portions in resolved silence. No use in dreaming of the feasts Stewardess Strong cooked up in their hearth at home. There could be no fire. No great takedowns of boars or shore cats for them to roast over a flame, fat crackling into the coals. They were to travel light, with swiftness, and beyond the realm of prying eyes.

"We'll be in Whitecliffe tomorrow, if we ride as hard as we did today," Rutland remarked. He licked at the last of the salted meat from his fingers. "We cannae enter the town, but there's a monastery, five or six miles inland. Abandoned. Property of Whitecliffe now that we've driven the Reliquary off our lands."

Hamish snorted. "Aye. Good riddance."

"That'll suit us for a time. I can return to Whitecliffe and secure provisions for us, but I cannae take too much, or 'twill draw eyes upon the cause. Too little, and we starve. If I return for more, soon we'll have those looking after our business."

"You raise an important dilemma," Law said. "We require more accuracy in our timeline."

"Huh?" Hamish asked, ripping the salted meat across his incisors.

"We need to understand when Ryan will complete his end of the mission," Rutland said.

"Oh, aye? Am I a mind reader?"

Law sighed. Rutland held out a hand, cautioning him.

"Hamish, I know ye have no vision into that cursed place," Rutland said, and in his amiable tone Khallum did finally see Rutland's use in all this, aside from the position of his land. "But ye do know yer son. Ye know Ryan. What he's capable of. He's been in there weeks now, and the day of reckoning approaches. What does your gut tell you when it speaks?"

Hamish scratched the back of his neck. Thinking. Khallum had finally informed Hamish that he had, of course, given Ryan a time by which his mission should be accomplished, but within that was the wild swing of reality, and the unpredictability of the prisoner himself, whom Ryan could not leave without. He had a deadline, that he could not jump forward on, but may require more time for. "He cannae do it a day sooner than th' hour assigned. My boy will be well aware o' that. But ye ask me what my gut tells me? It tells me I raised a capable man, and tha' capable man could talk a thirsting man out o' his own water. Aye, he willnae make us wait. He'll hit the day Khallum gave him as the day to see it done. We'll not be waiting long."

"Guts are not facts," Law said. "We do not make critical decisions based on emotion."

"Unless you have a raven capable of delivering messages inside the Wastelands unmolested, there isnae another thing working for us," Rutland countered. "If Hamish says his boy will be on time, we'll believe him until we have cause not to."

Hamish grunted his thanks.

The next words from Law looked as if they caused him great

pain, or a twist in his bowels. "And Lord Warwick, what are his wishes for the prisoner upon retrieval?"

Hamish took some joy in being the one to know something over Samuel Law, but it was a small thing as his belly went half-full and his bones clattered from the cold. "He's tah be brought back to Whitecliffe until the poison wears off and he's fit for travel. Then, we await word from Lord Khallum." From there, Hamish didn't know what his lord intended, but he wouldn't say that. Let them wonder what else he knew, rather than confirm what he did not.

"How will you explain two unconscious men in your keep?" Law asked Rutland.

"Nothing to it," Rutland said. "We get vagabonds from Oak Hill and the borderlands all the time. Refugees, castouts. Stewardess Rutland has an overly kind heart and takes pity on many of them. More than I'd like." He grimaced. "For this, I can only be grateful for her misplaced intentions."

"And are you usually the one bringing them in?" Law challenged.

"Let me be concerned with matters of my own household," Rutland countered.

Law, with a quick, sharp smile at Rutland, turned back to Hamish. "Where do we meet them? You mentioned a wagon?"

"Aye. Prisoners are returned to their families, when their promise is spent. For proper rites, ye know, as it were. They're carted out on wagons and then…" Hamish swallowed. "Far as I understand, left amongst the other dead as they await claimin'."

Law twisted his nose and lips. "There's no civilized handoff? We're expected to dig through piles of dead bodies to find ours?"

"Aye, so I hear."

"So you hear? What do you know?"

Hamish bristled. "I know my own son is inside, tryin' to save all of us. And I'll see you remember that."

"Easy," Rutland said. "It doesnae matter, does it? We know what we need to do. When we make camp at the monastery, I will send raven to Khallum revealing our chosen whereabouts. When Stewardess Strong gets her own raven, from the Wasteland guards, she'll give notice to Khallum, who will give notice to us. What we do when we get there isnae a concern until it is. We'll bring them home." He met Hamish's gaze. "Both of them. For one is valuable to the kingdom's salvation, and we'll credit the other with delivering that salvation to us."

Hamish flushed in gratitude.

"For tonight?" Rutland went on. "We rest. For there'll be plenty o' sleepless nights ahead o' us in the monastery as we measure the hours and days, painted against all the unknowns, and the manners o' which this could all fail."

"My son willnae fail," Hamish charged.

Rutland nodded. "Pray that we donnae fail him."

39

CRIMES AND DISTRUST

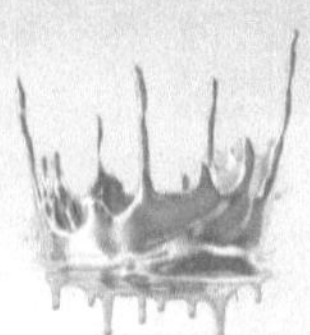

Valen and Drystan rode ahead, clearing enough distance between them and the girls that it seemed intentional. To Lisbet, the two men were in a world only they wished to be in, and the sense that she and Eavan were intruders only grew as they ventured farther into the strange woods of the Hinterlands.

And strange they were. The trees here were not the pine and fir that towered over her homeland. No trunks so large you needed four children to make a circle of arms around them. Here the soft, peeling bark bedecked long, graceful trunks that stretched into the skies, the tops of the tree line resembling blue-green clouds. Some bore fruit or flowers, which were also unfamiliar, in colors that were so unusual they startled Lisbet. Others simply shimmered in their odd, emerald effervescence. They reminded her of things she might see in a fever dream, but never in her waking world.

It was just like any other forest, and yet it was nothing like any other forest.

If she were welcome ahead, she supposed Valen would explain it all to her. Where the trees came from, how such rich and other-worldly colors were possible. He'd probably tell her it was *magic*,

446

because that's what every adult said when they had no better explanation. *Why do cherries grow in the Wintergarden, Mama? Magic, Lisbet. What else?*

If she wasn't jealous of whatever was happening between her brother and that peculiar man, she was practically green with envy that the two men weren't left to deal with the distressing changes in Eavan. She'd stopped her incessant preening and prattling over her life back in Whitechurch, and Lisbet almost wished she'd go back to that, because in its place she spun an odd tale of a childhood romance between herself and Kian de Medvedev and how she'd broken his heart. How he pined for her now, the one who got away. A story that had changed from the one Eavan told her years before, painted to make her seem the elusive catch Kian could not quite secure. That he must still long for, even now. It seemed to Lisbet that she'd crafted this version of the story for herself in direct response to what happened to her at the camp, projecting upon Kian her fear that no man would take her after that.

Lisbet almost hated herself for thinking it, but Eavan's acceptance of the horror might have been better than whatever disconnected reality she existed in now. A bliss that wasn't real, and would even more painful once realized. And Lisbet read enough between her cousin's words to understand that whatever had passed between Eavan and Kian, it hadn't ended well. Lisbet had her doubts that the young Medvedev would be as enamored now. As she read Eavan's truths between the words, Lisbet wished she'd questioned her cousin more before blindly following her down this path.

Yet there was no use in entertaining the budding sense of dread building within her. Kian wasn't the only Medvedev. And if the rumors were true, there was Medvedev blood running through the Derehams. Uncle Alric liked to say so, whenever he found occasion to slip it between the context of a conversation, though he was also the only man she knew who claimed to have been Beyond, so it was hard to know with him.

If nothing else, three of them were mere children. Surely they were in no danger here, except from the man leading them, with intentions he shared with no one.

"He loved watching me eat the apples. Oh, Lisbet, the apples here! They're twice as large as any apple you've seen, I assure you. No, don't tell me about the ones in the Wintergarden. I've seen them. No, these… these! The color is so vivid, and it will remind you of something ready to burst. And it does, in your mouth! Oh, how Kian would laugh when the juices ran down my chin."

"How nice," Lisbet mumbled, never taking her eyes off her brother.

"Nice doesn't begin to describe the sensation, but you'll discover this for yourself, soon enough. Kian loves to watch outsiders experience his world for the first time. I know he will want to do the same with you, Lisbet. Oh, but watch out, he'll give you an apple but steal your heart!" Eavan shook her head. "Beware, though. It belongs only to me."

"I will be on the highest alert," Lisbet said. It hit her then. Why should Drystan be the only one to hear the gospel of Valen? Why should she not get time with him, to better understand him? Dissect him? To better see through the veil that protected Drystan from the truth, and make her own assessment, as Drystan so assuredly had?

She was decided. It was Drystan's turn to watch over Eavan for a spell.

Drystan hadn't been pleased with the request, but Lisbet didn't much care. He'd had his opportunity to assess this man, Valen, and now it was hers. If nothing else, her sanity needed a reprieve, and Drystan might gain some appreciation for what she'd endured since they left the farm. He may even have a means to help her.

"Your brother keeps much of himself locked away," Valen commented after a silence filled with Lisbet's contemplation of all she wanted to say but struggled to articulate.

"That's not an especially astute observation. Anyone who meets him would know that."

"I never said it was. Only, I wonder if anyone knows how deep that locked room goes."

"Does it matter? Drystan's thoughts are his own to keep or to share."

Valen chuckled. "You came up here to discuss your brother, or me, or both, did you not?"

Lisbet flushed. "I came because one can only take so much of Eavan's nonsensical ramblings. And yes, to discuss matters with you. But I won't discuss Drystan. Only your intentions with him."

"You want to know why I'm so interested in your brother."

Lisbet didn't look at him. His striking eyes were so enchanting. She wondered if they had their own kind of magic. The kind that had enamored her brother and stolen away his judgment. "You wouldn't tell me the truth if I asked."

"Would you believe my interest is in helping all of you? Not only Drystan?"

"No."

He smiled to himself. "No. I didn't suppose you would."

"Is it true?"

"You didn't come up here for the truth. You came to sow a deeper distrust."

"And yet it's your arrival that has done that."

"I'm not your enemy, Lisbet. You have plenty to name without adding mine to the list."

"You vanquished some of them," Lisbet said. The next came out as an accusation. "In the most convenient and timely manner."

"Would you like me to tell you I had foreseen your peril?"

Lisbet laughed. "I wouldn't *like* anything, except the truth. I'd *like* to understand what your intentions are with my brother, and why you would give up your own life, whatever that is, wherever that is, to escort us halfway across the kingdom. I'd *like* to know your real name, where you really come from, and who you really are."

"I have my curiosities as well, Lisbet. I may be a mystery to you, but you are, as well, to me. I know your aversion to marrying the king. From what I know of him, your reaction isn't beyond understanding. But your bigger concern was for your brother. For his fate, which you believe to be more important than your own. And why is that?"

Lisbet hadn't seen it in quite this way until Valen said the words, but the message resonated. She had left more for his sake more than her own. She would have married Eoghan Rhiagain, much as the idea pained her, if that were the only problem settling over Wulfsgate Keep. But it wasn't. Drystan was the best of them all, and his behavior with Ravenna, which was not nearly as covert as he believed it to be, would have gotten one or both of them killed. He couldn't see this, but she could. And so only she could force him to action upon something that would give him what he most wanted, while protecting his life.

"You also keep much locked away," Valen said to her, cutting a hole through her introspection. "Must be a common trait among Quinlandens."

"You mean Derehams."

Valen said nothing. At first, Lisbet thought he was once again attempting to don his usual veil of mystique, but she watched him closely, seeing first how his brows furrowed, and then how the center of him caved inward, like a man who'd been punched unawares.

"Valen?"

"Turn around."

"What?"

"We must turn around, Lisbet. We aren't meant to be here. We're in danger."

"What are you talking about? We've been here for days already. Why are you acting like this?"

Valen's horse reared back, nearly throwing him off. "We've been detected and deemed a danger, and now we must go. Now!"

"How could you possibly know that?"

Drystan and Eavan came up to the strange scene. "Valen?" Drystan asked. "What's wrong?"

Valen reached a hand out and clasped it around Drystan's wrist. "We're not meant to be here. I feared this would be true, but now I know, and we must leave *now!*"

Lisbet slapped his hand away from her brother. "No one asked you to come with us. This is our journey, and we're not turning away, not when we're so close." She looked at Drystan. "Don't you see? Ever since he's come into our lives, we've been at his will. At his mercy. Now, he would seek to draw us away from our goal. Drystan! Open your eyes!"

Drystan's confusion danced across his face as his attention passed between his sister and his friend. Lisbet could see she was losing him; perhaps had already lost him. Even Ravenna's absence had been softened by the arrival of this man, and Lisbet would have believed nothing could pry Drystan from the feelings he was ready to throw his life away over.

"We can discuss this when we've safely crossed back into the Northerlands," Valen said. "You can decide then. Drystan, look at me. Look at me!"

"Who do you trust, Drystan? Your sister or a man you only just met!"

Drystan divided his eyes between the two of them, head moving so fast he grabbed his temples with both palms. "Stop! Both of you!"

"We're not in danger! Kian will be so joyed to see us!" Eavan offered.

A thousand sounds signaled all around them. Bushes assaulted by new activity. Leaves rustling at the intrusion. Valen's hand moved to his sword as they all searched for the source.

"Halt!"

They heard the voice, a lyrical high note that was soft and lilting, like a song. But the menace behind it kept Lisbet from feeling the safety Eavan had been hinting at for weeks.

The surrounding sounds turned to figures. Men, women, with long hair, ornate braids and plaits of colors Lisbet had never seen on anyone. They seemed to blend easily with the vivacious forest, magic and wonder married and flourishing in their hidden kingdom. Critters wrapped around their feet, soared above them.

Lisbet could hardly glean sense from it. But nothing in the incredibleness of the vision before her could erase the dread; that horrible feeling that her life, which had been hardly lived, was coming to a swift end.

"We mean no harm," Valen called. He'd left his sword sheathed, hands now held out to show his intentions. "We come in search of Yseult, and her son, Kian."

"Tell Kian it is me, Eavan! Eavan Quinlanden!"

"We know of whom you declare name," one replied, directing a venomous gaze at Eavan. A snake slithered around his arm. "And to Yseult we will take you, though no treasured guests come before our eyes."

"What's happening?" Drystan asked Valen, but Valen didn't answer. "What's he saying?"

"Don't fight this," Valen said to them all. "There's no running. Not now."

"You knew," Lisbet accused. "You led us here, to this trap."

"I'm either the one who turns you away or the one who drives you forward," Valen said sadly. His hands remained in the air. "I cannot be both, Lisbet. Even my transgressions are bound by limits."

"I don't believe you! You only told us to turn back once it was beyond our means. Once it was too late!"

"This wasn't my destination, Lisbet. It was yours."

The Medvedev closed in, forming an unbreakable circle around the travelers. Lisbet noted they had no weapons, but then a strange sensation came over her. Her arms were weighed to her sides, as if bound but without tethers. Her legs, as if one with her horse.

"Magic bindings," Valen explained, breathless, squirming in his own saddle. "You don't have the skill to free yourself from them. You'll only hurt yourselves to try."

"Kian will fix this," Eavan said, but some of the idealistic joy had seeped out of her voice, merging with reality. "We won't be prisoners for long."

"Your fate, decided by Yseult," the one with the snake said. "Look not to hope. Here, you'll not find it. Only for the crimes by which you will answer."

"Crimes?" Drystan looked at Valen, but for once, the man had no answers.

"You said they were your friends. That they took you in and were kind to you," Lisbet charged.

"They were," Valen said, and though she knew him to be lying, he sounded confused. "Something is wrong. Something has changed."

Consuming darkness replaced the surrounding confusion. She struggled to breathe through the rough fabric shoved over her head. She tossed her head back and forth to free the fabric from her skin, but it tightened at the back of her neck, securing into place.

Lisbet didn't compel her horse forward, but Starcaller moved, following the Medvedev, as did the others, all falling into a perfect line in the center of the Medvedev guard.

She wanted to demand they tell her where they were being taken, but there would be no answers until they arrived. Wherever they were being led, they were now prisoners of the Medvedev, and they'd be given nothing the Medvedev didn't wish for them to receive.

"It will be okay," Drystan called back to Lisbet. "I won't let them harm you, Lis, Eavan!"

It was her turn to reassure him, but Lisbet lost the words, buried in her fear, in the knowledge they were beyond the help of anyone.

They were on their own.

40

THE KEY AND THE BOX

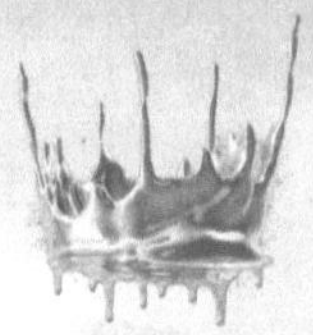

Asherley wished the little imbecile would hurry himself along. He seemed to drag it out on purpose, as if he had some seventh sense about how achingly sore her nipples were, or how little she enjoyed bouncing upon his bony lap. Once, she suggested he take her from behind, thinking to give herself some reprieve, and immediately realized her error by the dejected horror painted on his face. *But how will I drink?* She didn't propose it again.

When at last he finished, face stretched into a grotesque pleasure that would have turned hers sour had she been there for any of her own, he didn't immediately erupt into yawns and signals for her to tuck him in. He seemed more awake than before she'd come to his chamber. She glanced at the door, eager to return to the guard, to check for more scrolls.

Asherley pulled at her undergarments to secure them back into place. She loathed the sensation of his monster's seed warming inside her; needed to expel it before it took root. But the look he gave her, gazing up from the chair with his limp cock lying dead at the side of his leg, gave her pause. He didn't want her to tend to his naptime. He wanted to *talk*.

"Is my wife with child yet?" Eoghan asked.

"You would be the first to know, Your Grace."

"Well, I do not know, so I'm asking you."

"Not as I'm aware."

"Pity," he said. "I'm quite ready to strike her from my bed."

"She is eager to please you."

"Eager and capable are not the same," Eoghan answered. He turned his head to the side with a bored look. "If Quinlanden has sent me an infertile maid, I'll have his head served to his wife."

"Assana is perfectly intact," Asherley said, though Maeryn would be quite pleased to see her husband's head severed from his body. "These things can take time."

"How long after your own nuptials were you quickened with child?"

"Almost three years," Asherley said. She left it there. She'd been in no rush to procreate with a man she hardly knew, not when his children would be the next leaders of the Westerlands. She had to be certain. Those three years hadn't been the best in her marriage, but they had been the most important. A friendship had blossomed in the space of how little they shared in common. Asherley, who had never needed a man to complement the life she saw for herself, learned to enjoy Byrne, who was nothing like her. Nothing like any Blackwood she could recall. Not even like a Warwick. She didn't initially welcome his tempering of her fire, but it happened without either of them realizing it. When she'd come upon him reading a book in his chambers. As he spoke to the staff and servants on equal terms, even making jest with them, or asking after their children or spouses by name.

"Lord Warwick must have thought you were barren!"

"We were young enough that there were no worries from either of us, Your Grace. I bore my husband four children. The Guardians saw fit to bless our hearth." More, she thought to herself, if one counted those who hadn't lived.

"Yet only one son."

"Yes." Brandyn was her heir, but it should be Emberley. When she'd made this choice, she'd done it knowing there may be war in their lifetimes, and a lordship led by a man would be given more respect than one held by a woman. But that belief went against all she knew to be true about Blackwood women. She might yet correct this, if the Guardians allowed her to leave this place.

"And yet you, a woman, were left at the head of your Reach."

"The Guardians saw fit to bless my mother with only three daughters," she said.

"Your oldest. A girl?"

"Yes. Hollyn."

Eoghan flinched. She tried to read his whispers, but, as usual, they were tucked somewhere she could not find them. She had no reason to think he did this intentionally. In his artlessness, he saw no need to hide, and so his dark corners were vacant. Intentional or not, it was a constant source of frustration for her. She'd come to study him, not to fuck him.

"The one you were to bring to me, to be my bride."

Asherley was at a disadvantage. Without access to his intentions, she could only guess where he was leading her, but she knew, no matter where he was going, she must tread with great care. "It was with the greatest sorrow we learned the honor had been taken from us."

Eoghan snorted. His eyes glassed over, watching her. "Tell me about her."

Asherley again looked at the door. The sun was fading. Soon, she'd have no business outside, no excuse for being beyond the castle walls. "What would you like to know?"

"Anything."

"She was most eager to become your bride, and your queen," Asherley said, burying some of the sting from this truth. Hollyn's eagerness had been contained in a naivete and idealism of the world that she hadn't gotten from any Blackwood. Nor from Byrne, who, as any Warwick, had more than a healthy distaste for the Rhiagains. Asherley at first attempted to discourage her daughter's excitement, but ultimately allowed Hollyn to live in her delusions, for what awaited her might be more easily dealt with if accepted. Embracing her fate would aid in her survival when the time came to take her place at his side.

"What did she say about me?"

Asherley's confusion at the questions mounted. "That she had heard you were a most gracious king and could not wait to serve you."

"But did she speak of me? Of me, as a man?"

"I'm sorry, Your Grace. I don't understand the question. Hollyn didn't have occasion to know you as a man."

Eoghan yawned, but it was a feigned gesture, a strange contortion in the face of someone who had never actually watched someone do it. A desperate attempt to be rid of the moment. "I tire of conversation. See me to bed, Lady Blackwood."

"Yes, Your Grace."

With relief, Asherley attended to his naptime ministrations, reminding herself not to rush, not to draw attention to her eagerness to be rid of him.

His contrived snores followed her to the door. She felt his cloying eyes upon her back, and she slowed her pace. As she reached her hands toward the wooden handles of the doors, a thought struck her. It filled her with such terrible horror that she missed a step and was frightfully aware that he'd seen her do it.

But then, on a night where the rain hadn't stopped for weeks, Eoghan told me he'd met a girl. He never named her, and I never asked. To ask was to break his stream of thought, and to invite something worse. All he would say was that she was from a Great Family. One of the most great, in fact.

Eoghan, looking up at her with the hopeful eyes of a lover asking after news of his love. *But did she speak of me? Of me, as a man?*

Asherley slipped outside the door before Eoghan could witness her fight with the bile in the back of her throat.

Remembering the strange traveler who'd come through the summer before, claiming he was in search of a certain plant that grew only in the Westerlands. Asherley had paid him no mind, passing him off to Hollyn for her to hone her skills as a lady of the household. It seemed to her a traveler of no great house was the perfect opportunity to do so, and so she'd turned to more important business, as Hollyn spent weeks seeing after the stranger. She couldn't even conjure his likeness in her memory.

She'd never questioned his business. Never asked *which* plant he was after, and why. It was of no concern to her.

I heard tell of a family who had taken in my brother. I had to see for myself.

Not Darrick, Anabella had concluded.

Asherley lifted her skirts and raced against the receding sun, beseeching the Guardians that it be John Cantwell minding the sky dungeon on this eve.

AIDEN PACED ACROSS THE ORNATE RUG LINING THE FLOOR OF HIS tent. Over a hundred candles flickered, more than was required to light his spacious accommodation, but he, Aiden, was the light in this kingdom, and this must always be so, at all hours. The river rushed several meters beyond, the only barrier now between him and his prize. He'd traveled light—as far as men went—and despite Mads Waters' insistence he needn't be present for this mission, he would not have missed it. He had a specific image in his mind, of a man's final moments, expressed through eyes that would stay that way until the flesh rotted away from bone and returned to the ground, a promise so poorly spent.

Mads stepped inside. "Our scouts have returned, my lord. They have switched to their light guard duty for the evening at the keep. We shouldn't delay."

"We have enough men?" Aiden asked.

"Enough if we go now."

"Can we be certain we haven't been sussed out?"

"Had we been, they would not have relieved the guard duty to what it is now."

"And inside?"

"He's dismissed most of his servants. He is alone, save for one attendant." Mads' mouth twisted. "A woman."

"Is he a fool?" Aiden posed the question, although he was already most acquainted with the answer. The man was certainly a fool, and he would die a fool, but his death would create the display of power Aiden needed to silence those who would challenge him. He would neutralize this Reach, subdue it to his own command, and King Eoghan would reward him handsomely.

"He is grieving, I'm told, my lord."

"Grieving? Has there been news I should know?"

"No, my lord." Mads shifted. "Our scouts say he struggles in the absence of news of his children and wife. There has been nothing from his own search parties. He awaits their return, in agony."

Aiden grinned. Byrne Warwick was no man. He was the seed by which his masculine wife had brought more of her own into this world. He was an abomination to the Westerlands, to the Southerlands. Asherley had overplayed her hand, leaving this man to watch over a lord-less land. She would learn her lesson soon, powerless to do naught more than grieve her errant foolishness from her prison cell on Duncarrow.

Aiden fastened his sword belt. "Let us relieve him of this agony."

"Lord Warwick? Are you certain there's nothing else I can get for you this evening?"

Byrne looked up from his wife's chair. He hadn't spent the whole day there, and he was proud of this. He was finding strength in routine. Seeing to the business Asherley would, were she here. As he sat beneath the mounted sword of her people, The Betrayer—named so for its origins, wielded by the first Blackwood, Rhosyn—he began to feel a sense of peace in the way things were now. "No, Maye. You are free until morning."

Maye hesitated in the door. She was young... younger than his Gabi, though she'd certainly seen more in her short years, having been plucked from the alleys of East Derry, and bounced across several households before landing with the Blackwoods. In her eyes was her eagerness to please, to feel seen and useful. Byrne wished he had more to give her. More words to reinforce his gratitude at her constant presence. More smiles and encouragement.

"Yes, Maye? What is it?"

Maye gazed at her feet. "I wasn't sure if I should tell you."

"You should tell me anything you believe I should know."

"Only..." Maye twisted her hands. "In the market today, I overheard two of Clarissant Tyndall's handmaidens. I didn't know them at first. They're not among those I socialize with, is what I mean to say. They're new... that is, not from around here. The Tyndalls are staying in Longwood Rush, as you know."

"Yes." They were all closing in. The stewards and stewardesses of their Reach demanded answers, and he had none. His children were as gone as theirs. Even Asherley, who had sent them, didn't know to where they had gone.

"And they... they said their mistress believes her son is dead, and that you... forgive me, my lord, but that you know this and are keeping this secret."

Byrne sighed. "Thank you for telling me, Maye."

"It's not true, is it?"

"No," he said. "I would never keep such news from them."

Maye nodded, relieved. "They'll come back, my lord. This is their home."

He wished Maye was right in her prediction, but Byrne knew it could be years before he saw his children again. They wouldn't return until it was safe, and it would not be safe with The Pretender on the throne and Aiden Quinlanden, his sycophant, eager to do any bidding to win favor. Even if Khallum's plan blossomed to life, it would not change things overnight. There would undoubtedly be war.

Asherley had done right. He accepted that now. But the sting of their absence was no less keen. The dearth of their ringing laughter was a silence so loud it deafened him. He longed to hear their feet pounding against the old wood.

"Of course, Maye. And we will both celebrate that day, won't we?"

Maye's tiny face erupted into a smile. "Yes, my lord."

ASHERLEY FOUND JOHN CANTWELL AT THE GUARD POST, BUT HE didn't have more scrolls for her. Asherley asked him about this… what it could mean. Had something befallen the writer?

"I know nothing," he insisted. "I've heard nothing to suggest what you say. She doesn't write on a schedule that I have noticed, my lady."

"You're nervous," Asherley said, noting his jitters were more acute than the last time. "Something has given you cause for fear."

A young woman stepped forth from behind the cistern. One Asherley didn't know, but recognized from the faces milling about the keep. She was the same one who had run from her the other day, startled. The one who had most likely sent her the whisper that led her here.

"You. Who are you?" Asherley demanded.

"I am no one," the young woman said, affording her a curtsey appropriate for Asherley's position.

"No one, like John Cantwell?" Asherley reached for the young woman's face. Lifted it with the tips of her fingers, so she could see into her eyes. "I'm here because of you. Someone taught you how to deliver this message, and you sent me here. Now you will tell me why."

"It wasn't me."

"Then who?" Asherley hissed.

"T'was my master." The young maid trembled under Asherley's touch. "I was only doing their bidding, as I'm required."

"Who is your master?"

"If I tell you before it's time, they will have my life."

"Lady Blackwood, she's telling you the truth," John Cantwell pleaded. "We're sworn to secrecy. On our lives and that of our families."

Asherley ignored him. "Time? Time for what?"

"Tomorrow night," the girl said. "Tomorrow night, there will be a ship. No one will question why the ship is here, because we're expecting provisions from the Southerlands."

Asherley laughed. "There are no provisions coming from the Southerlands. Lord Warwick cut the crown off months ago."

The girl shook her head. "They're not from Lord Warwick. The king sent his own men to retrieve what Lord Warwick refused to send."

Asherley's eyes widened. "Did he now?"

"That is, the request was made on behalf of the king. But it wasn't made by the king himself, my lady."

"Your master."

The girl nodded. "There will be more provisions for all of us, and he will be most pleased. He will have no cause for care of a ship in his port."

"I care not about provisions, and neither do you. Your real reason for giving concern to this ship?"

John Cantwell stepped forward. "The ship isn't due to leave port again for a fortnight. This furlough means the captain and crew will stay in the servants' quarters within the keep, not aboard the ship."

"And?"

"It won't be so very hard for others to board, under the cover of night, as there will be no one aboard to stop them from doing so."

Asherley looked between the two conspirators. She wanted to

shake them both, to demand they stop being deliberately obtuse. But whoever had assembled them had only told them enough to get them to this point.

"Tell me what your master wished for me to know. The sun has faded. There will be a change of guard imminent."

The young girl gave her a curious look. "My apologies, I should be more clear. Lady Blackwood, you're to be on it."

BYRNE HAD ONLY JUST CLOSED HIS EYES WHEN THE LIGHT BUT STEADY footfalls of Maye sounded once again in the hall.

He'd been having the most wonderful dream. It wasn't like the dreams he had usually, because it was more truly a memory, and one of his favorites.

He and Asherley had taken the children to Wildwood Falls, on business with the Tyndalls. Hollyn was only seven. Brandyn was still being minded by a wet nurse. Ember and Gabi had entered a phase in their playfulness where one was perpetually seeking ways to outmaneuver the other, and this often meant they were running into each other, into walls, into the incredulous adults going about their business.

They'd taken a day to visit the falls. People came from all over the Westerlands for a spell at Wildwood, which was not one but a series of twenty waterfalls, cascading down the river until they eventually tapered off near the town center. It was so rare to see Asherley smile; to witness her unencumbered by the burdens of being the one responsible for the health and fate of the entire Reach. She'd looked so beautiful to him that day as she carried Brandyn on one hip and chased the girls through the water, actually *playing* with them. And he played right along, so eager to capture this moment in his mind's eye, to never forget it. To pull and stretch it into an eternity of time that he could live within forever.

It was such a small thing, but what remained the most potent years later was the way she kissed him over the top of Brandyn's head. A kiss from Asherley was a dutiful thing, something to be done in passing. But she'd let her lips linger that day; her eyes closed. He felt the moment she surrendered herself to the promise of a brief happiness, a respite from all that she was and must be.

When she at last pulled back, she offered a quick smile. Quick, but powerful enough to cause his heart to cease beating for a moment.

"Mama! Ember took my plushy wulf! She's gonna rip off the head!"

Asherley had shaken her head with a sigh, and once again was pulled into one of the many roles set forth for her; the moment sundered. But like those first years of their marriage, before the children, that day strengthened the unusual bond between them.

He had never known a love greater than the one he felt for his wife that day.

"Lord Blackwood!" Maye cried, and her words echoed across the room, dying on her lips as her head sailed through the air. It flipped several times as it passed across the distance before landing with a thud. It rolled across the floorboards and came to a rest at his feet, where her horrified expression was locked in perpetuity, fixed upon him with words that would remain unfinished.

Byrne looked up.

"If I'm to be on this ship, as you say, you will tell me why," Asherley said.

"All will be revealed when we set sail," John answered.

"I'm asking *you*. You, who does the bidding of your master," Asherley said to the young girl.

"You'll not be alone, my lady," the girl said. "John and I will be there, of course. As will my master."

"And why should I come, to serve a master unknown, to a place unknown?" Asherley laughed, leaning in. "You assume too much about my eagerness to leave this place."

"I know the king is fond of you," the girl said and immediately regretted her words, slapping both hands over her mouth in horror. "Forgive me, my lady. My master tells me I forget myself."

"He nurses from my breasts while I fuck him into insensibility," Asherley said evenly. "Unlike your master, I'm not afraid of my secrets. I fear nothing."

"Lady Blackwood," John said. His face revealed his fear that they were failing at a very important task. "There are those here who would see an order restored to this kingdom. As you would."

"We're hardly unique in that desire."

"Our master is one such person. The risk to their life is significant should they be revealed before they can retire to safer lands. Lands where there will be others like us."

"Does this have something to do with Dain Rhiagain?"

John frowned. "My lady?"

"As she writes in her scrolls! Of a long-lost son, delivered into the kingdom under secrecy."

"I know nothing of Dain's fate. I know only of a place where there are others who would see things restored to rights."

"Speak plainly, John Cantwell, or I will leave you to your failure."

John paled. "It will not only be my master and yourself traveling from Duncarrow, my lady. There will be others."

Asherley's impatience was only matched by her fear of the guard change. She waved her arms. "Who?"

The young girl reached out a timid hand. Within it was a key.

"What's this?"

"Please, take it."

"What is it, girl?"

The girl dropped her eyes. "This key opens every cell in the sky dungeon. There are those locked within who don't belong there. It is for you to retrieve them and ensure they are on the ship, on the night when the moon is at its fullest."

Asherley studied the key.

· · ·

"Aiden," Byrne said. He exhaled, resolved. Of course it was Aiden. He realized he'd been awaiting this moment, or one like it.

"Lord Quinlanden," Aiden corrected.

Ten men had come to kill him. Had he been more like Khallum, that would have been merely half of what was required. Instead, it was excess.

Byrne sighed. He set his book aside. Thought again of Asherley and the lingering kiss.

"Tell my wife—"

Aiden held Byrne Warwick's head aloft for the men to see. Of course he'd been the one to do it. There were only so many tasks he could source to others without losing respect. It should be him to kneel before King Eoghan and offer this, as a loyalty crafted by his own hand. No one but him should get the honor of Asherley Blackwood's first raw screams as she peered down into the gold box Aiden prepared for just this honor.

"Nicely done, my lord," Mads said with a nod.

"Rather more bloody than I expected," Aiden muttered. He kicked at the head of the servant.

"If I may, you did not allow him his last words."

"Was that a question, Mads?"

"Only trying to understand your strategies, as always, my lord."

"Last words are reserved for men. Byrne Warwick was no man. He's fortunate I gave him an honorable death."

Mads retrieved the box from one of the other men and held it out to Aiden. "My lord."

Aiden's head fell to the side. He looked deep into the hollow, lifeless eyes of Byrne Warwick, as if expecting some exceptional wisdom to pass through to him and awaken a fresh, new power. He admonished his own fleeting foolishness with a light *tsk*. "Now that I see him like this, he isn't so much of a prize at all."

Aiden dropped Byrne's head into the box.

. . .

Asherley regarded the key. "Why have I been tasked with this? Why not your master, if they are so certain of their own designs?"

The girl dropped into a bow. She held the key high above her, head lowered. "My master is forsaking all to save this kingdom. They would see that you, as well, will risk to see it done."

Asherley held her hand out. It was such a little thing, to take the key. She didn't have to use it. She could toss it into the White Sea and be done with this strange game of secrets. She could do things her own way, continuing her witchcraft with the king. She'd come so far with him in such a short time. It wouldn't be long before he would deem her indispensable, and her power would begin anew. Before she would use that power to do what these servants claimed their master intended.

But Joran's words haunted her. That night, as they conspired until evening turned to morning, as they compared the pieces of their individual visions, determined to understand how to take what they'd seen and turn it to action. *What you can learn, you must learn there. You cannot find it elsewhere.* Upon these words rested her certainty that it was she who must come to Duncarrow, and not Hollyn. Not any of her children. She alone could see this done.

And was the story written upon the scrolls not precisely that? What she could learn only here? And if so, had she any other choice but to go forth and see Anabella and Stefan delivered safely of the tyrant who would destroy them before letting them go? To deliver the ending to their vision, one which had been kept from both her and Joran, but now seemed laid before her with solid inevitability.

"The full moon. Dusk," Asherley repeated.

"Yes, my lady."

Asherley took the key.

. . .

"Send out the ravens," Aiden commanded Mads. "The Westerlands are under my command now." He hesitated. It was premature to add this next, but it was inevitable. King Eoghan would have no choice but to bestow this honor upon the man who had delivered one Reach and subdued another. The alternative was to make this same man his enemy. To delay the announcement would be to delay his gratification. "Both the Easterlands and the Westerlands are now under command of the Lord Chancellor of the Kingdom of the White Sea."

Mads' mouth parted in stunned reverence. He bowed. "My lord."

41

KIAN

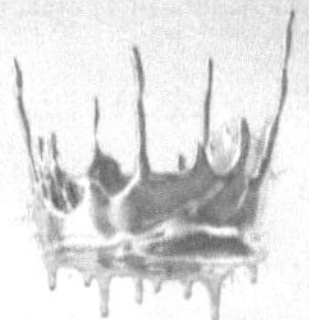

Eavan thrashed inside her bindings. She'd heard Valen's warning, but everything within her fought against this unfair restraint. The rough sack they'd shoved over her head scratched at her delicate skin, and she couldn't be certain, but she thought she smelled the distinct coppery scent of fresh blood. Kian would not stand for this. Kian would make them all pay for this slight, which could have been so easily avoided had the guards bothered to only *listen* to what she was saying. Oh, how angry he'd be when he learned of their rough handling!

It was all so unnecessary. She tried again to tell them on the ride to wherever they were going. *We were coming here all along. There's no need for bindings! We will come willingly.* None answered her, except Valen, who reminded her there was nothing that would sway them. And, sure, he had past acquaintance with the Medvedev and perhaps had reason for his concern, but he didn't know of her own history with Kian and Yseult, and how they had once called her *beloved ours.*

Valen was a most handsome man. She thought perhaps that was where Lisbet's fear of him was born, somewhere in her own discomfort around the other sex. Eavan was more advanced than Lisbet. She'd already experienced her own awakening to the way looking at a fair man made her feel, and what it caused her to think about, at night, tucked away in her bed. Valen was twice her age, but she'd let her mind wander to what it would be like to lie with him, and despite her agitated state, atop a horse she couldn't control, led away in blindness, she felt herself flush with exhilaration.

He reminded her of the beautiful men milling about Whitechurch. It was enough to overwhelm a young woman of her age, coming into her sexual awakening. There were no men like the ones in the Easterlands. No women, either. Valen was a true anomaly. An exception to the rule that the Quinlandens were created from the image of greatness, the true favorites of the Guardians.

A strange sensation came over her. It was as if they'd entered another room, or another place entirely. The air was different. Cleaner, for one, but on it carried the mingled scents of exotic flora and meals prepared over fire. There was also an even odder feeling, that there was life around her, yes, but that this life was not simply man or Medvedev, but in addition, something else, something that didn't exist in her world.

Ah, Eavan thought. Yes. That was it. She remembered now, feeling this when she was younger, when her mother and father still brought them to the Hinterlands. She should tell the others, as the only one—other than Valen, that was—who had ever graced these lands prior. She struggled with the desire to speak, though, and in the end kept this revelation to herself.

Voices she recognized from her time here before were like a chorus of whispers as they rode through lands she wished she could see. Without her sight, the scents cloying at her nose were at such high potency she almost screamed at them to stop, before realizing what a silly thing that would be to do. She was dazed with the assault of high fragrancy of floral and herbal competition. So much so that she didn't note right away that they'd come to a stop.

Drystan's offended cries sounded, mixed with Valen's placating tones, reassuring him, cautioning him. There were more signs of a struggle, and Eavan thought to herself how funny it was that she couldn't describe what a struggle sounded like but yet could recognize it. How only the shadows of movement around her were enough to make sense of the situation.

She couldn't help being pleased at these revelations.

Eavan made a surprised gasp as her horse again moved on. She could still hear Drystan's cries, but they were moving farther away. And then there were other, newer voices. Before she could strain to understand them, to test them against her recognition, she was pulled down by strong arms that wrapped around her from behind. She struggled against the intrusion, but like before, it was pointless. Even her legs wouldn't respond to the command to kick.

"You are making a grave mistake!" she cried out. Inside, she was screaming against her bindings, willing her anger to sever them. "Once Kian finds out, you will be punished." She groaned, drawing the sound out. "Don't you understand I'm trying to help you?"

"Eavan," Lisbet said, less of a warning, more of an annoyance. It reminded her of the way her mother sounded when she was fed up.

At last she was thrown. She braced herself for impact, but none came. She came to a stop, but it was sudden and without the contact of something solid. She was suspended in air.

"Seal it," a voice said.

There was no sound. No clinking of locks, or banging of steel. No other words were spoken. But moments later, she felt the dissolution of the magic holding her back from her own movements. She wiggled her toes, and then practiced pushing her arms away from her body. She made fists of her hands, and when she was sure, she reached for her head and ripped off the covering.

She saw Lisbet first. Lisbet, wearing a blank expression, huddled in the corner of the air.

The air.

Eavan looked down. There was no floor. No walls. She was

suspended above the earth. She scrambled in a panic, beating her hands into the invisible barriers of the prison cell.

"What?" Her question was clipped. She knew too little to understand what to even ask.

Looking up, she gazed into a sea of leaves. Trees. They were suspended beneath trees, in a forest. In a cell made purely of magic. Beyond that, more layers to the forest, but there were no figures. No men, no women, no Medvedev. They were alone.

Panicked, she looked again at Lisbet. "Lisbet! Are you all right?"

Lisbet looked not at her, but past her. She nodded into the distance.

"I'll get us out of here. Kian will not stand for this treatment," Eavan vowed. She swung her vision around again, waiting for someone familiar to step into it. "There will be trouble for those who did this."

"Oh, Eavan." Lisbet sighed and leaned her head against the unseen wall of the prison cell.

The world, Eavan, their new, fractured reality. All of it faded gently into the backdrop. Gradually, Eavan's insistences, the lyrical cries of animals that shouldn't exist, the strange buzz passing along the trees as the wind caught... these things blended into ambience, to a place Lisbet would go, but not yet.

She was thinking of the day she was told she would be married to Soren Frost. Soren was older than she was, Eavan's age. His father had once been the most prosperous trapper in the Northerlands, and Soren had the most precise shot with a bow that she'd ever seen. Her uncle, Rinn, was supposed to have been better, but he'd died before she was born.

What a different girl she'd been back then. This was before Drystan confessed that he'd fallen in love with Ravenna, something he'd experienced, he would tell her, because of his need to be specifically with her and no one else. Lisbet would be taken aback by that, because her reaction to her betrothal had been a quick assessment of Soren's skills, the suitability of the match, and the somewhat fortuitous, but not required, fact that he was nice to look upon. How well he would complement the Derehams, and what he could bring to the family was always the only thing that carried importance. The Frosts were a Great Family; one of the most wealthy. To be the one asked to unite the families was a great honor to Lisbet.

Never had it occurred to Lisbet that Soren might also be kind, or curious. That he might make her laugh, or talk to her well into the night, lighting within her something akin to happiness. Many times she'd heard the story of the first meeting of her mother and father at the Epoch of the Accordant, where they'd learned of their marriage and sealed it on the same day. They sometimes laughed when telling about how they'd been so very different, how challenging those early days had been, both getting to know one another and learning to be man and wife in the same breath. Lisbet thought this was all romantic in its own way. The process of discovery seemed to her something to look forward to.

Until the day she was told she was no longer to marry Soren Frost. That she would bring honor by instead marrying the king. Their sorrow was unspoken, as they lied to her about that honor with their words, but reflected the truth of their own horror in their eyes. She would remember this moment later, when she began to understand that her parents could not save her from this fate. It wasn't until she saw the love reflected in the happy expressions of Drystan that a powerful wave of realization came upon her, and she understood that love was not always hard won. It was not always thrust upon you, as you scrambled to know the person selected as your life mate. It could sometimes sneak in, spreading not from duty but something far deeper. Lisbet learned more about love in Drystan's joyful smile than in all the experiences and knowledge of her life thus far.

She didn't run from her duty out of any expectation she might find it, though. Marrying a king who had stolen his own crown had never felt right. But she, a woman, didn't get to make these choices. Valen's question had settled over her and taken root. *Your bigger concern was for your brother. For his fate, which you believe to be more important than your own. And why is that?*

The problem was, Lisbet couldn't say. She didn't know. It was a feeling, in a world where feelings were not to be trusted, especially those of women, who were prone to leading with emotion. But as she watched Drystan write in his daily ledger, or daydream during dinner, she couldn't set aside the powerful belief that he must be protected. It took a while before she could learn to separate her love from this belief, but once she did, she could be certain it was some-thing bigger... bigger than her, than him, than anything, which compelled her to think of a way to get him away from Wulfsgate before the inevitable clash between king and lords.

She'd told Eavan it was for Drystan and Ravenna; for them to be safe in their love. But Lisbet didn't need foresight to have seen Ravenna's defection as she spread her wings for the first time. Lisbet didn't believe Ravenna didn't love Drystan, but there were some things bigger than love. Ravenna had her own journey, and only the Guardians knew if her path would eventually intersect again with Drystan's.

What was she supposed to feel now? Now that her instincts had led Drystan here, to a place where they were unwelcome? More than unwelcome. Whatever she thought of Valen, she didn't think his fear was feigned.

Much as she distrusted the man, she hoped he was with Drystan, if only because he gave her brother comfort, and more than anything Lisbet didn't want him to be alone when it came time to face whatever consequence awaited them here in these strange lands.

For, though they hadn't ridden far, Lisbet was certain of one thing.

They were no longer in the kingdom as they knew it.

· · ·

"Eavan."

Eavan's blubbering came to a swift end at the sound of the voice that would make proper sense of all this. She snapped her head up so fast her vision blurred. "Kian!"

His body lightly recoiled when she said his name. She hadn't seen him in so many years, she hardly recognized him. He'd grown a head taller, maybe more, and his soft violet waves tickled his shoulders, which were now thicker, more pronounced, than they'd been when he was a young boy of thirteen. Aian, his familiar, flew overhead, soaring in protective arcs, passing his wings across the leaves of the overhead trees.

"You were asking for me, I understand."

"Asking for you! I came here for you!" Eavan's heart fluttered in anticipation, in confusion. Why had he not freed them yet? He only stood there, staring, and she thought he may have even taken a step back. "I came here for *you*, Kian."

"Disappointment," Kian said. "You shall feel it, Eavan, and it will not be half the pain felt by my own."

"You're being so strange. Let us out, please. I need something to drink, and this is terribly uncomfortable." She frowned. "This magic is very unusual. You can tell me about it later, and I shall tell you of those who used it against us in error."

Kian nodded to Aian, who flew away, out of sight. As they waited, he let the silence stand between them. Eavan was too anxious to fill it with her own pleas, for something was wrong, and a part of her wished she could return to the moment before he'd arrived, where she could still look to him as her savior.

When Aian returned, a young woman with spring green hair was with him. She carried a pitcher and two mugs. Kian took both from her and dismissed her. When she was gone, he held his hands out *through* the cell, through the magic, thrusting them at her.

"Take!" he demanded.

"Kian, I don't under—"

Lisbet reached forward and accepted the pitcher and mugs

herself, and returned to the corner where she shakily poured the water. Eavan thought she was probably questioning whether she should drink it. No one drank the water of the kingdom if they couldn't be certain of which stream it came from. But there was no water in the Hinterlands not meant for consumption. No water had ever tasted better.

"Shouldn't have. Come. You shouldn't have," he said. Sadness joined the anger in his face. This, too, made no sense. Was he still hurting from their last time together? Where he'd kissed her by the waterfalls, and she'd told him it could never be? She'd regretted this, too. If she had known her father would never again bring her, then she would not have left things as such. "You," he said, more aggressively. "*You.* You shouldn't. Have come."

"I will tell you why I did, if you only let me," Eavan said, using, without realizing it, the pliant, pleasing voice her mother affected when her father's mood was volatile. "If you give me the chance."

"I know. Already, I know," Kian hissed. "All know. Everyone. There is no secret now. Not even you."

Eavan looked back at Lisbet, but her cousin had her face buried in the delicious water. She hoped Lisbet's attentions were as equally distracted as this, for she was embarrassed. This wasn't the greeting she had in mind for the others to witness, and things were wrong now, all wrong, and she didn't know why, or how to fix it.

"I was young," Eavan pleaded. "I was only fourteen. Still a child."

Kian's face contorted into something both menacing and ugly, and as her words settled in over him, a third emotion was now painfully evident: disgust. "The petulant child. Thinks her charms have such impact. Kiss. You are not my only kiss, Eavan Quinlanden, child of trees. My last, neither. To be rid of you I would kiss them all."

The barrage of tears flooded inside her eyes and there was nothing Eavan could do to stop them from pouring over, painting her face with weakness when she needed strength. "I said I was sorry."

"Your father. He trained you well. Distracting me, and with pettiness of childhood? I care not, Eavan. Not. I cannot look upon, even, those times without great sickness. No longer."

"But will you not tell me why?" Eavan sobbed. "My heart is breaking, Kian, and I don't even understand the cause!"

"Your heart." Kian sneered. "Have you one?"

Eavan's tears blinded her. She could no longer even see the disapproving lines in his face. "If you loathe me so, then loathe me! But tell me! Tell me what crime I've committed that you can now look upon me with such hatred."

Lisbet laid a hand against her back. The soft comfort from her cousin made her double over in even deeper sobs.

"You dare come. Here. You dare," Kian answered. "The monster, your father, must care not for your fate. He has abandoned you, as he has forsaken us."

"My father!" Eavan cried, wiping at the tears and snot mingling into a horror upon her face. "What does my father have to do with this?"

Kian stared at her in furious disbelief. "All. All!"

Eavan pressed her hand against the invisible wall separating them. Tears flowed down into the bosom of her dress, staining the fabric. But what spilled inside of her was so much more devastating. There was a sundering between the reality of her own memories and whatever had happened to Kian in the intervening years, and she had come far too late to mend it. But she could at least understand it. "Talk to me as if I'm a child and know nothing. I beg of you. Just this, and I'll not ask for anything more of you."

Kian looked at her as if expecting to step into a trap of her design. Aian swooped lower, and came to a rest upon Kian's shoulder, and they both watched her. Reading her, she thought, but Medvedev could do so much more than that.

"Your father. Will not prevail. Is assured he will, with his confidence and cruelty. He has his magician. Magician from other world. He will see. What *we* have."

"I still don't understand. What does my father have to do with this?"

Aian opened his beak wide and squawked in loud percussion. Kian ran a hand over his belly feathers to ease him. "His subjugation of Saleen, answered by Drumain. By Asgill. By Mayke. He knows not what he has awakened. He will."

"Subjugation?" Eavan's sobbing came to a halt. "My father? The Saleen? What are you saying?"

"Beautiful fool."

Eavan winced at the words meant for her. "How? What has he done?"

"Taken, not his. Not his. Saleen fight under his magic. We fight under ours."

Eavan wanted to push back on this terrible accusation, which was coming into full view now. Kian was accusing her father of enslaving the Saleen for his own purposes, using some foul magic to overcome their own. And this was ludicrous, in every way. Her father could be cruel, but he had no power over the Medvedev. No one did. And wouldn't she have known, if he had the entire Saleen Clahnn under his sway?

Eavan opened her mouth to say these things, but memories replaced her words. Images of troops camped in the forests beneath their palace. There was something off about them; even behind their veil of armor, something that made them feel like they were *other*, different, not cut from the same cloth as the Easterlander men of crimson and gold who served the Quinlandens. But what was it to her? She had no interest in war, or soldiers. That was the business of men.

"I do not..." Eavan began, but couldn't decide if a rebuttal, a denial, or simply a horrified apology would be more appropriate. And what of her? What of what her father's actions had wrought upon his children, his wife, his name? No... no, it could not be true. He couldn't do such a thing, and yet... he could. She understood, in reflecting upon his terrible ambition, his chaotic desire for power, that he could, and had. He had done this terrible thing. There was no truth greater than the roiling anger burning under the surface of Kian's accusing face.

"You deny? You claim to not know?" Kian laughed. "What care of mine, what you know? Aiden Quinlanden takes from us. We take from him now."

Fresh tears prickled her eyes. "You don't understand, Kian. I am no prize to my father. I'm expendable. He will let me die here and lose not a night of sleep over it."

Kian shook his head. He flicked his finger against the clear wall where her palm still pressed. "If it is, then it is. Let us see if you die."

LISBET DIDN'T KNOW THE WORDS EAVAN NEEDED. SHE DIDN'T KNOW the ones *she* needed. None would dissolve the hopelessness she felt, trapped in a world she didn't know how to leave. Without weapons, without recourse, Lisbet had been hanging her hopes on Kian, despite knowing Eavan had embellished her hold on him. She'd been prepared for his indifference toward Eavan, but the venom in his words... the hatred burning in his eyes. Could it be true? What he accused Lord Aiden of?

A man who commits monstrous acts would still look upon himself and see not a monster but a man. Her mother had said this. She remembered it now, and it played over and over in her head.

Eavan thought the world of her father. Lisbet had no such blind spot for her uncle, as the daughter of the woman who had been tortured by that same man and barely lived to share the experience. But though Lisbet didn't deny he was capable of these atrocities, they seemed beyond his means to execute.

But Kian didn't come here with lies and games. He came here, aflame with the terrors inflicted upon those sharing his blood, ready to line Eavan up against the wall and let her pay for these crimes.

Lisbet reached for her mother's necklace, at her throat. That, at least, was still hers. She searched the gem for the strength of Gretchen.

As Eavan sobbed in her lap, huddled into a mass of limbs and tears, Lisbet thought maybe the best thing she could do was simply hold her.

"I didn't know," Eavan pleaded, but the man she meant the words for was gone. "I swear, I didn't know."

"How could you?" Lisbet asked, running her hands through Eavan's hair. "He's wrong to hold you to blame, Eavan. We shouldn't be held to the crimes of our parents."

"But why? Why would he do it?"

"Uncle Aiden?"

"Yes, why? He already had the largest force in the kingdom. Why this?"

Lisbet sighed. She pressed her lips to the back of Eavan's head, against her matted hair. "What more can you do when you have the numbers? You find the power."

Eavan howled into her lap. "What has he done? Oh, this cannot be, Lisbet. We must stop him."

Lisbet held back her laughter, regarding the suspended prison with half humor and half horror. "Someone will stop him. He's gone too far, this time. Kian said as much."

"It must be so terrible for the Medvedev to work together as one. My father must have done unspeakable things to warrant that. They never do that, Lisbet. Never."

"We've been in the dark on much," Lisbet said. "Matters in the kingdom are worse than we ever imagined."

"And I thought… oh, what a fool I am. A fool! A fool to believe I could come here. To walk away from a crown and trade it for… for…" Eavan rolled her head back and looked up at Lisbet. "Now, no man will have me. No man would."

Lisbet's breath caught. This was the first time Eavan had addressed the terror in the woods.

"Oh, Lisbet. I know what happened to me. And I know what you think of me."

"Shh. I adore you. Don't take yourself down another path that will harm you."

"I remember every moment! Not even one was mercifully taken from me." Eavan's glassy eyes peered up at Lisbet. "I won't ever forget the force of those monsters inside me. The heat…" She closed her eyes, wincing. "The searing pain. Even in the dark, their evil intentions glowed in their eyes."

Lisbet's own tears came. "I would do anything to take this memory from you."

"I know. I know you would, Lis. You've placated me, indulged my silliness, because you would do exactly that, would that you had the power."

"Ravenna killed them all. She even went back and claimed the lives of those who didn't come to our camp."

"I know that too. But she isn't coming back now to save us, is she?"

Lisbet shook her head. "She's on another path now."

"Poor Drystan."

Lisbet sighed. "Now what?"

Eavan closed her eyes and laughed softly. "Oh, Lis. I was about to ask you this very thing."

42

A CONFESSION AND A BETRAYAL

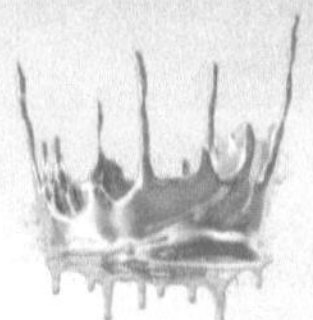

Brandyn decided he didn't like storms when stuck inside the Sepulchre. Back home in Longwood Rush, there was only rain, occasionally the roll of distant thunder, but never these high winds that seemed to make the entire structure sway, threatening to topple. Even at the base, in the falconer's quarters, where it howled so loudly, it was as if a monster was ripping through.

Aylen was oblivious. She sat at Hollyn's bedside with her wet cloths and periodic laying of hands. Neither did much of anything anymore, if they ever had. Brandyn one night had heard Aylen tell Christian that her healing was so powerless against Hollyn's affliction that it was the equivalent of blowing cool air on a severed limb. A futile effort that was no match against the inevitable.

They knew what it was now, but they weren't telling anyone. Both had changed toward Hollyn since, but also toward Brandyn and Storm. Storm accused them of letting Hollyn die with their secrets. When they didn't contest that indictment, Brandyn understood it was true, but not quite in the way Storm had insisted. Whatever they'd learned had confirmed the fear that Hollyn's illness was beyond any power they had. They were resolving themselves to their own helplessness in the matter.

Aylen rocked back in her chair. When she looked at Brandyn, her bleary eyes widened in panic. "Brandyn. Her breathing is slowing."

"What does that mean?"

Aylen's mouth drew to a close. She sighed inwardly and dropped her eyes. "It means her time is nearing an end." Fresh tears trickled down her cheeks. She looked up. "I wish more than anything in all the kingdom that I could have done more. Whatever the cost, I would've done it."

Brandyn tried to smile, but the sickening knot in his belly overpowered him. "I know, Magi Aylen. I know you did, and my family will be in your debt."

She shook her head. "No, Brandyn. There is no debt between us. There could never be, not for this."

"How long…" Brandyn winced as the sickness building within him competed for authority. He realized he'd been waiting for these words, but now said, he was no more prepared to receive them. "How long?"

"Not long." Aylen set the cloth back in the water basin and rose. "We'll leave you, so you can spend these final moments with her. I will be just outside if you need me."

Storm looked between them, as if unsure whether she should leave, too. Brandyn nodded his permission to stand down. Storm had protected them both, but her time as their guard was ended now. This duty Brandyn could only do alone.

They left, and with them, all the life and air the room once possessed. He'd never felt so alone as he had sitting at the bedside of his dying sister. This wasn't how he'd wanted to remember her. Once, she'd been so full of life, cheeks flushed with happiness and energy, not sunken in and colored like bile. Lips bleeding from being so cracked. She'd lost half her golden hair, too, and what remained had lost the blond sheen and looked more like the limp threads of the mops the scullery maids used to clean the floors, sticking in strange formation against the pillow.

Hollyn rolled her face toward him. Her eyes opened, but only halfway. Even that seemed to take whatever effort remained in her. She tried to lick her lips, but when she withdrew her tongue, there was nothing whetted, and she laughed to herself, struggling through each breath, and smiled with the corner of her mouth.

"You did so well, brother," she managed, through a gravelly voice. A rattle formed in the back of her throat, sounding as her words ended. "So well."

Brandyn reached for her bony hand and clutched it in his. He tried desperately not to cry. "I believed… I thought… if there was anyone…"

"I know, Brandyn. If there was, it would've been here. You did well."

"If I did so well, why… why…" He couldn't form the words.

"The Guardians have deemed my promise ended. Who are we to question this?"

"But it isn't fair!" As soon as the words were out, he wished he could retract them. How little he sounded; like a child, and not a boy on the verge of becoming a man. Not the heir to the Westerlands. Not the strength his sister needed in her final moments.

"I've received more care than a commoner. More than a child dying of a curable disease in a flea-infested alleyway. Fairness has many lenses. My passing is inevitable now, Brandyn. I'd prefer not to reflect upon whether my death is fair when my life has so little time remaining."

"I wish Mother were here," he said. Salty tears traveled over the top of his lips. "She would know how to ease you."

Hollyn attempted to laugh, but began choking instead. "No, I'm glad it's you, here, in the end. Mother has other matters more pressing right now. Ember would sass me, and Gabi would dissolve, while it would kill Father, I think, to see me this way. But you? You're just right, Brandyn. You have enough heart and imagination to hear my final words. A confession, I suppose, though only the Guardians can deem how deep a crime I've committed."

Brandyn reached for the wet cloth to dampen her lips, but she waved him away. "Don't minister me. The point in that has passed, and we can only count down against time. I only ask that you listen." Hollyn buried her face in her shoulder and coughed. When she pulled back, her nightgown was stained with blood. "What you do with the words when I'm gone will be your decision to make."

"Was it true? What you said to Brandyn?" Storm followed behind Aylen as she paced the halls outside the falconer's chambers.

"It would be cruel for me to lie about something so terrible."

"But why? Why haven't you told us why it is so terrible, and why she must die when we're surrounded by magic? What you learned when you visited the Sacred Halls?"

Aylen exhaled. She leaned into the wall, facing away. "What I learned was that there is no cure known to us. What I feared all along."

"That isn't the whole story."

"No," Aylen agreed. "But that story isn't mine to tell. I've given Hollyn her truth, and now it is hers to decide whether it dies with her, or carries on."

"Magi Aylen."

Both turned toward the sound. Storm didn't recognize the man, but by his silver robe she identified him as another Magi.

"Yes?"

"You've been summoned to see the Head Magus."

"Can it wait? I have a patient in the falconer's chambers in her final hours."

"No," he said. "Apologies, Magi Aylen. I'm afraid it cannot."

Aylen turned back to Storm. "I won't be long. Send for me if…"

Storm nodded.

. . .

Christian didn't turn at the sound of the doors opening behind him. It could only be Aylen. Aylen, and trailing behind her, his deep regret at not ending her request to read the scrolls before it had gone too far.

She sat down at his side, and he still didn't look at her, but he offered a tight smile. There were no reassurances to be given. They hadn't been called here to receive praise for their ingenuity.

Head Magus Tymagen nodded at the Magi who'd delivered Aylen. The man closed the doors, leaving Christian and Aylen alone with the Head Magus.

For such a prominent position, the leader for all magic practicers in the kingdom, the office was quite small and sparsely appointed. All four walls were lined with books so old they'd taken on a permanent musty scent, lined in thick layers of dust except where the fingerprints cut through, betraying which books had seen recent use and which had sat untouched. Christian was aware now how small the room was, how the books on all sides had an oppressive feeling, as if locked away in a box.

"You both know, I assume, why I have called you here," Head Magus Tymagen said. His desk was empty, save his hands, folded atop the old wood.

Aylen dropped her head. Christian sighed and nodded.

"I find it imperative that you should know it was not your uncle, Elder Rorric, who apprised me of Magi Aylen's midnight gambol in the Sacred Halls. Though I'm well aware he had a hand in your gaining entrance, he kept your secret." The Head Magus lifted the corner of his mouth. "Though I find myself curious how you managed to convince him."

"Head Magus, I beseech you not to punish Rorric for my crime," Christian said quickly. "I employed…" He didn't want Aylen to hear this, to blame herself. He chose his words carefully, though they were beyond the point where he could protect her from it all. "I used knowledge against him that was unfair for me to use. This put him in an impossible situation."

"I know the knowledge you reference," Head Magus Tymagen replied. "And it has not and would never be used against Rorric Dereham at the Sepulchre. His secrets are safe within the walls of this tower, where the rules of men end and ours begin. He knows this. Though I will take his long and exemplary history with us, and your confession of bribery, into account when considering how to address Rorric's slip in judgment."

"Thank you, Head Magus."

"But that," the Head Magus went on, "is a matter for another day. What's more pressing to me now are the crimes committed by the two of you, which go against all sense of order we've spent centuries working to preserve and protect. Do you know why we protect the knowledge written upon the scrolls in the Sacred Halls?"

"Not all are capable of possessing all truths," Aylen said, barely above a whisper.

"Yes, that is part of our reasoning," Head Magus Tymagen said. "But within those walls also exists knowledge even those who have achieved the honor of elder don't yet understand. It is the job of our elders to use all they have learned and experienced to study the words from our distant past and come to understand them in a way that is protected and precise. Do you know the true story of how the Rhiagains came to our shores?"

Both Christian and Aylen shook their heads.

"Nor do we," the Head Magus admitted. "This consortium existed long before the Rhiagains came to the kingdom. We have no less than a hundred accounts, all branded as eyewitnesses, of their arrival here. Among them exists a truth—perhaps some form of truth exists in them all—but discerning that, centuries after the events transpired, is a near impossible task. Can you understand what, if only one of these fell into the wrong hands, fear or lies might be created? How it might affect the kingdom as it exists today? Imagine if one of those truths cast the Rhiagains in a terrible light. The potential for war." He paused. "I could continue down this path, but do you understand?"

"Yes, Head Magus," Christian said. Aylen repeated the words.

"It isn't from a sense of parochial secrecy we keep these scrolls away from all but the elders, but out of caution. We hold within those walls truths that could spin their web into great power. Power can ultimately destroy, even when seized with proper intentions."

"I read nothing other than what I went in there to find," Aylen said. "I would not… I didn't even want to do this, but I had no other way."

"You did have another way," the Head Magus said, though his voice was kind. "Death is a way of life, Magi Aylen. No death is preventable in the end, and some come sooner than others. That this death will haunt you doesn't make it more deserving of violating the laws we all hold sacred."

Aylen dropped her head.

"Did neither of you consider coming to me for guidance?" the Head Magus asked. "To see if I could not steer you where you wished to go?"

"I'm ashamed to say I didn't approach you because I knew you wouldn't let us in," Christian confessed.

"No," the Head Magus said. "But I could have given you the knowledge you sought without entrance. I've read about the Virulent Spindle. I don't know the young woman's story, or how she came to have relations with a Rhiagain, but I could have identified that without either of you compromising yourselves."

"You knew?" Aylen asked.

"Not right away," the Head Magus said. "I didn't make the matter of Mistress Blackwood my own because there was no reason. Not until you broke into the Sacred Halls. But there are magic ties to the scrolls, and we can see who has read them. When I saw what you were after, the truth came together." He regarded them both with a strange look. "You haven't considered traveling to Duncarrow, have you?"

"No," Christian said. "Aylen and I both agreed that we had reached the limit of what we could do for Hollyn, once we understood what ailed her. We don't wish to bring the eyes of the crown upon the Sepulchre."

Head Magus Tymagen nodded. "A wise decision, in a sea of poor ones. You understand the predicament I am in? That two of my most promising and effective Magi have broken the rule that incurs a punishment of banishment?"

Aylen gasped inwardly. Christian laid a hand on her knee.

"It would be an incredible loss to the Consortium to lose the two of you. But if I turn the other way and allow the betrayal to pass, then it will drive a crack in the efficacy of the very foundation of who we are. Our authority in this kingdom is always under attack. The Reliquary waits for us to err in a way they can undermine, and chip away at, until we are no more. I know you understand that cannot happen."

"We do, Head Magus," Christian said. The knot in his chest grew. "That is not our wish, either."

"No," the Head Magus said. "I can see through to the intentions of you both, however misguided." He leaned back in his chair, which was the most ornate piece in the entire room. The wood curled into strange designs, like smoke, stretching near to the ceiling. "But I must enact punishment for a betrayal of this magnitude, no matter how I value your contributions and potential. All of the eyes of the Sepulchre are turned to me, and what I shall do. As I considered what to do, I also took into account the challenges your family has experienced as of late, Magi Christian. I realize you do not make the effort to communicate with your family, but I'm in regular contact with your mother and am aware of the Dereham trials, which, as you know, I've done my best to pass on to you, even in your apparent apathy. I could banish you both to serve your sentence in a small village with need of aid, but I believe your time will be better served in Wulfsgate."

Christian paled. "Head Magus, I would prefer no special treatment."

"It is my decision, not yours, and I have made it." He looked at

Aylen. "And as your wife, she can best serve at your side. You will both leave for Wulfsgate this evening and will remain there for a period of a year. When you have reached the end of your banishment, you will return to your posts and will swear your fealty and obeisance, vowing to never again break our sacred rules, the violation of which would subject you both to a permanent banishment."

Christian could hear in Aylen's harried breaths her attempt to abstain her tears. "We understand and accept your sentence," she said. "Yet would you permit me one final ask?"

"I will hear it."

"I believe Hollyn Blackwood has not more than one more night left until her promise is spent. I would see my charge to the end and be with her as she slips from this world."

The Head Magus leaned into his folded hands, considering. "It would be a great shame for you to leave that which is now to drive you away. See your charge to the end and then depart. I've already sent a raven ahead to Lord Dereham. They're expecting you both."

Aylen's relief filled the room, but Christian thought he would be ill if he didn't leave right at that moment. Wulfsgate. He would sooner serve out his banishment in the Wastelands than face the family he had forsaken with his choice. They had never understood it. Never visited. He received, from time to time, letters from his mother, but she had long ago stopped trying to beg him to return home, to change his mind and see reason.

How was he to serve a family he had abandoned so long ago?

"That will be all," the Head Magus said, pointing a sideways hand at the door, leaving them both to make sense of what they had done, and where it would now take them.

"Do you remember, Brandyn, when the traveler came to Longwood Rush? The one in search of a plant that he said only grew in our woods? You weren't yet at the Sepulchre."

Brandyn shook his head. "We get many travelers. I'd never remember them all."

"Nor would I, but this one was special. It was the first one Mother passed off to me to see after. She was preparing me, she said, for when I was head of my own household, as seeing to the needs of guests was one such duty. This was when it was expected I would marry a Tyndall. I was elated to do it, though somewhat less enthused at being assigned someone of such little importance.

"He was an odd man. Not much older than I was, though he claimed, in the beginning, to be closer to thirty in age, despite having no hair upon his face or the hard lines of living. He seemed gnarled by illness or injury, I didn't know, but he could hardly stand erect without aid. I didn't believe his claim of age, and later he told me the truth of that, as well as other truths." Hollyn's tired face stretched into a grotesque smile. "He was peculiar in many ways. He talked as if he'd never talked to anyone in his life, struggling so much with the task. He was both unsure and astoundingly confident, which I found very confusing. He asked some rather strange questions about a baby delivered to a family; a baby who would be old enough to be our father, or his. I didn't know what he was talking about and told him so. He was disappointed, and his enthusiasm for the plant he was after dimmed after that. I nonetheless escorted him through the Whispering Wood. As you might have guessed, we never found the plant. But you cannot find what doesn't exist, can you?"

Brandyn swallowed hard. His face flushed with his quickening pulse.

"I cannot say what made him open up to me that first time. Perhaps he was compelled by the Guardians, or was tired of keeping his true self behind a veil. He shared with me he'd never known his mother; that he once had a twin brother who'd taken all she had to give, and that taking killed her. I don't know why I said what I said to him, then, but had I not, would things have been different? I think they would."

Hollyn had found a fresh burst of energy as her story unfolded. Her last, Brandyn realized. For when she was done in the telling, she would be done with life, and while he was terrified of what she would tell him, he would hear it, would live in the moment with her, because when it was done, there would be no more. "I said he seemed incomplete. That what he craved was a mother. What had been taken from him. I then told him I would look after him for as long as he stayed, if he would let me."

"He said yes," Brandyn guessed.

"He very much did. And then he cried and asked if I would hold him, so I did that, too. And as I held him, I whispered to him that I would be proud for him to be my son. This man, who was older than I was, called me Mother then, and had I corrected him… but I didn't. I didn't correct him, I only kissed the top of his head and told him he was safe now."

"Wow," Brandyn whispered.

"Judge not others, brother, for you may find yourself the subject one day. We cannot know another man's struggles. What drove him to have them. He told me then that he had struggled to find a wife, for most women would not so easily understand his needs. And he could not in practicality marry a woman twice his age, for he required heirs.

"By this time, I was ever more curious. All men think of heirs, but he talked of his as if the absence of them would bring down a kingdom. I don't know why he told me the truth, but he must have seen in me that I could keep his secret, because I could. I did. He confessed that he was Eoghan Rhiagain, traveling under the cover of cloak, in search of something he had yet to find. And then he kissed me, and we…" Hollyn closed her eyes. "We lay together, in the Whispering Wood. Not only my first time with a man, but his, with a woman."

Brandyn swallowed the bile in his throat. She'd softened the blow of Eoghan's identity with her earlier confession, even if she didn't remember it. But it was no less revolting, that this man who would tear apart the kingdom had made a woman of his sister. "What was he… you know, in search of? If it wasn't the plant?"

"He believed he had an older brother who had been placed with a family. A brother who was believed dead."

Brandyn wracked his memory, searching through his studies for the answer. "Dain. Who died at two, right?"

Hollyn nodded against the pillow. "He had heard whispers that Dain had lived and had been sent to live elsewhere, his identify forever guarded. But I'd never heard of such a thing and felt like I'd failed him in saying so. It seemed more like a tale our nan would've told us, if we'd ever had the honor to meet her, you know?"

Brandyn nodded.

"He stayed weeks, spending them all with me, pretending to search, in vain, for his plant. At last he knew he must leave. He couldn't stay forever, much as we both wished for it. I loved him, though he wasn't handsome, and was a most strange creature. But he left me with a promise, in the guise of a plot. While we wasted away our afternoons in each other's arms, he had been thinking, all the while. He was expected to marry a commoner. To prevent usurpation, I suppose. But it was me he wanted to marry, Brandyn. Me, he wished to have at his side, as queen, one day. He knew if he returned to his father and requested such a thing, he'd deny him."

Brandyn's mouth gaped. "The Right of Choosing."

"Yes," she said. "He used his father's belief in the Epoch of the Accordant to plan what he'd say was the next reasonable move toward uniting the kingdom. The children of the marriages created in the Epoch, all united with the crown. And if you are King Khain, you see the reason in this, do you not? You see the genius in the suggestion, never looking beneath the surface to also see the intent. Khain died before he could see it done, but Eoghan never lost the desire for me. He waited, until the time was right, and then sent the ravens to the Reaches."

"He crafted the Right of Choosing to marry *you*?"

Hollyn nodded. Her sigh caved in her chest, and the rattle again filled her throat. "And I wished to be his queen so badly that I encouraged it, for my own selfish cause. I encouraged it, never knowing how it would tear apart the kingdom. And all for... for nothing. For an illness that's spending my promise. A queen who will never join with her king."

Brandyn floundered with the words jumping around in his mind. It was so fantastical, so entirely unbelievable that it could be nothing *but* true. And Hollyn wasn't prone to lies or deception. She had no motive for concocting such a tale, in her final hours, unless it was to outlay the last of all she'd held close, to pass in peace.

"I don't know what to say."

Hollyn squeezed his hand; her lack of force felt more like a twitch. "You need not say anything, brother. I didn't tell you for your wisdom. I told you because someone should know the story of Hollyn and Eoghan; to know the madness of love that had driven madness within the kingdom, and that I'm sorry, I am so utterly, deeply sorry that my selfish desires have delivered us to this point. In my death I beseech the Guardians for absolution beyond, for I could never find it here, not now."

Tears streamed down Brandyn's flushed cheeks. "I forgive you! Is that not enough? Not enough for your absolution?"

Hollyn was crying now, too. "It is enough! It is enough to know you yet love me, despite my crimes. But absolution is not yours to give."

"It doesn't work that way. You're not dying of your sins, Hollyn. You're dying because your body is wrought with disease!"

"A disease given to me by the object of my love."

"You think Eoghan gave this to you?"

"I know he did. I suspected it all along. Aylen has risked all her achievements here to confirm it for me. It is an illness the Rhiagains brought with them and have contained by their way of life, on Duncarrow."

Brandyn brightened. "If he gave it to you, then he can cure it!"

Hollyn shook her head. "No. We're past that."

"We aren't past that until your promise is spent. You're here, talking to me, still!"

"Brandyn. I'm asking you to be still. To say no more on cures or futures."

Brandyn breathed heavily, in, out, flummoxed by her revelation and the flash of hope he'd allowed himself to have. "What would you have me do?"

Wincing, Hollyn moved to the side, making room for him. "Lie with me, until I can no longer hear the wind whistle through the stone."

JUST BEYOND THE HOURS OF MIDNIGHT, AS THE WIND DIED TO A breeze, with all who had loved or tended to her at the Sepulchre standing solemn watch, Hollyn Blackwood slipped from this kingdom into the next, her promise spent.

43

LORD OF THE WESTERLANDS

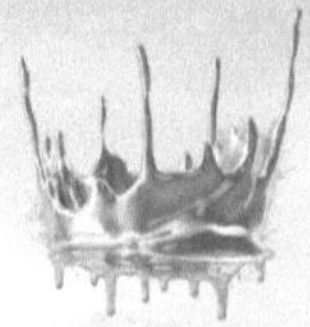

This was the third time Gabrianna had tried to open her eyes. At first it had been the invisible weight lying atop her lids. But then, once that lifted, the disorientation took hold. The fear spread its tendrils. The sense of having lost all aspect of time and space followed, and knowing that both fears were entirely founded, because she had lost these things and might never get them back.

The last thing Gabi remembered was talking to that boy with the beautiful hair. Kael. A Medvedev. With his striking violet hair and the hawk that answered to him alone. He'd come when she was feeling at her most hopeless, and even at the time she recognized that as the reason she'd eventually agreed to follow. The Sullen Siblings were too foolish to be afraid of him, but as Gabi agreed to let him lead them to the secret way to the Drumains, she'd known this aid would come at a cost. She'd summoned the courage of Emberley and gone anyway, because the one thing she *was* certain of was that Kael was Medvedev, and Gabi's mission was to find those same people and beseech them for help in saving Hollyn. Whether or not there was danger ahead, she had no other destination. No other plan beyond the one Emberley had given her, lacking in detail, brimming with confidence. She forced herself to ignore the pit of doom blossoming within her, because no matter what awaited, it was to the Medvedev she must go, and if there was even a chance that what he'd said was true, that she couldn't find the place without his aid, then she had no choice at all.

As she'd passed beyond the cave with Kael and the Sullen Siblings, an eerie calm descended upon her. And still—she wondered, briefly, if this was the Ravenwood in her—she knew this calm hadn't come from within her. Kael had delivered it, with his own magic, and that he'd determined it necessary to do so caused within her more alarm.

Then it faded.

Her fear.

Her confusion.

Her questions.

Her memory of anything that had happened from that last recollection of the cave and Kael's calming magic.

And now, if she would only open her eyes, she could confirm what she'd already known. That her awareness of her surroundings had only been returned to her as a result of their arrival at the place they'd set out to find. Except they hadn't found it at all. She suspected if she asked Brook and Meadow what they remembered, they'd have the same inconvenient gaps.

"Gabi!" Meadow cried. "Oh, you're awake. *Finally*. We have a big problem."

"Do we?" Gabi answered. Her head felt like it did after playing in the waterfalls near her home. Unsteady, unable to grasp onto something that would return her to rights. Her empty belly threatened to turn.

"Why are your eyes closed? Open them and look! Look at this… this… I don't know what it is, but I'm afraid and so should you be!"

The bright light assaulted Gabi through the tiny squint she allowed. The vibrant colors followed, and they caught her so off guard that her eyes opened all the way without command. Oh, the colors... she'd never seen such shades of green, of pink and blue. What trees grew like this? What plants...

That was when Gabi realized she was floating upon air, and so was Meadow.

She screamed, reaching for something to break her fall, but there was nothing to grab, and there was no fall. Meadow sat quietly, patiently, waiting for her to come around to what she'd apparently already discovered.

"What?" Gabi asked, unable to finish a question she couldn't form. "How?"

"We can't go anywhere. I already tried. It's like a cell, Gabi, but... I don't know. I don't know what it is, but it's not right, and we're trapped, like animals!"

"Where are we?"

"I'd hoped you would know."

She did know, but she didn't see Kael, who had led them there, or... "Where's Brook?"

Meadow burst into tears. "I think they killed him!"

"Killed him?" Gabi repeated. That didn't feel right. Why would anyone kill Brook? He was only a child. He's never harmed anyone. "Did you see them take him?"

Meadow shook her head. She buried her face behind her long hair.

"Then perhaps he was only lost, as we were."

"We were not lost, Gabi. We went with that *boy*, remember?"

"I remember." Gabi attempted to swallow, but her throat was so dry it caught halfway down. "I remember you told me we could trust him."

Meadow threw her hair back to the sides of her red cheeks and gaped at her, incredulous. "I'm not the leader."

"I'm no leader, either," Gabi said, but she'd already tired of arguing with Meadow. She needed to make sense of where they were and how they'd come to be there. Why. It's what Emberley would do, and that's who she needed to be listening to, not this guileless child sitting in the air across from her, awaiting those grown to save her.

There was no one grown coming to save them. That was the difference, Gabi realized, between a Blackwood child and other children. That ability to understand when to dissolve into fantasy and when to confront reality.

"We have to find him! We have to find Brook!"

Gabi closed her eyes again, this time for strength. "Meadow, if we can find a way out of this sky prison, then we would do that."

"There are others here. I heard them."

"Others? What do you mean you heard them?"

"When we got here. I heard others. Young ones, like us. What if they're kidnapping children from across the kingdom? *Eating* them?"

"I doubt that," Gabi said, but was troubled by Meadow's claim that there were others, like them. If so, who were they? And why were they here?

"There he is!" Meadow cried, rolling forward into a scramble as she pointed. "There!"

"No, that's not him," Gabi said calmly as another violet-haired Medvedev, somewhat older than Kael, approached the magical cell. He passed a pitcher through the barrier, which Meadow grabbed and hugged close to her. Gabi tried to send her own hand through the same way, but was unsurprised when she could not. It made sense, when nothing else did, that only a Medvedev could breach their own magic.

"We deserve to know why we're here," Gabi said, channeling her mother. "You owe us that, whoever you are."

"Kian. Son of Yseult." Kian watched her, his face blank. "You tell. Why you're here. Your intentions. Not ours."

Gabi's pulse surged. Son of Yseult. Emberley said it was Yseult who could aid them. "My sister is ill. She carries a disease no one can cure. She is dying." Gabi had hoped this might spur some empathy in the Medvedev's face, but he was impassive. "We were told your mother might help."

"Why?"

"Why?" Gabi repeated.

"She should help you say. Why?"

Gabi wasn't prepared for the question. How was she supposed to answer this? Yseult had no reason to aid them, but if anyone had come to Gabi for her power to save a life, she couldn't imagine turning them away. It wouldn't occur to her to refuse aid to anyone. "I don't know. Only that we love our sister and couldn't let her die without trying."

Kian looked away, toward the vibrant woods. When he looked back, he said, "I come to tell you a truth that has come to us. We are known of the death of your father, Byrne of Warwick. Done by hands of Aiden of Quinlanden, the most vile. He is now Lord of Westerlands."

Big dark spots filled Gabi's eyes as a powerful heat surged into her head. Behind her, Meadow gasped.

The howl Gabi sounded filled her ears; the last thing she heard before she again returned to a place where her father could still chase her by the riverbank.

"You can't leave!" Brandyn cried. "There has to be a way to change the Head Magus' mind."

Christian and Aylen sat before him and Storm, wearing the patient, resigned looks he'd known from his parents when they were simply humoring his objections. He supposed they'd given up their own fight on the matter before sharing the news with him. But there was also something else in their eyes; sadness. It was more than their inability to save Hollyn, which weighed heavily on them both. They were protecting him from something yet to come.

"No, Brandyn," Christian said. "I'm deeply sorry, but this is where things stand now, and there is no going back. Only forward."

"This is my fault. I shouldn't have come here with Hollyn!"

"We wouldn't have changed our actions, even knowing this was how it would end," Aylen assured him. "I have no regrets. I would do it again, even knowing it would be futile. Hollyn deserved no less."

Brandyn brightened as an idea occurred to him. "*I* could talk to him! I could tell him I coerced the two of you. I could take the full blame—"

Aylen reached a hand out and took one of his. "Brandyn. It is done. We leave today, and we will leave with more peace in our hearts if we know there is some in yours."

Brandyn tapped his feet against the wooden floors with increasing pace, trying desperately not to cry. He'd cried too much in these past days. A poor showing for a future heir of the Westerlands. He had to put aside that urge and in its place find strength, as his mother and father would when faced with trials.

"A full year," he said, sighing through his teeth. "What will I do without the two of you for a year? Without your guidance?"

"The years grow shorter as you grow older," Christian said. "And we will return, to guide you once more, before you've fully realized our absence."

Aylen nodded. "We *will* return, Brandyn. This is our home." She seemed to have something else she wanted to say.

Christian bowed his head over his folded hands. His sigh came from somewhere deep. "Brandyn, there is something else we've come to tell you. News I wish more than anything in all the kingdom that I didn't need to deliver to you."

Brandyn almost laughed. He'd just said goodbye to his oldest sister. His mentors were leaving him. There was nothing more that could hurt him now.

At his side, Storm tensed. She slipped a hand through his, squeezing. It didn't comfort him. Whatever Christian knew, Storm did, too, apparently. He sensed her angst.

"A raven came today, for you. The Head Magus knew something was amiss when it wasn't sent to his attention first, to deliver to you, as all other ravens coming into the Sepulchre do. It had come from the Westerlands, but not from your own family."

Brandyn slowed his breathing, working to control it. "All right."

"The raven came from Lord Quinlanden." Christian swallowed. His cheeks flexed. He struggled to find the words. "But first, I must tell you something about the Right of Choosing. Something the Head Magus has learned and believes you must know." Christian pulled an inward sigh. "The Westerlands wasn't the only Reach to arrive without an offering. The king saw fit to punish them all, by leaving with their sons. But your mother's son was here. And so it was her who went with King Eoghan to Duncarrow."

Brandyn's jaw went slack. "My mother is in Duncarrow? She's a prisoner?" He didn't wait for Christian's reaffirming of this terrible truth, but he didn't need to, for in his eyes he saw that Christian had seen this... had seen some form of it, before it had ever transpired. Seen it as only a magic dealer could. Christian's confirmation of what he had seen had unmoored him, and he was still coming to terms with this.

"I know this is a great shock. But what I have to tell you next will be more of one, and the only mercy I can give you is to deliver the news quickly. Lord Quinlanden's raven was sent from Longwood Rush. Announcing the death of your father, Byrne Warwick, and Quinlanden's assumption of command. He has declared himself the new Lord of the Westerlands." He paused. "And Lord Chancellor of the Realm."

Brandyn's mouth parted. He forced his eyes not to land on any of them, to look beyond and to go elsewhere, where he could think, and not be assaulted by the barrage of sympathy from people who loved him, who meant well, but would only drown him in the grief that would descend once he processed the utter shock of his father's death.

"Brandyn, we're so deeply sorry," Aylen said. "If only there were magic that could heal the heart."

"I'll murder him," Storm whispered, passing another squeeze

through their hands. "With glee. And not as swiftly as the men at the inn. I'll give him time to consider his cowardice and treachery."

Brandyn released her hand and stood, moving to the other side of the room. He pressed both hands to the windowsill, looking out into the empty field beyond the falconer's bedchamber. "He was killed by Lord Quinlanden, then. This is what you mean to tell me."

"Yes," Christian said. "He claims that the Blackwoods have abandoned Longwood Rush, and he has no choice but to assume leadership."

"Abandoned!" Storm cried out. "Only a man of great evil would murder the protector and then claim it was left alone!"

"He has no claim," Aylen said. "He knows this. Not as long as Lady Blackwood and her children live. He is goading Brandyn and his sisters to come out of hiding and challenge him, so he may murder them as well. Brandyn, you must not take that challenge."

Brandyn's breath fogged up the glass. Each exhale felt as if he were emptying the day's content of air from his lungs. But so he focused, *in, out, in, out,* remembering to control his emotion, not surrender to it. "And my mother? Has anyone heard of her fate in Duncarrow?"

"Not a word, though if she, too, had died, Aiden would be all too quick to announce it. It would only help his claim."

"So the Reach is undefended."

"Whatever defense your father had at his ready now answers to Lord Quinlanden."

Brandyn snorted. "They would *never* answer to a Quinlanden. *Lord Chancellor* or no."

"In the absence of a Blackwood, they may have no choice."

"Christian," Aylen warned. "Careful with your words. Brandyn may take them as an invitation to rise against a man who's far more powerful. He couldn't have made himself Lord Chancellor alone. He will have two Reaches and the crown behind him now."

Brandyn turned around. He felt in that moment as if the boy inside him had flown away, pressing itself through the glass and exiting into a world that had changed, for him, for them all. He wasn't a man, but the sensation that he was becoming one settled over him, taking root.

"I *will* retake the Westerlands from that coward, who would murder my father when he was at his weakest. *I*," he said, looking briefly at Storm, "will avenge my father, with my own hands, so Aiden Quinlanden can understand the strength of a Reach that rises higher than he ever will, as his life leaves him. Let it be my eyes he last looks into. I'll do this because I am the Lord of the Westerlands, not Aiden Quinlanden, and if my mother cannot defend what's ours, it falls to me."

Aylen released a sigh. "I suppose you must. It would be foolish to think otherwise."

Christian stood. "I will help you, Brandyn. However I'm able. If I can, I will stir the Derehams to your defense as well."

"My father and the Wynters will want to see this wrong righted," Aylen added. "There cannot be peace in the kingdom when lords are murdered in their own homes."

"I should return to Whitewood," Storm said. "My father would never serve a Quinlanden, and many other Great Families of the Western Reach will feel the same. If there is a resistance forming, he will know of it."

"It's too dangerous for you to travel alone. I'll go with you," Brandyn said.

"You're safer here," Christian said. "It may be the only place you're safe."

Brandyn felt the fire in his eyes as he looked at him and said, "Why do you think he addressed the raven to me? Aiden wants me to know he'll come for me, and then no one at the Sepulchre will be safe." He shook his head. "No, Magi Christian. I will only be safe where he cannot find me."

"He's right," Aylen said, exhaling. "The raven was a warning."

"But Brandyn cannot just leave. Can he? Won't they punish him?" Storm asked.

"An Adherent can leave under one condition. Death or turmoil in the family," Christian answered. "He will return to both. Brandyn, does anyone know Storm is with you, other than your family and hers?"

"I don't believe so."

"Then when you arrive in Whitewood, you'll be someone else. Aiden will have his men all over the Reach by the time you're back in familiar land, and there can be no doubt when he discovers you've left the Sepulchre he'll assume you've returned home. You'll need to know who you are before you get there."

"I have a brother," Storm said, looking solemn. "Shadow. He ran away to join the Reliquary when he was just old enough to mount a horse and was never heard from again. Foolish boy. We assumed… the worst. He wasn't six when he left. He would be about Brandyn's age."

"And others could believe this? That he'd returned home?" Christian asked.

"Many in Whitewood still beseech the Guardians in his name, to this day. Hope for his return is very much alive, for he is their only male heir. My mother and father would go along with the ruse, in the name of the Reach."

"Shadow Wakesell," Aylen said, with a small, sad smile. "Has the ring of a young man who will take back his home. The hero in the tales to be told in the future."

"Has it come to this?" Christian said. "Listen to us. How has the world changed so much since yesterday?"

"You would tell me, in class, that we should never ask how or why something has happened, but be ready to meet change with both eyes open, and then to ask, why it should continue," Brandyn said. "My father and sister are dead. My mother is a prisoner. I might never see my other sisters again. Nothing will ever be the same for me. But I will meet this new world of mine with both eyes open." As he looked at the three of them, Brandyn realized he was no longer fighting tears. He had no urge to cry. Only a powerful anger that he must either act on or be consumed by.

"I don't know what we'll find in the Westerlands, but it is my *home*, and if my father is gone, and my mother imprisoned, then the responsibility is now mine to do what I must, to protect it from this evil."

EMBERLEY LIKED HOW THE HEAT OF THE FLAMES BRUSHED HER CHEEKS, set against the shock of icy air. Aunt Earwyn insisted it was foolish to be outdoors when they could warm themselves within the keep, but didn't fight very hard when Ember pushed to have their conversation near the field. Ember had spent weeks outdoors and, while she had dreamed of leaving that behind, she struggled to do the same. She had become someone else, a woman, a warrior, in the wilderness.

"Your adventures make me envious," Earwyn said. Her aunt resembled her sister, Asherley, but instead of dark hair, hers was almost white, and as soft as silk. Close enough to make Emberley long for home, but different enough for her to appreciate the comfort of her own people without losing the strength she'd found without them.

"There are more to come," Ember said. "I just don't yet know where to start."

"You said you wanted to meet with the Ravenwoods."

"Have you? Living up here, I mean. You must have."

Earwyn smiled. She tucked her blond hair back off her face and huddled closer to the fire. "I've known some, yes. They send their youth to train in the towns, to practice their magic. There was one, Ravenna, who I had occasion to know well." Her smile faded.

"What is it?"

"The trouble with knowing a Ravenwood, Ember, is that to know them too well is to put them in danger. My nephew, Drystan, is perhaps learning this now, though I hope it turns out better for him than it has for others."

Ember cupped her cider in her palms. "I heard Lady Blackwood say Ravenna went with him when he ran off with Lisbet and Eavan."

"No one knows for certain. Only that Ravenna hasn't returned to The Rookery, and the timing of her absence is too similar to ignore." Earwyn looked at her. "And you, you've had changes of your own, have you not?"

"What do you mean?"

"Marsh."

Ember blushed. "It's nothing."

"Is it?"

"I'm glad it was Marsh at my side," Ember said. In the distance, a raven circled the sky, the lone creature navigating through the fresh snow. "He proved a good companion."

"You're at an age," Earwyn said with a light sigh. "There's no shame in realizing your childhood friends have come along with you as you've grown."

"You know why I've come here," Ember said to her aunt. "And now that I know Mother is in Duncarrow, it's even more important for me to focus on what matters."

"It all matters, Ember," Earwyn said. "Your mother is wise. I should know. It was her who guided Maeryn and me all throughout our youth. She has a gift for seeing ahead, and it isn't only her magic. There's a wisdom in her that runs through all Blackwoods, but especially Asherley. And yet… she cannot see all. She saw enough to send you into the world, but she trusted that you would, on your own, determine what should come next."

"You think a boy matters? Right now?"

"Only you can know that. I would only advise you to be cautious about dismissing the importance of anything or anyone the Guardians have chosen for you, for they don't choose accidentally."

Ember watched as the raven swooped lower, doing intentional, choreographed loops, as if putting on a show for them.

"Pay him no mind. He's been out there every day," Earwyn said, a note of disgust tinging her words. "Attention is what he desires."

Ember set her mug aside. "But who is he?"

"A Ravenwood. Ravenna's brother. Alasyr, I think his name is."

"What do you think he wants?"

"To warn us. He thinks we had a role in his sister's disappearance." Earwyn waved a hand. "Truly, Ember, if you keep staring you'll only encourage him."

Ember rose to her feet. "He's doing what I would do, if something happened to one of my own siblings."

"Ember, sit back down. Please."

Ember ignored her and marched through the snow, across the field toward the wagons where Alasyr was doing his acrobatics. As she drew nearer, the raven dropped lower, and as he did he unfolded, wings becoming limbs, beak becoming a perfectly arced mouth. She nearly gasped; her first sighting of a pureblood Ravenwood.

"Ember! Leave him be!" her aunt called.

"Hi. I'm Ember," she said. He watched her through lovely but wary eyes. "You're Alasyr, is that right?"

"Who are you?" he demanded.

"I just told you."

"You're no Dereham."

"No. I'm a Blackwood."

Alasyr recoiled. "A family of traitors."

"Emberley Blackwood!" Earwyn yelled.

"That must be what they tell you. I understand. But we're born who we are."

"Rhosyn Ravenwood was born Ravenwood. She chose to be a Blackwood."

"You're worried your sister has made a similar choice."

Alasyr sneered. "She would never. She is no traitor."

Ember shrugged. "I'm no help where this is concerned. I know nothing. I have my own problems."

"They all say that," Alasyr said. He had the most intense eyes, which glowed behind his black hair and sculpted face. He looked both familiar and also exotically foreign. "I should've known you wouldn't be different."

"Ember!" This time it was Gretchen. "Come back, please. I have news you need to hear."

"Hope you find your sister," Ember said, waving at Alasyr, who simply stared back with an incredulous glare.

Her light mood faded as she saw the way Gretchen regarded her. In her hand, she clutched a shred of vellum. Her cheeks flushed with an emotion Ember didn't yet understand.

Earwyn buried her face in her hands and sobbed.

"Emberley. Darling," Gretchen said. She didn't gather Ember in her arms, but instead held her at her shoulders. "I have to tell you something terrible, and how I wish it wasn't true."

Emberley glanced at her aunt, huddled into her grief in the chair. She didn't yet know the cause and was already grieving herself, already preparing to be in shock. She looked back to Gretchen. "Just tell me."

"Your father has been murdered," Gretchen said. She gripped Emberley's shoulders so tight, Emberley saw stars. "Murdered, at the hands of my brother. Lord Quinlanden."

Ember sagged, but Gretchen caught her in her grip. "No," was all she said.

"Aiden has declared himself Lord of the Westerlands. Lord Chancellor of the Realm."

"No," Ember said. She tore herself free. "No."

Earwyn rose and wrapped her arms around Ember from behind. "Oh, Ember. You poor sweet darling. Your poor mother."

A numbness passed over Emberley. She could hear Gretchen and Earwyn talking to her, a mix of sympathy and explanation, but their words drifted somewhere into the backdrop of the snowy landscape of Wulfsgate. They were elsewhere now, and Ember moved ahead of them, to a future that would be in her hands.

"This will not go unanswered. I swear to you. His crime goes against our way of life," Gretchen said, and now, finally, these were words that mattered. Emberley looked at her and, very slowly, nodded. Had her mother seen this? Asherley would have known that to share something this shocking would have destroyed Ember's confidence in her mission. But Ember couldn't reconcile that her mother would leave knowing it would mean her husband's death. She refused to believe her mother would sacrifice him for some greater good. For anything.

Earwyn hugged her tighter, but Ember stiffened in her embrace. There was no strength to be found in comfort. Earwyn should know. They'd both learned this from Asherley.

In the distance, Alasyr dropped his head and returned to flight.

KHALLUM HAD COME TO SEE HIS WIFE AS A BRINGER OF NEWS. SHE WAS always the first to be notified of an arriving raven, a fact that continued to confound and frustrate him. Gwyn was an outlander here, something Southerlanders never took well to, but they'd taken to her eventually, over the course of years. They'd cleaved to her kindness and admired her mettle. Gwyn, like any woman, could be emotional, but she could equally, and as often, be strong.

She'd been strong when she delivered the news about Byrne. For once, it was he who could not find his footing.

"We cannot suffer Aiden Quinlanden to live," Gwyn said. "For Byrne. For Gretchen. For Assana. For the Medvedev. For what he will do, even more than what he has done."

Byrne. His little brother. How Khallum had teased him for being less man than their sister, Yesenia. He'd found what few books existed in Warwicktown and hoarded them in his room, so no one would know. He tended to gulls with broken wings, by candlelight. He knew when it would rain, and when the sea would be too treacherous for a run. And yet, when Khallum called upon him to defend what was their right by birth, Byrne would rise and let the salt and sand wear proudly against his smile. He could be anything those around him needed of him, often without his loved ones realizing what they needed to begin with. But Byrne had known. Khallum had never known another like him.

And now, he was gone from the world. Ripped from this life unawares, no doubt, for a ratsbane like Quinlanden would not dare to have challenged Byrne man to man. He could only best him under the cover of darkness and surprise.

"He has taken what isn't his, in the Westerlands. What will be next?" Gwyn asked, though she knew good and well what answer she was after. Khallum grunted.

"What next, Khallum?"

"He wouldnae come here," Khallum said. "Nor the Northerlands. He struck where he perceived weakness. He'll nae find it again in this kingdom."

"Byrne was not weak."

"Asherley gambled, spreading her children over the kingdom and leaving it all to her husband. Oh, aye, ye didnae suss that out, did ye? Yes, wife. Asherley knew what she was doing. She's the type of woman who always knows, who never does a thing without that knowing. She gambled, and she lost." As Khallum said this, he wasn't so certain of the fact. There was more to her design. He'd seen it in her eyes as she was "forcibly" taken away to Duncarrow.

"The Westerlands isn't our concern, but it is. It is now, when what Aiden has done upsets the balance we have all respected for centuries."

"I know, Gwyn."

"What should we do? Find the Blackwood children? Use them to restore order?"

"Gwyn—"

"Tell me what to do. Tell me how to aid you."

"We can do nothing until Hamish and the men return with our prize."

"And when will that be?"

"I donnae know, for I thought when you arrived to bring ruin to my day that it was this you'd come to share!"

Gwyn recoiled. "It isn't me who's ruined your day. But I would see the one who has brought to ruin. And I would help you do it."

"I know you would," Khallum said. That hard burn in his chest was spreading. Unabated now. Soon he would be aflame. "Leave me."

"You push me away, when I can be of use."

Khallum's face erupted in crimson grief. "You cannae grieve my brother for me, so leave me!"

Gwyn watched him for a sign he meant for her to stay. He sent her none, and so she left him, alone with his grief, with his unmitigated rage. But he had to temper it, for now. If Hamish and the others met with success, Aiden's power would diminish to naught; Khallum could and would deal with the matter of his grasping treachery, but he would not be alone. He would stand, side by side, with Byrne's children, with Asherley, and together they would enjoy measuring the last moments of the craven monster. He would call upon his sister, Yesenia, and Corin, the Quinlanden who should have been heir. They would lay claim to the Easterlands, with the support of all the other Reaches.

But first, they had to rescue Darrick Rhiagain from the Wastelands and see him, and their kingdom, restored to rights.

44

HALF-MEDVEDEV

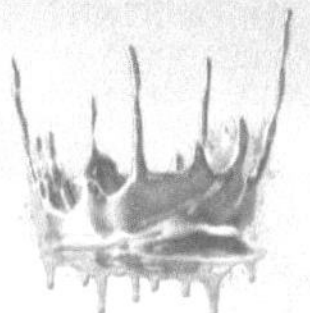

J esse had told Esmerelda about the pull. Although he had no magic in him, he supposed it might be something akin to magic, or even something deeper, innate. A sense that he was being summoned home. Esmerelda had said that as half-Medvedev there was no chance he was without magic entirely, and he'd gone quiet after that, because there was a truth in her words that he'd tried hard to bury.

If he was half-Medvedev, then where *was* this half of him? He'd grown his talents at the hearth, raised under the instruction of his buccaneer father. He'd taken to the trade well enough. Better than Ryan, who struggled to settle his attention on one thing for long. But they were Strongs, and there was no other future for them. Their value to their Reach, to their lord, lay in these ancestral skills, and their strategic position along the coast.

And how would one know they were magic, anyway? He'd heard stories of children ripped from their beds and sent to the Sepulchre; parents fearful of what would happen if they accidentally practiced this magic without authority. These children must have discovered their abilities on their own, and quite by surprise. Erran Rutland's daughter, Esther, was one such child, and Jesse would never forget the day they sent her off, screaming through her tears.

That discovery had never happened to Jesse, and as far as he knew, Ryan either. He supposed it may be something to do with the difference between Medvedev and men, but he belonged to the world of men and had no one to guide him through the half of him he'd been forced to keep hidden.

He'd told Esmerelda about the pull, but had said nothing about the foreboding. It swelled in tandem with the pull, as if the two things were tied to the very same place. Something whispered inside him to stay the path; that he was close, and he would know when he had fallen upon the place open only to those of his mother's blood. Alongside that were the screams, his own fears, that he should turn back before it wasn't his choice anymore.

He had no option but to move forward, toward the whispers, in spite of the screams. Ryan could only complete the task assigned to him if he knew Esmerelda was safe, and there was but one place in this kingdom where the Warwicks would never venture.

Or maybe two, Jesse thought, smiling to himself, visualizing the unsightly rocks guarding the fortress of Duncarrow as one sailed past.

"Help! Help me!"

Esmerelda came to a swift halt. Jesse turned his horse in a circle, searching for the source. The rustle of bushes being crushed underfoot sounded to his left. He turned, hand on his sword. But it was only a little boy, a child, red-faced and tear-stained.

Jesse removed his hand from the hilt. "Whoa. Whoa there. Slow down."

"Run. We have to run. *Run!*" The boy doubled over his knees, gasping for air, but he recovered quickly and tugged at Jesse's leg. "They're coming!"

"Who?" Esmerelda asked. "Who's coming?"

"Who are you?" Jesse asked. He looked around. "Where did you come from?"

The boy was incredulous at their questions, gaping mouth passing between the two as he decided which one to answer. He looked back over his shoulder and tugged again at Jesse's leg. "We have to go!"

Jesse looked at Esmerelda, who shook her head in shared confusion. With a grunt, he reached under the arm of the boy and swung him up onto the horse behind him. "I saw a cave a stretch back. We'll try to get some sense out of him there."

Even after they'd fed and watered him from their rations, the boy refused to calm. His startled, feral eyes had seen things he seemed unable or unwilling to share. He tore at his food as if he hadn't eaten in days, but was dressed like a child who'd come from a family of means.

"They'll find us here, too," the boy said. "We can't stay here."

"We willnae be long here," Jesse said, before he could remember to mask his Southern parlance. "We have our own destination to reach. But if you'll tell us where you come from, we can point you back to your own."

The boy rolled his head back as he took a generous swallow of the river water from the skin. "Windwatch Grove," he said, wiping his mouth. His lip quivered in time with his eyes watering with fresh tears.

"Windwatch Grove?" Esmerelda frowned. "The Westerlands?"

"Look at him. He's no Medvedev," Jesse said. But he, too, puzzled over how a boy, not more than a decade into his life, had ended up alone in the Hinterlands. "How did you find yourself here?"

"They took…" The boy bowed his head and sobbed. They waited for the bout to pass, and then, sniffling, snot stained, he looked up again. "My sister and I were on a most important mission. With someone… someone who's also important."

Esmerelda reached a hand out, but the boy recoiled, as if stung. "Tell us your name. We won't harm you."

The boy looked her up and down. "You're no Medvedev, either."

"No," she said. "My name is Elizabeth Dunn. This is my brother, John."

Jesse was proud of her for remembering their cover, even with this scared child. He'd nearly forgotten it himself. "From Greystone Abbey," he said.

"You speak like a Southerlander," the boy charged.

Jesse laughed. "I've spent some time there."

"We have to go get help," the boy said.

"Tell us who you are," Esmerelda said, soothing. "And we may be able to help you do that."

The boy looked conflicted about the request, but there was a hopelessness in his eyes, and it seemed to be this he answered with. "Brook Ashenhurst." He looked at his feet. "My sister Meadow and my friend… Gabi. They were taken."

"Gabi?"

Brook swallowed. "Blackwood."

Esmerelda gasped. She looked at Jesse, but he was equally bewildered.

"What were the two of you and a Blackwood doing in the Hinterlands?" Jesse asked. He ran his hands over his chin; his fresh beard.

"Gabi will hate me for not keeping her secret!"

Esmerelda touched his arm. "We're no harm to Gabi, or Meadow. We only want to help, if we can." She hesitated, mulling over her response. Jesse couldn't read her mind, but he didn't need to. She'd almost told the boy that the Blackwood children were her cousins, but there was nothing to be gained in the telling, and everything to lose if the child told another.

"You can't," Brook said. The tears started again. "You can't help. I… I need to go home. Get my father, and Lord and Lady Blackwood, and we need to return and *make* them give Meadow and Gabi back!"

"The Medvedev?" Jesse asked.

Brook nodded, sucking in his lower lip.

"But why would they take them?" Jesse inhaled. "Why are you here?"

Brook shook his head. "Gabi's sister is very sick. No one knows what made her sick. The healers can't heal her. No doctor understands it. Her other sister, Emberley… she sent us to see Yseult." He scratched his head. "I think that's her name. Chief or something. She thought Yseult could heal Hollyn, because there's different magic here, I guess."

"And where is Emberley now? And Brandyn and Hollyn?" Esmerelda asked, and Jesse could see the flush in her neck; the worry for her beloved relations.

"How do you know about Brandyn?"

Jesse's heart stopped, but Esmerelda recovered neatly. "We're from the Westerlands, too, Brook. Everyone knows who the Blackwood children are."

Brook squished his face into a frown but seemed satisfied with the answer. Or too exhausted to explore it. "Emberley went to Midnight Crest. Brandyn and Hollyn to the Sepulchre, where Brandyn is a student. Of, you know, magic."

Esmerelda paled. "You have all been on quite the adventure. Do Lord and Lady Blackwood know?"

Brook shook his head. "We left at night. They know now, I suppose. We left…" Brook searched his memory. "I don't know anymore. I don't know how long we've been gone. They took time from us."

Jesse pressed the boy for more. "How did the Medvedev come to take your companions?"

"We were in a cave." Brook looked around. "Like this one. Gabi was… Gabi was having a bad time. It was Meadow's and my fault. We were being mean."

"I'm sure it wasn't your fault," Esmerelda said.

"It was. We made her sad," Brook replied. "And then the boy came."

"What boy?"

"Kael. With the purple hair."

"A Medvedev. He found you in a cave?"

Brook nodded. "He said he knew where we were trying to go and only he could take us there. We pushed Gabi to go with him. She didn't want to, but we made her." Brook's mouth curled in anticipation of a new sob. "We made her, and then… and then I remember nothing until I woke up. Here."

"How long ago was that?" Jesse pressed.

Brook shrugged. "Like I said, they took time from us."

"They? Was there someone else with Kael?"

"Not at first. When I woke up, the girls were still asleep. Not really sleeping, but whatever they did to us."

Jesse nodded.

"But they were walking. I was walking, but now I was awake again. Kael was there. And four or five more, all with that strange hair. Purple. Green. And when they paused for water, I ran away and didn't look back."

"How did you wake yourself?" Esmerelda asked.

"I didn't. I didn't do anything. I just woke."

"Did they follow?"

"They yelled for me," Brook said. "One chased me. But I was quicker."

Jesse looked over his head at Esmerelda. "Just one in pursuit. We can handle this, if it comes to it."

She nodded in return.

"No!" Brook said. "One of them can charm you, like they did us! Ember said they're kind and peaceful, but it's not true. Why would they want to hurt children?"

"I can't make sense of it," Jesse said. "What could they want with children from the Westerlands?"

Brook didn't have an answer. Esmerelda stared off into the darkness. He wished he could speak to her openly in front of the child.

The news of her cousins had been a shock. He wondered what else had changed in the kingdom since they left.

Now he had to decide what to do with the boy. He couldn't leave him or take him. Despite the strange tale he'd told, Jesse had no other place to take Esmerelda. If he doubled back to the Westerlands, to deliver this child to his home, it would only increase the risk of Esmerelda being discovered.

"Do you hear that?" Esmerelda whispered. She tilted her head to the side, listening.

Jesse's hand moved to his sword. He looked at Brook and pressed a finger to his lips. Brook, wide-eyed, nodded.

He stood and slowly withdrew the sword. The metal made only a light sound as it passed across the sheath and into the open air.

The light in the cave dimmed as the entrance filled with men. Medvedev. You always knew them by their hair, he thought, but there was something more to it, he knew now. A presence harder to define in words.

He coaxed Esmerelda and Brook behind him. They scampered away and cowered behind the horses at the back of the cave.

"Bind him," one of the Medvedev said.

"Not adhering," another said.

"Again."

Jesse watched this strange exchange with mounting anxiety, but he held fast to his sword.

"Still no. You try."

The other closed his eyes. When he opened them, his face was marred with frustration. "Not for me."

"Who are you?" the first one, with the green hair, demanded.

"I've come here seeking aid from the people of my mother," Jesse said.

"You are no Medvedev."

"I'm half-Medvedev," Jesse said. He forced his voice to remain strong, to not waver in this confession he was no longer sure would be enough. "I am Jamesan Strong, son of Yanna of the Medvedev, and I seek asylum for the wife of Yanna's second son, Ryan."

"Chains, then," the second one said. "Yseult can decide."

"Jesse, why aren't they listening?" Esmerelda asked from the shadows. "Don't they believe you?"

"I donnae know," he muttered. He bore down on the sword's hilt.

The Medvedev moved into the cave. Then they stopped. One stumbled backward, back into the forest. The others turned to see and then they, too, fled, scrambling through the brush and scattering into the trees.

"What's happening?" Esmerelda asked.

"I couldnae tell you," Jesse said, breathless. He took several steps forward, sword still at the ready. When he reached the entrance, they were gone. All of them. He stepped into the sunlight and, sword in fighting stance, spun around to search for any signs of their intended jailers.

Something descended from the sky. A raven. He staggered backward as the raven unfurled into a new form. A woman. Hair, dark as night. Eyes, as bright as the flora painting the Forest of All.

His heart skipped. In fear. In… something else.

"You can put your sword away," she said.

"I'll put it away when I'm ready."

The priestess stepped forward. Jesse swallowed the dryness in his throat. He had an urge to look away from her, but equally found himself unable to do anything of the sort.

"I had heard the Medvedev feared the Ravenwoods, but it was a strange thing to confirm it," she said.

"Ravenwoods live in the North," Jesse said. His sword shook in his hands.

"I did live there," she said. "And then I left. Now I'm here."

"Stop," he said, when she moved closer. "Stay where you are."

"You have nothing to fear from me, Jamesan."

"How did you know my name? Are you in my head?"

She laughed. "No. I heard your speech to the Medvedev. Seems you're one, too, if you weren't lying, but you're not afraid of me like they are."

"What do you want?" he demanded.

"The same thing as you. Somewhere in this forest the Medvedev have taken men and women I care about prisoner, and I intend to do something about it."

"Who are you?"

The priestess came closer. She pressed a hand over his sword, lowering it. Jesse could hardly control his breathing as she came within inches of him.

"Ravenna Ravenwood. Once the intended High Priestess of Midnight Crest, and now someone else, someone I hope to discover before this is all ended."

Jesse let his sword fall to his side.

Ravenna touched his face with her soft, warm palm. "We can help each other."

45

A STORY OWED

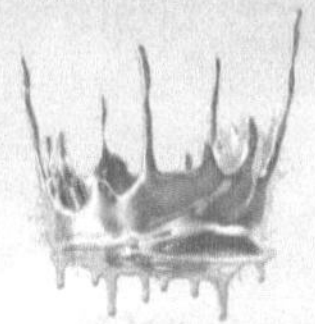

Drystan had screamed himself into exhaustion. It had been energy wasted upon gaolers who let the words slide over them, around them, unaffected. Aside from delivering food and drink, the Medvedev were notably absent. Immune to their pleas, indifferent to their suffering.

Valen watched as Drystan first spiraled into a muted anger, hurling his whispered insults into the wind as he slowly succumbed to his need for rest. He had words still resting upon his tongue when the soft snores sounded in the cell.

Valen reached a hand over. He let himself brush the hair, which had grown longer in their weeks on the road, back off Drystan's face. He stopped himself from doing more. There were first things he must say, that no one but Drystan could hear, and once heard, Drystan could decide the future of the words, if there was to be one at all.

These were not the conditions in which Valen foresaw him telling this story, but it was time to tell it.

· · ·

Valen's watchful gaze awakened Drystan. He felt it penetrate through the leather of his jerkin, and when he rolled over to face him, Valen seemed startled to have been caught in his thoughts.

"What is it? Did they come back?"

"No. They haven't returned since they brought supper."

Drystan was too tired now for his anger. The evening's meager portions only quelled the most persistent of his hunger pangs. None of it had replenished his energy. His left arm screamed at him with a fresh ache.

"Is it Lisbet? Eavan?"

"No one has given us word of either of them, though I have no reason to believe their present circumstances are any different than ours. If they wanted us dead, we would be dead already."

"But something's wrong?"

"Not wrong," Valen said. His eyes hung heavy, like a man in his cups. "Or no more wrong than it has been since they took us prisoner."

"I can see it in your eyes. Something *is* troubling you."

"I'd like to tell you a story, Drystan. I'd hoped to tell it elsewhere, but as I've lost sight of what will happen to us next, there are things I believe I owe you."

Drystan pulled himself up against the invisible wall. He blinked the sleep from his eyes. "I don't understand. What do you owe me?"

"A truth that has been denied to you. One which can only be told by two people, of which I'm one." Valen paused only long enough to draw breath and then said, "I once knew your mother."

"Many people know my mother. She's a lady of two great houses."

"I knew her very well… better than anyone else could have claimed."

Drystan opened his mouth, then closed it.

"Your mother called me Ash. Because of my eyes, she said. We were so young in those days, playing in the meadows and forests beyond Whitechurch, first as childhood friends, later as more.

Gretchen was different then. She had a light in her eyes that your uncle, Aiden, worked tirelessly to fade. He did fade it. I only saw it return when she became a mother, but it was a different one than I'd seen in her youth."

Drystan was wide awake now. "Ash? I've heard my mother talking to an Ash."

Ash didn't smile. "Have you?"

"Only when she sneaks…" Drystan stopped himself from saying too much. Valen, Ash, whoever he was, was finally going to share something about himself. Lisbet thought she was so wise, questioning him, but Drystan wasn't without questions of his own. He'd only had more patience on the matter, because he sensed Valen's presence portended something incredible to come, and he weighted those answers above any questions he might have. "Away from others."

"In the crypts?"

A chill rippled through Drystan. "Yes."

Ash nodded. "I might be able to shed light on this for you, though it will make little sense now. Shall I continue?"

Drystan nodded.

"I loved Gretchen. I could tell you why I loved her, or how it came to be that I knew it had grown to that, but it wouldn't matter. Coming from a Great Family myself, the Sylvaines of Rushwood, there was a chance for us to be man and wife, and we did all we could to hide our love from Aiden, who would've used it as another way to harm her. Gretchen worked to lay the roots for the idea with her father, and they started to take hold. Our fathers talked terms of betrothal.

"And then she returned from Termonglen one day to tell me she'd been bartered off to Holden Dereham. No chance for appeal. Too late to run off and make our own impassioned choices. She had only enough time to come to me with a handful of carefully chosen words, and then she was gone, shipped off to the Northerlands. She left me with the ghost of her. No time for a man as spent in love as I was for her to come to terms with any of it. So abrupt I never had time for grief. I was stuck on the idea of action. Stuck in the past that was still my present."

Drystan had known her mother had a love before his father, as many of the brides and bridegrooms of the Epoch of the Accordant had, but to hear another man speak of her this way was startling. *The before doesn't matter,* she liked to say, but now the before was sitting right in front of Drystan, announcing itself, mattering.

"I followed her to Wulfsgate. What can I say, other than that I was mad with my love for her and still so young? I later wondered, had things not happened so swiftly… had I had time to make peace with her leaving, would I have followed? I can never know. She can never know. But I followed, and while she should've turned me away, she was as distressed by our separation as I'd been, and we clung to what had never been given proper ending.

"We promised we'd only lay together once. Once, to form the proper goodbye that was taken from us. Holden was afraid of the crypts. She said there, we would be safe. She was right.

"But neither of us found the strength to stop matters there. She would come to me nightly, and then, weeks would pass before she came again. When she discovered she was with child—your brother, Christian—she halted her visits altogether for a while. She said she had to turn her attentions toward being a mother, but I saw the guilt eating away at her resolve. The strain of living a double life. As I'd been apprenticing with the blacksmith, as Ash, I buried myself in my own learning, but she returned to me when Christian was born, and with more vigor than ever."

"My father didn't know?"

"Holden sees what he seeks, and no more," Ash said. "He cares deeply for your mother, but that isn't the same as knowing her. Besides, he was in awe of his new son, who looked more Dereham than Quinlanden. Gretchen had done her duty, and would do it again, and that was all that mattered."

"Did he ever find out?"

"No," Ash said, "but he will remember the man who died upon the floor of your mother's bedchamber. The man who, they say, inadvertently drank the poison she used upon her enemies."

Drystan scrunched his face. "Those are only vicious rumors. My mother has never used poison on another. She never would."

"If you say so," Ash said. "Nonetheless, the man found it, so it was said. But that man was me, and no one forced me to consume it, nor did I do it accidentally. Your mother asked me to take it."

Drystan's jaw dropped at the terrible accusation. "I don't believe you. She would never do that. And if she loved you, as you say she did, then why would she?" He tried to imagine him or Ravenna making that request of each other, but couldn't even conjure the words. Though she had left him with so many questions, none answered, he still felt within him the love she'd gifted. Her necklace rested under his shirt, a reminder she might one day search for him again. Even in his tortured dreams, he saw her soar, never crash.

"It was her love that drove me to it," Ash replied. His eyes closed and a sad sound came out with his deep exhale. "We couldn't be rid of each other. I couldn't leave, and she couldn't ask me to go. I asked her what she would have me do, and, in a fit of emotion, she advised me where I could find the poison in her bureau and stormed away. She found me later upon the floor of her chambers, wrought with guilt at words that couldn't be unsaid."

Drystan was horrified. "But you know she didn't mean it, so why would you do it? And then let her believe she'd killed you?"

"We both needed a way out," Ash said, sighing. "Your mother needed to be free to be a mother and a wife, and I saw her impassioned plea as a way to be free of my own prison of love for her. I was the heir of Rushwood, and if I returned, I could still have a bountiful life of my own. A wife who could be mine, and only mine, children bearing my name. Anything would be better than the midpoint in which your mother and I existed, both something and utterly nothing."

"You didn't die, though," Drystan said.

"I did, to her," Ash said. "For I hadn't taken the poison at all, but a concoction that contained a potent mixture of deadly flowers from the Wintergarden. This mixture produces a sensation that is like death, but isn't death. It slows the pulse to a place where it cannot be felt by hand and shallows the breaths. I knew how to craft it, and so I did. And when the blacksmith's apprentice was removed from her chambers and sent to be burned upon the pyre with other deaths that winter, deaths of those bearing no name, I slipped away under the cover of night."

"You deceived her," Drystan charged. "You let her believe you were dead, and that she'd had a hand in it!"

"I freed her," Ash corrected. "I freed us both." His clipped laugh had a bitter note. "I should've known there was no freedom for either of us. I learned they'd sent her away after Lisbet was born, her grief turned to madness. Holden didn't understand what had control of her and was helpless to solve it, so he entreated the Magi of the Sepulchre to see her mind returned to her. Instead, she found a Magi who promised her he could return me to life, a life after death, and bind me to her for the rest of her days.

"When she returned, she labored under the irrepressible belief that, though I had died, I hadn't left. That my ghost lingered, and it was as if I'd never gone anywhere at all. She held fast to the promise of the charlatan Magi. Perhaps she found this arrangement better, even, then when I had come to her full of life, for if I was dead, then there was no one to stop us. No one but her could see me, and she could have both worlds, the one above, and the one below."

Drystan pressed these truths against his memories. His mother, slipping down into the crypts. *Ash, my beloved.* Speaking to air. Loving what wasn't there.

"You're remembering, now, the way your mother has been in the crypts."

"But it's not real," Drystan whispered. "And if it's not real, then my mother is... she's..."

"She's the cleverest woman I have ever known. There is a reason many fear her more than Holden. But, like all women, like all men, she is possessed of weakness, too. A weakness she perceives as strength. Through the ghost of Ash Sylvaine, she conceives of, and gains approval for, those things she already intends to do. He is her lover, her conscience, and her mirror. He is me, but more of what she needed. And it would devastate her utterly to learn that the deal she made with the Magi was naught more than her imagination, fed by her desire."

"And you…" Drystan shook his head, struggling to make sense of how this story, his mother's story, intersected with Ash's finding of them that night in the camp. "You looked after us, from guilt? Stalked my sister and cousin and me as we fled Wulfsgate, and then miraculously saved us from the brigands? Is that how I'm to understand this confession?"

"I left Wulfsgate when your mother was sent away. It was then that I had my encounter here with the Drumain. I lost my courage on the way back to the Easterlands and found something else instead. Yseult revealed to me a truth I had known all along, but had buried, for it was easier for me to believe I'd left nothing behind in Wulfsgate. Easier than accepting that I'd left everything behind." Ash tilted his head to the side. "I returned to the Northerlands when I heard the announcement of the Right of Choosing. I knew you would leave to protect Lisbet from the misery of marrying a king who stole his own crown."

"How? How did you know that?"

"Because it's what I would have done." Ash bowed his head. He again sighed, this time turning the ends of it into a light smile. "There was a night, months after you were born, where I stood at your cradle and watched you. Any child of a Quinlanden was beautiful, but I puzzled over your beauty, which lacked the cool hardness of the north. And when you at last detected me, opening your eyes in curious wonder, I looked upon that truth, the one I would spend years running from until the Medvedev pointed me true."

Drystan's mouth went completely dry. He felt strangely hot, like something alive was traveling his limbs and lighting him up, inch by inch. "What truth?"

Ash inhaled. When he released the breath, it landed into a smile, bigger and truer than the last. "I knew that I, Drystan Sylvaine, once known and loved as Ash, had looked upon a child, and that child was my son."

46

THE LOST WULFLING

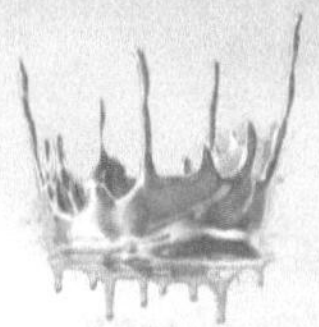

Christian dropped to the frozen ground. He took Moon's reins and led her from there. Aylen rode a little farther on Sun, and then did the same, joining him in the slow approach to the drawbridge that would take them across the stream and into the courtyard of Wulfsgate Keep. Men and women on all sides paused to see the return of the lost wulfling. Some bowed. Others simply stared, keeping their thoughts of his arrival to themselves. Later, they'd talk about it. It was no small thing for the former heir of the Reach to have come home again. He was glad not to know their minds. His own was occupied, convincing himself to take every step forward.

A tiny figure came running across the drawbridge, slipping around in the icy, packed snow along the surface. Hands waved in the air, followed by excited shouts, though Christian couldn't make out his words.

"Is that Torrin?" Aylen asked in wonder. "Little Torrin?"

Christian's shame at not recognizing his own brother deepened his dread, but he added it to the already long list. "And there must be Nyssa," he answered, pointing to the energetic girl who'd joined in, flagging her arms around with competing energy. She jumped out in front of him, determined to be first.

Aylen laughed. "Everything changes, and nothing does."

Behind the children appeared two more figures, and these Christian recognized without hesitation. His breath spiraled in the air, mercifully obscuring the image of his mother and father on their slow approach, delaying that which he would have delayed now for years more to come, but no longer possessed the choice.

Torrin and Nyssa slammed into him, and he stumbled back into Moon's flank. She chuffed in response. Tiny arms wrapped around him with all the force they could muster, and he couldn't help returning the embrace. He even laughed at how funny and familiar it all was, how, as Aylen had wisely just said, everything changed but nothing did. The twins had been barely speaking when he'd left, and yet, he knew them, and they him.

"Christian, I want to show you the cherries in the Wintergarden! They're bigger and juicier than ever this year!" Torrin exclaimed.

"No, Torrin, he doesn't *care* about your dumb cherries," Nyssa said with an exasperated look at her older brother. "But you should see the ponies that just came in from Darkwood Run. Mama says she doesn't know what Arranden is feeding them!"

"We'll have time for both," Christian said, planting kisses atop both their heads as his heart again filling. Aylen smiled knowingly over the top of the twins.

But a pall fell over his joy at the realization that Drystan, Lisbet, and Pieter would not be coming to greet him. Two of them, lost in the world, the third, a prisoner of the crown. How quickly everything had shifted for the Derehams, perhaps forever. When he'd decided to stay at the Sepulchre, he'd done it knowing it would mean distance from his family. But there had always existed the potential to see them again, when he chose, or when they did. Knowing now he might never see those three again hit him as he observed what remained of his once sprawling family. He strengthened his hold on Moon as his knees threatened to buckle. He bowed anyway, dropping into a crouch, struggling to breathe.

"Son," Holden said. Christian looked up from the huddle to see his father, holding out a hand. Christian took it and stood.

"Christian," Gretchen said. Her voice shook. She reached for him, but withdrew, instead wrapping her arms over her chest, where all her unasked questions lived. "You're home."

"Mother..." Christian's own voice choked as he searched for the long overdue words.

"No," she said. "Now isn't the time for that. You're here now. You and sweet Aylen. She's a sight now, isn't she?" Gretchen smiled at her. "Your father will be so pleased you're home again. How he's missed you."

Aylen bowed. "It's lovely to see you again as well, Lady Dereham."

"Aylen is my wife now, Mother. Father," Christian said. "And so home is wherever I am."

Gretchen's brows lifted. Holden grunted in surprised approval. "Is that so?" Gretchen said, and, still smiling, moved in to embrace Aylen. "Then I say to you as well, welcome home, daughter. Though, to do it without ceremony and celebration. Does that mean there is..."

"No, she's not with child," Christian said quickly. Aylen wouldn't like him answering for her, but their conversations around having a child left them at different ends of the question. "We wed because it was what we wanted to do."

"You chose well," Holden said. "Had you stayed, and taken my place, I might have chosen the same for you."

"Might have," Christian said, trying to smile. "And so I've chosen for myself, as my heart demanded."

Nyssa and Torrin squealed and danced around Aylen, each grabbing her hands and pulling her toward the destinations of their choice. She gasped and laughed with them.

Christian looked up to see his father looking directly at him. Holden nodded. Christian nodded in return.

"We've come to help," Christian said. "Tell us how we may be of service."

GRETCHEN FOUGHT WITH HERSELF. HER BATTLES WERE THE KIND WITH no end, as her persistent struggle between her heart and mind waged without reprieve. It was her heart that was spent with joy as she listened to her eldest son—at first, hesitant, but after some of the Northerlands' finest ale, more free—tell them about his life as a Magi. He and Aylen finished each other's sentences, smiling and laughing each time, both seeming almost desperate to share their tales with those from their old life.

Christian was still her son, but he was much changed. It wasn't only the silver hair that he and Aylen had been magically bound with as part of their vow of service. Nor the robes, which were somehow even more an anachronism of the world she recognized. Where he'd once been quiet and a young man possessed of his abiding desire to be alone, there was now a fresh confidence in his words. He wasn't afraid of himself. He feared only that what he'd left behind when he ran toward a different life would push him aside.

This instinct ran as strong within Gretchen as the one to hold him and assuage his fears. How she wanted to slap him! To slap that newfound confidence from his face before he could finish his words. To rip the wedding band from his finger and melt it over the blacksmith's forge. He talked of being needed at the Sepulchre, oblivious to the irony that he'd always been needed... *here.* When Gretchen had realized her heir had run off to find his own destiny, a new fear settled into her bones. Holden had largely ignored Drystan in favor of Christian, but when he turned his eyes to him, now from necessity, would he see beyond, to the truth? And could she live with knowing she would place a man who did not bear the blood of the Northern men in his veins? She couldn't pass him over for Pieter without revealing this terrible secret, and to do so would drive a stake through any chance of life or happiness for Drystan.

As she watched Christian's animated, happy retellings of the world he'd chosen, she continued this fight with herself. Smiling when she should, screaming within at him to examine his selfishness and return to the responsibility the Guardians had chosen for him.

"Gretchen, a raven has come."

They all turned at the intrusion of the soft, harmless voice of her brother-in-law, Alric. He ambled in, favoring the leg that hadn't been nearly chewed off by a mountain bear. There were times Gretchen forgot Alric lived in Wulfsgate, for he was so quiet and unassuming. Earwyn was a soft but powerful force, a presence you could not soon forget, but her husband spent his days in the library, or wandering the Wintergarden with that odd look that no one but him understood.

There was a simplicity in Alric that provoked Gretchen to ask her husband if he'd been kicked in the head by more than one horse. There was no meanness in the question. Only an attempt to understand the unusual man, who she had always tried to meet with kindness, despite how frustratingly obtuse he could often be when asked simple questions.

"Gretchen?" Holden repeated. "Not me?"

"No, brother. This is for Gretchen's eyes alone, per the color of ribbon tied," Alric said. He limped in a few more steps, holding it out toward her.

Holden's cheeks colored. "Am I not the Lord of Wulfsgate? What can be told to another that I cannot hear?"

Christian stood and accepted the scroll from Alric, then handed it to his mother. "I'm sure Mother will share whatever is inside, once she's read it."

Gretchen recognized the rough yarn of the Southerlands immediately. Khallum. He would send for her, he said, when the time came. A lump hitched in her throat. Her pulse quickened. With unsteady hands, she unrolled the vellum, too aware of all the eyes upon her.

When she had read the words, which pushed her forward into a new era, where what she knew changed her, and would change all those who read them, she looked up at her family.

"Well?" Holden asked.

"It was from Khallum. It's about my brother. He's found a way to glamour the Medvedev, and he's using them to build an army."

"Mother's blood," Alric whispered.

"That's not all," Gretchen went on. She wrapped the vellum in her shaking fist. She would burn it. She had no other choice. But first she would read it until she committed the words to memory, because these words changed everything. Everything. "Darrick Rhiagain lives. He has been a prisoner in the Wastelands these five years, and Khallum has found the means to retrieve him."

Holden's sudden intake of breath was the only sound in the room.

Aylen's eyes filled with tears. Christian gripped her hand, glassy-eyed himself.

"This is it," Gretchen said. "We have said we have no power against this kingless crown. No means to fight back, to determine our own destinies. Now, we have this chance. If Khallum meets with success in the Wastelands, then we are all, all of us, delivered of the madness that has taken over Duncarrow."

Holden bowed low over his knees, nodding to the floor.

"What now? What does Lord Warwick ask of us?" Christian asked.

"To be at the ready," Gretchen replied. "For once the realm knows that Darrick Rhiagain still lives and breathes, it will erupt into chaos."

"Will there be war?" Aylen asked.

"No," Holden said, at the same time Gretchen answered, "It would seem so."

"If there is, we must be ready," Christian said, standing. He looked around at the few people who knew the kingdom's greatest secret. "We must be on the right side of this battle."

Gretchen looked at her husband. "War or no war, your son is right. Khallum has chosen us to stand by his side, and we must not fail him."

Holden raised his head. "Wife, you forget who we are. We have no knights. Our armory dulls with the rust of disuse. Our force are farmers and hunters, grown fat and lazy by peace. Nothing has changed."

Gretchen stood over him. "Oh, you are wrong, husband. *Everything* has changed. Every man in the kingdom, from farmer to nobleman, will rise for Darrick Rhiagain. It is now upon us to deliver our loyalty to this cause. The men will follow."

"Mother is right," Christian said. "I've been beyond the Northerlands. I break bread with those from all Reaches, whose families suffer under Eoghan's raping of resources, taking of their men for labor under the guise of crimes that haven't been committed. No doubt Eoghan was behind whatever sent Darrick to the Wastelands. The realm's anger will be colossal, and their response, mighty. Any man can be a warrior if you give him a cause he believes is worth fighting for."

Gretchen's heart swelled with pride to hear her son speak as the heir he was born to be.

Ember came running into the Great Room, breathless. From her face, Gretchen deduced she'd been listening and had heard every word. "Take me."

47

BE WARY OF HOPE

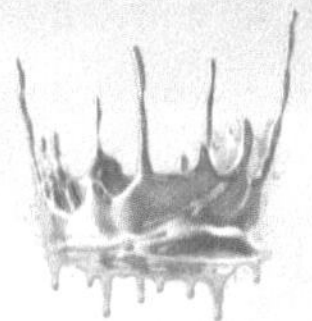

The letter said to burn the vellum upon reading. Someone slipped it under the cell door while they were sleeping. She'd almost missed it.

Whoever had sent it had no true notion of Anabella's circumstances in this sky dungeon or they would've known she hadn't had wood for the hearth for some time. The nights were so cold that Stefan had come upon a chill that she feared might take him from her. It passed, but the dark rounds under his eyes, the hollows in his cheeks... those had nowhere to go.

She couldn't send it down the drain where the rest of her vellum had gone. She'd seen the guard down there, speaking with the cloaked figure, and though she couldn't hear their words, she knew, in her heart, they were speaking of her, and that meant her words hadn't been for the Guardians alone. It meant that Eoghan's discovery of her treasonous tales was imminent, if it had not happened already.

For all she knew, this seditious letter was a ruse from the king himself. Designed to give her hope, so he could cruelly take in back in the final hours of her life. He had that in him. She'd seen glimpses of it over the years.

Anabella didn't think this was the case, though. Nor could she wrap her mind around the possibility she had an ally on Duncarrow. Five long years she'd suffered in this dungeon, watching the life first blossom and then slowly wilt away in her only son. Anyone who could have allowed that could be no true friend of hers.

She sighed, arms crossed over her pounding heart, observing Stefan enraptured by some new scenario he'd concocted with an imagination that had been born entirely from within.

No matter who sent it, there was an end ahead for both of them. She could be rescued, or killed, but her time in the sky dungeon was closing in upon its final hours, and she must face whatever came with bravery. Darrick would have. And wherever he was, she would make him proud in her own last moments of flesh and blood. She would shield Stefan from as much as she could, for as long as she could. Whether to her doom, or her destiny, she would leave this cell, tonight, with whoever came for her.

She could eat the letter. It might tangle in her bowels and send her to untimely death, or it might dissolve, never to show itself again in any form. She had no way of knowing, for she'd never had occasion to do it.

Anabella opened her mouth. She positioned the crumpled vellum upon her tongue, but hesitated. Not yet. Once more, first. Once more, for memory.

She read the words one last time. *Prepare yourself and your son for departure. Tonight. Allies will come for you. Burn this upon reading.*

Allies will come for you. She could interpret that any number of ways, but only one left her heartened.

Be wary of your hope, Anabella. It is not that which has kept you and Stefan alive all these years.

Her advice, Darrick's voice. Sometimes it was as if he was still at her side, in the Wintergarden, whispering promises and wisdom, his greatest gift. It hadn't been by choice that he'd left her.

Anabella swallowed the letter. It stuck in her throat and, gagging, she reached for what was left of the wine in the pitcher and washed it down. She could feel the jagged edges as they struggled down.

"Mama? What's wrong?"

Eyes watering in burgeoning discomfort, she knelt by Stefan's side. The vellum passed lower, and she was aware of it, fully. She pressed her hand to the spot just below her chest, where the truth lived. "Tell me how you bested the pirates this time," she said.

Asherley stormed through the halls, aware of the last of the setting sun beyond the windows to her right. Tonight she would either become the architect of the kingdom's salvation or the arbiter of her own doom. The one thing she would not be was anxious.

The eyes of gathered courtesans turned toward her frenetic strides. She slowed her pace, chiding herself for allowing others to witness the tempest brewing within her. Already she was losing some of her beloved control, and that could not happen.

Once safely ensconced within her own chambers, she went to the vase upon the mantle and shook out the contents. The key dropped into her palm. She regarded it as she rolled it across the surface of her skin. She had no lackey to shoulder this task upon. Either she saw this through, or no one would.

She almost preferred it this way, for there was no one's competence she trusted to be greater than her own.

Upon learning that Aiden Quinlanden was expected in the morning, she better understood the timing chosen by the mysterious ally. There was a need to be gone before he arrived, though she didn't have the full picture. Once aboard the ship, she would demand it.

Asherley slipped the key into the satchel sewn into her dress and went to extract the latest remnants of the king's enjoyment. With a rag, she scrubbed at her privates until the dark crimson of her own blood appeared on the surface. She had none of her own special herbs from her garden here. She had to do things the old way, to prevent the malformed king's seed from taking root in her womb. She would claw any child of Eoghan's out with her own nails before she allowed it to take form and be born.

She thought of Byrne. Although she would leave Duncarrow that night, she might not see her husband for some time. Careful planning, hiding away until it was safe to reveal the importance of their precious cargo, would all take precedence over returning to the Westerlands, where she belonged. But when she returned, with her would come a security the kingdom hadn't known in many years. Her reunion with Byrne, with the children, would be all the more a reward.

After so many nights in the bed of a boy, she craved the arms of a man. Her man.

There was yet another reason tonight's timing was fortuitous. Earlier, as she glided her hips over the king's misshapen body, he had looked up into her eyes with hawkish command and informed her she would become his wife. An order. That though she was nearing forty years of age, he knew she'd grown life only recently, for otherwise she wouldn't have milk to give. He would light her womb with life again, many times over. He said this, milk drunk, unable to mask the hungered venom in his eyes, and this time when he released his seed into her, he made her swear she would sleep with her legs up, to ensure a quickening.

How she'd managed not to lose the contents of her belly she owed to her hard-earned resolve. Thinking about it now, remembering the force of his seed entering her on the back of his demand, she wondered how she'd not seen this coming. Her charming of the king had come with the intention of uncovering secrets she could use to usurp him, but being so skilled, she had instead won him to the idea of keeping her. In a box, where he could take all he wanted, deliver into her what he needed, and then discard her when she'd dried up in use.

The shared visions of her and Joran had only brought her here. Beyond knowing her fate pulled her to the king's side, she had no further direction. All she had done since she'd stepped foot on Duncarrow had been born of her instinct, not her magic.

The key opened all the cells. That's what her young and nerve-filled co-conspirators said. When she'd asked how she would know which was the right one, that answer was not among the knowledge they possessed. Whoever gave them their orders had given them only what they needed to know to recruit her to their cause, and it was a lot less than she would've demanded under any other circumstance.

Asherley moved to the window and pressed her cheek against the glass. The last of the sun had disappeared beyond the horizon. Those recruited to sail the ship under the veil of secrecy would be readying it for sea now, and soon, beginning their vigil as they watched for the voyagers who made it all necessary.

Asherley whispered her prayers. But they were not to the Guardians. Not this time. She sent her words, in a language known only to those of Ravenwood blood, to the High Priestesses of Past, offering her plea into their hands.

STEFAN WAS FAST ASLEEP UPON ANABELLA'S LAP WHEN SHE HEARD THE key turn in the lock. She clutched her son tight to her, whispering her love, her promise that wherever they were going, there would at last be peace. She beseeched the Guardians that her words to him would not be a lie.

She looked up to meet the band of men who would deliver or assail her, but there was only one. Cloaked, like the one who had conversed with the guard below. Anabella couldn't see the face, and before she could think to say a word, they threw a blanket over her head. The stranger arranged the cover over Stefan as well, and then, to Anabella's utter shock, it was a *woman* who said, "Hold tight to him. We go with haste, or not at all!"

Anabella held back her fears and clutched her son's hand in both of hers as the stranger pushed her across the room and then out the door of the cell that had been her home for five years.

ASHERLEY HAD OPENED FIVE CELLS BEFORE SHE'D DISCOVERED Anabella's. Every prisoner within had come alive, first with fear, then with hope, and she'd almost let them go. She would have let them go if she wasn't certain they would draw attention to what she was doing. The entire kingdom depended upon them being far from Duncarrow before the plot was discovered.

She rushed Anabella and her son through the winding hall, past more cells. The guards would wake soon. She had only the herbs to put them to sleep, not to take their lives or spell them into a more prolonged rest. It wouldn't take much to rouse them. The excited, desperate pleas from the prisoners she'd left behind would be enough, and the solid oaken doors of the cells, revealing not even a whisper of the contents beyond until opened, had slowed her more than she liked.

They ran on, feet sliding upon the smooth stone floors. As they came upon the second set of stairs, the ones that wound all the way to the bottom floor and led out to the back of the keep, something quelled her haste.

"Please," a young man called out. "Please, whoever you are. The king is going to kill us."

"We're the children of lords," another said. "He'll kill us to hurt our mothers and fathers."

Asherley paused. Anabella stumbled over the halt in momentum, blind under the dark wool, but Asherley caught them both before they tumbled down the stairs to certain death.

"Tell me your names," she called back. She knew the answer. She still required confirmation.

Go. You cannot save everyone. No sacrifice is too great for the king-dom. You know this.

"Who are you?" she asked again, more demanding. Her pulse pounded in the back of her throat.

"Ransom Warwick and Pieter Dereham. We're the sons of the great lords of the realm, and we'll be put to death if we stay here. Please, ma'am. There will be a great reward for our return."

"Curse the Guardians," Asherley hissed, and fumbled in her dress for the key.

Anabella whimpered a question Asherley couldn't make out. Curled against her, Stefan cried softly into her dress.

Asherley fumbled with the lock. The key dropped, clanging against the stone. The sound seemed louder than any scream. She cursed under her breath and reminded herself who she was, reaching again for the key. Both boys cried for her to hurry, and she thought, if Ember had done well, she might be at the mercy of another lady of the realm. There were sacrifices she could live with, and then there was the idea of leaving heirs of the Reaches to die at the hands of a tyrant.

The lock clicked open, and both boys poured out, wrapping their arms around her, crying out their gratitude.

"Lady Blackwood! It's you!"

"There's no time!" Asherley nudged them. "Down! All the way to the bottom, and unless you wish to die, don't stop until your feet land upon the rocks outside. When you get there, hide, and go no farther until I'm with you."

The boys raced ahead, not needing any further encouragement, and she quickly lost sight of them. Her own descent would be slower because she had to ease Anabella and her son down. She could remove the blanket, but if she had miscalculated the guard exchange, and they were met with an adversary, then it would buy time for her to keep them from detection.

"Lady Blackwood." A new voice. Old. Foreign. She ignored it, though there was some glimmer within, some small tickle telling her to stop.

"The Rhiagain sorcerer," Anabella whispered. "Pay no heed to him."

"That I am," the old man said. "But an ally, too, I could be. One unlike any you've known before."

"I need no Rhiagain allies," Asherley hissed.

"Your enemies have need of them."

She opened her mouth, breaths heavy in the musty air of the sky dungeon, torn between his strange words and where she knew she needed to be. It was her desire to pause further that finally drove her back to action.

When Anabella tripped three times, focused too much on her son who stumbled in his fear, Asherley at last lifted the boy herself and carried him.

"We must be quicker!" she said, pulling Anabella along behind her. If the woman fell now, she'd fall upon Asherley, who could brace herself against the narrow walls of the stairwell.

"I cannot see!" Anabella cried.

"Trust to instinct. Your eyes will only take you so far in darkness."

Asherley moved more swiftly now, and Anabella kept pace, crying out only briefly as she connected with stone walls. Down they wound, and when they were halfway to the bottom, Asherley heard the first of the guards stirring above. His confusion echoed through the hall, and with a pinch of dread, she realized she'd forgotten to close the boys' cell door.

"Move!" Asherley urged, nudging Stefan over her shoulder so she could hasten her own pace. "Move, or we die!"

Anabella did as bidden, and faster they went, nearing the bottom, all the while listening to the guards begin their own descent.

Asherley exited into the night. Ransom and Pieter were waiting, huddled near the side of the keep. Next to them was John Cantwell. She didn't see the girl.

"Good boys," she said. "See that ship?"

They nodded. John accepted Stefan from her and broke into a sprint toward the dock.

"Run. And don't stop until you're all on board. If we're caught, you sail without us."

Ransom and Pieter bolted away, following John.

"No, you won't take my son from me!" Anabella yelled.

Asherley spun around. She lowered her hands under the blanket, clasped Anabella's in her own, and said, "Stefan is the son of the true king. If only one survives this night, it must be him."

Anabella, panting, hesitated, and then nodded.

"Now *go*, and, Guardians willing, we *all* survive this night."

ANABELLA BLOCKED OUT THE CHAOS BREWING AROUND HER. ONCE they'd reached the ship, she was pushed and shoved, nearly dropped down a set of stairs. She heard Stefan crying in the distance, and her fear at him being taken—that he was the true prize, and she wasn't needed anymore—was quickly subdued when he was laid back in her arms. Overhead, a door slammed closed.

She thought they might be in the cargo hold. The scent of dampened wood, of crates and rope, overpowered anything else. All the noise came from above, heavy boots storming around on the deck, a cacophony of voices competing. Her woman rescuer, yelling to push off, others screaming in fear. Anabella held tight to Stefan and made no promises, only reaffirmed for him that he was loved. Was born of love, and when the Guardians deemed his promise fulfilled, he would die of love.

They were thrown forward as the world shifted into action. The ship had left port. The choppy current made their departure from the dock agonizingly slow, but she had not the benefit of seeing who had made the journey. She could find no relief in looking back upon her prison and seeing there was no one in pursuit.

It seemed hours before there were feet on the steps, coming

down to where she hadn't let go of Stefan, or her hope, despite that it had never served her.

A sharp light pierced her vision as the blanket was pulled away. She moved her hands up to shield her eyes. Stefan buried his face in her dress.

Anabella squinted, opening and closing her eyes to gain use of them once more. She needed to face whoever had brought her here. To understand if she had traded one prison for yet another.

Two figures knelt before her. Both women. She had never laid eyes upon either of them.

"Anabella," the one with the voice she knew from her rescue said. Her hair was as dark as a raven's feathers, and her eyes, like the forests Anabella hadn't laid eyes upon for so long. "You and Stefan are safe now."

"Who are you?" she asked, looking first at the dark-haired woman, and then, at the other, who had an air of familiarity, though she had no recollection of ever meeting her. Her golden red hair signaled Rhiagain, but she couldn't be.

"Lady Asherley Blackwood," her dark-haired rescuer said.

"Princess Assyria Rhiagain," the other added.

"I don't understand..." Anabella said, breathless. She looked at both women, not grasping how they had come to be allied, or how either knew of her to come to her aid. From the wary curiosity emanating off Lady Blackwood, it was evident their alliance was freshly formed. Assyria, Eoghan's older sister. Had this always been her stance? How long had she known Anabella and her son were in the sky dungeon, suffering as they daily neared closer to death?

"Anabella," the princess said. She reached a hand forward and brushed the matted hair back from Anabella's forehead. Anabella cringed at her strange kindness, which as yet still made no sense to her. "You're not the only one who's suffered under the hand of my brother. His reign is a pox on this kingdom, and an abomination to the Rhiagain bloodline. You are Darrick's wife. His queen. Your son will be king one day. Do you understand?"

Anabella's emotions swelled up so quickly she had to clap both hands over her mouth to prevent a sob so loud it would rouse the whole ship. It could not be. It could not *be*, that this would happen to her now. It was a dream. Surely she would wake soon, and the cruel reality of the sky dungeon would return, reminding her that hope would kill her faster than hunger.

"There's more," Lady Blackwood said. "Darrick is alive. There are those who know where he is."

Assyria bowed her head. "We would see our king reunited with his queen."

48

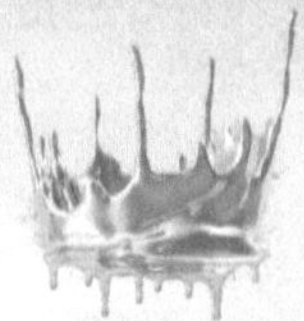

The raids on men by moonlight continued until there were only five of them left. Five, when there had been twenty a fortnight past. That only accounted for the damages in their own tent. Cap knew the others had fared about the same.

He'd mulled over the intentions of the guards for so long he'd lost any chance at precious sleep. In the beginning he'd believed they were culling the weak to spread the meager resources amongst those who could still produce in the mines. It was a chilling thought, even then. But now, when they hadn't ceased or even slowed their massacre, Cap understood that there was something much bigger going on. The inevitability of their own demise lingered heavy upon him, and when two more disappeared the night before, he accepted they were hovering before an impasse. They could die at the hands of the guards and be tossed away, forgotten, or take the leap toward a fate of their own making.

"Andy." Cap whispered the name. Without the chorus of snores from a filled tent, every sound resonated.

"Aye. No sleep here, either."

"We have an hour before the guards come, if the past nights are

548

predictive of future ones. You still have... those things you told me about?"

"Aye, I do."

"Bring them. Let us walk for a few."

Andy slipped out of the bed and moved to the tent door. Cap could feel his nervous energy from feet away. Andy leaned out, examining the surroundings, and then turned his head back and said, "Clear."

Cap joined him and they veered away from the guard station. He already knew where he was going. There was one place where a man could die in the Wastelands and be hailed as having died with honor. Dying there would ensure they weren't tossed upon the heap of discarded prisoners. When they were discovered in the daylight, there'd be too many eyes to allow such a thing.

"The mines?" Andy asked. "Yer a sick man, Cap. Anyone ever tell ye so?"

Cap shrugged. "We won't be swept away like rubbish. And I have some things to say. No one will hear them there. Not even the guards can stand to be here when they aren't required."

Andy said no more about it. On they moved, inhaling with each step the harsh red dust as a midnight wind passed across the valley.

There were several entrances to the mine where they performed most of their labor. Those younger, still filled with the vigor they came in with, worked at the greater depths, relying on an unsteady pulley to drop them to the bottom and raise them back to the top. Strangely, in a way Cap couldn't explain, he felt a call to this place where he had started his tenure as a prisoner of the crown. A time where he'd still had his hope, before they'd knocked it out of him. If he was to die anywhere in these cursed lands, he would choose here, where he could still remember when he wasn't Cap but someone who had been born to lead, to love, and to foster peace.

He operated the pulley with the ease of memory. Andy lost his balance, gripping the tiny cart with a sick look in his eyes. They'd never sent him here, for some reason. They'd paired him with Cap from the start. Had that never happened, it was unlikely they would've crossed paths. Perhaps the Guardians were present here, after all.

The cart screeched to a finish at the bottom, and then, with a light thud, landed. Andy scrambled out and then looked up to see how far they'd come. "Here? Ye couldn't have let us just sit easy in the north entrance?"

Cap pointed to a gathering of smooth rocks. He'd taken his breaks upon them many times, if you could call them that. They were given long enough to throw back the unclean water and relieve themselves. If they tried for more, violence replaced the desire.

"We don't have many nights left. Could be tonight they come for us," Cap said. "In fact, that's what my gut tells me."

"Aye. I've been feckin' saying as much. Good to hear ye listening to yourself, if not me."

Cap chuckled. He hadn't intended to do it. It felt nice. "These herbs, Andy. What are the odds we make it out?"

"Donnae know. About half and half."

"Equal odds we live or die?"

"So I'm told."

"That's an enormous risk you took, coming in here, knowing that was your only way out. You're still very young."

"As are you."

Cap dropped his eyes to his lap. "Darrick. I'd prefer you call me Darrick now. I'd like to call you Ryan, if you'd allow it."

"You can call me whatever ye like, but I wouldnae feel right calling you by the name your mother gave you."

"I'm asking you to."

"A'right, then. Darrick." He looked pained to say it.

"Before we do this, I feel compelled to share the story of what happened to me. How I came to be here. Until now it's lived only in my mind. Would you hear it?"

Ryan nodded. "Aye, it would be my honor."

Darrick leaned his head back against the rocks and began.

"I'D LIKE TO THINK I KNEW WHAT HE HAD PLANNED. LATER, I WOULD tell myself I did, to ease the bruise as it formed around my heart. Eoghan and I weren't on the friendliest terms as boys. He was cross, always, with everyone, but especially me. He blamed me for the deficiencies the Guardians gave him, and I refused to take that censure, though I was sad for him. It did seem unfair that our blessings had been so divided, but I cannot recall a time where Eoghan tried to overcome his, or rise above them. He preferred to wallow in a place where he could lay fault and curse the world.

"My relationship with my father was also strained. I was his favorite, as his heir, but it was Eoghan who shared his heart and mind. I had never been in favor of the choices my father made in his tenure as king. The Epoch of the Accordant was not visionary, but short-sighted. Murdering the elders of the Reaches was an act of a soulless man, an atrocity, one I could never reconcile when I looked upon my father. Never had I forgotten that we Rhiagains were interlopers to the kingdom. Our rule has been tolerated so long as it hasn't stepped beyond into the dismantling of the laws and customs the Reaches enjoyed long before our arrival. It was a tenuous grasp, and one that, I will say to you, though the thought will be unpopular, had no legitimacy. Our claim to have been sent by gods was a fabrication meant to save our lives, and then it grew into opportunity.

"We are not gods. We are not the same as you, but we're not very different, either. There isn't a Rhiagain alive, not aware of this, but most cling to these lies as if their lives depended upon them. Perhaps they do. My father and Eoghan certainly thought so.

"I kept these seditious thoughts mostly to myself, though they both were all too aware of my animosity about their overreaching. This Right of Choosing may have been Eoghan's creation, but it was where my father was aiming all along. Eoghan's belief in that plan made him more valuable than the son who found the faults in it.

"I may never know if my father was aware of Eoghan's plot to dispose of me. If he had an active hand in my intended demise. It is tempting to hold fast to my belief that though we had differences, he still had love for me. On good days, I still believe this. On others..."

Darrick dug for his waterskin and drank the last of the contents. He was so terribly thirsty. But he wouldn't need water soon. He only needed enough to wet his throat so the rest of his words could flow.

"They came for me in my bed. It took three guards to subdue me. In the moment's chaos, I wondered if there were three because that was all the loyalty Eoghan could muster on Duncarrow, but the night didn't turn out as I expected when I was dragged away in my nightshift.

"They took me to the end of the isle, where the rocks climb to a cliff so high the sea blurs and fades into the distance. They held me at the edge, the wind whipping us all around, and as the time ticked down I wondered, why have they not thrown me? What were they waiting for? Their feet slid along the damp stone, losing purchase, as the rain thrashed us all. Their own lives hung in the balance, and yet, they hesitated.

"I learned why soon enough. A fourth figure appeared, and when I saw who it was, my heart sank to the stones. It was my sister, Assyria. She had been my surrogate mother, my mentor, and, many times, the sole person who I could share my beliefs with. She nurtured the differences in me, offering caution on how to address them but never suggesting they were misplaced. That it would be Assyria to meet me and help deliver my end was the cruelest twist fate could deliver. Eoghan, I could understand. His hatred of me had burned from the cradle. But Assyria? I couldn't bear it.

"She leaned in and whispered to me words I couldn't forget even when I tried to put that night from my mind. 'Darrick,' she said. 'It's beyond my power to stop what Eoghan's envy has put in motion. Whence these guards return to him, they will announce your death, an accidental fall from the great cliff. But tonight is not the night you die. I wish there was elsewhere I could send you, that you would be safe. Years may pass, but it will not be forever.' She leaned in closer. 'He knows of your wife, brother. He will have her imprisoned here. I cannot stop this, but I *will* look after her. She will live here, but she will not die here. I promise you.'

"My Anabella, she meant. Have you ever loved someone with such intensity..." Darrick looked at his hands. "You have. You've told me about her."

Ryan nodded in the darkness. "Esmerelda. If my brother has met with success, she's safe with my mother's people now."

"I hope she is," Darrick said. "And I hope Assyria was able to keep her word, for there's no freedom for me if Anabella's was taken."

"If I can believe, so can you."

Darrick nodded. "Only... I never thought... no, I did. In those early days, before they'd beaten the hope from me, I still believed Assyria would come for me. Then I accepted that she'd either been caught or had realized the futility in the effort. I did. Guardians help me, Ryan, but I accepted that whatever life remained to me would play out here, in the Wastelands. I accepted it. I let Anabella's beautiful face fade from my memory. I forgot how soft her lips felt against mine, that first time I kissed her in the Wintergarden..."

Ryan touched his shoulder. "You did what ye had to. To survive in a place like this. You couldnae have known I'd show up one day with a way out."

"And how is it you? How has Khallum Warwick come upon news of my continued existence?"

"I cannae say."

"You've not even a guess?"

Ryan shook his head. "No one loathes The Pretender more than Lord Warwick. The entire kingdom must know that. He's made no secret of it. And the Wastelands were Warwick lands until not so long ago. Until your great-grandfather took them."

"He loathes the Rhiagains. This is a hatred that begins long before us."

"I'd not lead ye into a trap, if that's what ye think."

"I don't know what to think."

Ryan removed the two small bundles from his jerkin. "You said it yourself. We will die at the hands of the guards, or on our own terms. I offer something better. A chance we donnae die and find ourselves free of this wretched place."

Darrick accepted a bundle. He turned it over in his hand. "How incredible that something so small can perform such a monumental task."

"The hard work comes later."

Darrick smiled. "If the Guardians are with us on this night."

"I believe they are," Ryan said. "Ready?"

Darrick looked up. He wished, for a moment, his view was the night sky and not the jagged rocks of the mine that had taken so much of him. Somewhere out there, whether alive or not, Anabella knew the same sky. His queen.

"Ready," he said. He rested the bitter herbs upon his tongue. Met Ryan's eyes. Swallowed, before he could convince himself not to.

Ryan downed his own herbs. He stood before his king. Darrick's eyes welled with tears as the other man slowly dropped into a reverent bow.

"Until we again meet, it has been an honor to serve ye, Your Grace," Ryan whispered.

EPILOGUE

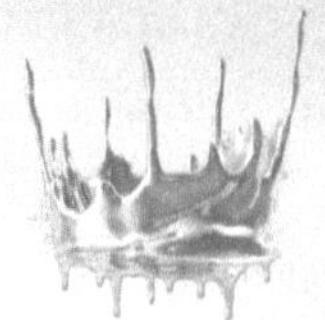

Gretchen's pulse battered in her chest as she fled down the steps with the ease that could only come from one who had taken a path many times. Someone new to the damp, winding stairwell would lose their footing, but not Gretchen. She needed no eyes to see, only her senses stained with memory, carrying her true.

When she reached the crypts, she tempered her breathing to adjust to the change in air. In the early days, she'd needed time to steady herself, but she'd learned to do that along the way, so that when she reached the bottom, she could do what she'd come to do with nothing holding her back.

"Ash," she whispered to the darkness. She passed her torch back and forth. Cobwebbed tombs danced in and out of her vision. Hadden. Torrin. Mylannie. Little Hughie. Names etched into eternity, condemned to the bowels of the keep, in a place no one but the outsider from another Reach would visit. Occasionally, she chided herself for not pausing to pay reverence to the ancestors of her children. But she'd known none of them, other than Holden's mother,

Mylannie. By the time they'd met, her losses had already broken her. The crypt called her name, awaiting a promise spent earlier than anyone expected.

Gretchen always said Holden was afraid of the crypts, and this was what made her meetings with Ash safe, but the place unsettled her, as well. Only the presence of her oldest and dearest love could quell the rising discomfort that threatened to turn to fear as she stood amongst the Derehams of past.

"Ash!" she hissed. Sweat beaded upon her brow, sliding into her eyes. She used her free hand to wipe it away, but more came. "I'm in no mood for games tonight."

He'd never made her wait. Not since he'd become her ghost. In life he'd challenged her often, but in death, that power had been taken from him. He was hers to command, to summon or to banish. If she called him, he had no choice but to come.

So where was he?

"I need you, you fool," Gretchen said, stepping deeper into the crypts. The farther back she wandered, the older the crumbling stone would be. She'd heard once that some tombs had fallen open, revealing bones and other horrors. She possessed no desire to confirm this with her own eyes.

The torch's flame wavered as the air thinned. She could venture on, but risked losing her light. She already knew he wasn't here. It wasn't only his lack of response, but the hollowness left by the absence of his presence.

She didn't sense him at all.

Had the magic worn off? If so, why now? Gretchen leaned against a mossy patch along the wall. A pile of spiders skittered away at the intrusion. They would normally unsettle her, but she hardly noticed them now. Her mind was a mess of questions.

"Ash, why now? Why would you choose now to abandon me, when I've never needed you more? My Christian has returned to me. My Drystan and Lisbet are out there, somewhere, alone and in danger of the same fate delivered upon Byrne, while Pieter toils in a dungeon. Our kingdom lies upon the brink of war, and the winner will be determined not by force but by cunning. I find myself at the center of it all, and I cannot do this alone. If you ever truly loved me, you'll help me understand how you could leave me on the eve of all this."

The answer came not from Drystan Sylvaine, but elsewhere. Somewhere even more familiar and intimate than his soothing wisdom.

You have never needed anyone, Gretchen.

"That's not true, Ash," she whispered, though she knew it was not Ash to whom she was responding. "And only you know this. Only you have seen me when my weakness is greater than my strength."

You'll need both for what comes next.

"But that makes no sense. Weakness serves no one."

The heart is not a weakness.

"This kingdom is not led by hearts."

No. But it will be saved by one.

THE FIRST THREADS OF THE TENUOUS TAPESTRY WEAVING THE kingdom together have been pulled, and now nothing will ever be the same. With secrets revealed and the realm on the brink of all out war, everyone must decide what side they fall on, and how far they're willing to go to protect what they love. Continue now with Book Two, The Broken Realm.

FEEL LIKE YOU NEED TO DISCUSS WHAT YOU JUST READ? JOIN THE Kingdom of the White Sea Official Reader Group on Facebook for book chats, giveaways, and exclusive series news.

· · ·

IF YOU ENJOYED THIS NOVEL, AN HONEST REVIEW IS ALWAYS appreciated.

Northerlands
THE NORTHERN REACH

Lord and Lady:
Lord Holden Dereham & Lady Gretchen Quinlanden Dereham

Capital:
Wulfsgate

Standard:
The jagged mountaintop

Children:
Christian, 19
Drystan, 17
Lisbet, 14
Pieter, 13
Nyssa and Torrin, 10

Greater Families/Stewards:
Aldenwood, Turick, Hardeham, Frost, Horne, Arranden, Wynter,
Haddenfoot, Claybourne, Weatherford

NORTHERLANDS

Key Towns:

Whitecap, Midwinter Rest, Westport, Eastport, Salthill, Darkwood Run, Witchwood Cross, Wulfshead Haven, Torrin's Pass, Dunwoode

Landmarks:

Northern Range, Icebolt Mountain, Torrin's Pass, Forest of Lycana

Notable Northerlanders:

Alric Dereham & Earwyn Blackwood Dereham of Wulfsgate
Aylen Wynter of Witchwood Cross

SOUTHERLANDS
THE SOUTHERN REACH

Lord and Lady:
Lord Khallum Warwick & Lady Gwyn Dereham Warwick

Capital:
Warwicktown

Standard:
The crested wave

Children:
Ransom, 19
Esmerelda, 17
Niall, 15
Garrick, 12

Greater Families/Stewards:
Strong, Rutland, Bradford, Clayton, Garrick, Holton, Leecaster,
Law, Nye, Thorpe

Key Towns:
Sandycove, Iron Hill, Sandymount, Whitecliffe, Stone Mawr,
Blackpool, Leecaster Bay, Hornsea, Goldthorpe, Port Worthing

Landmarks:
The Golden Coast, The Warwick Throne, Drummond's Cock

Notable Southerlanders:
Hamish and Andrija Strong, & sons Jesse and Ryan of Sandycove
Lem Garrick of Iron Hill
Barne Holton of Sandymount
Samuel Law of Port Worthing
Erran and Marie Rutland, & daughters Agnes and Esther of
Whitecliffe

EASTERLANDS
THE EASTERN REACH

Lord and Lady:
Lord Aiden Quinlanden & Lady Maeryn Blackwood Quinlanden

Capital:
Whitechurch

The Resplendent Reliquary of the Guardians is located in
Riverchapel
The Consortium of the Sepulchre in the Skies is located in
Briarhaven
The Council of Universities are in Oldcastle

Standard:
The oaken tree

Children:
Eavan, 18
Assana, 17
Cian, 16

Breandan, 13
Dorrin, 12

Greater Families/Stewards:
Oakenwell, Sylvaine, Forrest, Skylark, Rowan, Rosewood, Waters,
Edevane

Key Towns:
Streamstowne, Rushwood, Riverchapel, Oldcastle, Everleigh Pike,
Everhart Thicket, Greenfen, Briarhaven, Bythesea, Oak Hill

Landmarks:
Fionn's Pass, Gap of Ever, The Sparkling Beck

Notable Easterlanders:
Drystan "Ash" Sylvaine (deceased) of Rushwood
Joran Rosewood of Greenfen
Mads Waters of Bythesea
Wyat Edevane of Oldcastle

WESTERLANDS
THE WESTERN REACH

Lord and Lady:
Lady Asherley Blackwood & Lord Byrne Warwick

Capital:
Longwood Rush

Standard:
The providing mother

Children:
Hollyn, 16
Emberley, 15
Gabrianna, 12
Brandyn, 11

Greater Families/Stewards:
Tyndall, Glenlannan, Ashenhurst, Bristol, Blakewell, James, Stanhope, Richland, Derry, Wakesell

Key Towns:
Wildwood Falls, Pine Bluff, Windwatch Grove, Whispering Wood,
Valleybrooke, Greencastle, East Derry, Greystone Abbey,
Newcarrow, Whitewood

Landmarks:
The Seven Sisters of the West, The River Rush, Whispering Wood,
The Whitewood, The Hidden Cave

Notable Westerlanders:
Easlan James & son Kaslan, of Greystone Abbey
Clarrisant and Griffath Tyndall, & son Marsh of Wildwood Falls
Glen and Fleur Ashenhurst, & children Meadow and Brook of
Windwatch Grove
Jasmine and Mason Wakesell, & daughter Storm of Whitewood
The Great Rush Riders

HINTERLANDS
THE LAND OF THE MEDVEDEV

Chieftainesses:
Yseult de Medvedev, Drumain Clahnn
Ohsmha de Medvedev, Saleen Clahnn

Clahnns:
Drumain
Asgill
Mayke
Saleen

Yseult's Children:
Kian, 17
Kael, 15

Other Notable Medvedev:
Yanna de Medvedev of Clahnn Drumain (sister of Yseult, deceased)

DUNCARROW
SEAT OF THE RHIAGAINS

King:
Eoghan Rhiagain

Standard:
The crossed swords

King's Family:
Khain- Father (deceased)
Florian- Mother (deceased)
Assyria- Sister
Correen- Sister
Darrick- Brother (deceased)

Notable Rhiagains of Past:
King Carrow the Original
King Carrick the Dreamer
King Karsein
King Fynne the Good

Landmarks:
The sky dungeon, Isle of Belcarrow

MIDNIGHT CREST
HAVEN OF THE RAVENWOODS

High Priestess & Priest:
Varinya & Argentyn Ravenwood

Castle:
The Rookery

Sigil:
The raven

Children:
Alasyr, 17
Ravenna, 15
Ryandyr, 13
Ashara, 10
Nyana & Nevyn, 8 (twins)

Landmarks:
Courtyard of Regents

Notable Ravenwoods:
Adynora & Rillyn (Ravenna's grandparents)
Aryc & son Sandyr
Ailyn
Rhosyn (defected)

THE CONSORTIUM OF THE SEPULCHRE IN THE SKIES
THE ACADEMY OF MAGIC AND RULING COUNCIL OF ELDERS

Head Magus:
Head Magus Tymagen

Location:
Briarhaven, in the Easterlands

Adherents- students
Enchanters/Enchantresses- magic practitioners who have finished their studies and been assigned into the world. May also be called by their discipline (i.e. Healers, Seers, etc.)
Magi- Instructors of magic at the Sepulchre
Elder Magi- A position of tenure that allows access to the Sacred Halls
Head Magus- The head of the Sepulchre

Notable Magi:
Magi Christian Dereham
Magi Aylen Wynter
Elder Magi Rorric Dereham

Notable Adherents:

Brandyn Blackwood

Esther Rutland

574

WASTELANDS
CROWN LABOR CAMPS

Land seized by the crown and turned into prison labor camps, including Camp Atonement.

Notable Prisoners & Their Number:
Cap- WCNM999
Hill- SHNT1
Andy- SCST8769

Prisoner Numbers Decoded:
City- Reach-Crime-Number Correlating to Crime
I.E. Cap, from Whitecap in the Northerlands, was the 999th person
imprisoned for the crime of murder.

ALSO BY SARAH M. CRADIT

KINGDOM OF THE WHITE SEA

Kingdom of the White Sea Trilogy

The Kingless Crown

The Broken Realm

The Hidden Kingdom

The Book of All Things

The Raven and the Rush

The Sylvan and the Sand

The Altruist and the Assassin

The Melody and the Master

The Claw and the Crowned

The Priestess and the Paladin

THE SAGA OF CRIMSON & CLOVER

The House of Crimson and Clover Series

The Storm and the Darkness

Shattered

The Illusions of Eventide

Bound

Midnight Dynasty

Asunder

Empire of Shadows

Myths of Midwinter

The Hinterland Veil

The Secrets Amongst the Cypress

Within the Garden of Twilight

House of Dusk, House of Dawn

Midnight Dynasty Series

A Tempest of Discovery

A Storm of Revelations

A Torrent of Deceit

The Seven Series

1970

1972

1973

1974

1975

1976

1980

Vampires of the Merovingi Series

The Island

and more

The Dusk Trilogy

St. Charles at Dusk: The Story of Oz and Adrienne

Flourish: The Story of Anne Fontaine

Banshee: The Story of Giselle Deschanel

Crimson & Clover Stories

Surrender: The Story of Oz and Ana

Shame: The Story of Jonathan St. Andrews

Fire & Ice: The Story of Remy & Fleur

Dark Blessing: The Landry Triplets

Pandora's Box: The Story of Jasper & Pandora

The Menagerie: Oriana's Den of Iniquities

A Band of Heather: The Story of Colleen and Noah

The Ephemeral: The Story of Autumn & Gabriel

Bayou's Edge: The Landry Triplets

For more information, and exciting bonus material, visit www. sarahmcradit.com

About the Author

Sarah is the USA Today and International Bestselling Author of over forty contemporary and epic fantasy stories, and the creator of the Kingdom of the White Sea and Saga of Crimson & Clover universes.

Born a geek, Sarah spends her time crafting rich and multilayered worlds, obsessing over history, playing her retribution paladin (and sometimes destruction warlock), and settling provocative Tolkien debates, such as why the Great Eagles are not Gandalf's personal taxi service. Passionate about travel, she's been to over twenty countries collecting sparks of inspiration, and is always planning her next adventure.

Sarah and her husband live in a beautiful corner of SE Pennsylvania with their three tiny benevolent pug dictators.

www.sarahmcradit.com